OTHER NATURE

Book One

Kerry Williams

To Sarah, love Kerry x

Second Edition.

Copyright © 2024 by Kerry Williams

All rights reserved. No part of this publication may be reproduced, stored or transmitted in any form or by any means, electronic, mechanical, photocopying, recording, scanning, or otherwise without written permission from the author. It is illegal to copy this book, post it to a website, or distribute it by any other means without permission.

This novel is entirely a work of fiction. The names, characters and incidents portrayed in it are the work of the author's imagination. Any resemblance to actual persons, living or dead, events or localities is entirely coincidental.

Kerry Williams asserts the moral right to be identified as the author of this work.

Designations used by companies to distinguish their products are often claimed as trademarks. All brand names and product names used in this book and on its cover are trade names, service marks, trademarks and registered trademarks of their respective owners. The publishers and the book are not associated with any product or vendor mentioned in this book. None of the companies referenced within the book have endorsed the book.

Editor: Swish Design and Editing

Cover Art: Mellen Draws

Cover & Interior Design: Kerry Williams on Canva

For my sister, Roxy.

My first and number one fan.

Without you consuming my stories and demanding more this book wouldn't be in anyone's hands today.

Thank you. You gave me ALL the confidence to do this.

A Note from the Author

Dearest reader, please note, this work contains references to child neglect, scenes of peril and some closed-door steamy scenes.

My darling readers in the USA, I love you, but this book takes place in the UK and is edited to UK spellings. Hold on to your zzz's.

CHAPTER 1

Connie

Mostly I enjoy the heat, but today its clammy hands are wrapped around my throat, suffocating me.

I gaze out the window with longing. It's been the most glorious summer. The hottest on record for our part of the world.

Our tiny corner of the planet, Wixford, where I was born and raised. The perfect country village in the heart of England. A place where everyone knows everyone, and nothing ever changes. It's just so dull. I can't wait to escape.

When I glance across at Lorna—my best friend—she shares a dramatic eye roll with me as we wait for the rest of the students to file into the room. I give her a cheesy grin in return. The prospect of another year in the same place with the same people is like enduring a life sentence for us both. Wixford is beautiful but boring.

Other Nature by Kerry Williams

There's nothing but green and country roads with little more than a cluster of businesses—a coffee shop, a pub, a church, and an old, abandoned railway. Our school is a twenty-minute bike ride away, and although it also services the neighbouring town and villages, it comes with the same notion that everyone knows everyone's business. Sometimes even before they do. Not that it matters—there's a tendency to focus on the mundane here.

My year group hasn't changed much in all my seventeen years. I grew up with all these people, with the exception of my best friends. Even from a young age, the desire to have some excitement in my life, no matter how insignificant it may be, has always been there.

First came Brady. His family moved to a farm just outside Wixford when we were seven. It was long enough ago that I can't remember life without him anymore. Brady was popular right away. His flaming-red hair and Golden Retriever personality make him hard not to like. I can't recall him ever being angry, except with his brothers and sisters. He's full of energy and always fun to be around. Regardless, I was the first one to want to be his friend, which Brady never forgot. I've spent many hours on his family's farm because it was always the best place for playing games as we grew up.

Lorna's family moved here three years after Brady. Things had been different for Lorna, more difficult. At first, I didn't understand why. To me, she was the most incredible person I'd ever set my eyes on. Her silky jet-black hair travelled all the way down her back to her bum, and her dark round eyes were framed with thick, heavy black lashes.

Other Nature by Kerry Williams

She looked like a princess from a distant land. I didn't just want to be Lorna's friend—I *had* to be her friend. She's a beautiful contrast to myself. Tall where I'm short, and her hair always long, whereas mine bobs around my shoulders. While my hair is a shiny dark brown, it's nothing compared to her sleek raven locks. I love the way her tanned Indian skin contrasts my own paleness. Her eyes are dark and soft, whereas mine are green and bright. I think my eyes are the only thing I truly love about myself.

Now that I'm older, I realise the prejudice she and her family faced when they first moved here. I never fathomed the stares and the whispers she got.

That was seven years ago. Things moved on, and now Lorna and her family are cherished members of the village.

Other than that, nothing's changed since then.

This year, however, is a tad different. It's our last year here before Lorna and I move away to university. One year and then I'll be able to start a new life. If all goes well, a life with a bit more excitement.

For now, it's hard to keep that in mind as our schedules get handed out. A year seems like an awful long time. I'm only half taking in our head of year's speech about the importance of applying ourselves this year when the school administrator enters the room, somewhat flustered.

'Mr. Thompson, I have your two new students here.'
Two new students?

Everyone's attention snaps to the front of the room. It's obvious they're all thinking the same as me. In a village where everything is news, how could we not know about this? I rack my brain trying to remember any houses for sale but can't think of any. They must not have moved to Wixford but somewhere close by. Still, *two* new students.

To my right, Lorna's gawking at me with her wide brown eyes.

'*What the?*' she mouths at me.

I shrug my shoulders, every bit as baffled as she is.

It's comical how the whole room stares at the open door, taking a collective breath while we wait for the new students to step into the room, like we've never seen human beings before. I almost laugh as I recall a line from a television show my dad likes to watch. '*This is a local place, for local people.*' Maybe that's a little too on the nose.

As they walk in, a wave of empathy rushes through me. They're so exposed, standing in front of everyone like an exhibit on display. They are striking, made even more so by the fact that there are two of them. The girl is beyond beautiful. A waterfall of golden-blonde hair cascades around her face and down to her waist. Her face is delicate, pixie-like. While obstructed, in part, from view by her brother. She seems terrified as she takes in the sea of faces watching her like they're waiting for her to fall.

Her brother—an obvious twin—takes a protective stance in front of her, absorbing the full force of everyone's stares with his mouth set in a thin determined line. He's striking himself, in a different way than his sister. He has the same golden-blond hair made of thick, scruffy curls, a juxtaposition to her perfect waves. His tanned skin gives the impression of an entire summer spent outside.

'Ah, yes…' Mr. Thompson lifts his arm, welcoming them in, '… everyone, this is Peter and Anna Burke. I'm sure you'll all make them feel welcome.'

The twins look uncomfortable in their uniforms while they shuffle into the nearest available seats. Perhaps they didn't have to wear uniforms where they went to school before.

The room remains silent with anticipation, but Mr. Thompson continues his speech for a full twenty more minutes.

This is so disappointing. How could he not ask them anything? Not where they moved from or for them to give us an interesting fact about themselves. Nothing.

When the bell rings, Mr. Thompson motions for the twins to stay behind so he can talk them through their schedules. The whole class is abuzz.

Lorna hurries to fall into step with me as we leave for our first class. 'Connie, what the hell was that? Please tell me you know something.' She mirrors my thoughts, saying what we're all thinking.

'Thompson could've at least asked them a little about themselves, given us a tiny titbit. Something. Anything. He knows he's stoking the rumour mill by not saying anything, right?'

'I know. He was happy to ramble on about hard work and university applications for well over twenty minutes, but when it comes to something actually interesting…' I make a zipping motion over my lips for dramatic effect.

'It's suspicious,' she concludes with an exaggerated shake of her head, sending her raven's wing-shaded hair rippling around her.

I take an excited skip. 'Why do you think they came here? Why move for the last year of school?'

'Maybe they're in witness protection?' Lorna offers, her eyes widening at the sudden thought.

I stop in my tracks at her speculation. 'Do you think so? That would explain why none of our parents knew they were coming. I wonder where they're living. I don't know of anyone moving recently. Do you?' Reaching out, I grab Lorna's arm to stop her. 'Wait. Maybe they live in that old mansion outside of the village.'

'The one that's haunted?' Lorna laughs, taking my arm in hers and continuing to walk us to class. 'Now your imagination has got the best of you. Although…' she taps her chin, '… I could have sworn I saw a 'Sold' sign on the gates the last time I drove past with my parents.'

'Lor, their parents must be rich,' I exclaim before we dissolve into fits of giggles.

Every country village needs a good haunted house story, and the house in question has been abandoned for as long as I've been alive. It must be a wreck inside. The likelihood that anyone has moved into the shell of a home isn't high, but it's fun to speculate.

Lorna's a bit more practical than me, but she takes great pleasure in indulging my more fantastical side. We both love to escape into our imaginations. One of our favourite pastimes is still Far, Far Away from Here, a game we played when we were younger, which revolved around us being princesses saved by white knights. These days, our fantasies focus more on adventures in hot climates involving mysterious strangers, so the appearance of the mystery twins is too delicious for our imaginations.

We head to our classroom, and for the first five minutes of class, we're distracted, often glancing toward the door and hoping the twins will be joining us. Soon, it becomes obvious that's not going to happen so, with reluctance, we give our attention to our teacher.

After English Literature, we have a free period to enjoy before lunch. Still too excited by the new additions, we decide to head to the cafeteria rather than the library. We find a table in the corner, and our conversation drifts onto other topics.

As more people find their way into the cafeteria for lunch, we're not surprised to learn the twins are everyone's preferred topic of conversation today.

But not everything I overhear is kind.

'She looks like she's a model.'

'I heard that their parents died.'

'They're totally dumb.'

Lorna's scanning all forms of social media she has, intent on finding out what she can.

My thoughts drift back to the twins. The girl was scared, that much I'm sure of. Which, now that I think about it a little more, is weird. I recall how timid Anna was standing behind her brother, trembling and clutching onto his arm. Something bad must've happened to her, something to make her brother stand guard over her the way he did. Witness protection, while Lorna had been joking before, is now stuck in my mind.

Or maybe I just need to get out more, I think and turn back to Lorna, who's now frowning at her screen.

'What?' I probe.

'Nothing, literally nothing.' She puts her phone facedown on the table before throwing her hands in the air. 'How can they have no social media... *at all*?'

'Maybe their accounts are private?' I offer with a grin. 'Witness protection, remember?'

She looks at me, scepticism written all over her face.

My attention's caught by a flash of red hair from the corner of my eye, and I turn to see a beaming Brady heading in our direction. An immediate smile overtakes my face as it's impossible not to grin when he's around.

'So, what do we know?' he asks in his bright way, trusting that both Lorna and I know what, or who, he's referring to.

'Zilch,' I confess. 'They were a no-show in English Lit.'

'I can't find them anywhere on social,' Lorna adds, deflated.

'Ahh man...' Brady's face fills with disappointment, '... this is so frustrating. It has to be the most exciting thing that's happened here...' Brady looks around, searching for the right words. 'Well, in forever.'

'Guys, I seriously think we need to get some lives.' Even as Lorna speaks the words, her actions betray her. It's obvious she's scanning the cafeteria for the twins.

She gives up her search, and I turn my attention back to the pattern of circles I've been drawing on the edge of my notepad. *Why is it so hard to draw a perfect circle?* I jump a mile when Jamie blows in my ear, laughing at my reaction before taking the seat next to me.

Jamie.

Perhaps the one interesting thing in my life.

I've known him forever, but these days he's more Brady's friend than mine. He is certainly not my boyfriend. Nor does he want to be. Thing is, he has an awesome smile, and every now and then, I find myself kissing him. It's nice. Uncomplicated and fun.

'Did you all get a good look at the weirdos?' he asks with some modicum of glee.

Lorna scoffs. 'Real nice, Jamie.'

My bestie's not Jamie's biggest fan and has never quite understood the appeal Brady and I find in him.

'I was just speaking to Lauren Tatler, and she was telling me those two aliens are in her Foundation Maths class,' he continues, ignoring Lorna's remark. 'Apparently, they didn't speak for the whole lesson, and they can barely even add up.'

Jamie peers around at each of us for dramatic effect, like we should be horrified by this piece of information. After a minute, it's Lorna who breaks the silence.

'So? Is it a crime to be bad at Maths? I feel bad for them. It's hard enough being the new kids without having to worry about struggling with your classes.'

It's a sombre thought that they're struggling, for some reason. Speculation aside, Lorna knows what it's like to be new. Joining a new school for their last year must be awful.

Brady and Jamie strike up a conversation while Lorna turns back to her phone. My thoughts return once more to the twins and wondering why I'm so fascinated by them. Well, the whole school's fascinated, but that's not the point. Maybe it's because I've always been the one to befriend the new kid. Granted, the last new kid was Lorna seven years ago. But the point still stands, I'm two for two on befriending the newbie.

My mind made up. I make it my mission to make friends with Anna and Peter Burke. After all, what else is there to do around here?

The twins are a no-show in the rest of Lorna and my classes, much to my dismay, so the whole day passes without seeing them again. Gone. Like a figment of my imagination.

With the school day over and no sign of the twins anywhere, Lorna and I head to collect our bikes. Brady will sometimes give us a lift when our schedules match, but today isn't one of those days. The weather is still sticky hot for September, making a long bike ride quite laborious. At least the quiet country roads are fun to cycle around.

I stick my bottom lip out and unchain my bike. 'Is it bad that knowing the twins are in Foundation Maths lessens their mysteriousness to me?' I ask Lorna. It isn't that Foundation classes are bad, but it's the class kids take when they've failed their GCSEs. For some unfathomable reason, their struggling with lessons doesn't fit the fantasy narrative I've created in my mind. *You're being ridiculous, Connie,* I tell myself.

'Yes,' she answers, tossing her long black hair over her shoulder while she unlocks her bike without looking at me, and I feel guilty. 'It must be awful,' Lorna continues. 'To move somewhere new for your last year of school and start a new life, especially if you're struggling in your classes. I just wonder what their parents were thinking. Surely, they could've waited one more year to move.'

'Hey,' I say, an idea forming. 'You said that old house had a 'Sold' sign out front. Let's cycle out and take a look.'

'Connie, are you for real? They can't have moved to this village.' The glint in her eyes says she's up for it, though.

The ride isn't easy, and it takes us the better part of an hour with this heat something more suited to the Caribbean.

'If I could be anywhere but here...' I pant, '... I'd be lying on a sunbed in Saint Kitts with sexy Peter Burke rubbing my feet.'

Lorna laughs. 'Wow. That didn't take you long.'

I laugh with her, the sweat rolling down my face and along my chin. Lorna stares at me for a second, making me conscious of the likely gross state of my face, before looking back down at her handlebars. 'If I could be anywhere but here, I'd be *anywhere* but here.' She grunts with the next push of the pedals.

I glance back at her as she swishes the masses of hair off her face. 'What do you mean?'

She shakes her head. 'Nothing. I just mean I can't wait to leave. I'm hot and cranky. We should've changed out of our uniforms. I'm dying.'

The whole summer's been sticky and hot—stifling at times—but today's a whole new level. The heat clings to the air, suffocating. Our shirts are wet and sticking to us as we work our pedals to get up to the top of the hill. At last, our breath ragged in our throats, the house becomes visible.

My heart sinks.

It still looks uninhabited.

As we get closer, the ride becomes easier as the hill flattens, but our breathing still comes heavy with our silent progress in nearing the house.

It's bigger than I remember.

The old paintwork is chipped and decaying. Disappointment fills me at the lack of a 'Sold' sign. Not even a 'For Sale' sign. The gates are chained shut.

Lorna rests her forearms on her handlebars, hanging her head to catch her breath. I peer through the gate and down the long driveway. The garden is overgrown, and it's clear no one has lived here for many years.

What a shame.

'At least we know for sure now.' Lorna pants. 'It's getting late.'

'It was a long shot,' I affirm. 'You're right. If they moved to Wixford, we would've heard.'

We ride home in silence.

I'll just introduce myself tomorrow.

Little did I know it would be a whole week before I had the chance to speak to them again.

CHAPTER 2

Peter

As fast as my feet will take me, I stride down the steps and out of the school building toward the car park, making sure I'm staring straight ahead while searching for Sally and James' car. I can sense rather than see Anna beside me and try not to notice the faces watching us.

We did it.

We made it through the first day of school without incident.

Survived in one relative piece.

The exhaustion of being around so many people is something else.

Even as we walk toward the car, recognisable as our aunt and uncle's, Anna veers away from me, going around to climb in behind James, who's in the driver's seat, allowing me more leg room behind Sally. Our doors slam shut in unison, and we both let out a collective sigh of relief. It's done.

James doesn't drive off immediately, and neither of them says anything.

They wait.

For us to share.

If we want to.

They've said this a lot over the last three months. '*You can talk to us, you can trust us, we're here for both of you when you're ready.*' But everything has been so confusing. It's still so bewildering, and I'm not sure we even have the words to describe how we feel.

I lean forward and press my forehead into Sally's headrest, closing my eyes and welcoming the dark. Anna's concern emanates from her while she watches me.

Sally can't wait any longer. 'So, how did it go?' She tries to keep her voice cheerful, but the edge of worry is obvious.

Silence.

I'm not going to answer, so Anna does. 'Exhausting, loud, confusing, strange.' This is all she can offer. It's all she can process for now.

To be fair, it's a lot to take in.

Sally opens her mouth, then closes it again, and doesn't press for more.

James starts the car, and we drive to the place we're now supposed to call home. Anna's voice sounded gentle when she spoke, a relief for me to hear after a day of hearing so many voices. However, there's also a weariness to it I've never heard there before.

I roll my window down as far as it will go, allowing the full force of the breeze to hit me and letting it clear my head a little. Anna follows suit and, for a while, we drive in silence except for the whooshing of the wind in the car. Anna slides her hand across the backseat to find mine, and knowing where to find it without looking, I wrap my fingers in hers.

'Did you make any friends?' Sally ventures.

'No,' I say, my voice coming out harsh. 'They talked *about* us, not *to* us.'

Sally shifts in her seat to face us. 'I'm sorry, sorry that it's like this. It won't last for long, I promise. The excitement will soon die down, and you two will adapt and make friends, and it won't be so hard. I tried to prepare you both as best I could, knowing today would be difficult and that all eyes would be on you.'

I lift my head to her. Her round blue eyes swim. *Pity, the look is pity.*

She continues. 'We aren't... I mean, *they* aren't used to outsiders.' Sally faces the road again, falling into silence.

Perhaps she feels bad about the outsider jibe.

She isn't wrong, though. Anna and I *are* outsiders here. Strangers. Even to them, our own family. Sally said she met us once when we were babies, but that's where the acquaintance ends. Although James and her like to pretend they know much about our "situation," as they put it, they don't know *us* anymore. In truth, they know nothing, only what they've been told by others.

They believe they did the right thing by taking us in when we were "found" three months ago. With every fibre of my being, I wish they'd left us where we were.

In the beginning, I tried to tell them we were fine where we were, but they never listened. We couldn't go back, and I had to accept that. There is no going back. My breath becomes shallow. It's like I'm trapped in a nightmare, one I want to wake up from.

We cannot go back.

'I...' I struggle to get the words out. 'I-I feel like I'm suffocating.'

My head drops onto the headrest in front of me, and I try not to panic. I also attempt not to think about Sally and James exchanging worried looks. Sally wants me to talk about my emotions all the time, but everything I say or do prompts concerned stares and hushed conversations. I'm learning to keep them to myself.

The air around me continues to get thinner with the rising panic. Helpless, I clutch my hand to my chest, fearing my heart will give out at any moment.

Anna squeezes my hand. 'Breathe, Peter. Just close your eyes and breathe.'

So that's what I do.

Focus on Anna as she breathes in and out with me.

The journey seems to last an eternity, but once the car comes to a halt on the gravel drive, my door's open, and I scramble through the front door. Frantic, my bag gets tossed to the floor with a loud thump. I need this consuming suffocation to end. I kick my shoes off, leaving them discarded in the hallway, then continue forward, hopping between strides to remove my socks.

Damn socks.

I hate socks.

In the kitchen, I move toward the back door, removing my tie.

That feels good. Should have taken that off sooner.

Footsteps echo behind me, but no one makes any effort to stop me.

The back door flings open and, striding into the manicured garden with purpose, I gather the garden hose. After setting it to sprinkler and moving two rocks to rest it between—to allow the water to spray in the air—I unbutton my shirt with my free hand. It can't be long before my aunt and uncle say something, so I move with haste. When I turn the hose on, it sends a fine spray of water cascading everywhere. *Yes. Perfect.* Shirt is off, soon followed by the rest of my clothes and underwear. Why not?

Ah, at last.

I lay on the wet grass and let my body sink into it. The earth is ripe underneath me, and I dig my fingers into the dirt while the cold water drenches every inch of my body. *Relief.* For the first time all day, I relax.

My breathing returns to normal, but with it comes a slight twinge of regret. Sally and James are going to be annoyed. They've made it clear to me before—no nakedness in the garden. It's considered inappropriate. Still, I'm hopeful that, perhaps this one day—our first ever at school—they will make an exception. At seventeen years old, we've never been to school or interacted with anyone our own age. If ever there was a time to make an exception, this overwhelming and strange day has to be it.

Anna makes her way through the mist of water and sits by my side, calm and relaxed. She too has removed her tie, shoes, and socks, but otherwise is still clothed. My sister's doing so much better than I am. Anna peers straight at me with her dark brown eyes, so dark they're almost black. I don't have to talk through or explain my emotions to her. She already knows.

My pain.

My twin's pain.

Being a twin is like being an extension of another person—two halves who make a whole.

She starts humming a wordless tune like a skylark, my favourite. I close my eyes and focus on the sound of her voice, the mist of the rain I've created on my bare skin, and the dirt under my fingernails. If I try extra hard, it almost feels like home, but not quite.

After a while, she draws her song to a close, and I open my eyes.

'Better?' she murmurs, her voice not sounding so weary anymore.

'Better,' I reply to her, my own voice warmer now.

Anna gets to her feet and offers me her hands to help pull me up from the ground. Her clothes are soaked through, which doesn't bother her, but I wonder if Sally and James will be angry about this too. I collect my clothes piece by piece while we head back through the kitchen, me dripping onto our aunt's clean floor.

From her place at the stove, where she's busy stirring something or other, Sally's jaw drops at the sight of us.

Anna heads straight upstairs without saying a word.

Perhaps I should try and salvage what I can, so I stop in front of Sally, trying to convey all the sincerity I can muster. 'I'm sorry, Sally. It won't happen again,' I apologise in a rush before disappearing upstairs, trying not to laugh at her shocked expression or how her eyebrows vanished into her hair.

I don't get the nakedness thing. While I don't make a habit of being nude, I don't understand why it's such a cause for embarrassment. We've never been taught this, but it must not have been right.

In my bedroom, I lie across the single bed, not bothering to dry myself while I hear Anna running herself a bath.

When Anna and I were first brought here, I took the smaller room. Sally described it as the "box room." It has a tiny desk, a set of drawers, a single wardrobe, and a window big enough for me to climb through opposite the foot of the bed. I didn't care—it felt like a cage. The first few nights, we crept out and slept in the garden when Sally and James were sleeping, but they soon put a stop to that. It was something else that was "not right."

There's a light knock at my door. Anna would never knock, so I grab the towel on the back of the door and wrap it around my waist the way I've witnessed James do the same thing.

See, I'm learning.

'Come in.'

James inches the door open and peers in. 'Hey, buddy. Mind if we talk?' He sounds casual, like he's aiming at being my friend, but there's something about his tone that sounds loaded.

I nod, and he moves to sit next to me on the bed. It doesn't take a mind reader to discern the awkwardness rolling off him. *This is not good.*

'Listen, Peter, I know you and your sister's upbringing was, well, unconventional. Me and your aunt will give you the time and patience you need. We'll get you all the help you need. But there are some things that have to stop. Now… I know you prefer to be outdoors, and that's fine, but the naked thing must end.'

I bite my lip. Knowing I shouldn't laugh, I manage only to give him a smirk. I'm not a nudist or anything, but the clothes they've given us are so restricting. Of course, of all the things he could ask me to do, this is an easy request. Still, the idea that being naked is a bad thing is an unfamiliar concept, and I'm curious.

'I know. I will, I promise. But, James, why is it so bad?'

Our mother always taught Anna and me there's nothing more natural than our own bodies, that we should be aware of them and attuned to them, that our bodies tell us everything. Our bellies grumble when we're hungry, throats go dry when we're thirsty, eyes grow tired when we're sleepy. *'Listen to your body,'* she'd said. *'And more importantly, listen to your instincts.'*

Instinct—that pit in your stomach—always listen to it.

Other Nature by Kerry Williams

It's hard to differentiate now, the things our mother taught us. It all seemed so normal at the time, but now we're told nothing about our upbringing was normal. That pit in my stomach has been there for the last three months.

My attention is brought back to James, who's taking a while to answer as if his thoughts whir about his head like he's not sure of the correct answer.

'Listen, kid. It's great to have a teenager in this day and age with some body confidence. Honestly, it's a good thing to be comfortable, to have confidence.'

Strange, I've never considered it confidence before.

'But really, it's not a question of that. It's more—'

'Inappropriate, I know,' I finish his sentence.

'Right. It's just not what people do... get naked and lie on the ground. Not sane people, not in front of their family.'

'In my defence, it's been an extremely stressful day.'

'I know, I know. I can't even imagine how today felt. But it will get easier, and you *will* make friends here. Some of them might be girls.' He starts to get uncomfortable, shifting around, not knowing where to look. 'Did your mum, I mean... did she ever talk to you and your sister about, ahem... the birds and the bees?' He all but whispers the last part.

I'm lost. 'About bees? You mean the hive?'

'Oh God, kid.' He slaps his knee, looking around for someone to come to his aid, I assume. Finding no one, he lowers his voice to say, 'You may have been through a lot, but at the end of the day, you're still a teenage boy. Never been around any girls apart from your mum and your sister. You have hormones. These changes in your body. You're seventeen, for crying out loud...' he trails off, embarrassed.

What he's said is enough.

It clicks.

'Are you talking about sex?' I ask a bit too loud.

What is he thinking?

It's clear he's more embarrassed than I am. I have to nip this in the bud. While I have no problem with the notion of sex, it's not a conversation I'm in a hurry to have with James.

'I know you mean well, but please stop. Yes, my mother explained to me how sex works. I'm in no way about to try it. I'm simply attempting to take it one day at a time and tolerate being at that place with so many people. I promise I'll not take my clothes off around you, Sally, or anyone at school, okay?'

I think it's the most words I've ever spoken to James in one go. So much so my head hurts.

'Right,' he says, getting up to leave. His face is awash with complete relief that he doesn't have to explain what sex is to me. 'You know—'

'I know, you're here if I need you.'

'Right.' He dips his head and shuts the door behind him.

It seemed like he had more he wanted to say, but he didn't push.

The biggest misconception Sally and James—or anyone else we've encountered since we've been found—is that we were neglected in some way. Abused even. The idea surfacing that our mother hadn't cared for us. But she had. She may not have done things the way Sally or James approved of, but she taught us everything we'd ever need.

Maybe not what the authorities, or Sally and James, thought we needed. The things our mother taught us to believe make far more sense to us than this new world we've been brought into.

From my limited time in Sally and James' world, everyone ignores everything that matters. The food was the biggest thing at first. Anna and I were looked at like aliens for questioning what was in anything. Hell, we hadn't even seen food wrapped in plastic before. We ate what they offered, don't get me wrong. We were hungry, but we drew the line at meat. We've never eaten meat in our lives.

Our social worker informed Sally and James that we weren't malnourished when they found us. She called us *'Thin but healthy.'* We'd survived on the fruit and vegetables growing in the garden, plus we had chickens to provide eggs and a beehive that produced honey.

I think about the beehive all the time. The bees will be fine, of course, but the thought of all the honey building up, and being left to waste, makes my mouth water. The social worker told us when we were still in the hospital that the chickens had been rescued and the hive would be moved. Like we should've been glad we were all rescued. At the time, I didn't have the words to tell her how wrong she was.

Things only got worse.

When we were released from the so-called "care" of the hospital, we were brought to our new home at Sally and James' house. The main problem is the garden. It's tiny and lifeless. Not more than a patch of green grass.

I remember the first time I saw it, its three-high, wooden-fence box in the grass behind the house. I'd walked its length at a rapid pace, putting my hand out to stroke its rough texture before asking, 'Where is the gate?'

They were confused. 'What gate?'

'You know, to get to the rest?'

'The rest? Peter, this is it. This *is* the garden.'

My eager face had melted into a picture of horror at the knowledge that *this* was all the outside space we had. They'd appeared offended. I suppose they were right to be. In their minds, I was this poor neglected boy who'd been found sleeping outside, pretty much in rags, to be pitied. Meanwhile, there I was wondering how they could live with such a paltry outside space. It was all so unnerving. They ate their unknown food, polluting their bodies, and watched their television, concerning themselves with crimes committed sometimes hundreds of miles away. They worried about the way they looked and then told me the way *I* had been living was unnatural. That we were wrong when we said we'd been happy as we were.

But none of that matters now. The police informed us we are minors and so we cannot go back. Our Aunt Sally—now our legal guardian—is our mother's younger sister. I imagine out of some weird kind of guilt after hearing our tale of woe from the police, she agreed to take custody of us. We had no one else.

I'm so lost in thought it almost escapes my notice that Sally has been calling me down to dinner. Changing from my towel into some soft tracksuit bottoms and a T-shirt, I head downstairs. I'm in no mood for talking, but Anna makes polite conversation with our aunt and uncle while I hover around the garden after I eat.

Despite their initial reservations, Sally agreed to let me start cultivating their garden, which at least brings me some sense of normalcy. And even Sally admits that what I grow tastes better than what she buys from the supermarket.

Later, I stare into the blackness of my room. Sleep is not my friend. Tomorrow, we face the same grim reality, and the next day, and the day after that. All those eyes, faces, and whispers will carry on, and sooner or later, we'll have to answer questions.

My door creaks open. In the darkness, Anna's slender frame creeps into my room, her bare feet soft on the exposed floorboards. I flip onto my side so my back is against the wall to make room for her, and she climbs into bed without a sound. I don't know why our aunt and uncle find this so hard to understand. They'd told us that since we're teenagers now, we should have our own bedrooms, our own space. Yet Anna and I have slept side by side since we were born.

Anna examines my face before placing an understanding hand against my temple, her easy smile warming my loneliness.

'*Bzzz.*' In soft tones, she emulates the noise of a bee.

'So loud.' I gaze into her eyes, serious now. 'What are we going to do?'

Anna's face loses all traces of her warmth, but she holds my gaze, her words imploring. 'You have to *try*, Peter.'

We've never had to speak many words to understand each other. I know what she means—if I don't try, if I can't make it work, I'll be sent away. I think back to when I'd overheard Sally and James arguing about it not long after we first came here.

'*They're not right, Sal.' James' voice was harsh, and I can imagine the worry lines his forehead displayed from how he sounded. 'They barely speak a word, not even to each other. They should be in an institution, somewhere where they have the help that they need.*'

'*James, the doctors and psychologists all said they were medically fine. They were neglected for their whole life, all they saw was each other. What they need is a family who loves them, to give them some normality, who can help them integrate. All these years, she did this to them, and to think, I could have made a difference. If I'd acted when I had the chance, those children... well, it never would have happened.' Her voice was laden with emotion.*

James, softened by her tears, says, 'Sal, this is not your fault. Your sister was crazy.' He let out a loud sigh, full of defeat. 'We will try. We'll try to be that family for them. I will do that for you. But they're seventeen, Sal. The damage might already be done. Try to be prepared for that.'

They had moved on, and I had mulled over that word in my head, *institution*. I didn't know what it meant at the time, but it didn't sound good. So Anna and I, we applied ourselves. We took the time to talk to them more. We practised. Practised all manner of things. For the most part, we stayed at the house, acclimatising and baffling Sally and James often. We didn't know how to work a television, and never had a phone before. Crowds were the worst. That was the hardest part, something I'm still not great with. It's a good thing we learn fast. Everything's hard. I'm totally miserable and even more exhausted, but the late-night rows they think we can't hear have become less and less frequent.

'Hey, come back to me.' Anna puts her hand on my shoulder, bringing me out of my thoughts.

'How do you do it, Anna? How come you are coping so much better than me?' I roll onto my back, rubbing my eyes.

'I know this has to be more difficult for you.' Anna sighs. 'And in case you haven't noticed, I'm not dealing with this at all well either. I was physically shaking as we walked in there, I was so scared. I know you could tell. And Maths? I wanted to cry.'

Anna had been shaking this morning, terrified of the day in front of us, but I know—even though she would never admit it to me—her nerves had come from somewhere else too. She's excited. She's curious to meet other people our age, and she had felt a nervous excitement about the notion of making friends. Anna's doing what our aunt and uncle want, looking forward. Trying. The more she adapts, the more inquisitive she is about being a part of this new world we've found ourselves in. Yet I just want to go back.

I do need to try, though. For Anna's sake. For both our sakes. We'd found out all too soon what an institution means—a real cage. It's somewhere I cannot survive. I close my eyes and repeat to myself, *I have to try.*

I turn to Anna again, and keeping my tone light, say, 'You know, James tried to have the sex talk with me tonight.'

Anna's eyes widen, a broad grin spreading across her lips as her shoulders start to shake. She brings her hand to her mouth to suppress her laughter. 'What?'

'I know. It was because of earlier.' I laugh with her. 'I think he's worried I'll just start taking my clothes off in the middle of class.'

She's laughing now, unhindered, struggling to hold in the noise. 'I'm afraid you brought that completely on yourself. I mean, *I* wouldn't be surprised if you did.'

I can't help but laugh too, and give her a teasing push. I shake my head. 'Sex is the last thing on our minds. I don't know if I'll ever get used to so many people. It's like every one of my senses being on fire.'

'Brother…' Anna puts her hand on my face again, '… you'll be okay. *We* will be okay. We *will* get through this.'

'How do you know?' I stare into her eyes, which shine in the night.

'Have I ever lied to you before?'

With a gentle shake of my head, I pull her into a hug. Anna has *never* lied to me.

CHAPTER 3

Anna

Peter's chest rises and falls in the breaking dawn, his expression at perfect peace. Not the constant furrowed brow he tends to wear.

I wish I could tell him how it feels to be overwhelmed. Except I don't have the words. This scary new world is the sinking realisation with every passing day how different we are. How at risk my brother is. I'm caught, trapped between a new world and my old. He needs me to be strong. He's already been through enough.

All eyes are on us as we move like spectres through the school hallways. I can always sense the anxiety rolling off Peter when he tries to search for a way outside. He's always looking for a way out.

He wants to escape. We even tried it once. A blundering attempt to run away, followed by threats from James that we would be sent away. I know Peter would try again if it were not for me, but he would never leave me behind.

I never wanted to come here, but my own curiosity flares as the many faces glance in my direction, so many people, all so different. I've read a lot about the world and the people in it. They always seemed like abstract concepts. I tend to favour characters from different times, Elizabeth Bennet and Emma Woodhouse, to name a couple. Relationships I used to dream about but are out of my time. My mother told me the world was cruel and people always wanted something from you. No one was to be trusted.

We were safe where we were.

Until she was gone.

Then we were lost.

So lost.

Everything that came after the blue lights showed up one night changed. Years and years of conditioning being overridden, people telling us we were safe now. It was all so puzzling. At first, we saw danger everywhere, and I whispered to Peter on repeat, *'Don't tell them, Peter, don't tell them anything.'*

After a while of watching them, it became clear there was no danger. They *were* trying to help. They helped to clean us and gazed upon us with soft expressions. They found our aunt and uncle.

Sally clung onto us when she saw us, but we couldn't understand the heartbreak she experienced.

Every soft word and gentle touch felt alien.

I started to realise the world was not as broken as my mother had told me, but we had no idea how to be part of it. Relationships were difficult. Not at all like what

I'd always read about. My brother's different. He's never been interested in people, and plants are not complicated. But to me, people are fascinating.

Peter was right. Our mother did teach us about sex, but never relationships. My one real relationship is with my brother, who's more a part of me than anything else. I marvel at the people in our classes, how they speak to each other, and their exchanges of affection.

My favourite is to watch Sally and James when they're not looking. How they move about the kitchen when they cook together, a hand on a shoulder, a shared kiss. Actions I have only ever read in books. *Love*. Real love.

I hear them say it to each other and wonder how it feels.

I don't ask. I measure my words. Being careful is critical.

Peter doesn't notice. He hates being around them. And I don't know how to explain it to him.

'Do you think she loved us?' I ask Peter one day in our hiding place away from the crowds of the school.

'Who?' he asks from his perch, eating a banana.

'Our mother.'

Peter gives me a funny look, taken aback by the sudden question. 'I don't know. Do you think she did? I mean, she did take care of us all this time.'

I take a moment to gaze at his face, a little rounder than my own and sprinkled with a few freckles. Our mother was different to the mothers here, and from her sister. There was never any talk of emotions, only a lesson in all things. Lessons for Peter in particular.

With a shrug, I state, 'I wonder if we can feel it. Love, I mean. Do you think we can?' I don't want him to know what it means to me.

Peter shakes his head. 'You're getting real life mixed up with a book.'

I glare at him hard. Everything's so loud right now. In some respects, it's almost like we've been living underwater for a long time. We even have to go to a therapist. It's hard, like I'm unravelling bit by bit, and Peter always expects me to do the talking.

'Don't you want to?' I ask after a while.

'No.'

'How can you say that?'

'I don't want anything to do with these people.' He shrugs, looking bored with the subject.

'What did we just talk about?'

He cocks his eyebrow at me. 'I promised to keep my clothes on, not to make friends.'

'What about what I want?' With my question, he looks up at me again. There's something different in his face now, something enough to make my heart break.

'*Is* that what you want?' He moves to face me, taking my shoulders in his hands. 'I want you to be happy, sister.'

'So let's try,' I tell him, the excitement building in me. 'Let's really do this.'

CHAPTER 4

Connie

'They're like ghosts. I never see them anywhere. They must've found somewhere good to hide. Not that I blame them, with the number of rumours flying around.' The last of my cereal gets spooned into my mouth, and then the empty bowl goes in the sink as my mum makes her second cup of coffee for the morning. 'How else am I supposed to help them feel welcome if they never show their faces?'

Mum eyes me with suspicion, mulling over what she's about to say. 'What if I told you I know exactly who those twins are living with. Would it clear up some of the mystery rattling around in that head of yours?'

'I would say, *Mother, you must tell me everything you know right now*,' I demand. Mum has always said that I'm *"Away with the fairies,"* my head always lost in some fantasy, and from the smirk on her face, I can tell she thinks this is no different. She leans her elbows onto the kitchen counter, my conspirator, ready to dish.

'So I ran into Sally Tanner in the shop. Her maiden name was Burke, you know. Well, you probably don't know. Sally is quiet. What you won't know is that before you were born, before her parents died, Sally had an older sister. Bit of a strange one, from what I recall, but I was still quite young myself when she ran away. It caused quite the stir at the time.'

I look at my mum, waiting, as she takes a long sip of her coffee, enjoying having me on this hook.

'And?'

'And those children are her sister's, the one who ran away. Sally told me she was contacted by social services that her sister had died, and those poor things are her niece and nephew. As far as I know, Sally had no contact with her sister at all, but she did say she'd heard from her once when the twins were young. She'd thought they had travelled abroad. They're orphans. Their dad died when they were babies, and so when their mum died, they had no one. Sally agreed to take them in.'

'Oh,' is all I can say, and I take a seat on the stool at the kitchen counter. So sad. No parents, having to move in with people who are all but strangers to them. Awful.

Mum looks at me in earnest. 'Now, you didn't hear that from me. I would say they've been through a lot, so be kind.'

'Of course. The chance to even talk to them would be a fine thing.' My attitude deflates. 'Do you know how their mum died?'

'Good Lord, Connie, I didn't ask that. The twins only just moved here over the summer, so it can't have even happened two months ago.'

So that's the mystery solved.

I tell Lorna what I've learnt on the way to school, but Brady and Jamie already know, and there are whispers of orphans all over the school. While their story is out of the bag, the twins are still nowhere to be found. New speculations about the manner of their mum's death begin to circulate, and the sentiment against the twins begins to sour.

'I think they're stuck up,' Jamie says when the conversation turns to the topic of the twins while we're having film night at Brady's on Friday.

'You've never even spoken to them.' Lorna is quick to dismiss, keeping her eyes on the film.

'I passed them in the corridor today. They literally walk like no one is there. No eye contact, nothing. I think they've come from some exclusive school in some fancy town, and they think they're too good for us.'

I roll my eyes. 'Jamie, their mum died. Have some respect.' I glare up at him from my cushion on the floor to further reiterate my point.

He hangs his head over mine so I'm looking at his face upside-down. 'They are freaky,' he declares. He sings the word *freaky,* and I shake my head.

'You're hardly one to talk, Jamie,' I say and push him away. Instead of moving away, he lunges in to tickle me. I laugh and this time succeed in shoving him back in his seat.

'Guys, cut it out. It's getting to the good part.' Brady shushes us, and our attention returns to *Night of the Living Dead,* but Jamie keeps his arms around me.

Which is kind of nice, given that I'm liable to jump out of my skin every five minutes when watching a scary film.

It's easy to put the new kids out of my mind for the rest of the weekend. The weather is still muggy and hot for September, but there's a hint of a breeze on Saturday, so Lorna and I make the most of it by lazing about in her garden, listening to music. Then, on Sunday, we walk to the coffee shop for an iced mocha with Brady before catching up on homework on Sunday evening. A regular weekend.

By the time Monday rolls around, my brain is twin free. However, my mind does keep wandering back to the sensation of Jamie's arms wrapped around me. Comforting.

But is comforting enough?

Hardly the basis for a grand love affair. Besides, I'm not sure if I like him in that way, let alone if he feels anything similar in return. I wonder if I'm hoisting one of my fantasies onto him. Lorna hasn't mentioned anything, and she tends to pick up on this kind of thing.

'Lord,' Lorna exclaims as she plonks herself down next to me at break time, cracking into her cold can of Diet Coke. 'I thought the weather might actually start getting cooler after this weekend, but I swear it is hotter than hell today.'

'I know. I think my face is actually melting.'

Lorna snorts at my remark.

Jamie, still fresh on my mind, reminds me it's best to get her opinion. 'Lor, let me ask you something—'

'Oh my God!'

My head snaps up at Lorna's interruption, and I follow her gaze to the door of the cafeteria to see Brady walking side by side with Anna Burke. Brady's animated, talking to Anna about something. I can tell he's excited because his arms are up in the air, and he has the biggest grin on his face. Anna's enthralled and laughing as if this is the most normal thing in the world. Her body language is open, and her grin matches Brady's, her high ponytail bobbing about as she laughs along with him. She's luminescent.

I find myself looking to Lorna, and we both almost crack into laughter. She's thinking the same thing as me, that this scene looks like something out of a film. Brady and Anna walking and laughing, lighting up the room, every face turning to look at them as they go. Typical Brady. Only he can put someone so at ease.

He walks straight up to where Lorna and I are sitting. 'Guys, this is Anna,' he says as if we would have no idea who she is otherwise. 'Anna, this is Connie and Lorna.'

'Hi, Anna,' we say in unison, and she gives a small wave, looking a fraction more nervous now than she did a moment ago.

The difference is incredible to how she looked her first day. No more trembling and no cowering behind her brother, who's nowhere in sight.

Brady beams at her as he motions for her to sit with us, and her face lights up again. Anna looks like a different girl.

'So, how did you get chatting to Brady?' I ask her.

She flushes a little and looks down at her hands before answering, 'Oh, me and Peter have decided to enrol in Sports Science.'

Her answer is not what I expect. I didn't have her down as a sporty type. With her long gold hair, legs for days, and doe eyes, she's too perfect.

'I helped Anna with her fitness test,' Brady adds while gazing at Anna and smiling again.

She glances at him, blushing, then looks at her hands some more.

I turn to Lorna and raise my eyebrows to make sure she sees this is happening. *Are they into each other?*

Lorna gives her head the slightest shake, bemused too, and like me, scandalised.

While we've been dying to talk to them, the sight of Brady all gooey-eyed has thrown Lorna and me off somewhat, and now we are struggling for something to say.

'Is your brother not in school today?' Lorna manages to ask.

'Oh, he's here. He's just grabbing us some water.' There's a slight edge in Anna's tone as she scans the cafeteria.

I start to notice people are looking at us. I don't want Anna to be uncomfortable.

'So, Anna, you like sports?' I ask, hoping to sound casual.

She twists the end of her hair, relieved to change the subject. 'More like being outside, really, and being active. Plus, they said the course was also about nutrition. Peter and I liked that side of it.'

'Oh cool,' I say, thinking about how this is the complete opposite to Lorna and me. Both of us love being inside, reading a good book, and we could live on caffeine. As I look up, I spot Peter walking through the cafeteria doors with two bottles of water.

The swing of the doors alerts Anna to his presence, and she peers behind her to follow his approach. Peter keeps his eyes on her as he walks over to our table, his focus one hundred percent on his sister. For some reason, Lorna, Brady, and I all take a collective breath.

Anna gets up out of her chair and closes the distance between her and her brother. She places her hand on his arm as if he might shatter under a heavy touch and whispers something into his ear as they walk toward our table. The picture looks off like she's preparing him or something. His head gives her the slightest of inclines, then he sits in the chair next to her.

Gone is the Anna of moments ago, the girl who appeared relaxed and carefree under Brady's charm. Now, she seems guarded and reserved in her brother's presence. It's as though the air has been sucked from the room, and I resist the urge to shout for someone to open a window. Why do I feel like I can't breathe? No one's talking—not even Brady—and it could be hours, but I'm sure only seconds have passed.

My eyes fall on Peter, sitting opposite me. You can tell his hair is pale and golden from spending time in the sun. His tanned skin looks flawless, and my brain registering he's far too beautiful to belong in this village. His deep brown eyes lock onto mine, and all I detect in them is sadness and weariness. As he opens his mouth— I hadn't noticed his lips before, but they appear soft— my bottom lip gets sucked under my teeth, reacting to his proximity. How is he even real? It takes me a moment to realise he's about to speak.

'Hello, I'm Peter.'

'Oh, I know,' I say. My brain is mush, and I want to kick myself as a smile tugs his lips. 'I'm Connie,' I add. It sounds like an apology for some reason.

'Nice to meet you, Peter. I'm Lorna.'

Oh, yes, Lorna. I forgot she was here.

Air begins to refill my lungs, and my brain gives back my ability to form a single sentence. *What's wrong with me?*

'It must be strange to move to a new place where everyone knows your business, and you don't know anyone.'

'Very.' Peter smiles at her.

I'm glad Lorna's able to hold it together and break the ice, impervious to his killer smile.

'Your sister was telling us that you've joined Brady's Sports Science class.' Lorna sticks to a safe subject. 'So what sports do you like?'

Peter draws a deep breath as if preparing for what he's about to say. 'Yes, mostly athletics, like running long distance, that kind of thing. I'm not so good at team games.'

I can't help but grin. 'I'm sure Brady will try his best to change that. He's always forcing us to play games with him. Well, trying at least. I bet he'll be glad to have some willing participants.'

Anna beams at the idea I've suggested by accident. She turns to Brady. 'I'd love that.'

Peter doesn't seem so convinced. 'I'm always willing to try,' he says, sounding anything but.

'That settles it then,' Brady exclaims. 'This Saturday, the field by my house, rounders.'

'Ugh, Con, why did you have to give him ideas?' Lorna throws her head back with a sigh.

'We'll be there,' Anna says to Brady, something of her carefree countenance returning. At her response, Peter leans forward to rest his head in his hands, massaging his temples as Anna places her hand on his back, rubbing in soothing circles. 'It'll be fun, Peter.'

Her brother looks up at her, defeated, and gives a small nod. This time, she gives her brilliant smile to her brother.

It's strange interacting with the twins. I imagined Anna would be meek with Peter having to do the talking for her, but it's Peter who's reluctant and reserved. I'm overcome with an urge to drop the pretence and ask a question we're all dancing around. Peter isn't okay. He may be beautiful, but even from my distance across the table, it's easy to observe that every muscle in his body is tense, in fight or flight mode, ready to run. It seems unnatural not to acknowledge it.

'How're you two holding up?' I ask, the question leaving my mouth before I have a chance to think about what buttons it might press.

Peter sits straighter in his seat.

I regret my decision at once, but it's too late now. 'I'm sure you know people have been talking, but I don't know if anyone has asked you how you are. It must be tough. I can't imagine how devastating it is to lose your mum and then have to move home.' I'm rambling, and to my horror, no one is stopping me.

My little speech has come to an end.

Peter's eyes bore holes into me.

Anna flicks her gaze from her brother back to me, opening her mouth to speak, but it's Peter's voice I hear.

'It is...' Even the two words are measured. He takes his time to select them, while I wish the world would swallow me whole and not have him stare at me for a second longer. '... completely overwhelming.'

He turns to Anna, and I see the empathy on her face as she waits for what he's about to tell us. Peter glances at the ceiling as he speaks. 'Sooner or later, we need to talk about this, so it might as well be now.'

'You really don't need to tell us anything.' I try to take it back, guilty for prying. I don't want to force them to relive any past trauma.

Peter's expression changes into something maybe bordering on relief. 'No, it's better this way. At least then it's done.' He takes another breath, keeping his eyes on mine as if this story is only meant for me. 'Our mother was sick for most of our lives. Much of our time was spent caring for her. When she died, our whole world fell apart. We have no other family except our Aunt

Sally, who we didn't know until we moved here, when we came to live with her and her husband. After getting here, we came to realise our existence had been sheltered, and we were behind with school and other things. Sally and James worry about us, and we're trying to adapt. But it's hard.'

'That's awful. What happened to her? Your mum, I mean?' I ask, unable to stop myself.

Peter glances at Anna—away from me for the first time—their expressions unreadable, before he continues, 'We don't know for sure. Sally and James won't tell us much. We woke up one day and she was gone. We think *they* think they're protecting us.'

'Peter found her body,' Anna whispers, and his head whips back to gape at her in disbelief.

Sharing that part of their story was not part of what they'd planned on telling people, I guess.

All of us take a sharp inhale of breath.

'I'm so sorry, Peter.' I say, releasing the breath. *No wonder he's so guarded.*

'Man, that sucks,' Brady offers, shaking his head.

Peter runs his hand through his hair. 'Yeah, it does.'

Lorna looks over in my direction, her large eyes trying to ask me, *'What now?'*

I can only inch my shoulders a fraction up, bemused, hoping no one else notices our exchange.

Anna saves us from the awkward silence, glancing at the large clock on the wall and saying to Peter, 'We should get going.'

Peter stands to follow her, everyone taking the cue and standing to leave also.

Lorna picks up her bag and says, 'Con, I just need to run to the loo. Meet me outside?' I agree, then she turns back to Peter and Anna. 'It was so nice to finally meet you both,' she tells them and makes her exit.

I've taken a few steps before noticing Brady from the corner of my eye trying to linger behind. I can only imagine to be able to talk to Anna again. I fall into step with Peter, hoping to give Brady a window, but he senses Anna's not close by. With concern etched over his face, he looks for her. Up close, the few freckles he has sprinkled on top of his nose distract my attention.

Adorable.

'You know, Brady's a really nice guy,' I offer, considering his protective-brother bit stands out a mile.

'Hmm...' He makes a noise in response, not convinced, but looks back at me, studying my face.

The sudden scrutiny throws me off balance, and I have a need to break the silence. 'It might not seem like it now, what with all the gossip and such, but we're quite a friendly bunch when you get to know us. Soon, things will settle down, and people will find new distractions to gossip about. And then you'll understand things around here are quite boring.'

Why can't I stop rambling?

I'm cringing inside as the words fall out of my mouth. I'm not even sure if I'm making sense anymore, but Peter looks sort of amused. *At least he's distracted from Anna and Brady's conversation, so mission accomplished, I guess.*

'Do you find it boring here?' he asks, the corners of his lips turning up just enough to make my treacherous heart pick up speed.

Yes, he's finding my ramble amusing. Why won't he look away for a moment like a normal person? His constant gaze is making me squirm.

'Believe me, Peter, you and your sister are the most interesting thing to happen to this village in my lifetime. So, yeah, not a lot goes on here.' I laugh, hoping at casual.

'Hmm… maybe a little too interesting for you.'

'What's that supposed to mean?' I narrow my eyes at him, wondering if he's teasing me.

'I guess you'll find out.' Peter steps closer to me, just a fraction, but it's enough to have the desired effect.

His sudden closeness clouds my ability to think. His eyes are bottomless brown pools, and I find myself glancing down at his lips. A thrill dances along my body and sizzles on my skin like electricity. A strange pull toward him forms somewhere in my chest, hot like a flame. Something deep in my subconscious whispers, *Danger.*

Anna brushes past me. 'Ready, Peter?' she asks, red-faced, as she walks by me.

Without another word to me, Peter follows his sister, leaving me wondering quite what happened the moment before.

Brady's next to me in a heartbeat, looking buoyant, which is welcome light relief. For some reason, I'm a little rattled by my interaction with Peter. *What was that?* I shake it off, turning my attention to my friend.

'Mr. Timms, was Anna Burke blushing as she walked by just now?' I joke with him.

'Well, I kind of *had* to ask for her digits to arrange Saturday, the rounders match.'

'It looks like she was happy to give them.'

'Yes, Connie, I got her number. Happy?'

'Very. I couldn't think of a better friend for Anna to make than you.' I laugh, and Brady pokes me in the ribs, but his grin stretches from ear to ear, so he doesn't mind me teasing.

'You and Peter looked pretty deep in conversation yourselves,' Brady teases back with a loaded expression.

'I don't know what that was,' I reply, and Brady shoots me a quizzical look. It's true, though. I don't know what happened other than we said some words—which I'm now struggling to recall—and just kind of stared at each other. Relieved I don't have to explain my overactive imagination to Brady, I motion to the ladies. 'I better pick up Lor.'

Once in the bathroom, I find Lorna leaning against the sink, waiting for me.

'That. Was. Intense.' She pulls me deeper into the bathroom.

'I know,' I say in mock exhaustion, joining her and looking in the mirror to see if my face is showing any clear signs of stress. 'I'm such an idiot. What was I thinking asking questions like that?'

She puts a hand on each of my shoulders, turning me to face her. 'You were just saying what everyone else was thinking, Connie. Plus, now it's been said, and we can move on and be normal around them.'

'Something tells me those two will never be anything close to normal.'

Lorna nods. 'You're probably right. But I can tell you one thing for sure. I'm glad we met them for the first time without Jamie around.'

I wave my hand, dismissing her concern. 'You know Jamie... he's all talk. He'll be fine.' Part of me must agree with my best friend, however. Because Jamie does have the tendency of saying whatever comes to mind without any thought and was never as eager to meet the Burkes as the rest of us.

Lorna checks her reflection again, looking at me through the mirror. 'Is he ditching already?'

'It looks like it.'

'Have you heard from him?'

'No. Why would I?'

Lorna doesn't answer, instead raising her eyebrows at me in the mirror as if I should have every reason to hear from him. Maybe she did read into the whole arms-around-me thing over the weekend, but I don't want to bring that up now. Instead, I let her lead me out of the bathroom and to our next class.

The twins sit with us at lunch for the rest of the week, and it starts to feel almost normal having them with us. When Jamie shows up for school the next day, he isn't surprised by them being there, which means he's spoken to Brady.

Anna Burke is sweet. She laughs at all our jokes and joins in as much as possible, although it's pretty clear she only has eyes for Brady. I'm glad for him. He's never been short of admirers, or girls who would've liked to have called themselves his girlfriend, but I've never seen him look at a girl the way he looks at her.

Peter keeps to himself for the most part and rarely speaks unless anyone asks him a direct question. I don't have much chance to speak to him.

As the week goes on, I accept that Peter may consider himself an outsider and will, in time, drift away from our group, but I like Anna. I hope she sticks around.

Friday's lunch is spent talking about the upcoming rounders match. We decide it will be girls versus boys, despite Jamie and Brady telling Anna she will have a double handicap being on a team with Lorna and me, but Anna shows solidarity with her fellow sisters.

That night, I receive a text out of the blue from Jamie.

Jamie: *What are you up to?*
Me: *Just watching TV. You?*
Jamie: *Same. Looking forward to watching you try to hit a ball tomorrow!*
Me: *Ha-ha! Goodnight, Jamie.*
Jamie: *Do you think those weirdos are going to be able to even swing a bat?*

Me: *Don't call them that! Anna's genuinely nice. Brady's obviously into her.*
Jamie: *He looks at you a lot you know.*
Me: *Who?*
Jamie: *Weirdo brother! Who else?*
Me: *No, he doesn't. Don't be ridiculous, Jamie.*
Jamie: *I do think Anna is okay.*

I stare at my phone. Jamie hardly ever texts me. Then, thinking of the past week, it dawns on me that apart from our bizarre exchange on Monday, Peter hasn't spoken to me at all. I haven't noticed him even look in my direction.

A knot in my stomach starts to form.

CHAPTER 5

Peter

Today is not one I'm looking forward to.

It's only seven a.m., and the dry heat outside is already rising while I lie on top of my bed with the curtains and window wide open, the sun warming my face. I've been awake for hours—it's been a restless night—with shadows crawling in at the edge of my dreams, threatening to choke me. When the sun came up, I opened the window to cast the shadows of my nightmares away. Still tired from the lack of sleep, I've retreated to bed and am watching the dust mites float around the room and glisten in the growing light, already willing this day to be over.

Anna stirs next to me. Rubbing the sleep from her eyes, she croaks, 'You're awake.'

'Raring to go,' I respond in a dry tone, then turn to look at her, almost annoyed by the bright, earnest look on her face. 'Why do you look so excited?'

'You should be too. Today will be fun. We get to be outside, to run—'

'We could've done those things without four other people,' I interrupt her.

'That's kind of the whole point, dear brother.' She looks up at me. 'I think they're our friends now.'

'They're *your* friends, sister,' I remind her. *They almost never talk to me.*

'And what's wrong with having friends?'

I hide my scowl. 'Nothing at all.' The truth is, I don't want any of them as my friend, not really. But I do want Anna to be happy, and this Brady guy appears to be doing that. 'Brady's nice,' I relent. 'He seems to enjoy lavishing attention on you.'

'He does, doesn't he?' Anna gushes. 'He's so warm to be around, relaxing, like being in the bath or lying out in the sun.'

'You don't need to do this, you know.' I turn serious. 'You don't need to fit in. Who cares if we're different?'

'That's not what I'm doing. I just…' She frowns. 'There's also nothing wrong with being normal. I like Brady. He's friendly and easy to be around.'

'Nothing at all like your dear brother,' I tease her, a little guilty that she's upset.

She sits up and levels a serious expression on me. 'Peter, there's no comparison. You're the most incredible person I know. You're just…' she pauses to search for the right word, '… restricted here.'

'I don't know, Anna,' I say as I put my hands behind my head, trying to lighten the mood. 'You don't *know* a lot of people.'

Anna laughs and gets out of bed, then paces my tiny room. 'It's good to see you smile. Can you please be *this* Peter when we go out later?' She rests against the sill of the open window, blocking my sunlight while motioning to my laid-back form.

'I don't know,' I reply, rubbing my eyes. 'I don't think Jamie likes me.'

'I don't think any of them necessarily *like* you, Peter,' she says with no regard for my feelings. 'You don't speak to them. Just try to play nice, okay? For me?'

'Hmm...' is all I have to say.

'And this...' she motions toward the open window as she gets up and starts toward the door, '... has to stop. It's almost October.'

I roll my eyes, avoiding her gaze. 'I told you I don't have any control over it.' When I glance at her as she leaves the room, I can tell she doesn't believe me.

My focus returns to staring out the open window. I should be grateful for Anna's efforts. Sally and James are beside themselves that we're making friends, and we've had almost no concerned chats all week, so I'm off the hook by proxy. Anna's plans are panning out okay. I'd been annoyed with her on Monday when she divulged to Brady and his friends that I'd found our mother's body. That wasn't part of what we're supposed to say. Sally and James were quite clear about the version of the truth we're able to tell, and *that* was not part of it. I hadn't shouted at her at the time. We never shout at each other, but it was as close to an argument as we can get.

'What were you thinking, Anna? You tell me I need to try, then you go and say something like that?' I say when I confront her once we're alone.

'Brother, I had to. I had to tell them something to take the pressure off you, something that makes them think

they understand you.' She implored me, taking my hands in hers. 'If there's one thing I have learnt in our short time living here, it's that people fear what they do not understand.'

She'd been right. Knowing this small truth, however shocking to them, made me less of a threat and more someone to be pitied. The explanation Anna gave made my distance from them all an excuse. It bought me time. And it worked.

They gave me a wide berth. Anna did most of the talking while I sat and observed, accustoming myself. From my interaction with Anna this morning, I gather my time's up. She's expecting me to get involved.

I move to the open window and take in the morning sun, breathing in the warm air and letting the heat fill my lungs. Maybe it's time to cool down.

One big positive of today is not having to wear a uniform. Checking my reflection in the round bathroom mirror, I notice my skin has become lighter since moving here and having to spend a large portion of my time indoors. Anna's right. Things are moving forward, getting easier. If I'd been told two months ago, when I couldn't stand to be in the same room with someone I didn't know, that I would be going out to meet a group of people and play rounders, I wouldn't have been able to comprehend the idea.

Donning a pair of khaki shorts and a simple white T-shirt, I head downstairs and find Anna pouring some orange juice.

'Are you actually drinking that?' I ask. 'It's full of sugar.'

'I know, but it tastes nice.' She shrugs me off and leaves the kitchen to go into the garden.

Wow. I stare after her in disbelief. I knew she wanted to try, but she may be going a step too far in immersing herself in this new world.

'Good morning,' I greet Sally and James, who are now up, sitting at the breakfast bar and drinking their morning cup of tea. Their jubilation at our making friends appears to have faded somewhat and has been replaced by anxiety. 'Are you two all right?'

'Yes. Yes, we are fine. Thank you, Peter. Of course, we are fine. How are you?' Sally asks, concern etched into her forehead.

'Fine,' I reply, drawing out the word. They must think I'm going to have a breakdown about meeting Brady and his friends today.

'Because it would be okay if you're not,' she adds as I pour myself a glass of water.

'Sally, honestly, I'm fine. It's gotten easier being around other people. I'm not going to have some sort of meltdown. This'll be better, and away from the school and the crowd. Piece of cake.'

Sally attempts a smile, and I can't help but empathise. Sally and James have never had their own children, and now, without warning, they're trying to be parents to two strange teenagers.

My hands against the counter, I lean in and whisper, 'I promise to keep my clothes on.'

She laughs at my joke, and her shoulders ease back. 'I'm glad to hear it. I'm so proud of you and Anna. You've done so well under the most difficult of circumstances.' Her eyes fill with tears.

'Thank you,' I answer, not knowing what else *to* say, then go join Anna in the garden.

The morning passes without incident. Anna and I laze in the garden, and I'm surprised to find myself not all that nervous about an afternoon spent with Brady and his friends. Or, perhaps, Anna's excitement is starting to rub off on me a little.

During my week of observing them, they've become easier to be around. Brady is something of the leader. His personality is vibrant, and he's always quick to smile and laugh and put everybody at ease around him. I can see why Anna likes him.

Lorna is also confident but in a more measured way. Over the course of the week, she's asked me the most questions. Nothing too in-depth, a few things about school, which I tried my best to deflect, but she seems open and genuine in wanting to be our friend. She shared a little with me about when her family moved to the village when she was younger, how it had been hard at first because her parents are from India, and they were the first family from a different culture to move to the village. Lorna told me she's visited her parents' home a few times to see family, and every time, she has to adjust to how different life is there. She knows what it's like to be "the outsider," and I appreciated her efforts to put me at ease.

Connie might be the hardest to figure out. She's quiet but also the one they all look to the most. Like me, Connie comes across as being a little in her own head, always doodling on the edge of a notepad, humming to herself when she thinks no one is listening. What she hums gets stuck in my head, where it lives for the rest of the day. She has this transformative quality. Her delicate heart-shaped face is always set with a serious expression, framed by almost iridescent, shoulder-length dark brown hair contrasting her pale skin. But when someone makes her smile, her face transforms, and her jewel-green eyes sparkle, casting light all around her. A slight tug inside me suggests I want to be the person to make her light up, to make her sparkle.

I shake off the notion.

Then there's Jamie, who I get weird vibes from. He's loud in a different way to Brady and has an edge to him I cannot place. His humour comes more from teasing his friends, and I've observed him looking in Connie's direction a lot, not that she notices. It amuses me to consider there's a large chance she doesn't notice a lot of things.

All too soon, it's almost noon, and James comes outside to tell us it's time to go.

Anna looks me straight in the eye and asks, 'Are you ready?'

'As I'll ever be,' I reply, getting up from the grass and following James out to the car.

Sally joins us for the ride, where I filter out her babble of *'If it's too much'* and *'We're a phone call away,'* while a wave of nervous energy rushes through me.

This is it.

No more sitting on the sidelines.

It's time to join the game.

Anna shifts slightly in her seat next to me, suggesting I'm not the only one who's nervous.

Brady's parents' farm is only a ten-minute drive away, reached via narrow single-track lanes. The openness and green of the land as we approach makes me more comfortable than I've been in weeks. Upon our arrival, Brady's home looks like a hive of activity. An older couple—who I can only assume are Mr. and Mrs. Timms—are in the long driveway, lifting bales of hay off the trailer of a tractor. They stop what they're doing to greet us as we exit the car. I can tell I'll like Brady's parents—they're earthy people. They both have the same flaming-red hair as Brady. His mum's is piled up in curls on the top of her head. She maintains her position on the trailer, mopping her brow with the back of a gloved hand.

His dad strides toward James with his hand outstretched, wearing the same friendly expression Brady owns. 'James, it's been a while.'

James shakes his hand with genuine warmth. 'I've been a little busy,' he replies, glancing in our direction.

'Clearly,' Brady's dad says, turning to take us in. 'Nice to meet you two. Anna, I presume? Brady has talked a lot about you.'

'It's so lovely to meet you, Mr. Timms.' Anna beams, shaking his hand with vigour.

'Please, call me Jacob.' He turns my direction next, and I also extend my hand to him, following Anna's lead.

'Nice to meet you. I'm Peter.'

Jacob takes my hand to shake it, staring straight into my eyes. His blue eyes are warm but piercing, almost crystal in the sunlight. The opposite of the endless pools of brown Anna and I possess. A sudden irrational fear that those eyes can peer straight into my soul and will expose all my secrets overwhelms me.

'Nice to meet you, Peter.' He turns back to Anna without missing a beat. *I must be imagining things.* 'Brady and the others are already down in the bottom field. I'll show you the way.'

We follow him, waving James and Sally goodbye.

'Just give us a call when you need picking up, kids,' Sally shouts after us.

'How are you two settling in?' Jacob asks while we make our way to the back of their large driveway, then begin walking along a narrow hedgerow.

Like instinct, Anna answers for the both of us. 'We're doing okay. Thank you so much for asking. It's been difficult, but everyone's been so welcoming, especially Brady.'

Jacob grins at her as we reach a large wooden cow gate. He leans his weight against it until the gate relents under him, opening a little at a time. 'You just need to walk straight across this field, and they're waiting for you in the next.'

We thank him and carry on our way in silence.

As we reach the gate to the next field, Anna comes to a sudden stop while reaching for my hand. 'Just promise me that you'll be careful, okay?'

I pause, bewildered. 'Of course,' I say but can't help wondering why I'd need to be careful right now.

Without saying another word, Anna drops my hand, and we march on through the gate. The rest of the group is sitting down under the shade of a large oak tree on the other side of the field. Of course, Brady's on his feet the moment we catch his eye, bounding over to join us.

'Hey! You guys made it.' He sounds surprised. Perhaps they thought we wouldn't show.

'Of course,' Anna replies, smiling. 'Wouldn't have missed it.'

As we near the others, they get to their feet to say hi. Connie's holding a miniature speaker, which is playing music.

'Shall we get started?' Brady asks, already moving toward a little pile of bats and picking up some green cones. 'I'll mark out the stops.'

'Ready to get your ass kicked?' Jamie leers at Connie, who gives him a playful shove in response.

'I'm just glad we have a cool breeze today,' Lorna says, moving her hair in appreciation of the wind.

Anna catches my eye, her smile deliberate and annoying. I roll my eyes at her. She honestly thinks I have something to do with it.

I agree with Lorna, so I don't have to look at my infuriating sister, 'Yes, it's been a long, hot summer.'

'Oh, he speaks,' Jamie mocks, gawking at me, but this time, it's Lorna's turn to give him a shove.

'Shut it, Jamie.' She moves away from him and comes to stand by me. 'I swear it must be the hottest on record. I honestly can't wait for autumn to get here.'

Jamie sneers and turns his attention back to Connie, who's flicking through her phone, finding another song to put on.

'So, don't you like the heat?' I ask Lorna.

'To be honest, summer's usually my favourite. I love the heat and lazing around in the sun while reading a book, but this summer has been a little too hot. Almost suffocating.'

'I know what you mean.'

'So, yes, I'm looking forward to autumn. The beautiful colours, crunchy leaves, being able to wear a cosy cardigan with a warm coffee, and a good book.'

'Hmm…' I chuckle. 'Whatever the season, there's always a book involved?'

'Of course,' Lorna says like I'm stating the obvious. 'It's my favourite pastime. Besides, my parents say this year has been unusual as we typically have perfect seasons. They've said they have never lived anywhere like here. The summers are warm, the autumns crisp, snow every winter, and rainy, fresh springs. Like textbook.'

I laugh. 'What do you mean? The seasons?'

'Don't laugh at me. It sounds ridiculous, but it's true. You've only just moved here, so give it time. Wixford has perfect seasons. Where I used to live, in Luton, we barely had seasons, and it rained all through summer. Here, it's different. I guarantee you snow this winter.'

I don't say anything. Lorna clocks my look of confusion, and a question starts to form on her lips. I'm grateful when Brady interrupts.

'Are we playing or not?'

'Boys are batting first,' I say, making my getaway from Lorna to pick up a bat.

Despite myself, it's fun playing rounders with the group. Lorna and Connie don't want to bowl, so Anna's happy to put herself forward for the job. I bat first, sending my ball straight outfield, heading toward Connie, who instead runs away from the ball rather than touch it.

'Con, you're supposed to *catch* the ball,' Lorna shouts to her, doubling over in a fit of laughter.

'Are you crazy? That could've hit me in the face,' Connie shouts back before making her way over to pick it up.

As I arrive safe at home, Brady gives me a high five. Jamie is ignoring me and laughing at Connie and Lorna.

They make a snap decision Connie will take over bowling, and Anna takes her place outfield. As the game goes on, it's effortless to relax into them. They talk to each other with the ease of people who've known each other their whole lives. A pang of sadness ripples through me as I think about how Anna and I will never have that. We'll never enjoy the sense of familiarity with others.

Brady bowls for the girls. Connie's up last, her face lighting up for a fleeting moment when she hits the ball. A moment short-lived as I catch it with ease.

'Thank God for that,' she exclaims. 'It's time for a break.'

I follow Connie back to the shade of the oak tree, and Jamie starts play-fighting with Brady while Anna chats to Lorna. Connie flops to the ground, picks up her phone, and selects a song. Her eyes close against the music, which I recognise as one of the tunes she sometimes hums at school.

I sit down beside her, watching her head move to the music. 'Who is this?' I ask.

Her eyes snap open. She hadn't noticed me sit down. Of course she hadn't. She sits up, looking at me like I have two heads. 'Are you serious? You don't know this band?'

'No,' I tease the word out. 'Sheltered life, remember?'

'More like you lived under a rock. They're amazing and one of my favourites.'

'I can tell.' I swallow. She's beautiful. I stare at her sweet heart-shaped face. This close, her eyelashes cast shadows on her cheeks, contrasting against her pale skin.

'What makes you say that?' She appears amused trying to figure me out.

'Well, I recognise the tune. You hum it all the time.'

She laughs. 'I do not.'

'You do,' I counter, then start to hum the next part while her eyes go wide.

'Aren't you observant?' She half smiles, not enough to make her eyes sparkle but the colour rises in her cheeks.

Is she embarrassed I've noticed her humming to herself?

I reach out and graze my fingers over the blush of her cheek.

'What does this mean?' I ask, but Connie has stopped breathing. Her serious expression is back, and she's fixated on me. Maybe I crossed a line touching her without warning. Removing my hand from her face, my eyes don't leave hers. I don't remember moving so close, nor do I know why I'm drawn in. I forget there are four other people around us because all I see are emerald-green eyes.

I hear the crack before I feel it.

Then I'm moving past Connie.

Falling.

CHAPTER 6

Connie

The spell Peter's eyes have put me under suddenly breaks when his body lurches forward and lands on the ground next to me. Instead of his beautiful golden face, I see Jamie's, his mouth set in a grim line.

'Jamie, what the hell?' Lorna shouts.

Anna's beside me in a flash. The blood on the back of Peter's head indicates Jamie must have thrown the rounders ball at him.

'Peter?' Concern is all over Anna's face as she rolls him onto his back.

Awake, Peter moves his hand to the back of his head, studying the red liquid he finds, and then looks to Jamie while comprehending what's happened.

I stand and glare at Jamie, ready to yell at him, ask what on earth he is thinking, but Jamie's voice booms out, cutting me off.

'Were you going to let him kiss you?' Jamie demands, his arms gesticulating like someone possessed at Peter.

'Are you kidding?' I ask in disbelief. *How can he be mad at me right now?* Although upsetting, no words come to mind or out of my mouth in my defence. I'm too distracted by the thought.

Is that what was going to happen? Would I have let him kiss me?

'Jamie, you're an idiot. I can't believe you hit him with a rounders ball,' Lorna scolds.

'Yeah, I didn't think I was such a good aim.' Jamie laughs, glancing to Brady for approval, but Brady shakes his head.

'No, man, not cool.'

Jamie throws his hands up in exasperation over none of us finding anything remotely funny about this. 'Look, sorry, man. I didn't think it would hit you.' He holds his hand out to Peter, helping him up to his feet.

Anna rises by his side, her hand moving to smooth the back of her own hair as if she had been hit too.

'Come on.' I take Peter by the arm. 'Brady's parents have a first aid kit in the kitchen.'

'I think I should take Peter.' Anna stays put by her brother's side.

I try to give her my best reassuring look. 'It's okay, Anna, he's in good hands. You stay with Brady.'

Peter gives her a small nod, and after a moment's hesitation, she lets him go. Brady places a reassuring arm around her while I lead Peter back toward the farm. Jamie gets my best evil glare as we walk past.

He calls out behind me, 'Come on, Connie, don't be mad.'

But I don't look back.

I'm now hyper-aware of being alone with Peter—Peter who makes zero effort to speak to me. Every time he has, the experience has left me wondering quite what happened. I drop his arm, which I've had my own linked with.

'I'm sorry about Jamie.'

'Why are you sorry?'

'I don't know. He's my friend. I guess he's just a little crazy,' I offer with a nervous laugh.

'I'm presuming he doesn't like me much.'

He smirks, and his dark eyes glitter as if he relishes the idea, but at least he's not upset.

'I can't think why.'

'Can't you?' Peter asks.

It sounds like a challenge, and my belly does a little flip-flop at the sound, although I have no idea why. *Why does he make me so nervous?*

We enter the farmhouse. It's nice to be surrounded by the Timm's family kitchen, a full and cluttered farm kitchen. It looks the same today as it always has, as comforting and immovable as my friendship with Brady.

I show Peter to the bench at the table. 'Here, you sit right there,' I tell him, then go and grab the first aid kit from a cabinet. As I crouch down, I steal a glance at Peter. For a moment, he looks so childlike, so innocent, sitting here looking around the kitchen and taking it all in. The muddy boots lined up against the wall by the door, the large basket of eggs—some with feathers still stuck on them—and a large bushel of beetroots that lie on the countertop.

'Is this your first time on a farm?'

'Yes.'

'It's nice, isn't it?'

Peter agrees, and it makes me smile. I've always loved Brady's family home. 'Brady's family are really wonderful. This farm was like a second home growing up.'

I bring the first aid kit next to Peter and examine the wound on the back of his head.

'Tell me about that,' Peter requests, peering up at me through his thick, dark lashes that contrast his blond hair.

There's something exotic about his looks this close up that makes me ponder where his family is from. He's so distracting. I busy myself looking for an antiseptic wipe from the first aid kit.

'Not much to tell. Me, Brady, and Jamie would always play here when we were little. The farm is a great place for hide-and-seek. Brady's mum would make the most amazing cream cakes, and we'd sit at this table and eat so many we would feel sick.'

'Ouch.' Peter winces as I wipe the blood away from the injury on his head.

The cut is so tiny it's hard to believe so much blood came out of it. 'All of that blood from such a tiny cut. I think you're going to make it.'

Peter laughs as he turns to gaze up at me. 'Thank you.'

The flash in his eyes sends butterflies exploding through my stomach.

'So, what about where you grew up? What was that like?' I ask, desperate to change the subject.

'Oh,' Peter begins, glancing around, but his eye is caught by something, and he moves away from me and across the kitchen to get a closer look. As he reaches the fridge, I notice what it is.

Great.

'What's this?' he asks.

'Oh, just a flyer from the coffee shop Brady works at on the weekend.'

'Why does it have your name on it?'

Busted. Although I'm not sure why I'm embarrassed. 'I have a little spot there this Thursday after school. It's nothing.' The heat rising in my face burns.

'A spot?'

He's going to make me say it.

'Yeah, I'm going to sing a couple of songs, play the guitar. Just a few covers. Nothing special.'

'Ah… the humming. I should've guessed.'

There's something about him I've never noticed before, but now that he's talking to me, I can't explain it. He's a question—an impossible one. One I'm starting to want the answer to.

'So you're musical?' he hedges.

'I guess so. Like I said, not much goes on in this village, so you have to make your own fun.' Without thinking, I step closer to him. 'How about you? You musical?'

He marks my move forward, the corner of his mouth curling a fraction as he takes a deliberate step toward me. 'Me? Not so much. Anna is. I like to appreciate it, but unfortunately, I don't have the talent. Your friend Lorna… she's into books. Is that you too?'

'You got me.' I hold my palms up to him, now standing within reaching distance. 'What's not to love? I'm able to escape to faraway places, which is ideal when you've never been anywhere. How about you? Do you like books?'

'Not really.' He shakes his head. 'Again, more Anna's thing.'

'So, you aren't musical and you're not into books. What is your thing, Peter?'

We're now so close his freckles are visible. I'm gripped by the outrageous urge to count them. Something about him pulls me in like gravity, and I can't look away. Which is fine. I don't want the distance right now.

'My thing?' he draws out, considering his words. 'I like being outside, with plants. What's the word? Um... gardening.'

Was not expecting that.

'Gardening?' I laugh, taking a step back.

'Yes, gardening. Nature. What's wrong with that?' he asks, also laughing and taking a few steps back himself to run a hand through his hair. It might be the first time he's appeared unsure of himself.

'Nothing, nothing at all. It's just unexpected. Not many people I know my age enjoy gardening.'

'Right,' Peter responds in a quiet voice, bowing his head while his gaze lingers on the floor.

The tension in the air clears. He's not what I was expecting. Intense but gentle—a duality I'm not used to.

Peter turns back to the flyer on the fridge. 'So, Thursday? Can I come and hear you sing?'

I'm a bit taken aback that he's interested in hearing me sing. 'Yes, by all means. But don't expect too much. I just sing a few covers. It's no big deal.'

'Well, I enjoy your humming, so I'm positive I'll enjoy your singing.' His eyes are full of warmth as he gazes at me.

The butterflies threaten to creep back into my stomach.

'Hi, kids, what are you doing in here?' Mr. Timms asks as he comes into the kitchen, moving over to the sink to wash his hands.

My back goes ramrod straight like a naughty kid who's been caught, even though I haven't done anything wrong. 'We were using the first aid kit. Peter hurt his head.'

'Oh. How did he do that?' He steps closer to get a better look.

'Rogue rounders ball,' Peter answers, retreating from Mr. Timms, and although I could kill Jamie, I don't want anyone getting in trouble today. As far as I can tell, it's the twins' first outing with people from school.

'Hmm…' is all Mr. Timms has to say in response.

'I should probably call my aunt,' Peter begins. 'Anna and I should get going.'

I make toward the door. Although, I'll admit to being a little disappointed he's leaving. 'Sure. Let's get back to the others.'

Anna jumps to her feet without a word of protest when Peter announces they're leaving after we reunite with everyone. They say their goodbyes and leave.

With them gone, Anna is all Brady wants to talk about, and although I don't say anything, my thoughts remain stuck on Peter.

The afternoon turns into evening.

An autumn chill is in the air for the first time this year, so we all make our way home in the early hours of nightfall. I'm exhausted. An uneasy sensation creeps in, and that sensation is called Jamie. He and I have always been friends—nothing more. Maybe we act a little extra every once in a while, but it's never anything serious. Unsure what to do, I opt to call for a second opinion and FaceTime Lorna.

'Can you believe Jamie threw that ball at Peter?' I ask her so as not to make it too obvious what I'm calling about.

'Ugh, Jamie's an idiot.'

'I know. Did you hear what he said to me?'

'Something about you kissing Peter, right?'

'Yeah. Did you think it looked like that? Did it look like we were going to kiss?'

'I don't know, Con. I wasn't watching, but obviously Jamie was and is insanely jealous.'

I groan. 'Do you really think so, Lor?'

'Of course, dummy. Jamie's super into you. I can't believe I have to tell you this.'

I let out a big sigh. 'He's never said anything. We have kissed a couple of times, but he's never acted like he wants anything more.'

'Well, he is a guy.' Lorna laughs.

'So, what about Peter?' I hint, trying to be subtle.

What do I say about Peter? I know next to nothing about him. Except that when I'm with him, he's like a magnet to which I gravitate.

'What about Peter?' Lorna pushes when I don't continue.

I can't think of a way to describe how he makes me feel without sounding like I've lost every single one of my marbles, so I pivot. 'I kind of invited him to my performance Thursday.'

Lorna lets out a low whistle.

'To be honest, he kind of invited himself,' I continue after recalling our conversation in the kitchen in my head.

'So, do you like Peter?' Lorna asks matter-of-factly.

'I don't know, Lor.' I get up off my bed and pace around my room. 'I've had all of two real conversations with him, but he has this energy that kind of sucks me in. He's extremely quiet and then, all of a sudden, super intense. Am I making any sense?' I'm not sure I've done a good job describing what it's like to be around him. I shake my head. *This is ridiculous.* 'You know what, Lor, I'm acting crazy. Don't listen to me.'

My best friend laughs. 'Connie, don't overthink things. Look, Peter is hot, and he's new. It's easy to get carried away.'

I let out a large, surly breath, and I'm forced to agree with a begrudging nod of the head. My imagination's running wild. 'One piece of advice I would give, though. As your best friend, iron out what's going on with Jamie.'

'Nothing's going on with Jamie.'

'Does he know that?'

'Yes,' I say, but even I can hear the lack of conviction in my voice.

'Fine, but there will always be friction between the two of them if Jamie thinks you're his and he views Peter as a threat. Besides, maybe you're reading too much into things with Peter and this will all settle with time.'

'Yes, you're right. Totally right. Why make things awkward with Jamie when nothing's even happening with Peter?'

'Right.'

'Right.'

We end the call, and I'm almost disappointed Lorna thinks I'm reading too much into the connection between Peter and me.

Why do I crave it so much from someone I've just met?

I think back to our conversation in the Timms' kitchen, trying to replay the scene in my mind. How I talked about being musical, liking books, and gardening. I groan out loud, moving my pillow over my face. I *am* reading too much into this. How embarrassing I even brought it up with Lorna. She must think I'm crazy. There's some comfort to be had in the fact that she's my best friend and is aware of my vivid imagination.

I'm surprised when my phone dings to see I have a text from Jamie on Sunday night.

Jamie: *Hi, Con. I just wanted to say, I apologise about Saturday. I don't know what I was thinking throwing that ball at Peter.*
Me: *I think it's Peter you should be apologising to.*
Jamie: *All the same. Are we cool?*
Me: *Yes. We're cool. Night x*

I put my phone down with Lorna's words fresh in my mind. '*Iron things out with Jamie.*'

Me: *Hey, Jamie, why did you ask if I was going to kiss Peter?*

It takes Jamie almost half an hour to reply, and I begin to think he won't answer.

Jamie: *Because he looked like he was leaning into you. Connie, we've been friends forever. I was just trying to look out for you.*

I check my phone, relieved Lorna has gotten it wrong.
Jamie isn't into me.

If Lorna's words hadn't put the fantasy part of my brain to bed, the next day at school does, as well as the following days.
While Anna emerges like a normal part of our group, Peter returns to being quiet and withdrawn.

Except now he blocks the rest of us out even further by reading *100 Years of Solitude*, which is one of my favourites. It's shameful how much I want to talk to him about it, and I berate myself for obsessing over him. I don't know what's gotten into me.

I try to reaffirm to myself what Lorna has told me. *He's just new, interesting. You'll get over it*, I remind myself.

The only time I even notice him acknowledge me is on Wednesday when I catch myself humming the song stuck in my head all morning. On instinct, I glance at Peter, who looks at me with a smirk and then goes back to reading as Lorna gets my attention.

By the time Thursday rolls around, I figure all thought of him coming to my performance is forgotten and have convinced myself it's a good thing I won't have the pressure of him watching me.

As usual, Lorna and I are the first ones in the cafeteria.

'Serious question,' I say to her. 'How do you think I should wear my hair tonight?'

'Definitely up. In a high bun. Show off your neck. You have such a pretty neck.'

I chuckle. 'A pretty neck? Really? Is that even a compliment?'

'Absolutely,' she agrees with so much vigour I fear her head might fall off. 'It's dainty.'

'Ha. Everything is dainty when you are five foot two, my friend.'

As we laugh, Brady sits down at our table, dropping his bag to the floor. 'Hey, girls, what's so funny?'

'I was just saying Connie has the prettiest neck.' Lorna giggles. 'Wouldn't you agree?'

'Erm, sure. Ten out of ten in the neck department, Con.' He smiles at me, not having a clue what we're going on about.

'Where's Jamie today?' I ask.

Brady shrugs. 'Ditching, I guess. I haven't heard from him.'

We shake our heads. Jamie can pretty much get away with anything with his mum.

'I think he's still coming tonight, though,' Brady continues.

'Cool,' I reply. 'I appreciate the moral support, guys.'

'Of course.' Brady grins. 'I'll pick you up at five.'

'Are you bringing Anna?' Lorna asks.

'I haven't asked her actually. I've not seen her outside school since Saturday. Do you think I should ask her to come?' Brady looks back and forth between the two of us, suddenly unsure of himself. His insecurity is sweet.

'Connie invited Peter,' Lorna teases, and Brady's eyebrows shoot up in surprise.

'Thanks, Lorna,' I say, slapping her knee.

She giggles, trying to escape me.

'It was just in passing, and he's probably forgotten, so I wouldn't worry about it, Brady.'

He gives a sigh of relief.

'Besides…' I continue, looking around, '… where's Anna today? Her and Peter don't seem the types to ditch.'

Brady's expression becomes stoic. He peeks around to make sure no one is listening, and Lorna and I automatically lean in closer.

'They aren't here today. They have an appointment.'

'What kind of appointment?' Lorna asks.

'Grief counsellor,' Brady says, his tone sad. 'Apparently, it was one of the things their aunt had to agree to when they went to live with them. Something about traumatic circumstances. They have to go once a month.'

Lorna and I exchange a look.

'Anna talks to you about this stuff?' I ask Brady.

'Sometimes.' He shrugs, keeping his tone quiet as he explains. 'I try not to pry. Like I said, we just text. She misses her mum, misses her old house. I know she worries about her brother. She said he didn't take the move at all well.'

'Did she say where they moved here from?' Lorna asks.

We're hooked on Brady's every word.

He shakes his head. 'No. I get the sense there are certain things she's not allowed to tell me, that there's this big secret.'

'Like what?' I ask, my imagination already starting to go into overdrive.

'I don't know. It could just be sensitive, but there's never any detail. It's all general stuff.' Brady glances around again before moving closer until our heads are now in some kind of secretive triangle. 'Okay, so she said the reason why they missed so much school was because their mum was sick, but when I asked what she was ill with, she totally avoided the question. And when she was talking about missing home, I asked her where she lived before and she said, 'It doesn't matter because we can't go back.' There's just something off. And she has this weird habit of always saying we instead of I. Which I suppose could be a twin thing.'

We all dwell on the thoughts for a moment, and I can tell Brady feels guilty about what he's told us. I reach across the table and hold his hand.

'Brady, you're being a great friend to Anna. You should see how happy she is around you. It probably is trauma, and I'm sure that when she's ready to open up, it'll be to you.'

Brady smiles and rubs the back of my hand.

'Thanks, Con.'

So, Peter and Anna are in therapy. I suppose that isn't surprising, given their circumstances. I can't imagine what it would be like to lose either of my parents. To only be seventeen with no mum or dad. Even more, having been your mum's carers for most of your life. I guess the traumatic circumstances Brady referred to was how Peter had found her. When he has something like that going on, I can't blame him that making friends isn't at the top of his priority list.

By the time four thirty rolls around, I'm focused only on my performance. I've left it to the last minute to decide what songs to play so I'm packing in some last-minute practice. I sit on my bed, strumming on my battered old guitar, which used to be my dad's, humming along to the tune.

'Hey, honey.' Mum comes into my room. 'So I'm leaving now... I want to get a good spot. I'll meet you there.'

I grin at her. Although I'm only playing five songs, in my mum's eyes, I might as well be playing Wembley Stadium. She's always been proud I inherited Dad's voice.

'Thanks, Mum. Is Dad coming too?'

'Sorry, love.' She rubs my shoulder. 'He wishes he could be there, but he has to work late tonight.'

I bow my head and try not to let it bother me. My mum and dad have been together since they were around my age, but his job keeps him away a lot. An arrangement that appears to suit them both.

When Brady arrives at my house at five p.m., Jamie and Lorna are already in the car.

'Where were you today?' I ask Jamie as I climb into the back with Lorna.

'I had a headache,' he says with a cheeky grin on his face.

I shake my head at him, but I'm smiling. Jamie's cheekiness is part of the reason I like him.

Lorna gives him a stern look but says nothing.

The coffee shop is in the middle of the high street, a short walk from the car park. The wind bites tonight, and I wrap my arms around myself as we walk, clinging to the edges of my denim jacket and giving a shudder.

Jamie puts his arm around my shoulders and pulls me close. 'You okay? You're shaking.'

'It's chilly,' I respond, hoping it's not my nerves getting to me.

'I know,' Lorna exclaims in agreement, pulling her hands into the sleeves of her hoodie. 'Last week it was so bloody hot Connie's face almost melted off.'

We all laugh.

The warmth of the coffee shop is a welcome respite from the cool wind outside. It looks like the heat wave has finally broken.

I turn to Lorna. 'I'm going to go set up.'

'We'll be in the front row.' She winks at me.

I go to the front of the cosy café and start to get comfy, making sure my guitar is tuned and try to settle my nerves. I've done a spot here once before, so I know the worst part is getting going. Because of the shop's mini size, everyone's faces can be seen from the stage, which I don't mind, but I always expect the initial words to stick in my throat. So, for that first part, I close my eyes or look down at my guitar.

'Hi, I'm Connie Prinze, and I will be singing you a few songs tonight.'

My opening is met with cheering and whooping from Brady, Lorna, and Jamie. I can't help but laugh and shake my head at my friends, who also happen to be my most loyal fans. Having them here helps take the edge off my nerves.

Setting my fingers to the strings, I close my eyes, and I'm off.

The coffee shop is a warm and welcoming place to be. The interior has chocolate-coloured walls, a selection of round tables with wooden seats clustered in the middle, and two comfy booths in the window that have chequered cushions. Brady only works here on weekends, and often Lorna and I will come and occupy a booth to keep him company while we chat, read, and drink coffee.

As I finish my first song, more cheers erupt from the table of my friends while the other coffee drinkers clap along.

'Thank you to my adoring fans. Glad you could all make it,' I mock my gang.

Moving into my second song, I'm way more relaxed and confident. As the song goes on, a few more people arrive, ordering their drinks in quiet tones, some having hushed conversations, others sipping their coffee and watching me with varying degrees of attention. I find my mum's eyes and shoot her a quick wink while I sing.

As my second song finishes, my friends continue their clapping and rooting. I think my mum joins in too. I launch into my third and then fourth, which is another folky, upbeat song, my nerves now cast away.

I enjoy this song, always have. It sounds so cheery, but the lyrics tell of heartbreak. Glancing up, the door to the coffee shop opens and I spot Anna's golden hair as she walks in followed by her brother. My eyes drop back to the neck of my guitar, where I focus on my finger placement and try not to let their sudden entrance allow me to forget the lyrics.

When I peek again, Anna's looking around the coffee shop in search of our friends, but Peter's watching me. And I'm looking straight at him. Letting my eyes close, I try to remember to breathe. When I open them again, Brady and Lorna are motioning the twins over to their table while Jamie throws daggers their way. I continue my song while my heart pounds in my rib cage. I shut my eyes again, and in the hope everyone doesn't notice any hysteria in my voice, I choose to play off my sudden panic as passion and perform the rest of the song with my eyes closed, at last able to regain some sense of composure.

Damn him!

I breathe a sigh of relief as I finish, allowing myself to open my eyes to the round of applause and more cheers from Brady, Lorna, and Jamie. Anna is also giving a standing ovation. I take a sip of my water. Peter has not joined in the theatrics of cheering, but he's applauding and smiling at me. I silently curse him for the effect he has on my heart rate. At least I only have one more song to play.

My final song.

There's a slight pang of worry for it as it's more of a ballad, slow but beautiful. It's been in my head all day, and I haven't been able to shake the urge to sing it. *Too late to change my mind now.*

Relax, Connie, I think to myself. My heart's pounding like crazy. Pulling a deep breath in, I rest my forehead on the edge of my guitar and begin. The words aren't complicated, but they are sung slowly, subtle, and from the heart. At least they *are* coming out of me. I close my eyes and lift my head, gaining some strength. It's a short, beautiful song. *I can do this.*

My eyes open and find Peter's.

The world dissolves.

All hesitation is gone.

Right now, I'm singing only to him.

His warm chocolate-coloured eyes never leave mine, and his skin has a glow in the dim light of the fading day. I smile through my words, and he returns a hint of one, and instantly I experience the heat of colour flooding my cheeks. In this moment, I know what I've been feeling isn't my imagination—he's attracted to me too. We could be the only two people in the world.

I look back down at my strings to finish the tender song.

The coffee shop customers are applauding again, and my friends are, of course, cheering.

And that's when my insecurities flood back.

Did I just stare at Peter for a full two minutes? Well, that's embarrassing.

I try not to look at them while putting my guitar down.

'Thank you, everyone, for listening,' I manage to say before getting off my stool and heading toward the counter. I need coffee and a moment to compose myself.

Lorna's arm slides around my shoulder as I move. 'Wow, Connie, that last song was amazing,' she praises.

'Really?'

'Seriously. I still have the goose bumps.' She shows me her arms.

'I didn't know if I could pull that one off, but it's been rattling around my head all day.'

'It was gorgeous, Connie.'

I let out a sigh of relief. 'Thanks, Lor. Now I need coffee.'

She grins and lets me pass as she returns to the table with everyone else.

I'm sure Lorna would've told me if something was off or if I seemed to be serenading the new guy. *What is wrong with me?* I reach the counter and inspect the menu, thinking I might need something stronger than my usual cinnamon latte.

'I don't have to tell you that you sounded beautiful,' a voice says behind me, and I drop my purse in surprise.

'Peter.'

'I didn't mean to make you jump. Here, let me get that.' Without giving me a chance to stop him, Peter drops to one knee to pick up my purse from the floor.

Something about having him kneeling at my feet knocks the breath out of me. I turn back to the counter, taking the purse from him while using the counter to steady myself. 'Thank you.'

'I have been listening to that band you like. I'd hoped it would help me recognise the songs you sang. I didn't recognise that last one, though.'

'Really?' I ask, examining his face for signs he's making fun of me but finding none. 'Sorry to disappoint.'

Peter closes the gap between us—he must be six foot tall as he towers over me.

'That's okay. I enjoyed what you sang more.'

The ability to form words escapes me, so instead, I stare up at him. I have no idea what to make of him. He's two different people—a silent outsider or warm and confident.

Mike—who owns the coffee shop—appears, interrupting our staring contest and asks what I'm having.

I manage to order my regular cinnamon latte as my brain has nothing else to offer at this moment. Also I offer to buy a coffee for Peter, but he politely declines.

When Mike disappears to make my coffee, Peter continues, 'I only wish I'd been here since the start.'

'Brady mentioned your appointment when you and Anna weren't at school today. To be honest, I didn't think you'd come at all.'

Something shifts in his face. 'Yes, I thought Anna may have said something to Brady about it.'

'Does it help? Therapy, I mean,' I venture.

Peter shifts his head from side to side as if considering his answer. My hands stay put on the counter to prevent myself from fidgeting as I take in the contrast of his golden hair to his tanned skin and how good he looks in his pale grey jumper.

'A little, I suppose.' He places his hand on the counter next to mine, drumming his fingers before looking me in the eye. 'It's weird talking about our mother to a stranger. We're protective of our memories with her.'

'I can understand that. It must be hard.'

'Yes and no.' Peter's dark eyes bore into mine, and it's like the volume around me turns down. His head dips slightly, his voice going low as he confesses, 'It's more exhausting how we're treated like we're made of glass, everyone expecting us to break at any moment. Death is natural. But I'm always being told I'm not coping in the right way, not saying or doing the right things. That it's okay to cry, to share.'

'And you don't?'

'Why would I?'

Peter's voice is like velvet, his eyes deep enough to swim in. I move into sync with him. I breathe in, moving nearer, becoming aware of how close my hand is to his. Part of me wants to reach out and take it while his whole presence envelops me.

I almost jump out of my skin when Mike returns and hands me my coffee.

I'm not ready for my conversation with Peter to be over but sense we need to move to a safer topic than his mum's death.

I shift a little to the side of the counter. 'I noticed you've been reading *100 Years of Solitude*.'

'Mmm… you like that one?'

'I love it. It's so intricate and magical. It's a classic. Are you enjoying it?'

'I am. Is that what you like reading about? Magical people and places?'

'I like reading everything, Peter. Anything that takes me far away from here.' I relax at last. 'It's a pretty hard-going book, though. Not the easiest read.'

'Hmm… I think I can handle it.'

I look down at my shoes, wondering where I'm going with this. Still, I ask, 'It's just, aren't you in the Foundation English class?'

'Yeah,' Peter responds. 'So, what? Did you think I couldn't read?'

'No.' Apologetic, I hurry to add, 'Of course not. I'm sorry, I didn't mean to imply—' I stop.

Peter's laughing, making it obvious he's winding me up.

'That's not fair,' I say and give his arm a gentle push. 'It's kind of funny.'

Once my heart rate returns to normal, I take a sip of my coffee before continuing, 'Well, you seem in a much better mood. You know, you barely talk to us at school. I was starting to think you didn't like me.'

Peter's face turns serious. 'Can I tell you a secret?'

'Sure.' I hold my breath. Happy to be his conspirator.

'I hate school.'

I can't help but laugh, and Peter laughs with me. 'I think everyone hates school, Peter.'

'It's not the lessons. I despise the noise, and there are so many people. I don't like big crowds.'

'That must be tough. Our school isn't even that big. Where did you go to school before? I can't imagine anywhere being any smaller than here.'

Peter waits a beat, his dark eyes serious and taking me in as he decides what to say next. I get the sense I've put my foot in my mouth again somehow by pushing too far.

'Actually, we've never been to school before. I guess our mother was what you'd call a recluse, so she homeschooled us our entire lives. All Anna and I have ever known is each other and our mother. I don't remember meeting anyone else in my entire life until after she died. So when I said before that we were sheltered, I was understating it. We were completely isolated. No friends, no family. Just us. Also part of the reason for therapy. Adjusting to mainstream society. It's been one hell of a learning curve.'

'Peter…' I'm dumbfounded. 'I don't know what to say.'

'It's okay. It's kind of nice to say it out loud. You won't say anything, will you? Our official line is that we cared for our ill mother, not that she was crazy.'

'Of course, your secret's safe with me,' I promise, putting my hand on my heart.

'So that's the reason for the foundation classes, detective.' He shakes his head, his tone light, as he leans a shoulder on the wall beside him. 'No school, no qualifications. Our aunt wants us to have some normalcy, gain some sort of qualifications, have a chance in life, and get to meet kids our own age. It's getting easier, but the crowds still get to me.'

'If it's any consolation, Peter, I think you're doing amazing, given the circumstances.'

Peter flashes me a brilliant, dangerous grin. 'It's easier around you. I feel calmer. More myself.'

Just when my heart had been doing so well, his words knock the wind out of me. I set my coffee cup down on the counter and murmur, 'I think you have the opposite effect.'

'What do you mean?' His eyes search my face.

I hadn't expected him to hear, and for a split second, I only enjoy how he's looking at me by drinking in his chocolate eyes, the splattering of freckles, the warmth blooming in my stomach.

'Connie.'

My mum is at my elbow. Hearing my name in a voice other than Peter's makes me jump a mile—again. I'm all too grateful I'd put my cup down or I'd be wearing my coffee.

'Are you ready to go?'

The volume in the coffee shop has returned, and it clicks life's been going on around me while Peter and I have been talking. I glance over to the front table where Anna, Brady, and Lorna are all deep in conversation. Jamie, however, is nowhere in sight.

'Yes. Let me just go and say bye to the guys.' I motion to my friends, trying to pull my thoughts together.

Mum's eyes are taking in Peter's tall form. She is angling for an introduction even though she obviously knows who he is. It's a bit disconcerting that Peter up close is intriguing for anybody.

'Mum, this is Peter from school. Peter, this is my mum. Er… Suzie.' Again, I want to kick myself for almost forgetting my mum has a name.

'So nice to meet you, Peter.' Mum shakes his hand. 'I hope Connie's been welcoming.'

'She's been super welcoming. My sister and I are lucky to call her a friend.' Peter glances at me with a tug at his lips again.

'I'll meet you at the car.' I urge Mum to leave before I melt into a puddle.

At the front table, I interrupt a heated but jovial conversation between Anna, Brady, and Lorna to tell them goodnight.

I can't help but take in Anna. Sitting close to Brady, she seems so happy, laughing while Brady's hand rests on her knee. It's hard to believe that up until a few months ago, she'd never spoken to another soul, and yet, here she is, mediating a harmless argument, leaning into Brady. The mystery Brady revealed earlier is now solved, for me, at least. There's some guilt for being sworn to secrecy, but Anna will tell Brady when she's ready.

I collect my jacket and guitar, scan the coffee shop hoping to find Peter, then frown when I don't.

Damn, I wanted to say goodnight.

I resign myself to a night of overthinking and replaying our conversation from earlier, but no sooner than I open the door to leave do I see him standing outside gazing up at the clear night sky.

He tilts his body back toward me. 'Just getting some air.' He motions to the now bustling coffee shop.

A nod expresses my understanding about the crowd. 'It's a beautiful night,' I say, coming to stand next to him. The wind from earlier has subsided, leaving the air cool and fresh. All the stars are on display in the inky sky.

He faces me. 'It truly is.'

Once more, the world shrinks around us.

'See you tomorrow, Peter.'

'Goodnight, Connie.'

I drag myself away and walk toward the car park to find my mum. As I go, I turn to find Peter watching me leave.

Damn.

I'm in deep.

CHAPTER 7

Peter

Saturday morning comes with the sweet sound of rain.

I love the rain.

It's transformative.

Life-giving.

Cleansing.

I close my eyes, listening to the *drop, drop, drop* of the water on the frame outside my window. Imagining Connie's voice, letting its sweet sound wash through me, the song fills me from the tip of my toes right up through my chest. I can breathe it in, breathe in her words, her song. Those round green jewel eyes on me as she sang. The frustration of yesterday when she averted her gaze after she caught me looking at her and the sensation in my chest that I *want* her to look at me. When she sees me, for her lips fashion themselves into a smile. All these things fill me with wonder about what's to come.

I throw back the covers. I've lingered in bed for too long. Yesterday's T-shirt in hand, I pad downstairs, mindful of keeping my footsteps quiet. My pace becomes more urgent as my hand grapples with the backdoor handle.

Outside, air, rain—I need them all.

The wet grass between my toes brings me back to myself, grounding me. I open my arms and, turning my face upward, let the rain cleanse me. Wash the thoughts of Connie away.

I don't know how long I stand here with my arms raised, imploring the heavens.

'Peter?'

My sister is in her dressing gown and slippers, hunched from the rain. I must've been out here for a while as the cotton of my T-shirt and boxers cling to my drenched skin.

'Are you okay?'

'Fine. Just enjoying the first rain. Are they up yet?'

'Luckily for you, no. You should probably come back inside.'

I join my sister. She wraps her arm and half her dressing gown around me, then leads me through the kitchen, leaving wet footprints in my wake. *I need to remember to clean those up, or else I'll face the irritation of Sally.* Getting to my room, I wrap my own dressing gown around me and join Anna on my bed, leaning my soaked head onto her shoulder.

'You like her?' Anna asks, leaning her cheek on the top of my head, reading my mind.

'I barely know her. My thoughts just drift in her direction sometimes.'

'It's okay for you to want a connection, Peter. We've been so alone.'

'I have you.'

'It's not the same, my dear brother.'

'She would run a mile if she actually knew me.'

'Peter.' Anna pulls away to turn her body toward me, her hand angling my cheek so I can't help but look at her. 'It doesn't have to be that way. You can still let her know you, part of you.'

'How do I separate the two, Anna?'

'It gets easier. It just takes practice.'

I stare into her eyes for a second before asking, 'What part of yourself are you hiding?'

She opens her mouth but decides not to say anything, so I go on, 'I may have already told her we were homeschooled.'

Anna's expression becomes stern, so I bite the bullet and come clean. 'And that we actually hadn't met anyone else until we came here.'

'Peter.'

'You told Brady about the counselling,' I retaliate.

'Yes, because that's normal.'

'Who defines what's normal? Have you seen what they watch on TV?'

'Peter. Don't do that. You have to have some self-control.'

'Anna, do you really think they aren't guessing at what we're not saying?' I'm serious now. 'I only told her because she's already piecing together the holes in our story.' As I'm saying the words, I know they're only partially true. I *wanted* to tell her.

Anna lets out a deep breath, rubbing her forehead. She knows I'm right even if my intentions are a bit murky.

'Peter—' she starts.

'Anna. I barely see her except for school, and even then, it's across a table in a noisy cafeteria. I can control myself.'

Her expression implies she wants to say more, but she doesn't. For which I'm glad. When I think of the yin and yang that is Anna and me, Anna is the head and I'm the heart. While our new friends will start asking questions, Anna knows caution is the best way forward. The fact she is right is beyond frustrating, though. Nothing about our childhood was normal, and who we trust with that information—if ever—is not a decision to be made in haste.

'Anyway, isn't today the big date with Brady?' I ask, wanting to change the subject.

Mission accomplished. Anna beams at me. 'Yes. He's coming here around three, so we'll spend some time together, and I think he said we could order pizza and watch a film. Sounds great, right?'

'Yes, all great. Not sure about the pizza, though.'

'Me either, but I'll give it a try.'

I give my sister a gentle nudge. 'How does it feel to be normal?'

She giggles. 'I'll let you know when that happens. Not got much chance of that with you around, have we?'

'No,' I affirm. 'Not with me around.'

'Peter.' Anna looks down. 'I never want to be apart from you.' She stares at her hand, and I take it in mine. 'It's scary... really scary being here. I don't feel normal. But I don't want to be alone anymore. Either of us.'

'Look how far we've come. It's all because of you, Anna.'

'Thanks.' She releases my hand, getting up from her place. 'I think I'm going to take a bath. Get prepared.' It sounds like she's about to head into battle, not have a date. Although, they might be comparable.

I change into tracksuit bottoms and head back downstairs. After putting on some Converse and a waterproof coat, and cleaning the wet kitchen, I retreat to the garden. I hate how the coat creates a barrier from the rain, but I guess that's the whole point. I'll get less hassle from Sally if I have it on.

The morning must be wearing on when I hear her voice shouting from the back door.

'Peter, you'll catch your death out there.'

'No,' I shout back. 'The rain is good. It loosens the soil. I'll be fine.'

I get back to work, and Sally heads inside.

The end of Sally and James' garden has undergone a complete transformation. I've dug rows of beds, and now fruit and vegetables are growing nicely. Sally's initial resistance at me doing this lessened when I started planting things she could cook with. She was impressed, and now that she has more mouths to feed, free food seems to benefit her. My aunt was more than happy to buy the seeds I asked for and am now harvesting.

'You know strawberries aren't in season anymore.'

I look up to find Anna towering above me, an umbrella resting on her shoulder, saving her golden hair from the rain.

'Like they'll notice.' I shrug, going back to my task.

'Give me one, then.' She kneels next to me as I reach over and pluck one of the plump red strawberries and hand it to my sister. 'Mmm…' She devours it whole.

'You're not complaining.' I smirk and pass her another, which she accepts without hesitation.

'Your strawberries are the best,' she says through a full mouth.

'It beats the crap they buy at the shops.' I pop a strawberry into my mouth, the plump fruit juicy as it hits my taste buds.

Anna steals another berry in agreement, eating it in one mouthful.

'What's going there?' Anna points to the large bed I've been digging this morning.

'Red cabbage, maybe some leeks.'

'Sally won't have any garden left at this rate.'

I chuckle and move back to the bed of newly laid red cabbage seeds. Shoving my hands into the soil, I breathe in and out. The rain trickles down my arms and into the earth as the ground breathes with me. I take another breath, the energy building in the tops of my shoulders, and as I exhale, it flows down my arms into the ground. The power transferring back to the earth, giving life to the seeds.

I look back at Anna. 'There, that should do it.'

She glances back toward the house. 'Do you want some tea? You should come inside. You've been out here for hours.'

I nod and follow her back inside.

The warmth of the kitchen hits me as I enter, making my face clammy in reaction to the cold rain. Anna moves to fill the kettle and sets it to boil.

Sally is already busying herself making lunch when she says, 'Are you two hungry?'

'I brought you strawberries,' I offer, placing a handful down on the counter.

'Oh, lovely.' Sally beams at me, coming over to grab one, but stops at the sight of me making little pools on her kitchen floor. 'Peter.'

I take down the hood of my coat, my hair soaking underneath, and give it a good shake, sending water everywhere as Sally and Anna run for cover on the other side of the kitchen.

'Peter,' Sally shrieks. 'It's like living with a wild animal.' She laughs.

'It's your own fault for adopting strays.' I chuckle, taking my coat off and leaving it dripping on the coat hook, then kicking off my Converse to show my pruned toes. 'I'm going to get changed.'

Anna hands me my green tea as I make for the stairs, the ghosts of my footprints following me across the kitchen.

'You better clean this up,' Sally calls after me.

'Sure, sure,' I say, but I'm already halfway up the stairs.

By the time I'm washed and changed, I head downstairs to find Brady already here. I pop my head into the living room, where he and Anna are sitting on the sofa together, watching television. My aunt and uncle have made themselves scarce.

'Hi, Peter.' His arm removes itself from around Anna's shoulder.

'Please, don't mind me.'

I make my way to the kitchen and leave Brady red-faced. I intend to address the mess I left earlier, but I discover that Sally, or maybe Anna, has already cleaned up. So, instead, I set to my task in the kitchen.

When I return to the living room, Anna's head is resting lightly on Brady's shoulder. He looks my direction when I stand in the doorway.

'Whatever your aunt is cooking smells great.'

Anna peers up at him. 'No, that's Peter. He's been making a pie.'

Brady's eyebrows lift into his fringe. 'You cook?'

'Sometimes.'

'Peter's a great cook. He was always the one who cooked in our house since our mother was always too ill to cook for us. Are you joining us, Peter?'

I glance down at their entwined fingers. The ease of Anna's lie shocks me. Too ill to cook and too drunk to cook are two different things. I shouldn't stay. She doesn't need me here. I realise I've been quite selfish in wanting to go back to our old life, our old ways, and bring Anna with me. Time to let her live a little. I shake my head. 'No, I think I'll go for a walk. It's stopped raining.'

Anna and Brady look toward the window to confirm what I'm saying.

'Will you tell our aunt not to worry?'

Anna looks unsure, but I wave goodbye to Brady and leave them.

The farther away from the house I walk, the more the sickness grows. I push it down, deep into my stomach. The distance from my sister emotes like a knot at the end of a rope I'm being dragged toward. Walking away from her is uncomfortable, like I'm being pulled from my core back to her. The reality of our new life threatens to crush me, but I must get used to being apart from my twin.

One day, Anna will get married.

I walk without any real sense of where I'm going.

Above, the grey clouds appear ready to burst.

One day, she'll have her own family.

My feet carry me toward the edge of the village as the thoughts keep coming.

What will happen to me when Anna moves on?

My chest heaving, I stop at the corner and work to steady my breathing. Raindrops begin to hit my face. I almost hear Anna's logical tone telling me she's not gone and that it's all just practice, practice being apart.

Practice, I tell myself. *I have to practice being apart from her.*

One foot in front of the other, I increase the distance with a newfound purpose, testing that pull.

As I round the corner, a figure wearing a navy raincoat and thick black boots caked in mud, walking an old black dog on the other side of the lane, catches my attention. It takes me a moment to work out what they are doing as their arms flail about, but I soon realise they're dancing. Oblivious to any onlookers, their dog plods along beside them as they listen to an invisible source of music. The sight brings me out of my thoughts, and I laugh, even though they don't notice the sound.

Then I hear it—the unmistakable voice of Connie singing along to whatever she's listening to.

I cross and walk behind her while she bops along the path, unfazed by the rain shower now passing through. I almost feel bad as I watch her dance along, but it's hard to feel bad for such easy prey. Even with me making no effort to hide my laughing, she's in her own world. It's not until she lands an elaborate spin that she stops dead in her tracks.

'Oh my God, Peter,' she shouts. Removing her headphones from her head, she marches straight up to me and slaps me on the chest. 'What? Are you stalking me now?'

I roar with laughter, but her face is beet-red.

'How long have you been there?' she asks, composing herself, although the red in her cheeks refuses to budge.

'Long enough,' I answer, then scratch the head of the old dog now sitting at my feet.

'Traitor,' she mutters to the dog before spinning away, trying to make her escape.

I fall into step beside her. 'So, what was that song you were dancing to?'

'Freda Payne.'

I shake my head, oblivious.

'You know, 'Band of Gold'? Classic Motown tune?'

'No idea.' I hold my hands up as she shakes her head in disbelief at my musical ignorance.

'You need some serious educating.'

'Son of a recluse here. That has to give me some excuse for my poor education.'

'Maybe. A little, but *just* a little, a very little.' Her green eyes flash at me as we walk. 'Surely, you had a radio or something in that rock you lived under.'

'Oh, I can do you one better.' I laugh. 'We only had an old record player. Basically, a step away from a gramophone.'

'You're making fun of me.'

'I'm serious. We only had a record player. Our mother would play music in the evening for us sometimes. I don't think we had any records from after the sixties. Mainly lots of Ella Fitzgerald and Sam Cooke.'

'I love Sam Cooke,' Connie says, and I catch her smiling to herself. 'Sounds like you were stuck in a time warp. I don't think I'll ever be able to understand what it's been like for you.'

'You shouldn't feel sorry for us. It wasn't all bad. We didn't know any different. We were happy, and to be honest, life was simple. Now, not so much. Lots of thoughts, lots of emotions. A whole new world. Anyway, I'm in desperate need of some education.' I'm glad the rain has stopped because it allows me to see Connie's face better, witness the colour rise in her cheeks again. 'That is, if you are happy to give it?' I add when she doesn't say anything.

She comes to a slow stop to consider me, looking unsure. 'Why me?'

I mimic her actions, turning to her. 'Because I like you. I want to learn this world through your eyes.'

She starts walking, her face reddening again. 'How do you do that?'

Her question catches me off guard. 'Do what?'

'You say you were completely sheltered, literally from everything and everyone, but how are you so confident?'

'I don't know. I guess I don't know how to be anything else.'

She gives me a glance I can't quite read, then quickens her pace, her dog trotting beside her.

'Do you want me to leave you alone?' My tone comes out hurt.

'No.' She stops and lets out a big breath, regarding me, and I can't help but raise my hand to her face as the red begins to fade.

'Tell me why this happens?'

'I don't know, Peter.' She sighs. 'Biology?'

I tilt my head, confused.

'You make me nervous.'

'Why do I make you nervous?'

'I don't know. Maybe I'm sheltered too.'

'I know how we can change that.' My lips curl. 'Practice. We just need to practice you being around me, and then you won't be nervous anymore.'

Connie moves to rest her fingers on my hand, which is still holding her face. 'I'm not sure how much use that will be,' she whispers.

I swallow hard when she bites her lip, and my eyes are drawn to her mouth. Her green eyes sparkle like the stars, and she is close, so close, to me. I graze my thumb over her bottom lip, watching her with fascination as she takes a sharp intake of breath. My pulse quickens. I can't understand the effect she has on me. She's so near, but I don't move. A vague recollection of words spoken by my sister—something to do with self-control—pulls at the back of my mind, and I take a begrudging step back.

'So, it's a deal? Will you continue my education into this brave new world, make sure I don't make a fool of myself?'

Connie doesn't answer straight away, although she studies me.

It kills me that I can't read her mind.

Anna's right.

I want this connection.

Want it with Connie.

'I thought we were friends,' I say, knowing now I mean it.

Connie lets out a long exhale and walks on, I stick at her side.

'Okay, sure. Sounds good. I'll be your contact in the real world, but you probably won't need my help for long, Peter. You seem pretty well-adapted to me.'

I look down at my shoes. 'Maybe on the outside.'

In my peripheral, I see that she takes me in, likely assessing how true the statement may be. She can't understand how much truth it holds.

'So, this is me.' Connie motions to a quaint cottage.

'This is where you live?' It hadn't occurred to me that Connie has been walking with purpose, a destination in mind, and not wandering with no direction like I thought we were. The cottage, made of grey rock with wisteria growing up the front, suits her. It looks old and cosy.

'It's lovely,' I tell her.

'It's home.' Connie gushes.

We stand still and regard each other, but before the moment gets away from me, I say, 'Same time tomorrow?'

Connie seems taken aback for a moment. 'Erm. Sure.' She opens the front gate but spins back to me. 'Bring your earphones,' she instructs, giving me a sparkling smile before heading inside.

There it is, I think. *The Connie sparkle I have been angling for.*

I stay at the bottom of her garden and watch her go inside, our eyes meeting for the briefest moment before she closes the door.

I take my time making my way back to Sally and James' house. The sky has cleared to reveal a clear night. I don't know quite what to do with the knowledge that I make Connie nervous. I know I'm not good at reading others, and I associate nervousness with negative emotions, so it must be my strangeness coming through. Maybe she knows there's something wrong with me. I resolve to try harder to put her at ease. Granted, I'm not sure *how* to do that.

By the time I get home, it's pitch-black.

'There you are.' Sally's hysterical voice rounds on me as soon as I close the front door.

'Where's Anna?' I peer into the empty living room.

'She's upstairs. Where have *you* been?'

'I went for a walk.'

'For four hours? Peter, we were worried. You didn't take your phone.'

'I forget about that thing. I'm not going to run away.'

'Well, you don't have a good track record with that, young man.'

Sally hasn't been this mad in a while. This time, her anger is misplaced, though.

'It was once. And obviously I'm not running away. I came back. I was with Connie Prinze.'

'You were?' Sally's expression softens, turning curious.

I don't say another word, and instead, climb the stairs.

'You have to talk to us, Peter,' Sally calls after me.

What is with all the talking? Our mother never demanded to know every trivial emotion we felt or everything we did. Anna and I were, more often than not, left to our own devices. The lessons she taught us were about nature and biology. Our mother didn't have much time for emotions. She was more concerned about keeping them in check. But, then again, our world was much simpler when it was only the three of us.

I enter Anna's room, but she's not there. 'Anna?'

'I'm in here,' a weak voice calls from the bathroom.

'Are you okay?' I ask through the bathroom door.

'No. Pizza does *not* agree with me.'

'Told you it was poison.' I smirk.

'Don't be smug. I'm sick.'

The door flings open to a pale Anna with dark circles under her eyes, her hair all stuck up on one side.

'Wow.'

'And what the hell did you think you were doing?' she demands, becoming the second person to slap me on the chest today.

'What are you talking about?'

'Walking out like that earlier. I wasn't prepared for you to just leave.'

'I thought it was better to let you have some time with Brady. You didn't need your little brother hanging around.'

Anna rolls her eyes. 'Yeah, those twenty-one minutes make all the difference.' She wraps her arms around me. 'You have to warn me before you walk off like that. I felt like I was kicked in the stomach.'

'I know. Me too.' I hug her back. 'This is our life now, right? So, we have to get used to it. We can't be together all the time.'

'Don't say that, Peter,' she pleads.

I support my sister back to her room, where she flops to the bed, groaning and clutching her stomach. I lie next to her, putting my arm around her. 'Is there anything I can do?'

'I don't think so. Sally said my stomach isn't used to fast food.'

I watch her golden head rise and fall on my chest. Her breathing begins to slow, and my thoughts drift back to Connie and our conversation.

'Anna?'

'Mmm...' she replies, sleepy.

'How do you feel when you're around Brady?'

'It's hard to describe. It's like being warm and comfortable. Safe. Like I've always known him. But at the same time, I want to know him more, and every new thing I learn about him makes me like him even more. Why do you ask?'

'Connie says I make her nervous. That's a bad thing, right?'

Anna shifts her weight. 'You saw Connie?'

'Not on purpose. I ran into her when I was out. We walked, we talked, and I was under the impression she was enjoying my company, but then she said I make her nervous.'

'How do you feel when you're around her?'

'Calm.'

'Calm?'

'Like she's the quiet in the storm. All that noise in my head goes away when I'm with her. It's peaceful. I'm drawn toward her, the way I am to the trees and the outside. I do want her as my friend, Anna. You were right.'

Anna gives a click of her tongue. 'No wonder she's nervous around you.' She props herself up on her elbow, her sleepiness clinging to her through her sickness.

'Peter, you're you, so you don't understand that all these things you're feeling, it's easy for the people around you to feel it too. Try not to overpower her... she probably can't think straight around you.'

'What on earth are you talking about?'

Anna's head dips heavily onto my shoulder. 'I'm just saying... you have a way of getting what you want. I can understand why she finds you intimidating.'

'Not this again. I do *not* always get my way.'

'You always have.'

'We're not kids anymore.'

'I know. I can't remember the last time you really wanted something.'

'I really want to go home, but I can't have that.'

Anna's breath stops, and I regret saying it. 'Peter, our mother is dead. It was just a house without her. Our home died.'

She's right.

And I hate it.

'Do you honestly think I'm intimidating?'

'Just go easy on her, okay?' Anna urges.

'I think that pizza addled your brain, sister.'

Anna playfully slaps my chest again and then slips back into her slumber.

CHAPTER 8

Anna

My stomach still aches when I wake up the next morning feeling terrible.

Peter is already up and has taken the warmth with him. I press my forehead to the cold window to watch him in the garden below. He wraps a vine of strawberries around a trellis, and it starts crawling around the lattice from there. My heart does a pitter-patter at the sight.

He doesn't know how to be careful.

I retreat to my bed, unsure now how to help my brother.

I sink back into the pillow. It took me a while to get used to sleeping in a bed again when we came here, especially one as comfy as the ones Sally and James bought us. Of course, it was one of the easier things to get used to.

Soft pillows, bubble bath—easy to get used to.

Technology and other people—not so much.

My bedroom door swings open, and Peter strides in with a steaming cup in his hands. Sitting on the edge of my bed, he instructs, 'Here, drink this.'

I eye it with suspicion.

'It's just ginger and lemon. It'll help your stomach.' He places the back of his hand on my forehead. 'How are you today?'

'I'm okay,' I lie as he looks down at me. 'You don't need to look after me.'

'Of course I do.' He grins, handing me the cup. 'It's what I do.'

I falter a little. I can't help thinking of our mother, the role Peter has always had to play. Part of me wonders why he misses our old life so much. I suppose it was simpler. Now everything is so confusing.

'Why do you look so pleased with yourself?' I ask, noticing how the corners of his mouth turn upward a fraction.

'I'm going out.'

'You're leaving again?' My stomach starts to plummet.

'To meet Connie.' His grin slips when he notices my face. 'I thought you'd be pleased. You wanted me to make friends. I promise I'll be good.'

I plaster the best smile I can muster onto my face, unsure why it makes me quite so uneasy. 'I'm pleased. You should go. I'm glad you want to.' I look down at the drink he's made me. 'You're right... being apart takes practice.'

'See you later.' He plants a kiss on my cheek and leaves without another word.

The tears burn hot in my eyes when I'm alone.

Alone. I'm so alone.

My hand moves over my chest in an attempt to keep myself from splitting in two.

I should be happy for him, but Peter leaving is against my every instinct. I never fathomed that letting in the rest of the world meant figuring out who I am without him.

My phone buzzes on the bedside table beside me with a text from Brady.

Brady: *Hi! Hope you're feeling much better today. I had a great time with you before you got sick. Maybe we could try it again?*

I chuckle to myself, letting a little bit of warmth fill me again.

Me: *I told you pizza may have been a bad idea!*
Brady: *Definitely no pizza next time. Strictly pizza free zone.*

A loud laugh bursts out of me. Brady's so sweet. I almost do feel normal talking to him. There are no secrets with him, no words he doesn't mean. Another text message pings.

Brady: *I think a part of me couldn't really believe that you hadn't tried it before.*
Me: *Nope. All new to me. Anything else you think I should try?*
Brady: *Hell no! Let's stick to something safe, I can't have you throwing up on every date.*
Brady: *Although that would be a fun story for the grandkids.*
Brady: *Not that I'm thinking about having kids.*
Brady: *Please, stop me!*

Now I'm actually smiling. And biting my lip with a newfound giddiness.

Me: *Thanks for understanding, Brady. How about we try again, only this time let's have dinner in. I can vouch for my brother's cooking.*
Brady: *Now that's an offer I can't refuse.*

I'm a whole lot better having the solace of Brady. He eases the discomfort from getting used to not having Peter around so much.

Something that comes on even stronger later, when he returns, and I don't notice until I spot him from the kitchen window pottering around the garden. I squelch through the grass to him, not minding the rain. He sits on the grass, turning over the leaves of the plants like they're precious ornaments.

'How long have you been back?' I ask the back of his head.

'About half an hour.'

'How was Connie?'

'Fine.'

'Just fine?'

'Yeah, just fine. What else do you want?'

I don't know, some indication of how to do this. The feelings he described for Connie presented so big, way bigger than me. How do I know if I've found the right person or if I'm doing the right thing? My mother always told me I was a compass, and that Peter would always need me to guide him. Everything I ever did to indulge him was done in secret and always when she wasn't looking. He looked after us, and in return, we kept him safe. That responsibility is slipping from my fingers along with the growing reality—Peter never needed either of us.

'Brady's coming for dinner tomorrow,' I say instead. 'I told him you would cook.'

'Oh yeah?' He looks at me for the first time, his curly hair falling into his eyes. 'What should I make?'

'Pie.' I grin, and he reaches up to grab my hand, pulling me down next to him. I rest my head on his shoulder, in turn, he rests his head on mine.

'Whatever you want,' he tells me.

I only wish I knew.

CHAPTER 9

Connie

The bright October morning demands my attention outside the window of my English Lit class. The autumn colours are gorgeous, the leaves appearing more golden than I've ever noticed before—or maybe it's an emotional hangover from having spent two afternoons alone with Peter.

I have some marginal guilt about lying to Lorna yesterday when I blew off our Sunday evening call by telling her I'd promised my mum I'd help walk Barney. Mum had looked at me like I'd lost my mind when I said I would take him for his walk again considering she had to all but beg me to do it on Saturday. But the promise of meeting Peter again had seemed as fragile as glass, and I didn't want to jinx it by telling her I was going to meet him.

Plus, she would've had a million questions. It's been a long time since I had a new friend.

My mind wanders back to the image of him standing on the corner of the lane, his hands in the pockets of his hoodie. Waiting for *me*. His face when he saw me. That huge, dangerous smile. The instinct that had said *danger* when I first met him has been replaced by something else, something drawing me toward him instead. Even thinking about him makes the butterflies explode in my stomach all over again. His plan is doomed to fail. How will I ever not be nervous around him?

Our Sunday together felt a little different, more measured. He was less prone to saying things or looking at me in ways that made my brain fog and my heart race. The difference in approach was nice—at least I could think, although it meant he asked me a lot of questions. Wanting to know my favourite books, my favourite songs, my favourite foods. He didn't have any favourites, of anything, which was frustrating. He didn't know, or he'd never thought about it before. He could tell me a lot about my favourite flower, though. How Yarrow could help heal burns and scars, and how he used it to make ointments. That he made ointments for his mother when she burned her hands trying to cook. Peter might be the strangest person I've ever met.

I'd played him some more of my top songs as we walked. Of course, he hadn't heard of any of them. Every time our arms grazed through our coats, my stomach would explode with crazy butterflies. To think I'd been considering my feelings for Jamie before, wondering if I felt something more, was crazy now. Spending time with Peter was like a tidal wave. His proximity made my body hum. It answered my question about Jamie in *no uncertain terms* because nothing could compare to this.

Lorna's sharp nudge brings me back to the classroom and the realisation that I've been smiling like a lunatic out the window. She gives a questioning look, clearly thinking I've lost it.

I ignore her and try to give my attention to the front of class. It'd be best to tell her about spending time with Peter, but I have a protective instinct over my time with him. I have no idea what's going on with him. We're friends now, I guess. I've found myself privy to a secret that makes the basis of our friendship hard to explain. No one else knows their mum kept them away, isolated from the world. I don't want to break that trust, so I promise to keep the whole thing to myself.

Time spent with Peter is precious, private. Mine.

I've got the slightest twinge of nerves about seeing him today. Peter away from school is relaxed and easy to talk to—Peter at school is a different person. So I have to mentally prepare myself that there's a good chance he won't even talk to me today.

My nerves increase exponentially while sitting in the cafeteria with Lorna. It's hard to keep myself from glancing at the doorway.

As usual, Brady is the first to approach our table. 'Hello, ladies,' he sings as he bounds up to us.

'You're awfully chipper,' Lorna remarks.

'Why not?' He gleams.

Jamie walks over next, slapping Brady on the back before sitting down next to me. 'Brady, how was the big date?'

We all know Brady and Anna had a date on Saturday. I'd completely forgotten to ask Peter about it.

'Well, it was going well, but she ate one slice of pizza and *blurgh*—' Brady makes a puking motion with his hand. 'She got sick.'

Jamie howls. 'You certainly have an effect on women.' Brady laughs with him as he asks, 'What was the brother like. Did he just sit there and watch you like a hawk?'

Lorna shoots Jamie a scowl, and I cast a nervous glance back at the doorway, cringing inside.

'No, he wasn't there,' Brady reveals.

'You got her alone and she threw up on you? Man, you have the worst luck.' Jamie shakes his head.

'I spoke to her yesterday and she's doing much better, so I'm meeting her tonight again.' Brady positively beams.

That catches my attention. 'Tonight?'

'Yeah, she invited me over for dinner.'

'Ooh, dinner with the parents, or whatever they are to them,' Jamie taunts.

'Actually, I think Peter's cooking for us.'

Jamie's response waits because Peter and Anna walk in then, heading in our direction. My heart pounds in my chest, so loud it's the only thing I can hear. *Nerves again.* I hold my breath as he approaches, his dark eyes locking onto mine. As he draws closer, a large, brilliant smile breaks free, otherworldly in its effect. I finally breathe again and return one of my own. An acknowledgment this weekend was real, that it happened. We're friends now, whatever Peter's interpretation of that word is. I look away, noticing in the process that Jamie's also watching me, my cheeks reddening.

It would be great if this would stop happening.

Much to my dismay, my initial thoughts turn out to be correct. I don't get the chance to speak to him, although I'm dying to ask when I can see him again. Instead, I have to be content with chanced glances, sharing a secret smile when our eyes meet, and the butterflies creeping back into my stomach every time we do.

I don't think I utter a word to anyone during the remainder of lunch break, my brain trying to build the courage to say something to him from across the table. Anything. I'm drawing a blank. Before I know it, he's following his sister out of the cafeteria.

Why didn't I ask him for his number yesterday? Right, because I'm an idiot.

I'm heading out of the cafeteria, lost in my own thoughts, when Lorna grabs my arm.

'Just popping to the bathroom,' she demands rather than asks, pushing me inside. For a moment, she studies me, then asks, 'Did something happen with you and Peter?'

'What? No.' *Perhaps our smiles aren't so secret after all.*

'Okay. Well, he was looking at you a lot today. *A lot.*'

'Really?' I ask, turning pink.

'Yeah, and not just looking. I mean ogling you like you're a snack.'

I crack up. 'A snack? Seriously?'

We're both laughing now.

'Connie, that boy wants to eat you up. You're in trouble.'

'I don't know what you're talking about, Lor.' I feign innocence, the pink of my face turning full scarlet as I examine my mortified expression in the mirror.

'Mmm… well, I caught you giving him a cheeky look too,' she teases.

I give her a playful shove.

'I think Jamie noticed as well. He did *not* look happy. I think you should talk to him, Con.'

A sigh escapes me. 'I wouldn't even know what to say. Besides, nothing's happening with Peter and me.'

'Yet.' Lorna gives me a knowing glance before we set off to class.

I take a break from obsessing over Peter and spend the evening with Lorna, glad for the distraction.

The next day, I learn from Brady that Peter had cooked, which makes him even more appealing. The thought of Peter in an apron is too much for my imagination to bear. I also learn the twins are vegetarian—something Peter hadn't told me—along with the titbit he used to cook for his family. I somehow manage to stop myself from asking a million other questions about Peter, like, had he mentioned me at all? *Am I becoming borderline obsessed?* I resolve to put it out of my head.

Just calm down, Connie. You've spent two afternoons with the guy.

However, as soon as he walks back into the cafeteria, my resolve comes undone and I'm grinning like some stupid Cheshire Cat while he walks toward us.

I mouth, *'Hi,'* to him, which he mouths back. The butterflies make themselves at home in my stomach.

There it is. It's official. I am pathetic.

I'm not sure if I can keep this up.

How long can I keep stealing glances at him from across the table? It'd be a little too bold to outright ask him for his number in front of everyone. I'm sure Brady would tell me where they live. Then I could just go around and ask him to come for a walk. I could even take Barney, then I'd wait for the right time, and I would kiss him.

I snap myself right out of that daydream. The mere thought sends the butterflies into a frenzy.

'Earth to Connie.'

'Sorry, what?'

Jamie is waving his hand in front of me. 'You zoned out there.' He laughs with my spreading blush.

'Yeah, a world of my own. What did you say?'

'I asked what you were up to tonight. If you want to go for coffee?'

I focus on his hopeful blue eyes, trying to formulate an answer in my head, hoping not to panic. 'Oh, I have a tonne of homework to catch up on, Jay. I'm not sure I have time to come out.'

Disappointment floods his expression as he bows his head and turns away.

There's a problem here, and I so don't want there to be a problem here. I try not to think about it.

I lack the courage to march up to Peter's front door, and with the added guilt of rejecting Jamie, I decide to stay home and do my homework for real.

Although, I do text Lorna.

>**Me:** *I think you're right. I need to talk to Jamie.*
>**Lorna:** *What made you change your mind?*
>**Me:** *I think he tried to ask me out today.*
>**Lorna:** *What did you say?*
>**Me:** *I panicked and brushed him off. I feel bad.*
>**Lorna:** *It's his own fault, Con. He should've asked you out before Peter showed up.*

I clutch my phone to my chest. Lorna's words bring me some comfort.

Jamie *is* being territorial. If it wasn't for his irrational dislike of Peter, he wouldn't have asked me out.

>**Me:** *Thanks, Lor. Any ideas what I should say to him?*
>**Lorna:** *You're on your own there I'm afraid!*

Somewhat comforted, I stretch out on my bed, then glance over at the little digital clock on my bedside table. It's ten thirty p.m. I roll under the covers and my eyes begin to droop.

Click!

My eyes pop open, taking in the darkness of my room, everything still and quiet. Tucking my quilt up to my chin, my eyes slide closed again.

Click!

My back reacts first this time, jolting me upright. No doubt, I heard it this time. *What is that?* I wonder and frantically look around for the source.

Click!

Now I get out of bed with my heart racing. Our house is pretty old, yet I've never seen a ghost or anything before. I try to tell myself ghosts don't exist, but I—

Click!

I rush to my window and shove the curtain aside. My knees go weak at the sight of a figure moving in the darkness. I open my mouth to call out to my dad but stop when I realise the figure is waving at me. I squint into the darkness through the glass. I can't believe it. I throw open the window wide.

'I thought that window would be yours,' he says into the darkness without a care in the world.

'Peter,' I whisper as loud as I can, almost a whisper-scream. 'What on earth are you doing?'

He raises his arms to the starry sky. 'It's a nice night. Want to come for a walk?'

'Are you crazy? You almost gave me a heart attack.'

He takes a step back, and his confidence leaves with the sudden comprehension that throwing rocks or whatever at my window at this hour is not appropriate in the least. 'Shall I go?'

'No,' I hear myself reply. *What am I doing?* 'Just, wait there. I'm coming down.'

His lips curl as I close my window. I don't know why he looks so pleased with himself—I'm only going down to kill him. According to my clock, it's gone one a.m. My body's in action, putting on leggings, a large cardigan, my hat, and socks. I pick up my boots and tiptoe downstairs, grabbing my coat as I ease the lock open on the back door and grimace. Everything seems to creak in the dead of night. I take a moment to listen—there's no detectable movement from my parents' room. A pang of guilt runs through me as I pull on my boots and coat before inching the door shut behind me.

I try to act casual as I walk up to Peter, telling myself there's no way he can hear my thundering heartbeat in the darkness. He's standing in the middle of my back garden like it's the most natural thing in the world, wearing a simple black hoodie, hands tucked away in its pockets.

'You're lucky the dog's deaf. What are you doing here?'

'I wanted to see you.' He steps toward me, an amused look on his face.

'There's such thing as a phone. You could've called,' I suggest, all too aware he doesn't have my number.

'I hate those things. Besides, I prefer being outside, and I love the nighttime, so I wanted to share *my* world with you.'

I'm not doing a good job of being mad at him. The truth is, I'm glad he's here. Two days without talking has seemed like an eternity.

'You know my dad will kill you if he catches us.' It's my last feeble protest to whatever is coming next.

'So let's get out of here.' Peter flashes a devilish grin and leads me out of the garden and down the pitch-black lane. His golden hair and warm skin stands out even more against the dark sky, giving the illusion he is glowing, a light in the darkness, which adds to the enchantment.

'So, phones? Why are you against them?' I ask, attempting to bring myself back to reality, already half-knowing the answer.

'Never had a phone before.' Peter shrugs. 'They're kind of hard to get your head around. Sally bought both Anna and me one when we moved in. I think Anna uses hers a bit to speak to Brady. But, well, who would *I* talk to?'

'Me,' I reply like it should be obvious. 'You can call me or text me. You know, rather than waking me up in the middle of the night so I think there's some kind of psycho murderer in my garden.'

Peter laughs. 'Okay, fine. I'll find out the number. But tonight is just me and you, all right?'

Right when I think he's shocked my butterflies away, there they are again. Just me, Peter, and the night.

'Where are we going?' I ask, nonchalant.

'Not far.'

I follow him a little way down the lane, the autumn night nipping at my face. I once again take in Peter's tall form while he leads me forward. I'm bundled up, yet he's wearing a basic hoodie.

'Aren't you cold?'

'No,' he says. 'I love the cold.'

We turn into an empty walled field. For a while, we walk together in silence up the dirt path, further into the field. The illusion being we're miles from anywhere, even though we've only walked for about ten minutes.

'You're not a psycho murderer, are you?' I joke, and my voice blares out in the wide space. *I'm glad it's too dark for my blush to be visible.*

'No.' Peter stops and sits amongst the shorn wheat. 'Sit,' he invites, and I take a seat next to him, utterly perplexed. 'I know you said I make you nervous, and I want to be respectful of that. My sister warned me that I can come on too strong. But, Connie, I can't take another day of not talking to you at school. That place is so loud. I hate loud. I want you. I want quiet. So, I came.'

'At one in the morning?' I try to ignore his confession about wanting me. My damn imagination racing at all of the ways that he might.

'Yes.'

'You are so strange.'

Peter chuckles. 'You have no idea.'

'I'm beginning to learn.'

Now that he's forgiven, Peter lies back and motions for me to do the same. With some reluctance, I do. Above me, the sky is a black velvet canvas littered with twinkling stars. Lying against the cold earth with him takes my nerves away. I've never paid much attention to the night sky. It's beautiful.

'Do you know much about the stars?' Peter asks.

I shake my head.

'Perfect. There's some wisdom I can impart on you.'

He looks back to the sky and, taking my hand resting next to him, he raises it to a point. The sensation of his warm skin against mine makes my heart race, but I look toward the sky as Peter draws shapes with our pointed fingers.

'This is Pegasus. And this…' he continues to draw in the air, '… is Cassiopeia. You can tell from the W-shape.'

As he tells me about the different constellations, the planets, and what they mean to each other, I find myself gazing upon his face. He's unburdened, more relaxed than I've ever seen him. His words come to a halt when he catches me staring at him.

'Am I boring you?'

'No, not at all. There's nothing boring about you, Peter.'

He grins, relieved, his eyes resting on mine for a while. His eyes flick down to my lips for a moment, and the air becomes thick between us. Awareness of the heat of his hand still on mine strangles my breathing.

I will him to kiss me.

Instead, he looks back to the sky.

'You know, my sister and I were born under Gemini.'

'Huh?' My brain is confused by the sudden change of direction.

'Just a bit of cosmic irony, Gemini represents the twins.'

'Ah, yes.' I exhale, pretending it's obvious.

I glance at my phone, it's now a little after three a.m.

Reluctant, I say, 'Peter, we should go home.'

'Let me walk you back.'

This becomes the pattern of my life for a week, or is it two? During school, we almost never exchange words, only a few smiles across the table, followed by nightly walks to the field where we stargaze and talk. Sneaking out has become all too easy. My body is acclimatising, often waking up before the *click* of the acorn against my window.

It's like I'm existing in a dream or living a double life.

I haven't told Lorna what we're doing because a part of me doesn't think she'll approve, but also because one secret has led to another, and now everything seems clandestine. Even though it's all innocent.

We lie side by side, staring into the sky. I think Peter knows my life story by now—what it was like growing up as an only child, how I got my love of music from my dad, how I've known Jamie my whole life, the way I'd befriended Brady, and then Lorna, all those years ago when they first moved here.

'And now me,' he'd said one night, I forget which. 'You like outsiders.'

'I like mystery,' I replied, although I'm unsure if I chose him or he chose me. 'I can't wait to see the world, Peter. To get out of here.'

Peter hadn't responded. Instead, he'd seemed lost in thought.

The best things about the nights are Peter himself, more unburdened. Never revealing too much about himself, he talks about the stars and the Earth. How nature has an answer for everything. What plants cure a headache, what to eat if low on iron, how to recognise different birdsong. How he loves to watch things grow. The way he'd basically taken over his aunt and uncle's garden.

The time I spend with him under the night sky is like entering a new reality, something quiet and pure. The moonlight transforms Peter from an overpowering force into someone gentle and overwhelmingly lonely. The few things he does mention about his mother doesn't fill me with the notion his childhood was filled with love.

School, on the other hand, is beginning to feel loud and confusing. I'm starting to understand what Peter's been talking about. The lack of a good night's sleep is catching up to me. Luckily, no one has noticed the dark circles under my eyes. Except Anna. Her odd glances across the lunch table tell me her twin's absence at night has not gone unnoticed. The beauty of our moonlit meetings? Anna is the only one who's noticed, so, my life continues as normal.

My daytime life is as it ever was—homework dates with Lorna, phone calls with Brady. I'm almost too tired to notice Jamie has removed himself from my life—he doesn't bother to talk to me these days. Even my secret exchanges with Peter from across the table have come to a halt. I'm pretty much ready to fall asleep anywhere.

What's unfair, and somewhat irritating, is how Peter looks as gorgeous as ever and doesn't appear at all bothered by the lack of sleep. Something must give soon for me. I can't keep up with this. I'm vaguely aware today must be Friday because of the plans being made for tomorrow.

'I have an afternoon shift tomorrow. You guys want to come and keep me company?' Brady asks.

'Sounds fun. Autumn is definitely here, so sitting somewhere warm and drinking lots of coffee sounds perfect. Right, Con?' Lorna responds.

'Hmm…' I yawn into my hand. 'Totally. Coffee. I need coffee.'

'What is with you? You've been yawning all day,' Lorna remarks.

'I didn't sleep well last night.' I shoot a glance at Peter, who's avoiding looking at me. Part of me thinks he's enjoying the sneaking around.

'Are you okay?' Lorna starts to sound concerned.

'Nothing to worry about, Lor, just a nightmare. I keep dreaming there's some creepy psycho hanging out in my garden.' This time, I catch Peter smirk from the corner of my eye and have to suppress a grin.

'Yikes. Well, at least you get a lie in tomorrow. Anna, you should join us.' Lorna turns her attention away from me.

'Sounds good to me,' she says, taking Brady's hand in her own.

'Peter?' Lorna asks.

When I glance toward Peter, I notice Jamie momentarily stops scrolling on his phone or whatever he was doing before.

'I don't drink…' Peter starts before noticing me widen my eyes at him. 'I'll be there.' He bites his lip while I shake my head a fraction.

'Jamie?' Lorna invites him too, thinking nothing of Peter's response.

'Sure. Whatever.'

'Looks like you have the whole gang, Brady.'

Lorna confirms what time everyone should meet, but I forget almost as soon as she tells us.

I text her later to confirm the time, then my fingers hover over the screen. I'm tempted to text Peter to tell him not to come over tonight, but I can't bring myself to do it. It'll be better coming from me in person—and the perfect opportunity presents itself later that night.

'Are you okay?' he asks while we make our way to our spot in the field.

I've almost tripped over at least three times, my lethargy making it hard for me to pick up my feet.

'Yes. I'm just extremely tired, Peter.'

'I shouldn't have come.'

'It's okay. I want to spend time with you.' When we reach our spot, I say, 'We just need to work out a system. How are you not exhausted?'

'I don't sleep much anyway.'

'I love my bed.'

Peter chuckles. 'I'm sorry to be keeping you from it.'

He lies back and puts his arm out for me to lie on his shoulder next to him. One thing I've appreciated the last few nights is how Peter is a literal heater. It's easy to understand why he likes the cold. He's almost as comfy as a duvet.

'I brought a song I think you'll like.' I offer him one of the earphones, which he takes.

'Thanks.'

I play the song and listen to its melody as the starry night blurs in front of my eyes. Peter's so warm, and my eyes are so heavy. As the light fades to black, a stray thought crosses my mind. *Every time we've come out, there hasn't been a cloud in the sky.* I'd not noticed before.

When I wake, I'm in Peter's arms and try to gauge my surroundings. We're almost at my house.

'Hey,' he whispers.

'What time is it?' I'm practically asleep as he sets me back on my feet.

'I'm not sure. You fell asleep straight away.'

'Sorry.'

'Don't be.' He smooths my hair with a loving hand. 'I'll see you tomorrow, Connie.'

Without another word, I totter back into my house, and I think I'm asleep before my head hits the pillow.

CHAPTER 10

Connie

The sound of creaking floorboards pulls me from sleep. It's so snug under the covers, like I've slept for a week. I tug them tighter under my chin and curl into a ball, enjoying the warmth. The sensation that someone is in my room sinks in, and I open my eyes, half-expecting Peter to be here.

'Morning, sleepy head,' my mum says gently.

'Mum?'

'I thought I should come check on you. Is everything okay?'

'Fine,' I say in confusion, peeping out from my ball under the covers.

'I thought you were meeting your friends this afternoon?' When I don't answer, she continues, 'It's already gone eleven, love.'

That has me awake in an instant. My clock confirms what she's said—it's 11:10 a.m. I scramble to get out of bed. Although I feel like a new person for having slept in, I'm meant to be with everyone at midday, and my brain hasn't fully woken up.

'I brought you tea.' My mum passes me the mug, laughing at my visible confusion.

'You're an angel, Mum.' I take it out of her hands in appreciation.

This is not how I'd planned this morning. Now that my wits are about me again, I remember I want to look good today. I'm meeting Peter in broad daylight and out of uniform but now have less than an hour to get ready and out of the house, which is not ideal. With lightning speed, I shower and then get to work on my wardrobe. *What to wear?* I don't want it to come off like I'm trying too hard. I eventually decide on a black dress with dainty white flowers, thick black tights, and a chunky cardigan under my oversized denim jacket with my Dr. Martens. Cute but casual—I hope. I top it off with the bobble hat I've been wearing out at night with Peter. Being a boy, he probably doesn't even notice that kind of stuff, but it makes me happy. Connects my two worlds. My nervousness has melted away during our outings, but the prospect of seeing Peter in a new environment has brought them back with a vengeance.

My mum agrees to give me a lift but, still, by the time I'm at the coffee shop, I'm half an hour late. I hate being late. I did text Lorna to let her know I was running behind, but in my anxious state, I check my phone the whole way there, clocking how tardy I am. Also, in the back of my mind, I'm hoping Peter might text me. Of course, he hasn't. Even though he gave me his digits earlier in the week, he hasn't texted me yet, and I haven't had the courage to text him either. It's been almost a week of midnight rendezvous, and now that I'm no longer sleep-deprived, my neurosis has kicked back in.

I can't help but wonder what it all means. Is he my friend, or something more? All we've done is talk, but it's felt intimate. The secretness of it all makes it hard for me to get a handle on.

I enter the coffee shop and am immediately greeted by Brady's broad grin from behind the counter.

'You made it,' he exclaims.

My anxiety slips away at the sight of my friend. I stand on my tiptoes to plant a kiss on his cheek. 'I overslept.'

'Until midday? That's not like you.'

I give a shrug and peer around the coffee shop. Lorna catches my eye and waves me over to a booth by the window where she's sitting with the twins. Anna's looking radiant, her golden hair falling over her shoulders. From where I'm standing, I can only see the back of Peter's head, but the space next to him in the booth is free. I turn back to Brady and ask for my usual cinnamon latte before making my way over to the table. Another wave of nervousness washes over me at having Peter here in my domain. I realise I'm more than comfortable going to his nighttime world of stars and quiet, and now here he is in mine, my coffee shop, with my friends again. It all has a bit too much reality to it, and I'm not sure if I'm ready. Our stargazing has changed who we are to each other. To what, I'm not sure.

'Hi.' While not intentional, I say it to him more than anyone else.

'Connie. Where have you been?' Lorna demands.

I slide into the booth next to Peter and try to push the jittery feeling out of my stomach, then roll my eyes at my friend. 'I told you, I overslept.'

'More nightmares?' Peter asks, his face the picture of innocence.

'Actually, quite the opposite. It was just so blissful I didn't want to wake up. But I can't wait to get some coffee in me. It's essential.'

'Agreed.' Lorna laughs. 'This will be my second cup. I'll go grab yours while I'm at it, Con.'

With that, Lorna stands to get herself another coffee, leaving me alone with Anna and Peter, which is a first. Peter shifts himself in his seat, his expression telling me I'm the better view, but Anna's expression turns serious, her palms together in front of her. The atmosphere radiating off the two of them is palpable.

'You seem tired, Connie. Are you okay?' she asks after a loaded pause.

Peter lets out an audible sigh and gives Anna an exasperated look.

'Y-yes,' I stammer. 'I'm fine now.'

'Don't mind her, Connie,' Peter says. 'She thinks I'm being reckless.'

'You are being reckless, Peter.' Anna lowers her head, speaking in a hushed tone, clearly annoyed at her brother. 'What you're doing will have serious repercussions not only for us but for Connie if you're caught.'

'Yes, the key word there being *if* we are caught,' Peter responds to her with a devilish grin.

As I suspected, Anna is not only aware Peter is sneaking out, but she also knows he's been meeting me.

'Peter, this is serious,' Anna implores, looking at me for backup.

'Guys, please don't argue about me,' I interject. 'Anna, you don't need to worry about me.'

Peter gives her a smug look.

'Honestly, we've just been walking and talking. Nothing untoward has happened,' I add in a near-whisper.

Anna's expression softens. 'Connie, it's not you I object too. I want my brother to have you as a friend. It's the way he's doing it that I have a problem with. And I know he's hard to say no to,' Anna says with a hard look at her brother. 'What he's doing could make things very difficult for us.'

I'm confused by that. I look at Peter, but he says nothing, instead he glances away from me. 'What do you mean?'

Silence.

Anna shakes her head. 'Peter. I hope you know what you are doing.' Anna rises and heads toward the counter to talk to Brady and Lorna.

'I hope you and your sister aren't falling out over me?' I ask.

'No.' Peter shifts back to me again, and I'm hyper-aware of his closeness. 'It's just Anna being Anna. She's so cautious. She's the head, and I'm the heart.'

'Oh, so you mean you don't think before you act?' I say playfully. 'I would never have guessed.'

Peter laughs and gently boings the bobble of my hat. 'Nice hat.'

'You noticed.'

'Connie,' Peter says, serious now, looking me straight in the eyes. 'I notice everything about you.'

Damn.

I have nothing else to say or do except gaze into his rich chocolate-coloured eyes. His body so close to me, and the comforting smell of coffee swirling around us makes his lips look too inviting. His head tilts toward mine, and when he lowers his eyes to my lips, the butterflies take flight in my stomach.

'Here, Con.'

Lorna is concentrating on not spilling our two drinks, so she doesn't notice me sit to attention at her words.

Peter isn't fazed but instead gives a playful shrug, and for a split second, I'm annoyed. After all our nights together, *now* is when he tries to kiss me.

Really?

'Thanks,' I say and pull the coffee toward me, blowing on it as it's still far too hot to even contemplate drinking.

'No worries. I thought I should leave the love birds to it.'

At my quizzical look, she gestures toward the front of the shop where Brady and Anna are clearly flirting with each other.

Peter shakes his head at the sight.

As Peter takes a sip of his drink, I take it in for the first time. 'What on earth are you drinking?'

'Green tea.'

'Green tea?' I ask. Incredulous, my eyes go to Lorna to check I've heard him right.

'What's wrong with green tea?' His confusion is adorable.

'It's disgusting.' I make a face.

'Oh yeah? And what's that monstrosity you're both drinking?' Peter motions toward our drinks.

'Cinnamon latte,' we say in unison.

'I'm guessing those things are loaded with sugar.'

'You bet they are,' I say. 'Kind of the whole point.'

'You know that sugar is highly addictive.'

'Well, then, call me addicted.'

'Would you say that you have an addictive personality, Connie?'

'I guess you could say it's a personality flaw. I don't know what's good for me.' I shrug.

'Is that a fact?'

Peter's eyes dance over my face while I tilt my head provocatively in response to his question. Grinning, I'm lost in him.

Lorna's conspicuous, 'mm-huh,' brings me back to reality.

I turn back to my friend, feeling hot at her knowing look—time to change to a safe subject.

I shouldn't have worried. Peter is at ease here. Unlike at school, where he's a different person. He wasn't exaggerating about the crowds. He sits close enough for me to catch the warmth coming from him but not close enough to be touching. Every now and then, he tugs on my bobble hat as if it's something he can't help himself from doing.

Around half an hour later, our coffee-fuelled chatter is interrupted when Jamie plonks himself down next to Lorna.

'Wow. Those two are just too much.' He motions toward the counter, and we all see Brady and Anna still locked in conversation, sending adoring stares at each other. 'Have you ever seen Brady act like this?'

'He's in *lurve*.' Lorna does a little dance with the word.

'In his defence, he has known all the girls around here since he was five,' I add.

'Hmm…' Jamie snorts. 'I suppose she is something shiny and new. The novelty will soon wear off.' He glares at Peter as he says it.

'So nice of you to grace us with your presence, Jamie,' Lorna says, not hiding the sarcasm in her tone. 'And here I was thinking Connie was the late one.'

Jamie eyes me. 'Since when are you late to anything?'

'Look, I overslept, okay. Why the sudden interest in my sleeping patterns?' I avoid his gaze and take a sip of my fresh burning-hot coffee. Mistake.

Jamie throws his hands in the air. 'No need to be so touchy.'

Brady walks over with Anna in tow and hands Jamie his coffee. Sliding into the booth next to him, Brady forces him to squash into Lorna, who doesn't look happy.

'I'm on break, so I thought I'd join you guys.'

Anna copies Brady and slides into the booth next to me, forcing me closer to her brother. When Peter raises his arm against the back of the booth to give me more room, it's so hard to resist the temptation to lean into him. I take another sip of my coffee and wince. *Why did I do that?* Lorna gives me an odd look as I try to hide my burning mouth.

Having Brady join us changes the tone, since conversation always flows more freely with him around. He holds Anna's hand over the table while they chat happily to everyone.

I'm pleased for him. I wonder how much she's told him, what secrets of hers he is keeping. I stare into my coffee and contemplate why my situation with Peter seems so much more complicated.

A slight tug on the bobble of my hat breaks me out of my reverie. I consider him through my lashes, the faint curve at the edge of his lips. He's dangerously close.

'You seem lost in thought, or like the answer is at the bottom of your coffee cup,' he murmurs.

'Away with the fairies.' I shrug. 'That's what my mum always used to say to me. That I was away with the fairies, always lost in a daydream.'

'And what were you daydreaming about just now?'

'Wouldn't you like to know?'

'More than anything,' he whispers, causing the heat to rise in my face as my insecurities melt away.

I let myself lean into him a bit, for only the slightest touch of his torso against my side, but it's so intimate. I've been close to him before, but always with my coat and his hoodie between us. Here, wearing nothing but his T-shirt, I can feel his strong, lean body next to mine.

When Brady's break ends, he brings us over another tray of drinks. I'll pay later for ingesting so much caffeine, but I don't want the afternoon to end. Peter and Anna's earlier animosity has melted away.

Anna has been an active part of our group for a while, but seeing Peter come alive in front of everyone is something else. It's fascinating watching them interact when they're at ease. Sometimes it sounds like they're speaking their own language, the words arranged in a slightly strange order. Peter, alive and engaging, has everyone laughing, more like Brady than I would've ever thought. Even Jamie's prickliness has edged off. There's no getting away from their radiance. Something about their features, I can't place—too beautiful, almost ethereal. Lush golden hair and rich, dark eyes I could fall into.

All good things come to an end, and as Brady's shift finishes, he makes his way over to say his goodbyes. Anna has texted her aunt to collect them.

'I'll see you tomorrow then, Anna?' he confirms with her as she gets up, gathering her things with an enthusiastic nod in response.

I make my way out of the booth, instantly missing Peter's warmth.

As Peter passes me to join his sister, he dips his head to whisper in my ear, his hot breath sending a shiver down my spine, 'I'll see you tonight.'

My face must be scarlet it's so hot. Anna's right, he is reckless. I don't respond, not quite believing he'd dare to even whisper that in front of everyone. And then he's already at the door with Anna, waving goodbye to everyone.

'Do you need a lift home?' Brady offers, and I'm hoping my face isn't as beetroot-red as it feels.

'Actually, do you want to stay for another, Con?' Lorna asks before I'm able to reply.

'Sure. I'll catch up with you tomorrow, Brady. Bye, Jamie.'

Jamie gives Lorna and me a half-hearted wave as he follows Brady out. I start to tell Lorna I'll get this round—although I probably shouldn't have any more coffee—but before I can do anything, she's pulling me back into the booth next to her.

'Tell me everything,' she demands.

'What are you talking about?'

'Connie, I have eyes. What's happened between you and Peter?'

'Nothing.' I try to sound convincing. I can't remember why I don't want to tell her.

Lorna gives me a look of disbelief, her brown eyes all too knowing.

'Lor,' I say after a long minute. 'I don't even know myself.'

'You two seem so cosy. I can't believe nothing's happened. He's like a different person.'

I can't deny that. I've never witnessed Peter so carefree around other people.

'Okay, so I did run into him over the weekend,' I confess, needing to give her something to alleviate my own guilt. 'While I was out walking Barney. All we did was walk and talk. It was nice. And, well, I may have met him on Sunday too.'

'I knew it.' Lorna laughs, her playful slap landing on my arm.

'But I meant what I said, Lorna. I really don't know what's going on. It's complicated.' At least this part is true.

'You like him, and he likes you. Why does it have to be more complicated than that?'

I let out a big sigh. 'I don't know. When you say it like that, it shouldn't be. But he's a whole world of different. Even from Anna. He's had it tough growing up.'

Lorna regards me, thoughtful. 'It's not every day we get *different* around here. I should know.' She looks a little sad. 'Just go carefully, Connie, with him and with yourself.'

After getting off easy, I catch a ride home with Lorna's parents. Three coffees, and the thought of Peter coming over later, has me jittery. Maybe I would feel better if I'd come clean and told Lorna about the early-morning visits too. Obviously, Anna doesn't approve. I think Lorna would find it hilariously scandalous, then encourage me to stop and go on a normal date with him. If that's even what it would be.

I resolve to confront him about it tonight.

Put my foot down.

No more midnight visits.

If he wants to see me, then he needs to take me on a normal daytime date. I'm not a blunt person, so the thought of demanding Peter take me on a date is enough to make me want to be sick.

The night drags on, and I find I can barely sleep. I watch my clock count down to one a.m., then finally hear the *click* of an acorn against my window.

Practising what I've rehearsed in my head, I creep downstairs. I need to get this over and done with before he puts me off, or I put myself off by telling myself I'm an idiot for telling this gorgeous boy I can't lie under the stars with him anymore.

My heart pounds harder with each step I take toward him. Standing in the middle of my garden, his skin luminescent in the moonlight, he's so sure of himself.

I hold my nerve, stopping in front of him. 'Look, Peter, you can't keep coming over like this. As much as I want to spend time with you, I actually do need sleep to function. And, your sister's right, it's only a matter of time before we get caught. It's not like we're even doing anything wrong, so, really, would it be so bad if we just did something together during regular hours, you know, like normal people? A normal date, in the day.' I'm out of breath by the time I finish rambling. It's not what I practised, but it's close enough. I focus on my shoes, waiting for him to say something.

He doesn't.

Great work, Connie. You've ruined the first interesting thing to ever happen to you.

After what feels like an age, I peer up to find his face serious.

'Peter.' It comes out as a plea. 'Say something.'

He takes a step toward me, his movements slow and measured. His dark eyes stay on mine. His hand comes to rest on my face, his thumb running over my lips, causes me to gasp at the unexpected connection, the warmth of his hand in the cold night. 'Connie,' he murmurs my name.

I wait for him to continue or say it again.

Please say it again.

I dare not speak, afraid to break the spell.

A heavy breath escapes him, and Peter moves his face to mine. His lips find my own in a gentle, brief caress.

I freeze, the warmth exploding through me and taking me by surprise.

'Is this okay?' he asks, his words no more than a whisper.

I have no words.

If I speak, I'll wake up.

Instead, I nod, stepping closer to him.

I need more.

His kiss is soft and then urgent at the same time, his hand snakes around my back to clutch me to him. All my words, my resolve, falls out of my head, and I'm lost to him. I return his kisses, crushing my body to his. I've wanted this, him. I can't get close enough, can't get enough of him. My head swims.

Finally, he breaks away, breathless.

'I had to come over to do that,' he says. Smug. Still holding me close. 'You can go back inside to bed. Maybe I can give you a call tomorrow?'

'No, I don't want you to go. Not after that.'

Peter grins and leads me out of the garden and toward our spot.

'You totally tricked me. That's not playing fair, you know.' I shake my head.

'Actually, I'd planned to do that the whole way over. But, I can agree to your terms, no more night visits.'

'Not every night,' I relent. There's no way I'm giving them up now.

We sit down on what's now an extra flat patch of wheat. I wonder if whoever owns this land is baffled by its presence.

'And instead, we do this in the daytime?'

'Not exactly this, but how about a regular date?'

Peter moves his attention from me, giving it to the inky night sky.

He's lost in thought.

And I panic.

'That is, unless you don't want to go on a date with me.'

This makes Peter roll over and, taking my face in hand, push me back against the ground. His face hovering above mine, he declares, 'Of course I want to take you on a date, Connie. I want *you*, no one else.'

With a smile, my hand moves into his hair to guide his lips to mine again. This kiss is different, deeper, and the butterflies in my stomach go manic. There's no hesitation, no awkwardness. He breaks away from me, releasing a small sigh of satisfaction, which melts me.

'Hey, Peter?' I ask, a thought occurring to me.

'Yes?'

'With everything you've told me about your life, does this mean I'm your first kiss?'

'Yes, Connie. You're my first kiss, my only kiss. My first everything,' he tells me, eyes sparkling, sending the butterflies into somersaults. 'Was that your first?'

Now I turn red for a different reason and shake my head, trying to gauge his response.

'It was Jamie, right?' he hedges, and I bite my lip with guilt. 'So that's why he doesn't like me.'

I sit up and angle toward him. 'Do you think I'm an awful person?'

Peter looks confused. 'No. Of course not. You don't belong to Jamie. Do you?'

'No. I don't *belong* to anyone.'

'Good.'

His lips find mine again.

CHAPTER 11

Peter

As I climb back through my open bedroom window, I can just make out Anna's bumpy form in the darkness, under the covers, waiting for me. I remove my shoes and hoodie with as little noise as possible and climb in next to her.

She rouses for a few seconds, shuffling over to give me room. 'You left again,' she murmurs, her voice sleepy.

'Shush, don't wake up,' I coax.

Her eyelids flutter as she falls back under, and I stare into the darkness. Sleep threatens to overtake me. It would appear the late nights have finally caught up with me too.

So that was a kiss—that's what kissing Connie feels like.

With my eyes closed, it's easier to remember how she looked tonight, to remember her taste.

Something is growing inside of me—a need for her, a need to keep her close.

In the morning, my sister is already gone when I awake, and I presume she's downstairs making breakfast. I'm not quite ready to deal with her or another telling off for my behaviour and risking the easy life we've slipped into with Sally and James. I rummage under the bed for my phone, which has been left on charge. I won't meet Connie today, even though my first waking moments are filled with the desire to kiss her again.

We have school tomorrow and another week of late-night visits will see her falling asleep at her desk. Plus, I promised to stay away.

I find her name on my phone and press the call button.

'Hello?' she answers after two rings, sounding a little breathless.

'Good morning.' I smile at hearing her voice.

'Peter. You're calling.'

'Yes, I thought I'd call as I won't come to you tonight, you know, to let you get your beauty sleep.'

'Oh.'

At the disappointment in her voice, I offer, 'I can come over if you want me to.'

'No, you're right. I have homework to catch up on and then school in the morning. I will see you tomorrow, though, right?'

I bite my lip. 'I'll have a hard time not kissing you.'

'No one will stop you.'

'Hmm... probably not the best activity for a public place. Restraint isn't a quality I possess.'

'I'm beginning to learn that.'

'Connie, you have no idea,' I say, trying to keep my voice even. The line goes quiet, and I have to check my phone to ensure I haven't hung up by mistake. 'Are you there?'

I hear her blow out. 'Peter, I'm not going to be able to concentrate all day now.'

'Good. Then we'll both feel the same.' I laugh, pleased with myself for having some effect on her.

'Bye, Peter.'

'Bye, Connie.'

Today's going to be spent in the garden, but not quite yet. I'm still not ready to go downstairs and face Anna. I know there's only so long I can avoid her. I formulate my garden plans as I decide on having a bath. I've put an end to the strawberries, as I can't expect Sally and James to remain ignorant over having year-round strawberries. Meanwhile, I've promised Sally pumpkins for Halloween, so, something new to look forward to. Pumpkins make great soup.

The warm bathwater envelops my body, and I relax, the tension leaving me. I sink farther, deeper, until I'm submerged. When Anna and I were younger, we used to play this game in the lake where we'd hold our breath for as long as possible. I would always win.

I miss the lake. Floating, where minutes could pass like hours while Anna read her book under the tree. Beside her, our mother sat cross-legged on her threadbare blanket, drinking home-brewed gin and sewing our clothes. It was our own little corner of the universe.

My eyes open to Anna peering down at me in my watery abyss. The *woosh* of water fills my ears.

'Jesus, Anna, are you trying to kill me?' I push my hair out of my eyes, but the serious expression remains on her face.

'Are you ever going to stop?' she demands.

'It's called fun, Anna. You should try it sometime,' I quip, letting the water rise to my chin and exposing my knees to the cold air.

'I have fun. I have fun with Brady, but *my* fun won't get us in trouble.'

'It's just all so public.'

'It's safe.'

I roll my eyes at her as she perches on the edge of the tub. 'Brother, you know enough by now that when you're caught… and you will be… this whole village will hear about how you're some kind of deviant, defiling one of its beloved daughters.'

'Wow.' The laughter bubbles out of me. 'I didn't realise you had such a penchant for the dramatic. You read too much Austen. Besides, you heard her yesterday. We've just been talking.'

'That's not what people will believe, Peter.'

'Oh, who cares, Anna?' I splash her.

'I care.' She moves away to avoid being splashed again, then narrows her eyes at me. 'Something's different about you.'

I shrug.

'Something happened last night.'

'Don't do that.' I try to splash her once more, but she jumps to avoid it again. 'Don't pretend you can read my mind.'

'I don't have to. The smugness is rolling off you. You said you were just talking.'

'We were. Last night was the first time.'

'So now you really are a deviant.' Anna pushes my head under the water for a second, but her anger has dissipated. 'Tell me.'

'It was just a kiss.' I splutter from my momentary drowning.

She moves forward, crouching so her face is near mine. 'What was it like?'

I run my finger across my lip, remembering. 'She tastes like the first honey after a long winter.'

Anna laughs at me, shaking her head. 'Okay, Romeo.'

'What's the hold up with Brady? Don't you want to?'

'The right time hasn't presented itself.'

'That's your problem, sister.' I tap her temple, dampening her hair. 'You think too much.'

'As opposed to you, who doesn't think enough?'

'Between us, there's one perfectly balanced person.' I laugh, and Anna smiles weakly. I know she wants to be mad at me for my reckless behaviour, but I don't want her to be. 'Anna, I don't know how to be just part of who I am.'

Anna gives me a sad look, rubbing the lines on her forehead.

I can tell her annoyance is melting away.

'I hope you know what you're doing.'

Moving close to her I whisper, 'I have no idea. Which is why I need you by my side.'

'Always,' she whispers back without hesitation.

There's a knock at the bathroom door before Sally's concerned voice calls out, 'What are you two doing in there?'

Anna rolls her eyes. 'Ugh, we're talking,' she snaps, then gets up and storms out. 'What else would we be doing?'

'I don't like that tone, Anna.'

My sister apologises, then retreats downstairs.

Aunt Sally glances in my direction right before the door closes. There was enough time for her to register me in my now cold bath, my head visible to her, with concern etched over her face.

Despite their initial jubilation at our making friends, there's been a growing tension in the house. In the beginning, it was all talk of sharing and openness, but their expectation that Anna and I will share everything with them is not something we are familiar with.

Always in the back of Anna's mind is the worry we'll be carted off to some sort of institution, where James wanted us in the first place. The reality is that, when she says we, she means *me*. I'll be taken away. Hence the annoyance at my nightly disappearing act and my inability to appear normal.

I get the impression Sally and James are waiting for something.

What, I don't know.

I know I've earned Anna's complete forgiveness when she joins me in the garden later, offering to help to plant the pumpkin seeds.

'You know, I looked it up online…' Anna begins as she pushes a seed into the ground with a finger, '… and pumpkins should take around three months to grow.'

I pause. 'Do you think they'll notice?'

'No, but I do think you should be more careful. We live in the countryside. All it takes is for them to tell one of their farmer friends that their nephew grew perfect pumpkins in three weeks, and you would have some serious explaining to do.'

'I could grow them in three minutes if you asked me to.'

'Peter.' Anna raises her eyebrow at me.

I should stop pushing my luck with her.

'They'd probably think I'd just bought them, that my whole caring-about-nature thing is just a big lie,' I say flippantly, rotating the cool earth with my hands. It's too dry—we need rain soon.

'You're out here every day.'

'You're giving them too much credit. They would make every plausible explanation before they believed the truth.'

'I'm not so sure about that.'

'Anna, anybody who eats all that shit without any thought about what's in it has to be willing to live in some kind of welcome ignorance.'

Anna looks thoughtful, mulling over my words and abandoning her task of helping me, instead sitting cross-legged beside me.

'What do you think Connie would say?'

What would Connie say?

I stop what I'm doing and sit back on my heels to look at her. It's a question I've considered a lot over the last week. But, every time I have, I can't find a way of articulating the words in my head, let alone out loud.

'Like I said, I think I can trust her.'

'So you're going to tell her, then?' There's an edge of panic behind Anna's words.

'I don't know. How do you explain something like this? Would you tell Brady?'

'It is not my secret to tell, Peter.' She avoids the question with tact.

'But if you were me?'

She shrugs. 'No. Not yet, anyway.'

My head tells me Connie would run a mile, that she *should* run a mile. I think about the tension in the house, casting my mind back to some of our mother's more gin-filled evenings when her ramblings weren't even the least bit coherent.

'Do you ever wonder if any of the adults in our lives have told us the full story?'

Anna smiles, putting a comforting hand on my arm. I grin back and glance toward the kitchen to check that no one is watching. 'Want to see me make this garden look like something out of *Cinderella*?' I challenge, willing her to egg me on.

'Didn't I just tell you to be careful?' Anna reminds me.

'Kill joy.' I snigger. 'Okay, that's a no to *Cinderella*,' I say more to myself as I dig into the fresh earth and breathe in the fresh autumn air, letting it fill my lungs. It fills all of me, gathering my energy, and I let it build. Connecting with the earth, I breathe with her, and push out, passing on life. The seeds spring into life, germinating quickly with my transferring energy. Tiny shoots appear above the ground.

Whoops, a bit too much push there.

'Peter,' Anna exclaims, her face flashing displeasure.

'Oops.' I take my hands out of the earth, holding them in the air. 'I didn't mean to push that far.'

Anna glances back to the window, double-checking that no one is there.

Great. She's mad at me again.

'You need to get yourself under control,' she grinds out before storming back inside.

I stare at the tiny pumpkin shoots, feeling in a bit of a mood myself now.

Why is being different such a bad thing? It's not like what I do hurts anyone.

I decide to call it a day.

To try and placate Anna, I sit inside and watch television with her. It's not long before my eyes are heavy, perhaps due to overusing my energy in the garden.

The next day, I wake to the sound of rain on my window. The clouds are fat with water, and grey covers every inch of the sky.

School again today.

One thing I never accounted for with joining the *real* world is the boredom. Never has more been expected of me. And yet, I've never been so bored in my life. The only thing I have to look forward to today is a short hour at lunch where I get to see Connie.

Her brilliant jewel-coloured eyes glance over at me across the table. The way she looks at me, a dare. I recall what she said yesterday. *'No one will stop you.'* The challenge in her words makes my chest ache.

My morning passes in a haze.

Boring, all so boring.

At least now it's boring rather than the overwhelming sensation of being surrounded. The chatter around my sister and me has died down, and we can fade into the background. The world has become a sea of grey. Meaningless, endless grey.

As Anna and I enter the cafeteria at lunch, I know I can't spend another day looking at Connie from across the table. As usual, she's flanked by Lorna and Jamie. Her green eyes stay on me the whole way as I walk over, her friends chatting around her.

'Hi, guys,' Anna says when we reach them, sitting in her usual seat next to Brady. They all say hi as I remain on my feet and make a snap decision.

'Hi,' I say directly to Connie as the chatter continues.

'Hi,' she says back.

I was wrong. The world's a sea of grey, with Connie in the middle, my guiding star.

'Can I talk to you?' I ask.

It's enough to stop everyone's chatter, and they all look at me like I have two heads.

'Connie, can I talk to you? Alone,' I clarify as all faces turn toward her.

The colour rises in Connie's cheeks when she gets out of her chair.

I walk around for her to join me, guiding us toward the front of the cafeteria. A glance behind shows everyone still watching us as we go.

'Let's get a drink,' I suggest. When we're out of earshot, I say, 'I didn't mean to put you on the spot.'

'It's okay. I don't think anyone's heard you say more than two words at school.'

I laugh. 'Well, I hate it here. But at least I get to see you. I didn't want to waste that time today.'

Her cheeks bloom a faint pink again.

'Thanks. I must admit, I missed you last night. I didn't miss the lack of sleep, but I missed you. Good thing you didn't come, though. It rained all night.'

'Did it? I fell asleep on the sofa. Looks like those late nights finally caught up with me as well.'

She laughs. 'So, you *are* human after all.'

We reach the counter, where I grab a bottle of water. 'What do you want?'

Connie looks at the selection for a while. 'Coke for me, thanks.'

I hand her the drink, refraining from pulling a face at her choice. I try not to think about what so much sugar is doing to her insides as she drags her feet back to the table.

'So, I was thinking about what you said, about having a daylight date.'

'You were?' she quips.

'Yes, and I want to take you somewhere on Saturday. Daylight hours.' My brain barely registers the words before I say them, my mouth making decisions for me. I stop and grin at her.

Her green eyes sparkle when she peers up at me. 'Where are you taking me?'

'It's a surprise.'

'Okay, mystery man. It's a date.'

'Good.'

'Good.'

She's within reaching distance. One movement, and she'd be mine. She bites her lip, unsure.

'And tonight?' I ask.

Much to my disappointment, she shakes her head. 'It's a little rainy.'

'You're killing me.' I lift my hand and tug out the lip she's chewing with my thumb.

'The feeling is mutual.'

'So…' I let out a breath, '… are these assigned seats or something?'

'What do you mean?'

'Can I sit next to you? Or is it some unwritten rule you sit next to Lorna and Jamie every day?'

'Just habit, I guess. You have to get here a bit quicker. Did you get my text?'

'Text?'

'Yes. I texted you last night?'

'Oh. That thing lives under my bed. I never think to check it. What did it say?'

Her face reddens again, but I don't push the subject as we reach the table. She sits back down, and I move to take my regular seat next to Anna, but somehow reading my mind, Lorna turns to me before I can.

'Do you want me to move up, Peter?' Lorna offers.

'You sure?'

'Absolutely.' She looks almost gleeful.

'Thanks.' I sit down next to Connie, who's now gone scarlet. I whisper to her, 'So, what did it say?'

'Peter.' She leans closer, although the conversation has continued around us. 'Don't make me say it.'

'Hmm... now I *really* want to know what it says.'

'Well, maybe you need to actually start using your phone, like a normal person.'

'Fine. I'll be normal.'

'Yeah, let me know how that works out. Besides, do you realise what you've done?'

'What's that?'

'Lorna's going to pump me for information later.'

'What have you told her?'

'Nothing.'

'How come?'

The corners of her lips twitch, and she teases, 'I like having you to myself.'

I breathe her in, and my eyes drift to her lips. 'You're irresistible,' I say quietly.

In the spirit of self-preservation, I force myself to join the main conversation and drag my full attention away from Connie. I dare not touch her at all. Instead, I return a conspiratorial smile from Lorna, which confirms Connie's earlier sentiments—she'll get a grilling from her friend later.

When I leave the cafeteria with Anna, I look back to where Connie's giggling with Lorna, who's dramatically fanning herself with her folder and I grin.

'You know how to make an impression, brother,' Anna teases.

'I thought you'd be happy. Less sneaking about. I even made a date with her on Saturday, during the day.'

Anna gives a mock-gasp but relents. 'That's good.'

When I get home, I check my phone to find a single text from Connie.

Connie: *I can't wait to kiss you again.*

It crosses my mind to go over anyway. Except, I'm just getting back in Anna's good books. I'll have to wait until tomorrow to see Connie.

Instead, I stare out of the window at the sweet, beautiful rain. It's been about two weeks since we've had any.

I consider going out to the garden, plunging my hands into the dirt, forcing the pumpkins into life, and encouraging the green vine to take over the garden until huge gold orbs—like some fairytale nightmare—burst forth. In part for the look of horror on Anna's face—it would be pretty funny—but also to help force sleep to come.

I don't, though. Instead, I let the boredom take hold. The shadow nightmares return, chasing sleep away, and time stretches on.

The next day, I count the minutes on the clock until lunch. Today, I don't ask to speak to her, though. I simply sit in my usual spot after saying hello to everyone. I catch her gaze when I pull out my phone to send her a simple text.

Me: *Tonight?*

She takes out her phone, then looks my direction, the briefest smile passing her lips.

Connie: *Still raining.*

At her response, I meet her eyes, shaking my head.

Me: *How about I meet you after school? That's daytime right?*

She immediately picks up the phone, smiling at it.

Connie: *Okay. You know the address!*

I'm relieved I'm going to be able to kiss her again soon. The thought of it is starting to consume me. Every time she looks at me puts me on the verge of shifting toward her. My movements, my focus, are starting to shift.

Beyond my control, my resolve has set upon Connie—on having her and making her mine.

As we leave for our next class, I make a snap decision and tell Anna I'll catch up. I lean against the wall of the cafeteria doors, waiting for Connie to exit. It occurs to me I have all but disregarded my sister's previous advice to take it easy on Connie, which bothers me almost as much as the fact that she's also right.

I'm *completely out of control.*

Connie and Lorna are some of the last to leave. I grab Connie's arm when she passes, making her jump a mile.

'I didn't mean to scare you.'

'Peter.' Connie clutches her chest. 'What are you doing lurking there?'

God, do I lurk?

'I just…' I pull myself up from my place on the wall, towering over her. *I have no idea what I was going to say.*

Lorna looks between the two of us.

'I'll see you in class, Con,' she states with a quick departure down the hall, not wanting to play gooseberry.

'Are you okay?' she asks me with genuine concern.

I must look a bit frazzled.

'No. No, I couldn't wait.' I crush my lips against hers.

Her reaction is instant and, dropping her bag to the floor, her hands find their way into my hair and pull me closer. Her kiss is ecstasy, something I can't get enough of. My hands drift from her arms, finding their way down her body to her hips. After rotating her body to push her to the wall, her breath leaves her chest hard before I continue to kiss her, pressing my body to hers.

Wanting her.

Wanting everything.

Her hands move up my chest and push against me. 'Peter, stop.'

I stand back, both our breaths ragged, and look up at the ceiling. 'Sorry.'

Take it easy on her, Peter.

She may know I'm not well-socialised, but she doesn't need to know I'm all but feral.

'No, you don't need to be sorry.' She smooths out her hair. 'It's just… this is school. You can't kiss me like that here.'

'Okay. Later?'

'Yes. I will see you later.' She looks at me, rooted to the spot.

I shouldn't kiss her again.

So, instead, I walk away, leaving her standing there.

CHAPTER 12

Connie

Even though I don't know what I was expecting, I'm somehow still surprised to find Peter standing at my front door when I answer his knock. I guess I'm getting used to secrets and sneaking around. Not that I don't like it—it's fun, but it's also nice to know he isn't embarrassed to be with me in the light of day.

It's still raining. His simple jacket is soaked through and his wavy hair is dripping water on the ground, but he stands there with a grin, looking at me in a way no one ever has. His smile is so charming it's dangerous.

'Nice night,' he says without a hint of irony.

'Yeah, looks it.' I shake my head, laughing.

He takes a step back from under my porch, stretching his arms out wide, and his palms catch the downpour while the water splashes off his face. 'I'm serious,' he says to the heavens. 'I love the rain.'

'You're crazy.' I walk out and grab the front of his jacket, retreating into the shelter of my hallway, pulling him with me.

He stumbles forward until we come to a stop. With his tall form looking down at me, his eyes bore into mine and his hands snake around my back, his hair dripping onto my face.

'Let's take a walk.'

'You're joking?' I escape his drips just in time as my mum enters the hallway, curious about who has arrived.

'Peter? Is that you?' She looks aghast at his drenched form.

'Hello, Mrs. Prinze.' He gives a brilliant smile.

'Please, call me Suzie. You look soaked to the bone. Come inside. Take your jacket and shoes off, though. You're getting water everywhere. Do you want some tea?' Mum starts making her way into the kitchen.

Peter kicks his shoes off, hangs his jacket on a nearby hook, and squelches in after her. I take a deep breath and wonder what kind of can of worms my mother is about to unleash.

'Connie, why don't you go and grab a towel for Peter?' she asks.

I hesitate, not wanting to leave the two of them alone, but can't think of a good enough reason to refuse, so I dart up our narrow staircase to retrieve a towel from the airing cupboard at the top of the stairs. When I return, Peter's leaning against the kitchen counter. After his many midnight visits, it's strange that he's standing here in my well-lit kitchen, talking to my mum like he belongs.

'Nice of you to come by, Peter. I have to admit, Connie talks a lot about you.'

'Mum,' I whine, handing Peter the towel.

He looks pleased with himself. 'Does she?'

'I do not.' I shoot Peter a glare.

My mum gives Peter a wink, handing him a green tea. 'It's all good stuff, I promise.'

'And you wonder why I don't have people here,' I scold her.

Peter lazily dries his hair, and I can't help but notice how his black T-shirt clings to his body.

'Come on, Peter,' I say and start to lead him upstairs before my mum can do any more damage.

'Thanks for the tea,' he says before following me up.

'Door open, honey,' Mum calls after us.

As I open the old oak door of my bedroom, my heartbeat picks up as Peter steps inside and looks around. *Peter is in my bedroom.*

'Why don't you have people over?' he asks, perusing the world map on my wall. Carefully, he presses some of the bright pins in it.

'Oh.' I shrug. 'I live in the smallest house. I suppose it just always worked out that way. I like getting out of the house.' I manage to stop the oncoming ramble before it picks up momentum.

'I like it. It has character.' He moves to look out the window he's been throwing acorns at and gives it a thoughtful smile.

'What was your house like? The one you grew up in, I mean.'

'Different.' He looks at the pile of books on my bedside table.

I nod at his frustrating answer.

'So, what do the pins mean? I thought you hadn't travelled.' He gestures to the map as he dries his hair.

'I haven't. I've never been on a plane. They're all the places I want to go.' I join him to look wistfully at my map. 'This world is so full of wonder, and I've seen none of it.'

'Where would you go first?'

'Paris. I know, not the most exotic, but I'd just love to visit. Walk along the Seine, sit on the steps at Montmartre, drink great coffee, eat great cheese, fall in love.' Against my will, the heat rises in my cheeks. 'Where would you go?'

'It would have to be Paris,' he says with a smirk

I let out a sigh. 'You're only saying that because I said it.'

'You made it sound so appealing. I want to do all those things too. Maybe not the coffee part, though.'

He drops the towel onto my bed.

'Seriously, Peter, you're going to get my bed all damp.' I move around him to pick up the towel and I swear I catch him rolling his eyes. From the corner of my eye, I see him lifting his soaked black T-shirt over his head, revealing his chest. 'What are you doing?'

'Drying off.' He takes a step forward, taking the towel out of my hands and dropping it to the floor. I instinctively put my hand on his stomach, which is flat and lean, and hot. He is always so warm. His body isn't too muscular, more naturally athletic, and even though he's been out in the rain, his skin is warm to the touch. He guides my free hand onto his chest and breathes in like I'm his air. His ochre eyes turn even darker.

I lose the power to breathe, to think.

Before I know it, his hands are in my hair, bringing my face to his. Kissing me. My hands run up his chest and make their way around his back, holding him closer. My feet move in reverse, my back hitting the cool of the window. His kisses become more urgent, moving from my mouth down my neck, and immediately my knees go weak.

'Peter. Stop.' I manage to breathe. Although he backs away from me, I miss his touch instantly. I try to collect my thoughts, watching my open bedroom door. 'We need to slow down a sec.'

Peter takes a deep breath, rubbing his forehead. He moves to the window and pushes his head against the cold glass. 'I'm sorry, Connie. I keep doing that, don't I?'

'Don't apologise.' I take my dressing gown and drape it around his shoulders in case my mum does decide to come and check on us, then go and sit on my bed. Best to put a bit of distance between us as his self-control is non-existent, and mine is hanging by a thread. 'It's not that I don't want to kiss you, Peter. Believe me, I do. But my mum would go nuts. Besides, things are getting a little out of control, so maybe we could just talk for a while.' I sound pathetic.

My heart almost breaks at the sadness in his eyes.

'Do you think I'm out of control?'

'Yes, I think you are absolutely, one hundred percent out of control,' I tease him. 'And I'm trying to go with it. However, it's not something I want my mum to witness. You're pretty wild, Peter.' I smooth my hair out, giving him a grin. 'Kissing you is wild.'

He pulls his arms through the dressing gown and moves to sit down in front of me on the floor. The sadness in his eyes is gone, replaced by an earnest expression.

'I'm glad you feel it too. I can't stop thinking about you. Kissing you is the most addicting thing I've ever tasted.'

His words send a thrill through me. I give my head a small shake. 'How are you even real?'

'What do you mean?' He cocks his head at me.

'You.' I motion to his cross-legged form. 'You just came out of nowhere. Apparent son of a total recluse. A boy who knows all the constellations and the things in my garden that can cure my headache. You tell me I taste addictive. You're... I can't find the words to describe you. How can you be real?'

'I don't know,' he replies, looking down.

A distance is growing between us.

He's pulling back.

So much unsaid.

He has the ability to tell me just enough without giving anything away—bits and pieces, not enough to solve the puzzle.

'Tell me something, Peter. Something real, something about you.'

His eyes search mine. Maybe searching for trust or for the right thing to say. I realise how much I want him. Not only physically to be near him but to *know* him, to know whatever pain he's hiding.

'Something real,' he says. Taking another long pause, he admits, 'Talking is hard for me.'

'I know. Talking is always hard, especially when you've been through something horrible.'

'You don't understand. Talking is *physically* hard. When I talk to most people, I have to think extremely long about what I'm about to say. I have to concentrate on finding the words. Anna has it too. Although she doesn't find it as hard as I do. She's adapted quicker, but it's there.'

'What do you mean?' I can't quite wrap my head around what he's trying to say.

'We were raised alone, Connie, with only our mother. And she did speak to us, taught everything we needed to know, or at least what she thought we needed to know. But looking back now, the older we got, the less she spoke. Well, the less she spoke real words and not ramblings. Anna and I, we only had each other. How we spoke to each other, it was different. Even now, if you hear us when we're alone together, it won't sound like this, like how I'm talking to you now. You could probably tell we were speaking English, but maybe not. We'd sound garbled, I suppose. So, when speaking to you, I think about every word before they come out.'

I sink to my knees in front of him, waiting for him to continue.

His gaze holds mine, waiting for my reaction.

'What nobody knows is that before we came to live with our aunt, after our mother died, we were taken in by social services, and we spent weeks in a hospital.' With his voice barely a whisper, he adds, 'They first thought we would have to be institutionalised because we couldn't speak. Not like I'm now.'

'Oh, Peter.' I take his face in my hands, the tears burning hot in my eyes.

He takes my hands in his. 'We could understand them. Because the words we were speaking were still English… they just sounded different. It didn't take us long to learn how to make ourselves understood. In the end, they tracked down our aunt, and she agreed to take us in. They thought it was the best thing for us to go and live with her. Give us the chance of a normal life, and here we are.' He gives a definite nod. 'And that is something real.'

'I'm so sorry.' The tear threatening to spill escapes my eye, rolling down my cheek and dropping onto Peter's hand.

'Don't be.' He wipes another tear from my face. 'We didn't know any different. Connie, the reality is… I've lived most of my life outdoors, so adapting has been hard, unbelievably hard. The funny thing is how I keep waiting for the penny to drop. For when everything clicks in my head between my reality and what everyone has been telling me is true. We were neglected, our mother was crazy, and I'm broken to believe this wasn't the case. We lived like that for seventeen years, my whole life, and I can't reconcile how it was wrong. It's *this* world that makes no sense to me.'

I'm unable to stop the tears from falling. My skin prickles against the cold. Peter was not only isolated but neglected in ways I can't fathom. When I don't speak, he pushes my head up, forcing me to look at him, his eyes searching for signs of horror.

'I want to tell you, Connie, everything. I feel so heavy with all this weight of who I am. I want you to know it all. I'm beginning to suspect I want you more than I've ever wanted anything in this world, and I don't know what will happen when you recoil away from me.'

'Peter, why wouldn't I want you?' I move my hands to the back of his neck. 'You're a god. Of course I want you.' I kiss him. 'You can trust me.' I kiss him again. 'You can tell me anything.'

He slips his hands around my back and pulls me close, kissing me deeply. I smooth the hair off his face as I get into the rhythm of our kiss. I want more. He lifts me onto his lap, his hands finding the skin of my back, and his hot palms dig into me, holding me tight.

I'm wanted, needed.

It's hard to resist.

'Peter.'

'Connie.'

'Peter.' I manage to pull myself away. 'Not here,' I say reluctantly, my legs like jelly.

He gives a low breath. 'My self-control is in tatters.'

'Right. Like you had any to begin with.'

He places a chaste kiss on my lips and shifts me off his lap. *How can I miss someone who's in the same room with me?* He moves to the safer position of sitting on the chair in front of my computer desk, and I ease myself back onto the edge of my bed. I must be crazy telling him to stop. I'm on the verge of instructing him to put a song on when I notice he's still wearing my fluffy dressing gown, his bare chest showing.

'You look ridiculous.' I laugh, the mood lightening.

He chuckles, looking down at himself. 'I like it. Much fluffier than mine.'

I grab my phone. 'Say cheese.'

He gives a half smile as I take a picture. Of course, he kind of looks like a rock star instead of ridiculous. Then, unable to help myself, I turn the camera around and sit on his lap to take a picture of us together.

'We look good together,' he says when I show him the photograph.

I agree.

I always thought my life in this village was disconnected from the real world, that I was missing out on so much. It's unfathomable to imagine Peter and Anna's childhood. I can't help being mad at their mum for doing what she did, and for everything they missed out on.

'Do you want to talk about it?' I ask gently. 'What it was like for you growing up.'

'No.' He shakes his head a touch. 'I want to hear more about you. Why did you start learning to play the guitar?'

I can't blame him for wanting to avoid a painful subject, and he's already shared way more tonight than I ever expected him to, so I humour him. 'My dad. He plays and sings too. He's an amazing singer. That's how he and my mum met. They went to the same university, and he played in a band. She saw him perform and was crazy about him. The rest was history.'

'Does he still have a band?'

'No, that finished a long time ago. Before I was born. In fact, he barely plays at all now. He works away a lot and is always tired when he's home. He likes that I play, but I know it makes him sad.'

'Why?'

I glance down at my hands. 'My mum says he always used to talk about "making it," but he never did. So when he hears me play, it makes him sad. I think it reminds him of those dreams, forever out of reach now. He has to take care of my mum and me. Responsibilities and all that.' My eyes prick with tears again. 'You know, I've never said that out loud to anyone before.'

'You can tell me all of your secrets too,' he whispers.

The time passes too fast, though, and before I know it, Mum is calling up the stairs. I'm grateful my mum trusts me enough not to come up to check on us.

'Peter, it's after ten. Do you want a lift home?'

'Shit.' Peter jumps up, patting himself down.

I imagine for his phone, which is absurd, given he's still in my dressing down.

He peels off my gown, throws on his T-shirt, which has been drying on my radiator and heads downstairs, where he grabs his jacket and grapples in his pocket for his phone. I can see it has a bunch of missed calls before he hits redial.

'Hello. I left my phone in my pocket. I know it's raining. I'm inside, at Connie's. Yes. Yes. Yes, her mother's right in front of me. No. I'm coming home now.' He clicks off the line. 'I'm sorry, Mrs. Prinze, I didn't realise the time. Don't worry, I can walk.'

'Don't be silly,' Mum says. 'It's pitch-black outside and you'll get soaked again.'

'It's fine, I don't mind.' He turns to me. 'Connie.'

And before I know what's happening, he leans down and kisses me. My brain, not fully engaged, tells my mouth to kiss him back. Then he's out the door, into the night.

Mum stands there dumbfounded.

I would laugh if I wasn't in such a rush to get out of her sight to avoid the grilling. Instead, I stride back upstairs as fast as possible.

'Is that boy your boyfriend, Connie?' she shouts after me.

'No, Mum!'

CHAPTER 13

Peter

The gravity of what I'm going to do weighs heavily on my chest.

I haven't seen Connie outside of school all week, mostly because I'm trying to stay in Sally and James' good books after Monday night. Not only had I not answered their calls, but I'd left Connie's house in such a hurry I forgot to put my shoes on. They were not happy about me turning up in the pitch-black, wet to the bone and barefoot.

Despite the rain drying up, I've also refrained from sneaking out during the night, mostly to stay in Anna's good books. So by the time Saturday rolls around, it seems like I'm in everyone's good books except Connie's. I hadn't planned on not being alone with her again after Monday night, but our conversation reaffirmed my decision to tell her everything. I needed time to digest what I'm going to say on our date. Plus, I feel guilty that I haven't told Anna my plans.

I sit and breathe in the fresh morning air, watching the breaking dawn. There's a good chance Connie will not want to be my friend anymore after this afternoon. *Connie.* It's been too long since I've felt her lips on mine. Seen her jewel-like eyes sparkle up at mine when she smiles. My heart aches at the knowledge I'm the one who she saves that sparkle for now.

I've made my decision. Come what may, it's better she knows, and not because I can't bear the weight of the secret anymore. At least, that's what I tell myself. I don't want to be alone, but I can't keep this secret from her forever. Yes, it's better she knows, and then *she* can make her decision. I've promised myself if she rejects me, then I'll let her go and not bother her again. Although, I'm beginning to learn selflessness is not in my nature.

I've had days to plan my speech, but nothing ever sounds right.

Anna stirs under the covers, her eyes flicker as she takes me in sitting at the window. 'It's cold,' she murmurs.

'Just trying to clear my head,' I answer. 'Anna.' I move back over to the bed, lying down to face her, hoping to catch her attention before she falls back to sleep. 'Do you think I'm a bad person?'

'What?'

'Do you think I'm selfish?'

'Sometimes,' she says, battling sleepiness.

'Do you think there are others like me?'

'Selfish?'

'No, silly.' I give her shoulder a bit of a shove. 'Different. You know, who can do what I can? It's a big world... there must be others, right? I can't be on my own. There has to be a name for it?'

Anna opens her eyes. 'What's this about, Peter?'

'Don't you ever wonder?'

She takes time to consider her answer. 'Of course. Honestly, it scares me. I think you're one of a kind, and I don't want to think about what they would do to you.'

I pull her in for a hug and let her drift back to sleep, warmer for having me close. My thoughts remain busy, swirling things. I leave for Connie's way earlier than I need to, choosing to wander and meander my way to her home. The cold October air is biting, but it's good to be outside. I repeat the words over and over in my head, reworking them to sound less like a horror story.

As I ring Connie's doorbell, my heart beats rapidly in my chest, threatening to break out. I wonder if I'll be able to keep my nerve.

Connie's face is alive with her smile when she opens the door. In an instant, she's in my arms, her warmth melting away my anxiety, and I drink all of her in while I still can.

'Peter, you're early.'

'Mmm... I couldn't wait to see you.'

Without wasting a second, she's on her tiptoes, bringing her mouth to mine. And I'm hers. She deepens her kiss, pulling me into the house and slamming the door behind me. Once closed, she pushes me against the closed door and leans her body hard into mine, her hands grasping around the back of my neck and pulling my mouth to hers.

All too soon, she pulls away from me. 'I missed you too,' she says with a grin.

'I can tell.'

She gives me a playful shove. 'So, mystery man. As you're here a little early, tell me, what should I wear?'

'Something warm. I thought we'd just go for a walk.'

The slightest flicker of disappointment flashes across her face. I already know a walk is not Connie's idea of a date, but I'm going to stick to my plan.

'Okay, well... I'll just grab my boots and then we can go.'

'Are your parents in?'

'No, they've gone shopping,' she calls from upstairs.

'Will they wonder where you are?' I shout up to her.

She appears at the top of the stairs. 'No. I'm not usually in the house on Saturday. Normally, my Saturdays involve staying warm and hot coffee. It's a good job you're cute, that's all I'm saying.'

I give a small laugh, then take her hand and lead her out of the house, my nerves beginning to rise. We slip into silence and stroll along the lane toward the outskirts of the village. Soon, we meet the crossroads where we can enter the woods. I begin to lead Connie off the path and into the trees, but her hand roots me in place, pulling me back. Her green eyes are looking past me into the dense trees.

'Peter, where are you taking me?'

'It's easier if I show you.'

'You're not taking me into the woods to kill me, are you?'

Connie says it as a joke. She's trying to lighten the mood, to make me laugh, but I know the smile I give her doesn't reach my eyes.

'No, killing is definitely not my style. Look, Connie...' I take in her face, '... what I want to show you, there's no going back after. You may never see me the same way... you might not even want to be my friend. I want you to know, but if you want to turn back, then I understand.'

I want to will her to say she wants to turn back or to suggest retreating to the coffee shop. But she doesn't. Instead, with a dip of her head, she tightens her grip on my hand and walks forward into the woods.

As we continue, the silence returns and I take the lead once more, guiding her further and deeper.

The denseness of the woods shelters us from the biting wind, but the absence of the blowing only increases the volume of the silence between us. Lost in my thoughts, it takes me a second to realise Connie's hand is no longer in mine. She's stopped a few paces behind me.

'Peter, we've been walking for half an hour. You're starting to worry me. Where are we going?' Her heart-shaped face is etched with worry.

'Do you trust me?' I ask her.

'Yes,' she replies though the word shakes.

I retrieve her hand and urge her forward. 'We're so close.'

My heart hammers. We are too close. Practically there now, and I'm nauseous.

Breathe, I remind myself. *Just breathe.*

I plant my feet firmly onto the ground as we round an all-too-familiar row of trees with a hedgerow growing in front.

Here goes—the words are stuck in my throat.

Connie speaks first as she takes in the sight in front of her.

'Is this?' she questions but trails off as she moves toward it, looking back at me incredulously. 'Have we walked right out of the village? This is the old haunted house, right? I never knew you could get to the back. You're not thinking of breaking in, are you?'

I shake my head. 'This is my house.'

Connie laughs. 'What are you talking about? This house has been abandoned for years.'

'I grew up here. This is where we lived. Where our mother kept us hidden for our whole lives.'

Connie laughs again, more uncertain this time. Not an easy laugh, it's more of an uncomfortable, unknowing laugh. Looking from me to the house and back again, she starts, 'But...' Connie shakes her head, trying to take in my confession, '... how can that be possible? How can no one have known you were here the whole time?'

I shrug, trying to ignore my shaking legs. 'I don't know. The same way we didn't realise we were near anyone. Our mother told us the world was a cruel and corrupt place, that it wasn't safe for us. So we accepted her words. She kept us in and everyone else out.'

'But her sister lives in the village?'

'Apparently, they had a big fight when we were still babies, so my mother let her believe she had left the country with us.'

Connie's eyes are wide as she looks back at the decaying house. 'None of you ever left, not for your whole life?'

'Never. In the end, we barely lived in the house in a practical sense. We only used three rooms. Our mother raised us to be completely self-sufficient. We grew all our own food. We had chickens, a hive...'

'But the water and electricity, how did she pay for that stuff?'

'I wish I knew.'

She turns back to me, cautious. 'You've been here the whole time.' Her green eyes hone in on mine. There's no sparkle now—they're serious, searching. 'What happened?'

'She died.'

I take a breath and look at the house. *My house.* The home I've long wanted to run back to. Seeing it now, it isn't my home, just a place to hide. The grim reality that I don't have a home stings. I close my eyes against the unease in my chest, trying to recall the words I've been practising.

'Connie, I need you to understand.' My focus returns to the girl in front of me. 'Everything we were taught as children... it was *all* to do with nature. How to survive and how to grow. Everything my mother ever valued came from the earth. She believed in an eternal cycle of nature, and that we came from the earth, and when we die, we return to it. All energy is recycled, nothing is truly wasted. Our lives are not our own, all borrowed from the universe, we're all part of something bigger.'

'Okay,' Connie says, measuring her response while wrapping her arms around herself. 'I think I understand.'

'Good.' I push past the feeling of churning bile in my stomach. *Keep going.* 'We were always taught death is a natural thing, not a bad thing. Nothing truly dies. Not in the grand scheme of things.'

Connie waits.

I'm sick to my stomach for even trying to justify this. 'It wasn't unusual for Anna and me not to see our mother for days at a time. She would sometimes take to her bed and not get up for a few days. In the last few years of our lives together, we basically lived outside for all the warm months. Earlier this year, as spring turned to summer, our mother took to her bed. I don't know how long it had been, but one day I climbed the stairs to check on her. I thought she was sleeping. As I got closer, it didn't take me long to realise she was gone. Her eyes were open and staring at the ceiling... they looked like two glass marbles. Shiny. Dead. I knew our mother was gone. All that remained was a shell.'

Connie's knuckles are white from clutching her coat, and she swallows hard. 'I'm sorry,' she whispers.

'Don't.' I turn, undeserving of her pity. 'I must've stood there for hours. Just looking at her. When Anna came to find me, she was distraught. I had to drag her from our mother's room, kicking and screaming, from our mother's side. I told her it wasn't our mother anymore, that she was gone, and we were on our own now.'

I chance a look at Connie, who's now letting the tears run freely down her face, and shake my head. 'Connie, I stopped Anna from grieving for her mother. I was being selfish. I didn't want things to change. I wanted Anna and me to stay the way we were. I was too selfish to get help or to even bury my mother's body. I'm the one who left her there.'

And there it is.

I turn my eyes to the ground, my voice a mere whisper as I remember my final memory of my mother.

'I left her to rot. It wasn't even three days before the whole house filled with the stench of death. It was everywhere, clung to everything.' I force myself to look at Connie so she can see me, see who I truly am. 'Eventually, Anna begged me to bury her body. It must've been the heat. We could already hear the noise of the flies from the stairs. But we went in anyway. What we saw wasn't our mother, it was rotting flesh.' I wear my self-disgust in my expression. 'And flies, thousands and thousands of flies. Her eyes were gone.'

Connie's hand clasps over her mouth, her eyes closing against her tears. I have a strange sense of relief now that the words are out. Now that she knows. I let my fingers catch the tears rolling down her cheeks. 'I never even cried. I'm a monster who left my mother to rot in her bed. And I didn't cry, not one tear.'

'Peter…' Connie steadies her breathing, peering up at me. 'You're *not* a monster. You didn't know what to do. How were you supposed to know what to do?'

'I should've buried her when we had the chance. I left her there. I thought it didn't matter. But it was so horrible, Connie. I can never unsee that… never forget the smell, that sound. She was my mother.'

Connie wraps her arms around me tight. I don't think she could hold me any closer. The weight of my shameful secret is now her burden too. I give in and return her embrace, pulling her to me.

'Connie, you should run. Run far away from me,' I whisper against her hair, knowing it's the furthest thing from what I want.

Except, she's not running, not letting go.

'I'm not going anywhere.' She brings her lips to mine.

To kiss me.

The weight I've been carrying reduces as she deepens her kiss. I feel lighter and lighter. Less myself—or more myself, I can't tell which. Until the kisses aren't quite enough anymore. I want her warm skin next to mine. My hands act without me having to tell them. The cold October air bites, the sensations amazing on my skin, bringing me back to life.

She's mine and I'm hers.

All of me.

'I didn't plan on that happening,' I say, running my finger over her bare shoulder. 'I thought you'd never want to see me again.'

'You're not the monster here, Peter. You should never have been in the position you were put in.'

I watch my finger travel down her arm, loving the way she looks at me. It's more than I could ever have expected.

'You're only seventeen. It was your mother's job to protect you. She kept you away from everyone. For no good reason.'

I look into her eyes. *Maybe that isn't entirely true.*

'You know what's weird?' she asks, looking around her as if taking in her surroundings for the first time. 'Aside from being naked in the woods.'

'What?' I laugh.

'It's October, and I'm not cold right now.'

I groan, rolling my eyes.

'What? What's so funny?' Connie demands.

'It's nothing. Just something Anna would certainly have an opinion on.'

'Anna would have an opinion on my nakedness?'

'No, not that.' I take a deep breath. 'I have one more thing to tell you. Or show you. A final secret.'

'Are you kidding?' Connie pulls my T-shirt over her head and sits up to look at me.

'Just this last thing… and that's it. Then you'll know everything.'

'I don't know if my heart can take any more, Peter.'

'This is different, I promise.' I get up to retrieve a nearby acorn. An acorn is fitting.

'Can you at least put some clothes on?'

'Seriously?' I roll my eyes at her but do as she requests.

This secret is different. The anticipation of showing her sets my blood on fire. I sit in front of her, enjoying the perplexed look on her face.

'Acorn.' I hold the acorn in front of her face.

'Acorn,' she confirms.

'Watch,' I say and can't help but smirk. With my mother gone, Anna is the only person in the world who knows what I can do. Well, not anymore. Not after the next few minutes.

In five... I dig a shallow hole with my hands and place the acorn in the centre.

Four... Connie gives me perplexed glances while I fill the hole with earth again.

Clearly, she thinks I've lost it.

Three... I place my hands over the acorn's nesting place, and I watch Connie's face.

I wish I knew what she was thinking.

Two... I breathe in, drawing my energy up through my palms and into my shoulders.

Here we go.

And one... I breathe out, pushing the energy down. Down past my palms and into the earth.

Connie gives a sharp gasp as she gawks at the fresh seedling of an oak tree sprouting through my fingers. I laugh at the look of delight on her face.

'I told you this secret was different.'

'What? How did you do that?'

I hold my hands up and wiggle my fingers. 'Magic.'

'I'm serious.' She bends her head closer to the ground to take a closer look at my seedling. 'What is this?'

'An oak tree, of course. Well, the start of one. It'll take a lot of years for it to be fully grown. I just gave it a bit of a shove in the right direction. I don't think I could grow a fully-grown oak tree. Or maybe I could, but I would probably sleep for a week.'

Wow. It's so good to say it out loud. I can't stop the stupid grin on my face.

Connie caresses its green leaves with gentle fingers. 'This is a trick. How did you do it?'

'No trick. I've always been able to do it.'

'What? Grow oak trees?'

I nod. 'Grow all things, actually.'

'Just like that?' Connie clicks her fingers. 'Magic?'

'Not real magic. I was kidding about that. It's me... I make it grow.'

Connie narrows her eyes, waiting for the punch line. 'What does this have to do with me being warm?'

'This is Anna's theory, not mine. She would tell you that it's me keeping you warm. When our mother died, we lived entirely outside. We stopped going in the house at all. We weren't found until months later. We slept outside, every night, for months. Anna believes I kept it hot enough so we didn't freeze.'

'But the whole village had that. It was our hottest summer.'

I shrug my shoulders. 'Anna's theory, not mine. She thinks I do it without realising.'

'Huh.' Connie keeps her eyes on the seedling, leaning closer to examine it.

'You don't believe a word of this, right?'

'The stars,' she says more to herself.

'What?'

'Every night we went out to look at the stars, there was never a cloud in the sky.'

'You believe me?' I almost can't believe it.

'No, I mean, yes. I don't know.' Luckily, she's laughing—an easy laugh—and smiling at me, one which reaches her eyes. 'Peter, you know this isn't a thing, right? People can't do these things.'

I nod. 'Yes, I realise. I understand this isn't normal. And I suppose I don't need to tell you to keep this a secret. Even from Lorna and Brady.'

Connie nods. 'So, you can make things grow, and maybe control the weather.'

'Yes, and maybe,' I confirm.

'Huh.' Connie nods again—slow this time—running her fingers over the tiny seedling's leaves.

CHAPTER 14

Connie

Slowly I draw my fingers across my lips, feeling the remnants of him. Still a bit swollen. I could trace the echoes of his body on my own. His absence is as cold as the autumn air. Remembering it makes me want him again—for him to be mine once more. Even thinking about it sends a thrill through me.

I want to call Lorna to tell her about what happened. But I can't.

To tell her would be pulling at a finely spun thread of secrets—so many secrets—most of which are not mine to tell. Peter, who's now mine in a way I've never known. Peter, who was neglected. Peter, who has abilities I cannot explain. I can't separate this one secret I want so desperately to share with my best friend without unravelling it all.

I finally flop down onto my bed. It's a lot. Lots to digest in a small amount of time. Peter, on the way home, had been as animated as I'd ever seen him. Babbling on about the trees and their root networks and other things I didn't understand. I'd been trying to process it, and I don't even remember saying goodbye to him.

I try to wrap my head around the incredible trauma he's been through—is still going through. His mother must've experienced paranoid psychosis to keep them locked away from the world, then convinced them of her delusions.

How could that explain what he'd shown me, though?

How is it possible?

How can he be possible?

The buzz of my phone brings me back to reality, making me jump a mile. *Lorna*. Of course she wants to know how it went. The thought of talking to Lorna is strangely alien after being alone with Peter. Who seems to take me out of this world and into another, making my normal life a stranger when I return.

I answer her FaceTime.

'Hey, girl,' she chimes at me, a huge grin on her face.

'Hey. How's it going? What have you been doing today?' I hope I don't sound too desperate to avoid her questions.

'The usual. Hung out with Brady. He had a shift at the coffee shop. Anna was there. It was kind of nice to get to know her a little better, although she was quieter than usual.'

'Oh really?'

'Yeah, but then I realised I've never seen her without her brother. They tend to be a package deal.'

I tilt my head thoughtfully. I wonder if Anna already knew Peter was going to tell me everything, which would've been enough to make her nervous. Part of me understands why she's been so wary of Peter sneaking around with me. She's protective of him. So much of their relationship is unexpected. Anna is the protector, the thinker. As much as he'd never want to admit it, Peter is vulnerable.

'Enough with the small talk, miss. What I want to know is how *your* day was. The date. Where did you go? What did you do?'

'Actually, we just went on a walk. A really long walk.'

'You don't look too thrilled about how it went.'

I try to give her a convincing smile, masking the storm of thoughts in my brain and laugh. 'Well, you know me. Walking isn't exactly my thing. I swear next time, I'll be taking him for a meal or something.'

'That means there is going to be a next time?'

I can't help but blush and nod. *How I want to tell her.*

'Has he asked you to be his girlfriend?' she continues.

'No.' I shake my head. 'Then again, as far as I can tell, Peter isn't big into labels.' I make a strangled sound. 'Lorna, I'm in so deep.'

She gives a fraction of a frown. 'What do you mean?'

'It's hard to describe. It's coming on so strong. Like falling, willingly, and I don't know if he can catch me.'

'Connie, why would you possibly say that? I wish I could show you how he looks at you.'

I try to hang onto that thought. 'If I could tell you everything he's been through. My heart breaks for him. He's incredible how he is, but I don't know if he can ever truly recover from it.'

I've said too much, as Lorna looks almost alarmed. 'Jesus, Connie. What happened?'

'I can't tell you.'

Lorna considers me for a moment. It's not like me to keep anything from her, but she knows enough about me to know I would never betray anyone's trust. She doesn't push me for more, instead saying, 'Just be careful. I want you to be happy, but make sure he treats you how you deserve to be treated, Connie.'

I make plans to see her tomorrow.

More grounded now, thanks to my bestie, I roll back onto my bed. I glance at my phone and wonder if I should text Peter to make sure he is okay and to apologize for being so quiet on the way home. All the excitement of the day has taken its toll, and my eyes are drooping.

No, I'll text him tomorrow. I let sleep take me.

At the gentle *click* of an acorn on my window, my eyes snap open. My body's in action, the invisible connection between Peter and me tugging me toward him. Now an expert at moving like a spy through my own home, I pull on my clothes and leave. Sleep has given me some clarity from the fog I was in earlier. I know when we go out to our spot that there'll be no chance of rain. The night will be clear and cloudless. Because Peter wills it so.

Peter glows in my garden, where he stands under the moonlight waiting for me as he always does. His features are soft, and relief blooms across his face when he sees me smiling at him. The warmth coming with him gathers in my chest. I'm not in deep—there's *no* coming back from this. I am lost to him, and there's nothing I wouldn't do for this boy. I'm his. I want to be only his. My pace quickens with my lengthening strides, and I throw my arms around his neck, almost knocking him off his feet while pulling him into a kiss. His initial surprise only lasts a moment before he kisses me back.

His smile sparkles in his eyes. 'I just wanted to come and check on you. You were a little quiet when I left.'

'Better now I'm with you,' I say and take his hand in mine to lead him out of the garden and to our spot in the field.

I lie my head back on Peter's arm as we take our usual place under the stars. I'm full of energy and excitement, and a thousand questions fly around my head. 'I have so much I want to ask.'

'Okay. I'll try to answer as best as I can.' Peter's big brown eyes look down at me expectantly, and I attempt not to get distracted at having him close once again.

'First question, if it's not a trick...' I look away from him to maintain concentration. 'Say I believe you have abilities, the power to make things grow. How does that even work?'

Peter's brow furrows as he examines the stars, searching for how to explain the unexplainable.

'It's like this... it comes from within me. It's *my* energy to start with, I just transfer it. I can move it out of my body and into the earth and...' he shrugs, '... then things grow.'

'How's that possible?'

Peter takes my hand, twisting his fingers around mine. 'It's all about connection, Connie. Everything's connected. You and me, and the stars and the moon. Energy is borrowed. It can all be moved, transferred.'

Like an enchantment hanging in the air, it's almost tangible. The warmth in his hand he projects all around us, it's all from him.

'How do you know this?' I ask.

'My mother. She said I have a gift that Mother Nature has given me, a gift humankind has forgotten they have or is even possible.'

'Does it hurt? When you transfer your energy?'

He laughs. 'No, of course it doesn't.'

I look down at his hand in mine, sensing I'm about to ask a stupid question. 'I mean, does it take some of your life? Will it mean you won't live as long?'

He doesn't answer straight away. Then he says, 'I guess I've never thought about it.'

My heart is in my throat. The thought of Peter not living makes my chest ache. My face obviously gives away my worries as he sits up and traces the edge of my cheek with his fingers.

'Don't be scared. It makes me tired sometimes, but I get some sleep and then I'm fine again. It's not going to kill me.'

'What about Anna? Does she have powers too?'

'No. Just me.'

'Why you?' I reach to stroke the side of his face, and he closes his eyes against my touch.

'No idea. I'm special, I guess.'

'That you are.' I look down at his lips. 'Peter, you're unreal. How can I possibly keep up?'

Peter's mouth turns down with the hint of a frown before grazing his bottom lip with his teeth. Anticipation rushes over my body as he lowers his head to mine, his breath hot in my ear. 'Connie, I'm going to take you so high you're never going to want to come down.'

His soft lips find mine, his kisses different from the fevered ones we shared this afternoon. Now, they're strong and slow, and certain. His weight shifts on top of me as my hands find their way under his shirt and run achingly slow along his strong back, pulling him closer to me. The rest of my questions melt away, save for one word escaping my lips. *'Peter.'*

As sure as the sun that rises or the ebb of the tide, I am his.

I'm caught in Peter's golden glow.

Time passes differently with him, and I can't remember life before he was in it. Now, he fills my every thought, my every waking moment, and even my dreams.

The days blend, defined only by the time spent with Peter and the time I long to be with him again. The time without him feels cold and dull compared to being around him when it's like I've never been seen before.

I'm hooked. He's addictive, too addictive. It's never enough and yet all too much at the same time. I always want more, so much more. I'm going to get burned, yet I want it, welcome it. I want to burn for him, to be consumed by him.

I'm sort of aware there's a filter on the rest of my life, and I'm neglecting my friends. Has it been two weeks or three? The sweetness of Peter is hard to resist. He tells me his mother taught him that he and Anna are part of a whole, but to me, Peter could be *my* other half, a part I didn't know was missing.

Much to my mum's delight, he's taken up a regular residence in our kitchen, charming her as much as me. We sit under the halogen glow of the kitchen's breakfast bar and talk for hours, until he has to walk home. The promise we'll meet each other again under the cloak of darkness, while not every night, is enough to balance my need for sleep and to keep the need for each other satisfied. Every time, the night sky is clear, and despite the autumn air against my bare skin, I'm never cold. I think Peter seeps into everything, making his surroundings his own, bending them to his will, and now, this includes me and my body, perfectly in tune to him.

Times when I'm on my own, I feel myself floating back down to Earth, almost teetering on the edge of reality. I have a pang of guilt when I notice a text from Brady.

Brady: *Hey, we never catch up anymore. Miss you x.*

I forget to text back.

At Peter's aunt and uncle's house, I sit in the garden and marvel at the overgrown wonder he has created. He shrugs when I ask if his aunt and uncle suspect anything,

'They wouldn't believe the truth even if I told them and would probably just have me committed.'

I have to agree. It's occurred to me I should have myself committed, that my mind has snapped, and Peter and all he can do are a figment of my imagination.

He places a little pumpkin into my hands, wrapping his hands around the other side so his fingertips are touching mine. His eyes flash—he enjoys doing this, showing off what he can do—as the weight of the pumpkin increases, and before my eyes, it turns more orange under my fingers. The pumpkin vine travels up my wrist and wraps around my little finger.

Cute.

I let out a laugh of disbelief and hold up my vine-wrapped finger. 'Did you mean to do that?'

'That depends. Do you like it?'

How can I resist? My kiss is my answer.

At school, it's hard to keep focus. I'm not sure if Jamie is even my friend anymore, but I can't bring myself to care. He's stopped sitting with us at lunch. Brady and Lorna try encouraging me to talk to him, but I honestly don't even know what to say. He's never admitted to me he likes me, and as far as I know, he doesn't like Peter because he thinks he's weird. No other reason. Well, Peter's ability to make things grow by touching them is weird, I suppose, but Jamie doesn't know that.

As Peter and Anna enter the cafeteria today, Peter lingers in the entrance, waiting to catch my attention. He motions with his head for me to join him.

When I reach him, he takes me by the hand and leads me outside without a word, to the field at the back of the school. Around the back of the huts where I think they teach art, there's a little wooden box that must be used for storage of some sort and is the perfect height to sit on.

'I didn't even know this was here,' I say.

'This is where Anna and I would come to hide for the first week. Away from the noise, away from everyone's prying eyes.'

Ahh. Another mystery solved. 'So, what am I doing here?'

Peter advances on me, the back of my legs hitting the wooden box. His eyes are hungry.

'As I'm not going to see you tonight, I want to kiss you today.'

He kisses me hard, my breath catching in my throat as I stand on my toes to deepen our connection while his arms snake around my back.

'Hmm…' I whisper through our kiss. 'Remind me why I'm not seeing you tonight.'

Peter gives a dramatic sigh. 'You're meeting Lorna, remember?'

Oh, yes. Lorna. She made me promise I would come over. My friend has been more than gracious about my somewhat ridiculous inability to be apart from Peter.

When I do venture over later, she's more annoyed that he hasn't asked me to be his girlfriend yet.

'Does it matter?' I laugh at her. 'We're always together. Who cares what it's called?'

'Okay, who are you, and what have you done with Connie?' she jokes.

'I don't know, Lor. I just feel good. Really, really good,' I say and stretch out on her bed, lying my head on my hands.

'Hmm…' she muses. 'Last time we spoke about it, you said you were worried about being in too deep. I see you've firmly jumped off that precipice.'

I close my eyes, thinking of him. 'You have no idea.'

'So why don't you tell me?'

Her question pulls me out of my thoughts.

Why can't I tell her again?

The longer I leave it, the harder it'll be. I start collating the words to express exactly what's going on. My head swims as the heat rises in my face. *What is going on?*

'Connie, I'm happy for you,' she continues when I don't respond. 'He obviously makes you happy. But I'm still your best friend. Don't forget about me.'

'I know. I'm sorry. I promise we'll hang out more.'

Which I plan to do.

I can have my cake and eat it too, right?

We make plans to spend Thursday together, which is Halloween. Just me, Lorna, and Brady, like the old days. Except, no Jamie. Lorna doesn't bring him up, for which I'm grateful. I'm on cloud nine right now and don't want the bubble to burst.

It's weird to think the twins have only been in our lives for two months.

The next day, I babble away to Peter as we make our way to our little spot.

'So, tomorrow night. It's Halloween, and I told Lorna—'

He isn't listening. He's stopped and stares into the pitch night behind us.

'What's wrong?'

Peter shakes his head, wrapping an arm around my shoulder. 'My mother called it an instinct.'

'What kind of instinct?'

'I'm not sure. The feeling you get in the pit of your stomach. You know, when your instinct tells you something your eyes can't see.'

I had that sensation the first time I met him. It lasted a flash of a second. Or maybe it was part of the addiction Peter brought with him—the unknown, constantly leaving me wanting more. The danger is part of his appeal.

He shakes his head, pulling me down next to him on the ground.

'I'm obviously losing my mind,' he says as we recline to star gaze.

We haven't discussed Peter's abilities much, but the talk of instincts has sparked a thought in my mind. 'Peter?' I ask, looking up at the dark night and twinkling stars. 'What would happen if you transferred your energy to me?'

Peter takes his head from where it has been resting on my shoulder. 'Why? Do you want to grow a few inches?'

'Is that a short joke?' I gently slap his arm.

'Why would I give you energy?'

'What would happen if you did?'

'I don't know. I don't think it works on people. I think it has to be connected to the earth.'

'But I thought you said everything was connected?'

'It is, but it's complicated.' Peter's face sparkles in the moonlight. His amused eyes take me in as he eases me onto my back, placing gentle kisses along my neck. 'I can't believe you want me to use my abilities to make you taller.'

'I do not,' I protest, enjoying his lips on my skin, his hands working to remove my coat. 'I'm just curious about what it'd do. I mean, how do you control the weather? How are *you* possible?'

He takes my face in his rough palms, looking into my eyes as he shifts his weight onto me. 'I don't think about it.'

'Never?'

'Never.'

Peter never thinks about it. Or so he says. How can he not wonder what he is, and why he was chosen for these gifts? In the grand scheme of probability in the universe, there must be someone else like him somewhere. Or maybe many others.

I don't think I take in a word anyone says to me the following day. Other than Peter's text message at lunch asking if he can come over later. Of course, I don't think twice about saying yes.

I'm so tired from the night before that I suggest we watch a film and promptly fall asleep on my sofa in his arms. Surely, it's only been moments when he's lifting me from his chest.

'Hey, sleepyhead, I'd better get going.'

'Already?' I ask, checking my face to ensure I haven't been drooling on him.

'It's after ten. I need to go before my aunt and uncle worry.'

I move to allow him to get up, instinctively patting myself for my phone.

'Here.' Peter hands me my phone. 'It's been buzzing a bit.'

The screen shows five missed calls from Lorna and a bunch of texts asking where I am. I look up to Peter, confused. 'What day is it?'

'Erm, I'm not sure. Thirty-first, I think.'

My face drops. I'm in trouble. I'm officially a bad friend.

'Is something wrong?' he asks.

'No, nothing. Just some brain fog. I can't keep track of the days. You go, I don't want you to get in trouble again.'

I say goodbye to Peter and then text Lorna back in a frantic state.

Me: *I am so sorry. I fell asleep. I'll make it up to you, I promise.*
Lorna: *Were you with Peter tonight?*

I bite my lip, the guilt rising like bile in my throat. It's true I'd fallen asleep, but I'd already forgotten our plans before then. I've been neglecting Brady too. I can't even remember the last time I talked to Brady or Anna. I don't even know if I'm Jamie's friend anymore.

I'm lightheaded. Woozy. *Do better,* I think to myself.

Me: *Yes, but I fell asleep. I'm sorry, Lor, I forgot we made plans tonight. I forgot it was Halloween today and invited Peter over. We were watching a film and I fell asleep.*

Lorna doesn't text me back. I chew my fingernail, thinking back to Peter and how comfy he was to sleep on. Despite us spending many nights together, I've never woken up next to him. It was nice.

'You look lost in thought,' my mum says, coming to sit next to me. She fusses with flattening my messy nap hair. 'You looked pretty cosy. Things must be getting serious between you two.'

'Yeah, I guess so.' I give her a weak smile.

'What's wrong, honey?'

'Nothing. I think I've been neglecting my friends a little.'

'Yes. You and Peter have been seeing a lot of each other.'

Another pang of guilt shoots through me. *She doesn't know the half of it.*

'He's your first love, darling. It's all new and exciting. One friendly bit of advice, though. Boyfriends will come and go, but good friends like Lorna and Brady are hard to come by. Apologise. They'll forgive you.'

My mum places a sweet kiss on my head, and I hug her in return before retreating to my room. There's still no text from Lorna.

Peter won't come back tonight. I miss kissing him, so I text.

Me: *I love waking up next to you.*
Peter: *I love that too.*
Me: *Will you come to me tomorrow?*
Peter: *I'm yours.*

The words make my heart flutter and I bite my lip. *I can't wait.*

CHAPTER 15

Connie

Lorna is decidedly not talking to me.

'Lor. Hey, Lor,' I whisper at her during English Lit. 'I messed up. I'm sorry, okay?'

Nothing.

'Lor!' I whisper shout as loud as I can without drawing attention. I throw my pen lid at her, hitting the side of her head.

She thrusts her head in my direction, launching the pen lid back at me.

I hold back the urge to laugh.

Lorna's dead serious as she bites at me in a hushed tone, 'It's one thing to ghost me and ghost Brady for weeks for some boy, but to stand us up like that, Connie. It's crossed a line.'

Her words are quick. But I'm glad she's talking in any capacity at this point.

'I know, I know. I've been bad.'

Back to the silent treatment.

'Come on, Lor, you have to forgive me. I swear I'll do better. Maybe we can catch up tonight?'

'No, Connie. It's not the same. Look, I'm mad right now. Just give me some time to cool off.'

I nod. That I can do. Determined, I resolve to make more effort in showing Lorna how sorry I am and to prove I've not totally lost my mind over Peter. I hate her not talking to me. I can't remember the last time we fought. Probably not since we were kids.

Although I try to pay attention to the rest of class, instead, I find myself looking out the window into the fresh autumn day. It's dry, of course. I'm seeing Peter tonight. It's always dry on those days. My personal microclimate. I notice Lorna looking at me and grasp I must be smiling at myself.

'Are you seriously thinking about him?'

'What? No. Don't be ridiculous.' My face has to be turning pink.

Lorna rolls her eyes.

I dutifully follow her to the cafeteria during our break, expecting her to continue her silent treatment. But, instead, she turns to me, much to my surprise.

'Are you going to grace us with your presence or sneak off with Peter as soon as he gets here? Where do you two even go anyway?' Her tone is so frosty it could freeze the fiery pits of Hell.

'I thought I would sit with you today, if that's okay?'

Lorna shrugs. 'You don't need me to tell you what to do.'

'I want to stay.'

We make our way to our usual seats, and I know she's thawing when she doesn't take out her phone and use it to ignore me.

'We walk to the field at the back of the school. Peter and me, that is. We just talk.'

'Is that all?' Lorna eyes me, and I wonder if she thinks I'm lying.

Brady enters the cafeteria, but instead of coming to join us, he makes his way over to the table where Jamie is sitting. It stings. Brady's never mad at anyone.

'I guess I deserve that,' I say to Lorna.

'You do. He's upset.' Lorna's gaze softens at the look on my face, then she rolls her eyes with a flip of her hair as she continues, 'But he'll be back over as soon as Anna comes in. I swear, you two are so whipped.'

The corners of her mouth twitch, and I chance a smile at my friend.

'You have no idea.'

Peter catches my eye as he walks in, motioning for me to join him, but I give a gentle shake of my head. When I stay rooted in my seat next to Lorna, he makes his way over, bewilderment on his face.

Anna takes the seat next to Lorna, not even looking at me, and launches into conversation with her about something I'm out of the loop on. It never occurred to me that while I've been busy with Peter, Lorna is getting closer to Anna. Although ridiculous, a pang of jealousy shoots through me.

'Hi,' Peter says, leaning over me, his face close to mine while his hand grips the back of my chair.

'Hi,' I reply in a shy voice as he kisses me with confidence. The stress of falling out with Lorna melts away with the warmth his touch brings. I forget why my friends were upset in the first place. They would understand if they knew how I felt.

He takes a seat next to me, and I try hard to listen to Lorna and Anna's conversation.

Peter's fingers push their way through my hair at the nape of my neck which is impossible to ignore. My head relaxes into his hand.

'Hey, what's going on?' he asks me as Anna and Lorna continue their conversation. 'You're all tense.'

'I did something bad.' I look up into his bottomless eyes. 'I was supposed to meet Lorna and Brady last night, and I forgot.'

Peter sticks his bottom lip out in a pout. 'And now they're mad?'

I nod. 'I've been a bad friend, Peter. I need to make it up to them.'

He gives me a devilish grin. 'I did try to warn you that I'm incredibly selfish.' His thumb runs along my bottom lip. 'I just want you all to myself.'

Once again lost in his haze, I forget where I am, and I bite his thumb before saying, 'You know I'm yours.'

'Hmm… I thought you didn't belong to anyone?' His voice is like silk sliding over my skin.

'We both know things can change, Peter.'

My mission has failed already.

Everything, my whole body and all my attention, is firmly on Peter.

'Girl, you have it so bad,' Lorna says, pulling me out of my thoughts as we walk to our next class.

'I know.' I rub my eyes, trying to wake from my reverie. 'Have pity on me, Lor. I have zero control.'

She laughs. 'Okay, okay. You're forgiven. It's a good job I love you. You can make it up to me tomorrow.'

'Yes!' I jump up and down beside her. 'Thank you, thank you. All the coffees are on me.'

'That's great.' She shakes her head. 'But, fair warning, none of this vague crap, Connie. I expect you to tell me what's going on with you.'

Okay. Which means I have all of one night to figure out what *is* actually going on. The last two weeks have been a golden, hazy, Peter-filled blur, filled with all warmth and magic and moonlight. Not reality. I'm so lost in him right now, but saying the words out loud to Lorna should help anchor me. She always gives good advice.

'Hey, Peter,' I begin when I'm with him later, his warm hand in mine as we walk to our spot under the cloudless night sky.

'Yes, Connie?'

'What am I to you?'

Peter flops to the ground, his face drawing into a frown as he looks up at me. 'What do you mean?'

'What is this? Us? What are we? Am I your girlfriend?'

Peter's face is unreadable. 'I don't know what that means.'

'Peter, I just need to know I mean something to you.' I sit down next to him, hating how I sound right now. 'I know you've been through a lot, and I don't want to push you, but I don't want to get hurt either.'

'Connie, I would never hurt you. You're the only thing here that has made my life bearable. I seek you out because I don't want to be apart from you. You're my light in all this darkness.' His eyes dance over my face, gathering hunger. 'I chose you, Connie. I don't just want you… I need you.'

My breath is shallow. *How can I not be consumed by him?*

'Peter, how I feel about you. I have never felt anything like it before—'

I don't have the chance to finish before his mouth is on mine. All my questions are lost, and all of my insecurity is gone. The need to have him overtakes me, and I am his. Lost to him.

His name on my lips, 'Peter,' always.

Then I can't understand what I'm seeing.

Blinded.

By a brilliant white light.

In the absence of Peter, I'm cold. So cold.

The full force of the November air hits every inch of my body. It's so frigid I can't think straight.

'What on earth is going on here?' a harsh, angry voice demands.

'Who are you?' Peter's voice sounds above me. He must be on his feet.

I scramble on the ground, trying to cover myself with whatever I can find.

'I own this land.'

'Oh my God,' I manage to whimper. Understanding hits me right in the stomach, sending rolling nausea, and my eyes adjust to squint at what I now know are the headlights of a truck pointed at Peter and me.

'Take your hands off me,' Peter snaps, but I don't dare look up.

Please don't let this be real.

'Peter,' I whisper, pulling my coat around me. 'We should go.'

Panic.

Panic is rising in me.

I know we need to get out of here.

I should stop saying Peter's name.

Peter is at my side, reaching toward the ground for his clothes. I try to find my boots. What a nightmare. This has to be a nightmare. I must wake up.

'I don't think so. I'm calling the police.'

'No,' Peter starts with a strong edge to his tone as he moves toward the other voice.

I still can't make out his face from the glare of the headlights.

'Please.' I stop Peter, pull him back, and then move toward the stranger in the dark. 'Please, no police. We weren't doing anything bad. We were just...' I can't bring myself to finish.

'Connie?' the stranger says, registering my face.

The fact that he isn't a stranger makes the sickness double. It's Todd, and he's known me since I was little.

My stomach lurches as I steady myself on Peter, who's now watching me with obvious concern. I must have pulled his T-shirt on because he's wearing only his tracksuit bottoms. All his warmth, which has been protecting me, has vanished.

'Connie Prinze, what on earth are you doing out here in the middle of the night? And Peter? Is that Sally's boy?'

'I'm not Sally's boy.'

The ice in Peter's voice sends a chill down my spine.

'Jesus. Have you two been coming out here to my field to do this? Anything could have happened to you. I could've shot you.'

'I'm really sorry. I think we should just go,' I say, pleading with my voice.

'You must be joking. There's *no way* I'm letting you walk around this village half-dressed at one in the morning. Get in the truck, the pair of you.'

'No, I don't think so,' Peter tries to protest.

'Peter, please,' I implore.

There's no need to make this worse. The horrible reality of what is about to happen weighs heavily, and the golden haze of a bubble I've been living in is well and truly shattered. I force my boots on and climb into the cab of the truck. Peter slides in next to me, his shoes in his hands and hair all ruffled from my hands running through it. He looks a perfect mess. After a glance toward my bare legs under my coat, his eyes meet mine, and a wave of warmth passes through me. Despite everything, I lean in closer to him to claim the full effects.

The drive to my house is painfully awkward and short, my frantic brain scrambling to avoid having my parents find out about this. One saving grace, my dad is still away for work.

I go on autopilot, walking like a person condemned to my front door. Farmer Todd is in step beside me, with Peter close on my heels. He, thankfully, has pulled his hoodie on. My eyes stay on the ground. Sickness has been replaced with numbness as Todd knocks on my front door. The sound echoes all around, breaking the stillness of the night and shattering the dream I'd been living in.

How can I have been so stupid?

The house springs into life. An upstairs light comes on, and I hear my mum rustling on the other side of the door before it swings open to reveal her, flustered and wrapped in a flannel dressing gown. It takes her a minute to register that it's me she's seeing.

'Connie?' She steps onto the porch, taking in my form.

I'm lightheaded.

'What's going on?'

'I hate to wake you in the middle of the night, but I found these two in my field and wanted to get them home safe. I'm sure you can appreciate I didn't want to get the police involved, not with Connie being your daughter and all, Suzie.'

I can't bring myself to look at my mother.

'The police? What's been going on, Todd? Connie?' Her voice becomes more demanding the more she wakes up and is aware of what's in front of her—my bare legs and Peter, who's doing, I don't know what, shifting about uncomfortably behind me.

'Mrs. Prinze, I think maybe it's better if your daughter explains. I'm going to get Peter home.'

I chance a glance back at Peter, who silently mouths, 'S*orry,*' as Todd escorts him back to the truck.

My mum slams the door behind us and squares on me. The light off the hall is too bright, too accusing.

'You better start explaining why Todd is escorting my teenage daughter and her boyfriend to my front door at god-knows-what-time in the morning.'

My eyes stay fixed on my boots. 'I sneaked out to meet Peter. We went for a walk, and Todd found us in his field.'

'And what exactly were you doing, Connie?'

Tears threaten to spill, and I can't bring myself to say the words.

'Look at me, Connie.'

I reluctantly comply.

'Were you having sex with that boy?'

My body is alive with shame as I dip my head down a fraction. The only way I can answer her question. She turns away from me as the air is sucked out of the room, her hands covering her mouth. It takes her a full minute to compose herself, and a tear spills and rolls down my cheek. I let it. More follow. My mum, who's never been anything but good, understanding, and proud of me, is devastated. I deserve her disappointment.

'Constance, what on earth were you thinking?'

'Mum, I'm so sorry. I don't know... I wasn't thinking.'

'Tell me... this is the first time you've done something like this?'

'I—'

'Don't you dare lie to me,' she interrupts.

'No. It's happened before.'

'How can you be so stupid, Connie? Has he been putting you up to this?'

'Peter hasn't forced me into anything, Mum.'

'I didn't raise you to act like this. Sneaking out in the dead of night, keeping secrets. It's freezing outside. What possessed you? Actually, don't answer that. At least tell me you were safe?'

I don't catch her meaning at first, and my confusion is visible on my face.

'Were you using protection?'

I glance at my shoes again, my stomach doing another swan dive when I shake my head.

'Jesus, Connie.' She goes to sit on the bottom stair, her head in her hands. 'You stupid, stupid girl. Is that what you want? To be seventeen and pregnant? To have your whole future ruined?'

Her words hurt.

They're like an attack.

Maybe that's how she felt about me. When she fell pregnant with me when she was at university, not more than a couple of years older than I am now. What if she and my dad only stayed together out of some duty to me? I wonder if this is how she truly feels, that getting pregnant ruined her life. The tears continue to roll down my face.

'Mum, I'm sorry. I—'

'Connie, I can't even look at you right now. Go to bed.'

I wipe the tears from my face with shaky hands. I feel wretched, but I know I have gotten off light for now.

She calls up after me, 'I'm taking the keys out of the locks, so don't even consider going out again.'

The second my head hits my pillow, I let the tears cascade in rivers of regret. To disappoint my mum so much physically hurts. I can't help thinking about Anna's warning to her brother the day we went for coffee. How his actions had consequences for me too. I'd never thought them through. I've been too carried away with the sense of abandon Peter brings with him, the certainty he has in himself and his actions. Never any hesitation. I've never lived a life like that before.

I wonder what this means for Peter. *Will his aunt and uncle try to send him away?*

I awake at about five a.m., hot and uncomfortable, still dressed in my coat and boots, and curled up on my bed. Groggily changing into some fuzzy pyjamas, trying to satisfy my need for comfort, I climb back into bed and go back to sleep.

When I open my eyes again, the red numbers on my digital clock blink ten a.m. I'm not ready for the world, so I roll back over and go back to sleep.

The next time my eyes open and it's almost one p.m., I lean off the bed and pull my coat from its position on the floor to check my phone. Nothing from Peter. I squint at the brightness of the screen and text Lorna.

Me: *Lorna, you're going to hate me, but something has happened, and I can't come out and meet you today. I can't explain now, but I will tell you EVERYTHING on Monday.*

I hit send and let my phone fall back onto the floor. I will tell her everything. Part of me knows the reason I never did in the first place is because she would've told me what a horrible idea sneaking around in a field was. Sleep takes me again, in and out, letting me dream of Peter. Only Peter.

When my bedroom door creaks open, for half a second, I think it's him.

'Connie?' Lorna says, her voice soft.

'Lorna?' I sit up and take in the sight of my best friend.

She's wearing an empathetic expression. Looking perfect and composed in her skinny jeans and an oversized cardigan, her long black hair pulled back in a French plait, she's the opposite of me. Tear-stained and puffy-faced, my hair is all over the place from being in bed all day.

'You're here.' I am obvious and ridiculous... and stupid. I forgot stupid.

'Yeah. You okay?'

I eye her, suspicious. 'Why are you being nice to me? What did my mum tell you?'

Lorna takes a seat on the edge of my bed and gives me a long look. 'Connie, your mum didn't tell me anything. Brady did. Is it true?'

'Wait, what? What did Brady tell you?'

'He said you and Peter were caught last night. In the wheat field not far from here. That Todd almost shot you both.'

I rub my eyes. *This is unbelievable.* 'How on earth does Brady know that?'

'Is it true?'

Great, my light head is back.

'Yes.'

Lorna's face falls.

'Does everybody know?' I whisper, my tears threatening to spill again.

'I don't know. Brady asked me if I'd heard, and when I got your text, I knew something was up, but I didn't think it would be true.' Lorna moves closer, taking my hand as my tears start to fall again. 'What happened? Did Peter? Peter didn't hurt you, did he?'

'No, of course not. We were just stupid. I've been so stupid. Lor, this has been going on for weeks,' I confess in a small voice.

'What?'

'I've been sleeping with Peter for weeks. Sneaking out, keeping secrets from everyone. I've been so wrapped up in him and have been so stupid.'

Lorna's face is full of surprise. 'How can you not have told me this? We tell each other everything.'

'One secret led to another,' I admit through blurry tears. 'It got completely out of control. It just felt so right. I didn't stop to think.'

'Constance Prinze.' Lorna brushes the hair from my face. 'What a mess.'

The love in my friend's eyes causes a fresh spring of tears. I'm so happy she doesn't hate me. *How can I be so happy and yet so disgusted in myself at the same time?*

'I don't know how to stop myself when it comes to him.'

She takes my face. 'You could try talking to me, Connie. I know I was mad before, but I'm not now. I'm saying this with all the affection I can muster. I love you, but this isn't you.'

I look at my hands. Ashamed. Then Lorna starts laughing, giving me a gentle shove.

'What?' I shove her back. I didn't think it would be possible to laugh today.

'It's pretty wild, Connie. You. Peter. In a field. You do know that I'm so going to have to kick Peter's ass when I see him at school.' Lorna laughs.

'School.' I groan. 'Lor, it's going to be hell, isn't it?'

'I won't lie, it won't be pretty. There will be stares, and there will be gossip, but it will pass. And you, my friend... *you* will be on your best behaviour.'

'Yes, this is enough drama to last me a lifetime. Thank you for coming to see me.' I lay my head in her lap.

'What are friends for?' she says as she strokes my hair.

A little later, my mum is a whole different kettle of fish. Even though she let Lorna up, she's too quiet when I build up the courage to creep downstairs. I know she knows I'm here, but she's making herself look busy around the kitchen.

'Mum,' I mumble. 'Please.'

'Did Lorna know what had been going on, Connie?' she asks as she wipes down an already immaculate work surface.

'No, no one knew.'

'Then how did she find out? Did you tell her?'

'No, Brady told her. I don't know how he found out.'

My mum gives a big sigh and turns to face me. 'I don't know how we'll keep this from your father.'

I lean my hip against the cupboard. 'What do you think he'll do?'

'I have no idea. But I can't imagine he will want you to continue seeing Peter.'

'And you?'

'Connie, I know better than demand you make promises that will break your heart. You'll be eighteen soon, and you're growing up. Of course, I knew you'd have a boyfriend in time. But you've made it so difficult to trust you.'

'I know. It won't happen again.'

'And there are some things you need to sort out, young lady. Contraception for one, that is, if you're not already pregnant.' She turns away from me, again unable to look at me, her eyes wet.

Perhaps she does see too much of herself in me. After all, she always said she'd been infatuated with my dad. Overwhelmed by his talent, by his attentions. She always talked about it before like it was a romance novel. Only now do I read between the lines. Her infatuations led her to make some poor decisions, to get pregnant too young, too early in their relationship.

I don't know what to say. I consider myself a reasonably intelligent person, but the thought never occurred to me. Peter never mentioned it either. It just happened naturally. No hesitation. The thought I might be pregnant makes my stomach twist in knots.

How would someone like Peter react to that news?

I retreat to the sanctuary of my room.

I can't sleep.

My lengthy sleep earlier and lack of activity has left me restless.

It's just after two a.m.

I can tell my mum has finally gone to bed, satisfied I won't try to make a break for it. I know she's taken both door keys to bed with her. I stare at my phone. It's 2:06 a.m. I start texting Brady, hoping to repair some of the damage there.

Me: *Hey. Sorry it's late. I know I've been distant lately, and I know you've already heard, but can we talk? Maybe tomorrow?*

My thumb hovers over send, but before I have chance to press it, I jump out of my skin at the sound of a faint knock. On my window. *He cannot be serious right now.* Even if it isn't the same click of the acorn, it's a definite knock. I get up and look out into my garden—*nothing*. I open the window, and as soon as I do, I see him holding onto my windowsill.

'What the hell are you doing?'

'Shh. Can you move back?'

'Are you flying?'

Peter can't hold in his laugh as I take a step back from the window, and he hauls himself through it. 'I really hope that's a joke. Your trellis is ancient, but the ivy growing up it is strong.' His voice is light, like nothing has happened. He straightens up to look at me, his smile annoyingly irresistible.

'Are you actually crazy?' I cross my arms.

'Maybe,' he says, moving closer to me, letting his hands rest on my hips with the lightest of squeezes. 'But I had to check that you were okay.'

'A call would have worked, Peter.' I put my extended hand on his chest, determined to maintain the distance between us.

'I wanted to see you too.' He takes a step forward.

I step back. 'This isn't okay, Peter. I'm in trouble. My mum is furious. We've been stupid.'

He continues moving toward me, his hands tightening their grip. My hand slides up his chest, and my mind starts to swim. I'm losing this battle.

'Let me make it up to you,' he murmurs.

'Aren't you in trouble?'

'You're worth it.' He closes the distance, kissing me as I pace back.

The backs of my legs hit my bed, his warmth saturating the air around us and filling my body. I'm in dangerous territory.

'Peter, you can't be here.'

'Don't send me away.' His arms engulf my body while his kisses travel down my neck. 'Can you be addicted to a person? I think I'm addicted to you.'

Falling back, my hands wrap around his neck as his weight settles on top of me. His kisses come more frequent as they travel down to my chest.

'That's the problem, Peter. I'm starting to feel consumed by you.'

In the darkness of my room, his eyes look black.

He whispers into my ear, 'Then, let me.' His breath hot, he begs, 'Let me consume you.'

The clock reads just past four thirty in the morning when I awake, on fire.

How can it be so hot?

I fling the covers off my legs to try and cool down, relishing the cool air. My hair is sticking to my forehead, and pushing it back, I discover the source of heat is Peter's chest, flat against my back, scorching me.

It all floods back.

Peter is here in my room.

In my bed.

He climbed through my window.

I cannot be trusted alone with him.

I look at his sleeping face. His stupid, beautiful face. He doesn't care, not the same way I do.

'Peter. Peter, wake up,' I whisper.

Groggy eyes open long enough for him to wrap his arms around my waist and haul me closer.

'Peter, you need to leave.'

His eyes flash open. He looks around, taking in where he is. 'I fell asleep?'

'Obviously.' I push him up and out of bed with desperate urgency. 'You can't be here.'

'Connie, it's okay.' He starts collecting his clothes, pulling his T-shirt over his head.

I scramble out of bed, wrapping my dressing gown around me. 'No, it's not, Peter.' I'm starting to sound shrill through my whispers. 'Nothing about what we've been doing is okay. I need you to leave.'

'Connie, we haven't done anything wrong,' Peter tries to soothe me, taking hold of my wrists. 'What we've been doing, it's natural.'

'How can you say that?' I say and push him away from me. 'Do you believe that? Peter, you need to go.'

'Connie...'

It's hard to watch Peter's face crumple with my rejection, but the thought of my mum finding him here is too much for me to bear.

'No, Peter, you need to go. I can't deal with this right now. You need to leave.'

'Connie, don't you want me?'

The vulnerability in his words cut me. Fresh tears spring into my eyes, forcing me to turn away from him, threatening all my resolve. Inside, I want so desperately for him to stay, but instead I whisper, 'Peter, please go.'

Peter doesn't make a sound as he respects my wishes.

He's gone.

I look out in time to watch him cross my garden. He doesn't look up.

My arms clutch my body, cold without his presence.

CHAPTER 16

Peter

The clouds twist and turn in front of me. Tortured. Threatening to break.

Anna casts me a glance before she hops down from her place at my side. I remain silent, lying on my back and cursing the sky above me. She lets out a large breath of obvious annoyance, throwing away the core of the apple she's been eating harder than necessary.

'Honestly, I can't believe you're throwing her to the wolves like this.'

I don't say anything. I almost will the clouds to open and send the rain to cleanse me of this wretched emotion. Except, I don't want to give Anna the satisfaction of knowing the stormy weather has anything to do with my bad mood.

'So, what? You're giving me the silent treatment too? That's perfect, Peter. Well, while you're out here hiding,

Connie is probably in the cafeteria wondering where you are and feeling like the whole world is looking at her, judging her. She's probably never had to endure that before. The least you could do is be by her side.'

'She doesn't want to see me, Anna. She made that perfectly clear.'

'Ugh.' My sister shoves me so hard that I almost fall off the wooden storage box I'm lying on. 'I know you don't care about what our aunt and uncle say, but what everyone is talking about… that matters to *her*. You can be so unbelievably selfish.'

I sit up to look at her, the annoyance rising in my chest. 'Give it a rest. She was more than a willing participant.'

Anna's eyes flash with a fit of anger I rarely witness in her. 'Typical. As usual, you take no responsibility for yourself.'

'What's that supposed to mean?' I jump down from my spot to confront her. Anna's only about three inches shorter than me and not easily intimidated.

'Don't you get it?' She takes my shoulders. 'It's you. It's always been you. You affect *everything*, and *everyone*.'

Her eyes stay on mine, the anger dissipating and being replaced with something softer as I struggle to understand.

'You think I *did* this to her?'

Anna's voice is quiet now. 'I'm saying you can control more than just the earth and the trees, brother.'

I step back out of her grasp. 'You're crazy. I have no control over people. I don't *want* control over people. I didn't force her into… do you think I'm capable…' My voice croaks.

'Peter—' Anna starts toward me, but I maintain my retreat away from her, horrified, and interrupt with, 'Why would you say something like that to me?'

The heat rises in Anna's face, her eyes becoming glassy. It's easy to see she regrets what she said.

'I'm not saying she doesn't like you, Peter. It's obvious she does. It's not like you mean to, but when you want something, you can sway the outcome. Perhaps, you cloud her judgment.'

'Stop.' I drag my hand down my face. 'Where's this coming from, Anna? Why now?'

'I didn't believe it myself until last night.'

'Anna, what aren't you telling me?'

Anna gives me a long look and, taking a deep breath, confesses, 'Peter, our mother told me you could do it.'

My stomach plummets through the floor, followed by a roll of thunder rumbling in the distance. This time, it's Anna who takes a step away from me as she casts a nervous glance at the sky.

'What?' I grind out, my voice barely above a whisper. The strong instinct to flee rears its head deep inside.

'She'd been drinking. A lot. She never mentioned it again, so I thought she'd made it up. I didn't believe it until I saw you last night. It's like this.' She motions toward the sky. 'You don't know you're doing it. You can't control it.'

'Anna, what else did our mother tell you about me?'

'Nothing. That's the only thing she ever told me that you don't already know. I promise.'

I turn away from her, leaning against the box to sink my head into my hands. Trying to think, to recall all the times I'd met Connie. Been intimate with her. Sickness blooms in my stomach, considering any way I may have forced her to be with me—that it's only my will that's kept her close.

'You've known I've been seeing her this whole time,' I say through my fingers. 'Why didn't you tell me I could do this?'

'Like I said, I know she likes you. It only takes seeing you two together to know it. But these reckless decisions you two have been making, I think they're yours, Peter. I think Connie's being pulled along. Her judgment is clouded when it comes to you.'

Sitting back on my haunches, Anna takes her place next to me. I look into her brown eyes, so much like my own, a mirror I can't look away from.

'When did you realise? That what our mother had said is true?'

'Friday. Or Saturday morning, when the farmer brought you home.' Anna glances down at her hands. 'I thought James was going to kill you. I've never seen anyone so mad. Peter, why do you think they haven't sent you away?'

I shrug. 'They were furious. Still are, as far as I can tell.'

Anna gives her head a shake, rolling her eyes. 'It was crazy. I wouldn't believe it myself if I hadn't been there. Everything changed when you opened your mouth. It felt like a wave when you started talking. It washed over everyone, and calmed everything down. James was ready to hit you. Then you started talking, and it all went away.'

I shake my head in disbelief. 'Jesus. What am I going to do?'

'Peter, you need to control your emotions.'

'How? I have no idea what I'm doing.'

'Let's start by finding Connie. It'll make you feel better.'

My head swims like the clouds above me. Anna has kept something from me, I didn't know that was possible. I desperately try to wrap my mind around being able to exert my influence through my emotions. The fact I might be able to infect everything around me makes me want to be sick.

Maybe Connie is right to keep her distance.

I allow the cold November air to penetrate my bones as I try to prepare for the weight of a hundred eyes once more, but as we approach the school building, the back doors swing open, and Connie steps out with Lorna by her side. From a distance, her attention is on her friend, and she hasn't noticed me walking toward her.

Relief floods my body. Connie knows where to look for me, which means she's come to find me. She can't think I'm a total fiend, then.

The breeze catches her hair as she looks in my direction. Upon spotting me, her beautiful smile spreads across her face. I'm undone. The tension building in the sky bursts and the first drops of rain kiss my cheek. I quicken my pace toward her, and she does the same. Five paces apart, and she runs into my arms.

She's like home.

The home I've felt torn from for months.

Someone who knows me, accepts me. I have to do better for her knowing what I know now, but I can't accept this isn't real.

'Tell me you aren't mad at me, Connie,' I whisper into her ear.

'I'm not. I freaked out.' She motions toward the school building. 'It's pretty crazy in there. I don't blame you for not wanting to face it.'

Lorna, who is trying to shield her hair with a book, cocks an eyebrow at me, and I smirk. When I open my mouth, she cuts me off.

'Hey…' she holds up her free hand, '… it's not me you're corrupting.' Lorna's tone is light.

She doesn't hate me either.

Anna was right. Seeing Connie has made me feel better, but as I look back at my sister, her face is etched with worry. I follow her gaze back to the cafeteria doors where a furious-looking Jamie is marching in our direction, closely followed by Brady, who half-jogs to keep up.

'Are you kidding me, Connie?' he shouts as he makes his way over to us.

I move my body to shield her, putting my arm out to ensure he keeps his distance, but he solidifies his gaze on her, ignoring me.

'You're going back to him? After what he's done to you?'

'Jamie, get a grip,' Connie spits back. 'Peter hasn't *done* anything to me. Honestly, it's none of your business if he does.'

'Wow. He's seriously done a number on you.' Jamie shakes his head and rolls his eyes. 'He's made you look like a *total slut*. And you say he's done nothing.' His voice drops a tone, almost imploring. 'Can't you see he's controlling you? This isn't you, Con.'

I use my warning hand to give him a slight shove away from her, and for the first time, he acknowledges my existence. The hatred boils on his face as he clenches his fists at his sides.

'Really, freak… you don't want to push me.'

'Oh, no, I think I do. You have something to say, then you say it to me. Leave Connie out of this.' My voice is controlled, but his rage is contagious.

'I have plenty to say to you. Don't you worry.' Jamie gears himself up, moving close to my face. Ignoring the falling rain and the swirling storm, he adds, 'I should kick the shit out of you right now, for what you and your sick sister are doing to my friends.'

I was *not* expecting that.

'What are you talking about, Jamie?' Connie's voice asks from behind me.

'You lured one of my oldest friends out of her home like some kind of predator, you twisted freak. Defile her like it's nothing. And even though you've already ruined her, you just keep on coming back for more.'

His words hit me full force. 'Have you been following me, Jamie?' I say through my teeth, and my blood starts to boil.

Anna is at my side. Cautious, she takes my arm, lowering her voice so only I can understand what she's saying. *'Get your emotions under control.'*

It's too late, though. As I focus in on Jamie, everything else drowns out. All I can see is him laughing right in my face.

'For about a week. This is a small village, you idiot. You didn't stop to think your route to her house goes right past mine. You really are some freak creature of the night. I saw you. How else do you think that clueless farmer knew where to find you?'

'You did this?' Connie's voice sounds distant.

Anna glances at me, shaking her head.

'I did this for you,' Jamie shouts into the rising wind. He motions to Brady. 'You too, Brady, this concerns you. He is so depraved.' He shoves his finger at my chest. 'Do you want to know what he's been doing when he's done with you in that field, Connie?'

Anna's grip tightens on my arm as Jamie looks straight into my eyes, burning with the satisfaction of what he's about to say.

'He slithers right into his sister's bed.'

My world decelerates, goes into slow motion, and I'm vaguely aware several things all happen at once.

Connie's breathless, *'What?'* comes from behind me.

To my side, Anna reels back a few steps, her gaze fixed on Brady while shaking her head at the accusation in Jamie's words.

I don't have time to explain myself to any of them.

There are no words.

All I have is rage.

Blind, burning rage.

The energy rises like vapour through my legs and into my chest, and in that instant, I know I'm going to hurt Jamie.

A lot.

'That's right, Connie...' he turns his gaze to her, '... after being with you, your boyfriend has been screwing his own sister.'

My palm turns into a fist.

This is going to feel exquisite.

Except, my fist never connects.

A deafening sound explodes in my ear, shuddering the world around me in a pitch of blackness. Pain splinters down my body in agony. My feet leave the ground, and then, silence.

The quiet doesn't last for long, but the world has gone underwater.

Voices sound far away. I can zone into Anna saying my name, but it's faint. I try to pull myself to the surface. The rain splashes on my face, and a hot liquid trickles from my ear and down my neck. My whole right side is almost paralysed in pain.

The voices in the background are clearer now. Jamie is swearing. Connie's crying, while Lorna calls out in panic, 'We need to call an ambulance.'

'No,' Anna and I say in unison.

'Peter.' Connie is at my side. 'Oh my God, I thought you were dead.'

I lift my hand to my ringing ear to find the warm liquid is blood. The pain of moving my arm makes me wince, and it hangs heavy.

'I'm okay. No ambulance.' I can barely hear my own thoughts, the pain in my head clouding any ability to think. To understand what has happened.

I sit up, and Brady is in front of me. My vision is blurred, and bright flashes keep him in and out of focus.

'Dude, that was crazy. You need to go to the hospital.'

I try to focus on him.

'Peter, your eyes.' There's confusion in his voice.

'You can see that?' I ask him, but my voice doesn't feel like my own. I shake my head to try to shake away the golden flares. It hurts.

Anna is pulling me to my feet, which is impressive, given how heavy I am. I let her draw me up, then sway on the spot. I wrap my arm around her— unable to focus.

'I just need to get him home,' Anna says.

'You have to be joking. He clearly needs medical attention.'

Jamie.

I try to focus on him when another flare crosses my vision, and I clutch my eyes.

'Jamie, don't you think you've done enough?' Lorna asks.

'What? I control the weather now, Lorna?' he replies.

'Please, I just want to get my brother home,' Anna pleads.

'I can drive you,' Brady offers.

'I'll come with you,' Connie insists.

'No, Connie. I just need to get him home. He'll be okay. Trust me.'

Brady's strong form appears on my left side. He takes some of my weight, and we're moving. The movement sparks a series of flares across my vision, so I close my eyes and let my sister and Brady guide me. On my right, Anna's words are barely audible. Hot liquid begins to trickle from my nose, down my lip, and into my mouth. I taste the metallic texture on my tongue. It tastes burned.

'Anna, are you sure this is a good idea?' Brady asks her again once we are out of earshot of the others.

'What's happening?' I manage to get out.

Anna is quiet. It's Brady who answers. 'Peter, you've just been struck by lightning.'

'Anna,' I say. 'My eyes... I can't see.'

'We need to get him to a hospital, Anna.' Panic now evident in Brady's voice.

'I said no, Brady. Just take us home, please.'

We reach Brady's car, and my limbs are so heavy they have to bundle me into the back, where I sprawl across the back seat. I drift in and out of consciousness, catching snippets of Anna and Brady's conversation.

'Anna, I hate to bring it up, but what Jamie said—'

'Brady, of course I am *not* having sex with my twin brother. That you even have to ask makes me feel sick.'

'I'm sorry, it's just... why did he say that?'

'He's clearly deranged and wants to hurt Peter.'

I don't get the rest.

The next thing I know, Brady and Anna are heaving me out of the car and into my aunt and uncle's house. They drag me up the stairs, my feet like lead, until they're able to flop me onto my bed. Every muscle strains under the extra weight I have acquired. My eyes are so heavy I can't open them as I cling to the fringes of awareness.

'I hope you're sure about this,' Brady says, but his voice already sounds like a faraway dream.

Blackness.

Sweet relief.

※

Crackling in my ears wakes me with a start.
I was hit by lightning.
The swiftness of sitting up causes shooting pains down the whole right side of my body, from my neck to my toes. I clutch the nape of my neck at the agony.

'You're awake.'

Anna is at my side when I open my sore eyes. After a few blinks, her blurry form comes into focus.

She leans forward and rests the back of her hand against my forehead. 'You're still ridiculously hot.'

I refrain from saying something smart. Instead, I say, 'I smell.' Knowing the singed stench is coming from me.

'Yes, it's gross.' Anna wrinkles her nose, the worry lines fading from her forehead. 'You seem better. I didn't know if I'd done the right thing. Don't ever scare me like that again.'

'I don't plan to. What was that?'

'Lightning.'

'Obviously. I mean, why did that happen? One second, I was going to punch Jamie in his ridiculous face, and the next, I was on my back.'

'Ugh, he's a horrible little person. I wish you had punched him.'

I give the hint of a smile. It's not like my sister to ever condone violence, but what Jamie accused us of is heinous, even for us. We've slept side by side forever, but to suggest it's been anything but innocent is insane. Our inability to do otherwise may reflect the shared trauma of our upbringing, but we're innocent nonetheless.

'How did you know I would be okay?'

Anna's shoulders shift with a shrug. 'Instinct. They all thought you were dead.'

'But not you?'

'Peter, if you died, I'd feel it deep in my soul. I knew you would be okay. Somehow.'

I rub my neck again, comprehending that I ache everywhere. The heaviness is still with me. My skin tight. I wonder if this is all normal for being hit by lightning. How many people make a full recovery? The flashing in my eyes has stopped, and my hearing is back to normal. I've only been out for a few hours.

'Are you okay?' Anna asks.

'What's happening to me?'

My sister doesn't have the answers, so gives me another shrug.

I've always enjoyed my gifts, being in touch with the earth, with nature. It's part of who I am. I've been proud of it even. But these new abilities, I'm not so sure.

My question hangs in the air. All answers died with our mother. She never meant for this to happen. She'd meant to keep me safe. Hidden from the world.

Yet, I can't help but wonder if she knew about the control. Did she also know about the weather? That my emotions seep out of me and influence everything around me. The people, the earth, the weather. It's too big to comprehend.

When she died, I didn't understand how exposed it left me with no idea what to do.

Or what I'm capable of doing.

I'm lost.

'Take a shower, brother. Try to rest.' The kind kiss Anna places on my head breaks me out of my thoughts.

CHAPTER 17

Connie

'You're out of bed,' I say.

'You're here?' he replies.

Peter stands in the middle of his bedroom, his palm raised in front of his face in an expression of wonder. Maybe the lightning did fry his brain. The last time I saw him—over twenty-four hours ago—he could barely stand. From a distance, you wouldn't be able to tell anything had happened to him.

'I had to come. Anna said you'd mostly been in bed.'

He gives a fraction of a nod. 'I need to show you this,' he says, moving a pace toward me, his eyes bright. He holds the palm he was examining moments ago in the air.

I'm not sure what I should be looking for, but then I see it. What can only be described as a ripple of electric current that washes across his hand.

'How are you doing that?'

'It's from the lightning. I can feel the electricity coursing through my veins. In my blood. My blood is humming, Connie.'

I take a step back as he steps forward.

'How is that possible?'

'How is any of this possible?' His eyes sparkle. 'Magic? Connie, you asked me before about what would happen if I shared my energy with you. Do you still want to try?'

'Will it hurt?' I can't help but take another step back as he steps forward.

He shakes his head. 'No, it's pure energy. It felt like a weight at first, but I have control of it now. It's another extension of the earth… I can flex and bend it. But it must leave my body. I can share it with you. You'll only ground it. It won't hurt. I won't give it all at once.'

'What will it feel like?' My heart hammers in my chest as my back hits the wall.

Peter laughs. 'I have no idea. I've never been hit by lightning before, never used electricity the way I can use the soil. This is something new.'

I'm not sure about this. Peter seems a little manic. Can't say I blame him. I have no idea what it's like for my blood to hum. But the idea of being so connected to him sends a thrill through me. He reaches for my hand, raising it so my palm faces his, maybe an inch apart.

'Do you trust me?' he asks me, his focus on our palms.

'Yes,' I whisper.

I can't help but gasp when I see the first tiny lightning bolts pass from his palm to mine. It doesn't hurt, far from it. Instead, the sensation tingles, filling me with warmth, and an intoxicating power grows beneath my skin. A few moments elapse while a hundred tiny lightning bolts connect our hands while emitting a faint glow in the dim light of his room.

I hadn't noticed him move so close to me, his face now only inches from mine. His dark eyes are hungry.

'Tell me how it feels.' His voice is rough and low.

It's indescribable so, instead, I close the distance between us. I want more. He returns my kisses, leaning me against the wall. My hands find their way to the hem of his shirt, pulling it over his head. What I find stops me dead in my tracks.

I push him back to arm's length to take in what I'm seeing. What the long sleeves of his shirt have been hiding. I bring my hand to my mouth. There isn't an inch of Peter's skin that isn't bruised—he's tinged yellow everywhere. Peter gives me a slow twirl so I can view all of his body, see the purple bruises of lightning forks down his torso, back, and arms.

'Would you believe these actually look a lot better than they did yesterday?'

I reach out and trace a finger down one of the purple forks. A spark of static follows my movement. I've never seen anything so horrific and so strangely beautiful at the same time. As I move my fingers back up his arms, I watch the sparks follow while Peter watches me. Waiting, for something? My reaction. For me to be freaked out. To run away. I can tell he's holding his breath.

Slowly, he takes hold of my hand, his fingers entwining mine. The electricity rolls down his arm, passing from his skin to mine, undulating off like a wave. The warm, powerful feeling of Peter. I close my eyes against it.

'More,' I demand in a whisper.

His lips find mine, the electricity reeling off him now and into me.

Too good.
Inhumanly good.
I need him.
Now.

My hands run through his hair. The electricity now shared between us, I could run a marathon, or five. The bare skin between us is no longer shooting sparks, but still warm to touch. As we lie tangled together on his bed. I hope to always feel this way, that this sensation won't fade with the electricity.

'What are you?' I ask, although at this point I'm too far gone to care.

'Isn't it enough that I just want to be yours?' he asks, placing a soft kiss on my shoulder.

I would usually find this a frustrating answer, but I know he isn't being evasive. The truth is he doesn't know.

'Peter.' Anna's at the door, talking fast. 'Our aunt and uncle have just pulled up. You two better get down here.'

For some reason, I'm not nervous or scared about being caught. Confidence courses through me. *Is this what it's like to be Peter?* I look at my hand to see a ripple of electricity pass over my palm.

Peter gazes upon my smiling face, then he steps closer and closes my palm in his hand. As quickly as he's given me his power, he can take it away.

We are down the stairs in seconds.

I throw myself down on the sofa next to Lorna right as the key moves into the lock of the front door. Peter lingers in the living room doorway, his black hoodie zipped up to the top, hiding the mass of bruises covering his body. In the bright light of the living room, I can see faint bruising under his eyes that I hadn't noticed before.

'Peter, you're up. Are you feeling better?' Sally asks. Buried under the weight of her shopping bags, it takes her a moment to spot me. 'Connie? Lorna? What are you two doing here?'

'Checking up on me,' Peter's quick with a smooth reply.

'Actually, I wanted to talk to you.' The words barely leave my mouth before I know it, fuelled by my new sense of confidence.

Both Sally and Peter look at me in surprise.

'I just wanted to say sorry to you, Sally. For what's happened, for any trouble it's caused you, James, and Peter. I really like Peter. We were stupid, but I hope you won't object to us continuing to see each other. Obviously, what happened won't happen again. We promise.'

I look to Peter to confirm what I'm saying, and he runs his hand through his hair before turning to his aunt. 'Yep. Best behaviour from now on, I promise.'

Sally eyes Peter suspiciously before turning back to me. 'I appreciate you coming to apologise, Connie. You probably should get on home now. I don't want your mum worrying about you.' She gives Peter another glance before following James into the kitchen with their haul.

'What was that?' Peter asks as I move toward the door.

'Look, we need to let things cool down for a while. Okay?'

His fathomless eyes burn. I tilt my head, urging him to speak, but instead, he dips his head to mine for a simple kiss and tells us goodbye. Lorna and I walk to the end of the drive and collect our bikes from where they're leaning on a nearby fence.

'So, he seemed okay?' Lorna asks, her words loaded.

'Yes,' I say nonchalantly. 'He looks good, right?'

Lorna laughs at me as we mount our bikes and ride in the direction of my house. 'Yes, he looks good as always. Not quite as good as you… you're all glowy. Please tell me you two weren't doing it?'

I shrug. 'Okay, I won't tell you.'

Lorna laughs, shaking her head.

'Lor, thanks so much for covering for me and coming with. I just needed to know he was okay.'

'Of course. I was worried too. He's lucky to get off so light. He should see a doctor, though. There may be consequences we can't see yet.'

'Yeah, I'm sure he will,' I lie.

After a short bike ride to my house, Lorna instinctively gets off her bike and follows me inside. She knows part of her accompanying me tonight was to give me cover, as my mum would never have let me go out if she thought I was going to Peter. Lorna's doing her final part to show my mum I hadn't run off to Peter again.

I put the key into the lock and invite Lorna inside, asking her if she wants a coffee. I've barely finished my question when Mum calls out from the kitchen.

'Connie?'

'Yeah,' I shout back.

'You have a visitor.' My mind jumps to Peter for some reason. Stupid brain, I've just left Peter, so it can't be him. I look to Lorna for a clue of who it could be, but she gives me nothing.

My mum pops her head out of the kitchen, soon followed by Jamie. Lorna's takes a sharp breath beside me. My insides turn to ice. Jamie wasn't at school today, but the power still running through my veins sends the hairs on the back of my neck on edge. I've never physically wanted to hurt anyone before, yet it takes everything in me not to close the short distance and slap Jamie across his face and wipe the sheepish expression he's wearing right off it with one strike.

Noticing the tension, my mum looks from me to Jamie.

'What are you doing here, Jamie?' I ask, trying to keep my voice level.

'I just wanted to talk to you, Connie. Can I have a minute?'

He has me cornered. All my mum knows is we've been friends forever. It would raise more questions to tell him I don't want to speak to him.

'Outside,' I say.

'That's my cue to leave. See you, Mrs. Prinze,' Lorna calls to my mum and makes a swift exit as we walk toward the door. 'See you tomorrow, Con.' She gives me a reassuring look, followed by a death glare at Jamie.

I stand on my porch and close the front door behind me, thankful to still be wearing my big coat. I'm in no mood to talk to Jamie, but the lingering confidence allows me to stand my ground. Jamie can be feisty, nasty even, but I'm ready for whatever he's come to say.

'You have five minutes,' I snap at him.

'I'm sorry I outed you, Con.'

Okay, wasn't expecting an apology.

'I shouldn't have gone about it like that. I should have confronted you first. I didn't want to hurt you.'

'What did you think would happen, Jamie? You know where we live... you knew full well what people would say about me. You even called me it yourself.'

'I know, and I feel horrible about that. I thought it would shock you into seeing the truth.'

Ah, so this isn't a real apology.

'What truth?'

'About him, Connie.' Jamie steps closer, taking my arm. 'About what he's doing to you.'

'You're kidding me, right?' I jerk out of his clutch.

'There's something very, very wrong about him, Con. You should see how you are around him.'

I shake my head in disbelief and turn to go back inside, but he stops me before I can.

'It's not only him. Anna too. Don't you think it's weird how they both turned up out of the blue, and within weeks, somehow brainwashed you and Brady? It's like they clicked their fingers and they had you. You need to snap out of it, Connie. You need to see what's happening.'

'You need to leave, Jamie. I'm done here.'

'What happened to us, Connie?' He puts his hand on the front door, preventing me from opening it.

I look into his blue eyes, scan his rugged face that I would've once called cute, mischievous. He's a friend I've known forever, so I soften a little at the sadness in his eyes.

'Us?'

'It was always me and you, Con. I've known you my whole life. I thought we would end up together.'

'Jamie, you never said anything to me. I thought we were just friends.'

'Is that all you've ever thought of me?' He inches his other hand to the door so both his arms block me in at either side.

'Maybe, at one time, I thought we could be more. But that was before.'

'Before him?'

'Before him,' I confirm.

His eyes dance across my face, then glance to my mouth. My stomach dips.

'I like you, Connie. I want you to choose me, not him.'

I blink. *There it is.* I breathe out slowly, averting my gaze to my boots. 'It's too late.'

He moves at once, turning to look out into the winter night, his breath coming out in a cloud that dissipates into the still evening. We stand for a moment in silence before I continue.

'Jamie, did it ever occur to you that I don't want to just *end up* with someone? That I want to be wanted by someone?'

'Would it have even made a difference?' The cool edge has returned to his voice. 'Even if you and I had been together, would it have made a difference when he showed up?'

I close my eyes, taking in a deep breath, thankful for its coolness. 'Impossible question,' I say, drawing on that confidence. 'You think you know him, but you don't. You've never taken the time. One thing I do know is that if we were together, he never would've asked me to choose. And to be honest, if you think loyalty means so little to me, then you don't know me at all.'

There's nothing else to say to him.

'He's bad news, Connie,' Jamie adds, but I'm already halfway inside.

The door slams behind me, and I dart up the stairs and into my room. Shutting Jamie out of my life hurts more than I imagined. We haven't spoken in weeks, but the tears spill, knowing this is my fault.

Lorna warned me.

I should've spoken to him first.

But I couldn't deal with rejecting him, and now it's all blown up in my face.

Things do get better and faster than I could've hoped.

I expect school to be horrible, but much to my surprise, the gossip dies out within the week. Peter and me being a couple is accepted, and people carry on with their lives.

Life goes on, albeit in a slightly different way.

I can't put my finger on it.

Things are different, like a carefully balanced equilibrium. Life is poised on a knife-edge, although I'm not sure why. Something of a normal existence returns, but with Peter in it. Proving he's trustworthy, he makes an effort to come over and spend time with my parents. He talks a lot to my mum. Luckily, we've managed to avoid telling my dad. Sometimes, I go over to his place and have dinner with him and his aunt and uncle. Though, truth be told, I try to avoid this as much as possible—they are wildly uncomfortable. Peter never says much, and I often catch Sally and James watching him. I wonder how he can bear it. He's even making an effort to spend time with everyone, with most of our free time now being spent with Lorna, Brady, and Anna at the coffee shop.

There are no night visits, and I might pop because we never seem to be alone anymore. The electricity well and truly grounded, with all traces are gone from my body.

One positive is I'm not pregnant. Thinking about it now, I can't believe I was so stupid for so long. I think that's the biggest weight off my mum's mind, although she's coming round to him a lot faster than I expected her to.

I stare into my coffee mug. It's been almost a month of no alone time with Peter. We're widely accepted as a couple now, yet he's never asked me to be his girlfriend.

Now, I seem to be the only one not subject to his charms. I'm annoyed with myself for being so upset by it, about being jealous of my friends, of my own mum, for the attention Peter is giving them. I feel like a brat, but I miss the haze of being so close to him all the time and decide I have to take action.

'Hey. Can I talk to you?' I ask, rudely interrupting the conversation he's having with Lorna.

He looks taken aback while Lorna's eyes boggle at me. No doubt she thinks I'm acting a bit bizarre. I feel it. What's wrong with him?

What's wrong with me?

'Outside,' I add, then march out of the coffee shop.

There's a thin layer of snow on the ground, and despite hating the cold, I do love the snow. It has a magical, quiet quality about it. Peter follows me, and for a second, I want to hit him in his beautiful face for looking confused.

'What's going on?' I demand.

'With what?'

I love the freckles on his nose. The blond of his hair is a little longer now, curling into his eyes a touch, so he has to shake it out of his vision. I adore the tan of his skin. What I had at first assumed was the result of summers spent outside is now evident that it's the remnant of a heritage that he never talks about. Despite his secrets that I carry, there's still so much left unsaid. So much that he guards.

'With us. You seem distant.'

'Distant? I thought this was what you wanted. Didn't you want things to cool down?'

I glance around at the snow and laugh. 'When I said cool down, I didn't mean become arctic.'

He cocks his head, not following.

'Peter, I so appreciate all the effort you've been making but...' I trail off.

'But?'

I stare into his deep brown eyes full of warmth.

'Connie, I'm not great at subtlety. You need to tell me what you want.'

I rest my hand on his chest, taking a step closer. 'I miss you. I miss you keeping me warm.' I bite my lip.

I'm taken off my feet in the next second as Peter lifts me. His lips find mine as he pushes me back into the wall of the coffee shop. His kiss is urgent and unrelenting. Eventually, he peels himself off me.

'Wow.' I let out a breath, blowing my hair off my forehead. 'You're enough to give a girl whiplash.'

'What does that mean?'

'It doesn't matter.' I laugh and kiss him again, pushing my hands through his hair. The warmth I've been missing fills me instantly. I have no sense of shame in how much I crave his attention. 'Peter, I never want this to stop. Why can't we be both? Be normal... dinner with the parents, hanging out with friends, and... be this.'

'Connie...' Peter pushes his forehead to mine, closing his eyes, '... I find it hard to control *this*.'

'Who says you need to control anything?' I reply, not knowing what I mean, only knowing I want him back. *All of him.*

'Okaaay.' He drawls the word like he knows I have no idea what I'm asking from him. 'Whatever you say.'

'I say that you should come and see me tonight.'

'There's snow on the ground. Not sure even I can make that disappear.'

'What happened to the ivy being strong enough for you to climb up?'

My favourite devilish grin spreads across his face. He nods and kisses me again.

CHAPTER 18

Anna

Things are coming to a head. Something starts to bubble under the surface of my skin that I don't have a name for.

I realise the longer my brother and I are here, the more our emotions unfurl, the more lost to our surroundings we become. But whereas he cannot stop himself, all I seem able to do is hold back. I have to. Peter's emotions have always been so much stronger than my own, so strong they can overpower me. And at the moment, they are more heightened than ever.

I can't avoid it, and in a way, I know it's the same for others too. I can see it in their stares when we walk down the crowded corridors at school. The relationship between him and Connie has changed the energy he emits. Now when people look at him, I see the desire in their faces. Not only at him but also at me. It's like I'm an extension of him, the longing looks of others hugging the curves of my body.

He doesn't notice.

He's so sure of himself.

All he sees is Connie.

Sometimes I wonder how it must feel to be her, to bear all that crushing desire. Although I sense their stares, I still obsess over how it feels to be so *wanted*. To want someone so much in return. I wish I could say it's good, but it only confuses me.

How do I tell my brother, when he's trying so hard, that this is all because of him?

Instead, I retreat to my safe space.

'Are you okay?' Brady asks as he looks up from making hot chocolate.

I must have looked lost in thought from my space on the kitchen counter. The peaceful glow of his family kitchen has become a kind of refuge.

'You thinking about your mum? This'll be your first Christmas without her.'

I look into his eyes, so genuine and full of kindness. 'Yeah,' I lie. 'More like thinking about how different my life is now. I…' I so desperately want to share what I'm going through with him. 'Sometimes I feel guilty that I don't miss her more. Do you think that makes me a terrible person?'

Brady looks thoughtful, then shakes his head. 'I don't think there's any right way to grieve. Especially when you were the carer for your mum. You never got much chance to be a kid.'

I swallow the lump in my throat at his words. He doesn't even know the truth, and yet he understands.

'Anna...' he sets my hot chocolate down in front of me, '... you know I'm always here. You can talk to me whenever.'

I push my hair from my face, my eyes hot. 'I know. It's just so complicated. I don't know what to do, Brady. Peter has been all I've had for so long, and now, he doesn't need me anymore. What do I do?'

'Hey.' He pulls me in for a hug, and I let him. Allowing his arms to envelop me.

In return, I wrap my arms and legs around his body and hold him close. All I want is to stop thinking for one second. If only my mind would stop for a moment.

He places a tender kiss on my neck, which sends a current through my body.

In the next heartbeat, I don't think, only act. I bring his lips to mine and kiss him with everything I have. I want all the confusion to stop. Some time to not think. Only feel.

Brady's breath shallows as he deepens his kiss, and I squeeze my legs tighter. He is so good. I want to lose myself the way I know my brother can. Little by little, the anxiety leaves my body. I want to keep going, to exist only in my body for as long as possible.

'Oh my God,' a voice shrieks from the doorway.

I jerk back to see a girl with the same flaming-red hair as Brady standing with her hand on her hip, looking scandalized.

Brady's face turns bright red at the sight of her. He picks up the nearby roll of kitchen towels and launches it at her. 'Get out of here, Jen.'

She snatches it out of the air. 'Were you going to do your girlfriend on the counter? Dad is in the next room.' She laughs.

My face goes scarlet too.

'I was not… that's not what was h-happening,' he stammers as Jen continues to laugh at him.

He gives up trying to explain and instead tries to force her out of the kitchen, an action that results in using some kind of wrestling move on her.

After I watch them tussle for a while, I come to my senses, and it clicks that this is Brady's older sister, home for Christmas from university. Right when she has Brady pinned, his dad calls for him. Brady huffs to his feet, leaving me alone with Jen, who laughs and makes her way over to the refrigerator.

I hop down from my spot trying to compose myself. 'You know we really weren't—' I start, but she waves me off.

'Please, anything to wind my little brother up. It's beyond fun. It really is fine.' She looks back at me. 'I'm Jen, by the way.'

'Anna.' I beam, holding out my hand for her.

Her hair is wild, falling all around her shoulders in waves, and her milky skin is flawless. The way she looks at me makes my skin flush again. *It seems I certainly have a type.*

'I guess I'm not much like that with my brother.'

'You should try it,' she says, seeming unable to look away either. Her teeth skim her rosy lower lip.

'Try what?' I ask, completely forgetting what I've just said. Her hand still in mine.

'Hey, kids.' Brady's dad pokes his head around the door. 'The carols are about to start.'

Jen whips her hand from mine, her face reddening too, and leaves the room in a rush.

I have the sudden urge to splash my face with cold water and desperately want Jacob to leave, but instead, he hovers in the doorway.

'How are you holding up?' he asks.

My heart pounds as I try to figure out what he means.

'This will be your first Christmas without your mum. Must be hard on you and your brother.'

'Oh.' I almost sigh with relief. 'We aren't Christian. My mother didn't believe in God.'

Now it's Jacob's turn to look confused. 'You never celebrated Christmas before?'

I shake my head, wondering why he's looking at me like I've sprouted two heads.

This becomes a common theme when I meet Lorna the next day, and we take the train to the closest town centre.

'I'm so glad the snow has melted. This would've been miserable otherwise,' she tells me, although she looks pretty bundled up in her thick woollen scarf.

I study her closer. Her hair looks even shinier against her fluffy white beret, and she can do the most amazing cat flicks with her eyeliner. *She looks cute today*, I think before snapping myself out of it.

What is wrong with me?

I'm out of control.

I blame Peter, believing it's all his fault that I can't look at anyone without falling in love with them.

She doesn't seem to notice.

'I met Jen yesterday,' I say, mainly for something to fill the silence, and so Lorna doesn't notice me drooling at her.

Lorna's eyes flash up at me. 'Oh yeah. What did you think of her?'

Erm, gorgeous. Apparently, I have a thing for redheads.

I clear my throat. 'She seems nice. How she is with Brady, it's so different from Peter and me.'

Lorna considers me for a while before she looks out of the window at the passing countryside. 'Brady has a great family. But his brothers and sisters drive him crazy. Especially Jen. She's kind of the wild child. She's the only one to have left. Mostly, the Timms stay on the farm.'

'Why did she leave?'

'Not much choice after she came out.'

I scrunch my face at Lorna, whose eyes widen.

'Not that there's anything wrong with that, she wasn't run out or anything. I literally mean not much choice. Like, it's hard to be gay 'round here when you are the only one.' She picks a chip at the edge of her nail varnish.

'Oh, I didn't realise.'

Lorna chuckles. 'I'm surprised. She's an awful flirt, and she loves doing anything to wind Brady up.'

My face reddens again, thinking about the moment we shared, and guilt floods my body. Lorna must mistake my blushing for embarrassment because she changes the subject, going back to her phone.

'So I have pretty much everyone figured out except my dad. Dads are always so hard to buy for.' She slows her speech as she glances over at me. 'Sorry. That's pretty thoughtless of me.'

'What are you talking about?'

'You know, your shopping list. What are you getting your brother?'

'What do you mean?' All thoughts of how cute she looks are firmly banished.

'For Christmas?' She laughs.

'I have to get him something for Christmas?' I ask.

Lorna wears the same bewildered look Jacob had yesterday. 'Don't you celebrate Christmas?'

'Yes.' She laughs again. 'I may be the only brown person in this village, but Christmas happens to be my favourite time of year.'

'I didn't mean—'

'Don't worry about it.'

She smiles with genuine warmth, and a bit of that compassion catches in my chest. 'Have you never been given a Christmas present?'

I shake my head.

Lorna doesn't make me feel guilty or strange about it, however. Instead, she endeavours for us to squeeze every Christmas-related tradition into one day. I help her with some of her shopping, but mostly she forgets about that. We buy candy canes and walk around to view the decorations. She even takes me to Santa's Grotto.

I've never felt so childlike.

'Thank you so much for today, Lorna,' I tell her on the way home. 'It's been a weird few weeks. A weird year, actually. Today has made me feel almost human again.'

She beams brilliantly. Not saying anything, she holds out a small bag.

I take it from her and peek inside to see a delicate ornament that looks like two flying doves.

'It's pretty cheesy,' she says, embarrassed. 'I stole the inspiration from my favourite Christmas film. Turtle doves represent friendship. Anyway, I guess I wanted you to have your first Christmas present.'

I can't fight the smile beaming from me.

CHAPTER 19

Peter

Everything is different now.

The abilities I was born with, which have always been so familiar—skills I simply coexisted with in harmony—now blister under my surface.

My skin itches with the need to use them. It's as if the lightning strike broke a dam inside me.

Still on the outside of my swan-like exterior, my life is as close to normal as it has ever been.

Connie is, well… she is blissful. I'm managing to find balance for her. The nights I get to spend with her are what I live for. Hidden in the golden glow of her room after stealing in through her window, I'm happy for the first time. Funny thing about happiness—one doesn't know what was missing until happiness has a face, and she's beaming. All the bits in between, I'm learning to live with more and more easily. Focusing on school, spending time with her friends and getting to know them, repairing the damage done with her family, and becoming the person Connie needs me to be—a part that fits. I focus my energy into making her happy in return.

Who would've thought I would be trying to fill my time by spending it with others? These days, I need a constant distraction to focus on. Something, anything, to take away the desire to use my abilities.

Tending Sally and James' garden is no longer enough. It allows only a trickle to escape, where I need a waterfall. The built-up pressure turns into splitting headaches. It takes three lightning storms to figure out they're happening every time I get a migraine.

Something has to give.

So, I take a walk. Deep into the woods, where neither Anna nor Connie knows I go, and I plunge my hands deep into the earth and let it out.

The energy flows from me and into the ground. Everything around me bursts into life each time. The flowers that should be long dead bloom full circle, the vines of the undergrowth wind up my arms, the leaves on the trees grow, turning green and then brown before shedding again.

The release leaves me shaking.

These are the nights I sleep the soundest.

Then the build-up begins again.

While I struggle to keep the powers I've always known in check, I'm beginning to learn how to flex a new one, or, at least one I never knew I possessed. *Influence*. Which isn't an exact science. I try to imagine using my influence like planting a seed in someone's mind and letting it grow. The main problem is I have no idea if it's worked or not. The other problem is I don't have any idea if I'm *not* using it either.

One issue at a time.

My main goal is Connie, making her life as easy as possible, making her mum not only like me but willing to let me stay there, so I don't have to sneak in anymore. No more risks for Connie. I need to make her happy, and keep her content.

On the night before New Year's Eve, I have my confirmation it has worked. I'm staying at Connie's officially for the first time, which means no sneaking out. No more sneaking around for her.

Here I am, Connie stretched out on her stomach beside me in her bed in a state of complete relaxation as I trace patterns of the constellations across her back. Bliss.

'That feels good.' She arches her back into the caress.

I ache for her, running my fingers up her back and into her hair. Her skin is so soft.

'Are you excited about New Year's Eve tomorrow?'

'I don't understand why everyone makes such a fuss about New Year's Eve. But, yes, Anna and I are excited about the party. We've never been to a party before.'

She bites her lip and laughs, and I give her arm a tiny squeeze for laughing at me.

'What's so funny?'

'Nothing, just don't get your hopes up too much. It will only be Anna, Brady, Lorna, and us. Not much of a party. But there will be music and drinks.'

'Well, I have nothing to compare it to, so I can't be disappointed.'

'What did you used to do for New Year's? When your mum was alive.'

Her eyes gaze into mine. She asks far more questions about my past these days. Knowing my influence might have stretched over her in the early days of our relationship sits in an uneasy pit in my stomach, even if it was unintentional.

'We didn't do anything. It was just another day. We rarely even knew what day of the week it was. It didn't matter.'

She runs her hands through my hair. 'It's so hard for me to get my head around what your life was like. How recent all this change was, how weird it must still be.'

'Yeah.' I lean my head back into her hand. 'You know, I'd never seen a banana until six months ago.'

Connie giggles.

'Seriously. I mean, I knew they existed, but I'd never seen one.'

'Wow. That must've been a revelation,' she teases.

'It's true. A thousand little things you've taken for granted, I'd never seen. Like, a horse, or being in a car, and I've never seen the sea.'

This whole time I've wanted to return home, to run away, I'd held fast to the notion that our mother never neglected us. Little by little, I am beginning to understand I have been in a cage my whole life.

'It's a big world, Connie, and I know nothing of it.'

New Year's Eve.

As comfortable as I've gotten around our friends, I still would rather it be Connie and me, alone. Plus, the faint unease of my skin being too tight flares in my veins.

This isn't the best time to be with everyone.

Anna and Lorna arrive at Connie's house to begin the "getting ready" ritual. I never realised girls have a process for getting ready that begins hours before the actual event. I retreat downstairs and camp out on the sofa for most of the afternoon with Connie's old Labrador.

After a while, my sister finds me downstairs, her cheeks tinted a light pink. She flops down beside me. 'How's it going?' she asks.

'Okay. What's that you're drinking?' I motion to the pearly liquid in her glass.

'Oh, this?' She holds the glass in the air, spilling some of the liquid onto the floor. 'It's wine. It tastes good. Warm.'

'You're drinking now?' I raise my eyebrows.

'You're not the only one who gets to live a little, Peter.' She smirks at me. 'Do you want some?'

'No, I don't think that's a good idea.'

'How come?'

'Do *you* think it's a good idea to give alcohol to someone who has issues with restraint?'

'You've been doing so well. You can give yourself a break.'

Anna's wide-eyed honesty only inspires guilt, and I rub my head, knowing I should come clean. I haven't told her anything, not about the power surges or using my influence to make Connie's mum tolerate me. *Screw it.* I take the glass of wine out of her hand and drain what's left.

My cheeks warm. She's right, there is something toasty and welcoming to the sharp flavour.

Connie and Lorna join us downstairs, both bearing the same flush in their cheeks. Connie fetches me a glass from the kitchen and fills it. Staying close by my side, she continues to laugh with her friends. We finish the bottle before Connie's mum drops us around at Brady's house. Anna and I never drank before—our mother's homemade gin never tempted us. The alcohol takes the edge off the itch I need to scratch. I'm a bit blurred at the fringes before we even arrive at Brady's.

Brady has decorated the barn with twinkling lights and set up a small sound system so we won't disturb the rest of his family in the main house. Anna has been using my arm to keep herself steady as we walk in. We're laughing and talking together, reminding each other how bad the bathroom used to smell when our mother was brewing gin.

'How much have you two had to drink?' Brady smiles as he plants a kiss on Anna's cheek and hands me a beer.

'We only shared a bottle of wine at my house.' Connie laughs.

'They've been doing that the whole way here. I think they have their own twin language,' Lorna explains.

'Were we doing that?' I ask, and Anna giggles. I hadn't even noticed.

'Yep.' Lorna nods, turning to Connie. 'Put some music on, Connie.'

She doesn't need telling twice.

No one seems bothered by Anna and me talking our own language. We drink more, and the tequila Lorna gives me makes my vision blur. Truth be told, I haven't felt so relaxed in weeks. Unburdened by trying to maintain appearances, Connie stays clutched to my side as we laugh and talk. Normal, totally normal.

We sit on old bales of hay that are stacked high. Lorna climbs to the top, wobbling on the spot while staring into the hay pit on the other side.

'Hey, Brady, remember when we were kids, and we used to spend hours jumping off these bales?'

'Yeah, we'd probably just hit the floor now.' Brady moves up to join his friend and peers over the edge.

'I think we could make it,' Lorna jokes.

'Don't, Lor.' Connie pulls her friend by the arm.

'I'm kidding.'

Lorna and Brady sit back down. It sounds like fun. Anna climbs up to the top bale and teeters on the ledge, smiling to herself. 'It reminds me of the lake,' she says without thinking.

I know she's talking to me.

'You grew up by a lake?' Brady asks, not missing a beat.

The colour floods her face, not having meant to reveal anything about our past, but she continues anyway, the warmth of the alcohol spurring her on. 'Yes. We would swim in it in the summer. Peter would always find the highest branch to jump off and do backflips from.' She turns to look at me. 'You were such a show-off.' Her laughter tinkles in the air.

'Not much has changed,' I say and climb up to stand next to her. The drop isn't too far. The alcohol has thrown me off balance, but I would guess there's enough loose hay to cushion the blow. I look at Anna, and her smile stays on her lips. I'm guessing she knows what I'm thinking—I want to jump. I want her to jump.

'Be careful, you two,' Brady calls out.

Even as his words leave his mouth, Anna's feet are already in motion. She takes one step, two steps, and then her feet leave the hay bale, a loud shriek escaping her as she falls through the air.

Brady, Connie, and Lorna are on their feet to join me at the top of the stack, rushing to look over the edge to see Anna lying in the pile of hay at the bottom and laughing.

'You're crazy,' Brady shouts.

I laugh. My turn. I turn my back to the edge before the others notice what I'm doing. Anna rolls off the pile, still giggling. I hold my hands in front of me and crouch down for half a second before propelling myself backward through the air, landing feet first in the hay. I can't remember the last time I did this.

'Show-off,' she shouts at me as I roll out of the way.

'You're both crazy,' Brady yells down at us.

'You don't know the half of it,' I call back. 'Are you three coming down or what?'

They all exchange looks before they hurry to follow suit, jumping into the hay to join us on the ground.

More shots.

More dancing.

And Connie.

She fills my vision. Singing along to the song, pulling me in. Her fingers entwine with mine, her green eyes gazing up at me through her dark lashes. I tug her closer to press her body against mine. This song is one I know, so I sing back to her.

Who knew drinking could be such a release? Everyone's inhibitions melt away. Even my sister, who's dancing close with Brady. I put my arm around Anna's neck, pulling her closer, and her eyes seem blurry. Or maybe mine are.

'I feel good,' she says into my ear.

'Me too.' I laugh back at her. 'Maybe our mother was onto something all those years.'

Anna makes a face, pushing me away at the notion. I have to admit, it was godawful stuff. I leave Anna to dance with Connie, moving back to the table first and trying to focus in on what bottle is the tequila. *I want more.*

Brady is at my side, slurring in my ear. 'Look at that.' He uses his beer to point over to Anna dancing with Connie.

My sister is almost as tall as me, so she looms over Connie. She appears to be enjoying Connie moving her body against hers, both of them lost in the music. I raise my eyebrows at the sight. This isn't like my sister. I start to respond to Brady but don't have a chance.

Lorna's screams echo through the barn. I spin around to see Brady already rushing to her side. I stumble over, not quite registering what I'm seeing. There's so much red.

'What happened?' Connie drops to the floor next to Lorna's leg, which is thick with blood, her bone clearly visible through the break.

Brady is white. 'I think she jumped from the top and fell. Her leg.'

I look on in horror as the tears start running down Lorna's face.

'Con, have you got your phone? We need to call an ambulance.'

Connie wastes no time, running to fetch her phone.

'Peter, do something,' Anna says.

When did she join me?

My eyes drift back to the blood. I've never seen so much. I gawp at my sister in disbelief. Her face this close is all fuzzy. 'What? I can't fix this,' I whisper back.

Connie runs back over with her phone, clutching onto Lorna. To Brady, she says, 'Maybe you should get your parents?'

Brady nods, looking like he's going to be sick.

While the blood pools on the floor.

I might be sick.

'Peter,' Anna whispers, her words coming out slurred. 'We both know you can do this. You can do anything.'

I inspect Lorna's splintered leg from afar, and my brain swims. The itch for release rises to the surface again, fighting against the alcohol in my blood. I flex my neck. *I can give it a try.*

I step toward Lorna, trying to say something, but the words come out as blurry as I feel. Connie and Brady look at me, not quite knowing what to think as Lorna continues to whimper.

'I meant to say… I think I can help,' I manage to get out.

Connie looks from me to Anna, who's swaying behind me in my peripheral vision. 'Peter, I—'

'What are you talking about?' Brady asks. 'I'm going to get my parents. Connie, call an ambulance.'

'No,' I say, my voice sounding much more confident than I am. I nod at Anna. 'I can do it.'

I join Connie on the floor with Lorna, kneeling beside her leg. The bone looks shattered. The tequila lurches in my stomach, and I fight back the urge to vomit. Connie's eyes are wide, watching. Everyone stares at me for what seems like an eternity. Lorna's breath is shallow, and confusion contorts her face. My mind flicks back to my mother's body, already starting to purple.

I hadn't been able to save her.

Hadn't even tried.

I can't cheat death… it's natural. But this isn't death.

It's flesh and bone.

I can control the earth, the weather, minds—why not flesh?

I put my hand onto Lorna's leg, triggering fresh screams. The wound is hot, and she's losing blood fast. Power flares in my blood. Anna's right—like my connection to the soil and the earth, I can also connect with flesh. I close my eyes and find all the shattered pieces of Lorna.

Putting a person back together is different from giving life to the earth. It is more like pulling than pushing.

Drawing her back together, I focus. The energy burning hot, and she screams again with the agony of having her bone forced back into place. I open my eyes to ensure I'm not scorching her skin. I'm not. There's a blinding hot sensation cradled in my palm. So hot that white light begins to glow between my fingers.

'What the hell?' Brady says the words, and I agree absolutely.

What the hell?

As the white light burns, it fixes Lorna's leg, and her screams start to lessen.

Something clicks, and my breath leaves my body. Hard.

Lorna's body is whole again, but I can't let go.

The white light changes, takes on a form, weaving like a snake around my fingers.

I should let go.

It is *amazing*.

Overwhelming.

The light moves again, snaking around my wrist, and travels up my arm. I only hear the hammering of my heartbeat, it's so loud.

Lorna has stopped screaming now.

I close my eyes, letting the euphoria wash over me, while the light wraps around my arm like a vine. I lick my lips and almost taste it.

Anna's firm hand pulls me backward, forcing me to release Lorna, who lies unconscious in Connie's arms, her leg no longer showing any trace of a break.

I stagger to my feet. Everything is quiet now except for the sound of my ragged breaths. The light that has been travelling up my arm absorbs into my skin. I shake my head, trying to clear the effects of the alcohol and the light flooding my veins. Absorbing into my blood stream, it rushes through my body, shifting and turning. *Oh so good.* I try to steady myself against it.

'Peter?' Anna tries to approach me.

I hold up my hand, urging her to stay back.

Different from the pure energy of the lightning, this is something else. It doesn't make my blood hum. It makes it sing. I might come undone it's so good.

So. Damn. Good.

My shallow breaths change into laughter. 'I'm all right.' I can't stop laughing. 'I'm okay.' More laughter.

Nothing's even funny, but I can't stop laughing.

A rushing sensation pushes me backward.

My feet are moving, and I'm going to fall.

I lose consciousness before I hit the floor.

CHAPTER 20

Connie

'Peter,' I coax his name, caressing his face as he starts to wake. It's almost midday. He looks so peaceful when he sleeps, it seems a shame to wake him. To force him to face today.

'Connie? How did I get here?'

'You don't remember?' I ask, sweeping the hair out of his eyes.

He rubs his head, coming to and sitting up in my bed to look at me.

'Wow. I had such a strange dream.' He takes my hand and draws it across his forehead, pressing the tips of my fingers to his skin. 'My head hurts.'

'Yep, you had a lot to drink.' I try to smile. *He doesn't remember.* 'So, what did you dream about?'

He shakes his head. 'I'm not sure, but I think I dreamed Lorna broke her leg and there was a lot of blood.'

'Lorna *did* break her leg, Peter. And you fixed it.' I watch him carefully.

He was manic last night. Even Anna said she had never seen anything like it before. After he lost consciousness for a few seconds, he came to in a haze. Delirious. His words coming out in jumbles about his mother, about power, and he could barely stand. It was chaos.

Brady was also drunk and causing a riot, demanding to know what was happening and what was wrong with Peter. Eventually, Anna took Brady back to the main house, leaving me with an unconscious Lorna and a nonsensical Peter. Not knowing what else to do, I called my mum and told her we'd all had too much to drink, and we needed to come home. She was strangely chill about the whole thing as we bundled them both into the back seat—Lorna barely opening her eyes and Peter bobbing in and out of awareness.

I haven't slept much. I texted Anna a few times for an update, but none came.

Peter takes some time to register, to recall what happened.

'Shit. I did that. I didn't know I could do that. Where's Anna?'

'She's still with Brady. He was pretty freaked out.'

'She told me to do it.' Peter stares at me, his expression blank, impossible to read.

I tilt my head, unsure of how to offer him comfort. 'Yep, she was pretty drunk too. We all were. I think Lorna tried to do a backflip off the bales and missed the pile of hay. Everyone panicked.'

'Shit, shit, shit.' Peter drops his head into his hands. 'Connie, this is bad… this is so bad. Lorna and Brady, they saw. They saw what I can do. How can we explain this?'

'Well, I'm not sure what Anna has said to Brady, but Lorna is still asleep on the sofa downstairs. You were pretty out of it. She's been sleeping, but she seems okay.'

Peter gets out of bed and paces my room. He stares down at his hand, the one that healed Lorna to not even a scratch remaining. Peter's powers had always seemed like a glorious mystery to me, romantic and beautiful. In the cold light of the new year, combined with the sleep deprivation and Peter's wild behaviour last night, they now seem scary.

'Peter, what are you?' I don't mean for it to sound like an accusation.

In two steps, he's on his knees in front of me, his eyes pleading and desperate. 'I'm just a person, Connie. I didn't ask for any of this.' Peter takes my hand, focusing on entwining his fingers with mine, holding on with everything he has. 'Connie, my whole life, my mother said the outside world was bad and she was keeping us safe. But what if she had it all wrong? What if it's me who is bad? What if I'm what the world needs protection from?'

He lowers his head into my lap.

Lost. He is so lost.

'Connie, I have no idea what I am. I just want to be with you.'

'Peter, I love you.' I hadn't planned on admitting those feelings to him, and I don't know why I chose this moment to say the words, but his vulnerability scares me and I can't bear it.

'You love me?' His dark eyes are like black pits staring up at me, ones I'll fall into at any moment.

'I do. I love you, Peter. That is not who you are. I'd been so consumed by you that I lost myself, and I can see you are trying to do the same. But I'm my own person, just like you are. You need to find your place in this world. You owe it to yourself to find out.'

His body trembles. 'Connie, you don't understand. The last few weeks, I've felt like I'm losing control. I don't think I want to know.'

'You can't hide forever, Peter. I can help you, but you have to help me understand.'

'What if I'm a monster, Connie?'

'Peter, you're not a monster. Do you think I could fall in love with a monster?' I force him to look at me. 'But we can't do this on our own.'

As the words leave my lips, an idea is forming, and I know it's the right thing. I grab my phone and call Anna, throwing Peter's T-shirt at him. It rings for an eternity, but right as I think it's about to click off, she answers.

'Connie?' Her voice is thick with sleep. 'Sorry, I dozed off.'

'Is Brady okay?' I ask as Peter gets dressed, eyeing me with curiosity, his features pulled into a serious expression.

'He's asleep. Is Peter okay?'

'He's fine. Listen, we're coming to you now. Tell Brady to meet us under the tree,' I say with certainty. I need to make this happen before I lose my nerve. Peter and Anna's instincts are to hide, and even though Peter has been opening up to me, I'm sure it is never the whole truth. Before I think about it too much, I quickly type out a text, hit send, and hope for the best.

I pull on jeans, a T-shirt, a big cardigan, and my favourite bobble hat, then take Peter by the hand and lead him downstairs.

'What are we doing?' he asks.

'We're going back to Brady's. You need allies, Peter, and your allies need to trust you. That starts with being honest.'

Peter is obviously far from convinced. 'Can we just take a moment?'

I don't answer him, and I don't stop. Downstairs, Lorna's awake. Her silky hair is a bird's nest on the side of her head, and her usually perfect eyeliner smudges down to her cheek from where she was crying in agony only a few hours ago.

My mum hands her a cup of coffee.

'Hi, guys,' Lorna says, her voice hoarse. 'Wow, so I totally overdid it, right? I can't even remember getting back here. Sorry, Mrs. Prinze.'

'Please, you're only eighteen once.' My mum shrugs it off and begins to leave the room.

'Actually, can you get your coffee to go, Lor? I promised Brady we would head back over. Do you mind?' I give my mum my best puppy dog eyes.

She reluctantly agrees.

Lorna grumbles about her hangover and having to move but pulls her shoes on, commenting how she was sure she was wearing tights before.

The ride back to Brady's is strained. Peter's tension pulses through the car as he stares out the window. I wish I knew what he was thinking. I'm sure I am right, though. He needs answers. Living with his head in the sand will only make things worse.

When Lorna researched lightning strikes and found out most weren't fatal, I managed to sort of explain things away. In reality, I want answers too.

We walk down to the field where we'd all met a few months before. Everything is so different now. The anticipation of what I'm about to do makes me jittery. I'm not a confrontational person. I don't know what I will say or do if Peter and Anna decide to flat-out deny everything.

Too late. Anna and Brady see us from where they are sitting cross-legged on a picnic blanket beneath the tree. They both look tired.

'Have I missed something?' Lorna asks. 'Why is everyone so on edge?'

I let my breath mist the air in front of me, then look from Lorna to Peter, as Anna and Brady come to join us. No one says anything. Brady's eyes are on Peter, Anna's are on me, and Lorna is looking to anyone for an explanation regarding this bizarre get-together.

'What are you doing here?' Peter says, catching sight of someone else approaching, then defensively putting his body in front of me.

'I was invited.' Jamie's voice drips with disdain, squaring up to him.

Peter looks down his nose at him, not backing down.

In the end, I put my hands between the two. I made this happen, time for me to step up. I look up at Peter and reveal, 'I asked him to be here.'

Peter's face twists into a frown.

'Peter, I've known Jamie my whole life. He may not have acted like it recently, but he *is* my friend. Plus, he knows what it's like to have a troubled home life. And we need allies.' I push Peter back, then shift to face everyone.

Anna's face is pale, almost white, looking to her brother for help with what to do.

'I know things have been weird...' I start, '... but no more secrets. We need to trust each other.' I take a deep breath, look at Anna, and say, 'It's time for both of you to come clean... to all of us.'

Anna chokes for a second, all faces turning to her. 'No, Peter.'

'They saw, Anna.' Peter raises his hands in the air in exasperation. 'And, honestly, it's getting worse.'

The words seem to make sense to her. Her eyes are wet, and I feel a pang of guilt for how sick she looks. This goes against everything in her nature.

Jamie's demeanour changes from hostility to one of bewilderment. 'Er, what's going on?'

Peter exhales. 'I don't even know where to start,' he says more to me than anyone else.

'At the beginning,' I suggest.

He looks at Jamie. 'You saw me and Anna together. What you think you saw, it wasn't like that.'

Jamie shifts uncomfortably.

'But Anna and I, we've slept beside each other our whole lives. I thought when we came here we were trapped, but I've come to realise our whole life before was a cage.' He looks at his sister, the moisture spilling out of her eyes and trickling down her face.

Brady glances at her.

'Only...' Peter continues, '... we didn't understand it was a cage at the time. Now I believe it wasn't a cage for *us*. It was a cage for *me*.'

Anna closes her eyes, unable to fight the tears.

'What's going on?' Lorna quips. 'I don't understand.'

'Peter and Anna have actually lived here this whole time. They were born here,' I explain as Peter moves to comfort his sister. 'They grew up in the big house just outside of the village. Their mother, she...' I take a huge intake of air, '... she kind of kept them prisoner there.'

'That's not possible. It's been empty for years,' Brady argues.

'It's true,' Anna confirms, her voice trembling. 'But it wasn't like that. We didn't know we were prisoners. We were okay, for the most part.'

'Why would your mum keep you prisoner?' Jamie directs the question at Peter.

The visible vulnerability in Peter makes me shake, like an exposed nerve. Of all people, he's explaining this to Jamie, but maybe it's easier to say it to him.

'Our mother used to tell me I was born special, that most people have lost their connection to nature, to the world around us. They didn't know how and didn't want to. She said I was different.' His eyes find mine. 'It's just a connection. She said I have a connection to the earth people wouldn't understand. She never gave it a name.'

'And this connection, that's how you did that thing last night?' Brady asks.

Peter nods.

'What thing?' Lorna looks to Brady.

'You don't remember? You jumped, Lor. You broke your leg, and the bone was poking out. Peter fixed it. There was a light, then it was all healed. Not even a scratch left.'

'How's that possible?' Lorna whispers.

'I don't know,' Peter admits. 'Honestly, I've never done that before. I didn't even know I could.'

'And the lightning? Is that part of it?' Jamie asks.

'I think so, but that was the first time that happened too.' Peter rubs his head. 'A lot of these things have only started happening since our mother died. Before, it was just making things grow.'

'You can make things grow?' Lorna asks.

Peter gives her a shaky smile. 'Only plants. I've always been able to make plants grow. It's only recently I can do other things,' he reiterates and gives Anna a slight glance. 'Or, rather, have learned that I can do other things.'

'So why are you so special?' Jamie asks, the edge in his voice is back.

'I'm trying to explain.'

'Well, try harder.'

'It's different now. Things have changed, everything has an influence.' Peter paces, trying to organise his thoughts, to make them into words. 'I honestly don't know why I am the way I am. Our mother never told us. When you're raised in isolation, trust me, you don't even think to question anything. Since joining the village, it's more than making things grow now. The lightning and what happened last night. I've never experienced anything like them before.'

He turns to Lorna, almost lost in his own thoughts, as he looks at the hand he healed her with. 'Lorna, the power of fixing your leg. It was like I could see all the atoms in your body and, like a jigsaw, I had to put it back together. It was as easy as a puzzle. I saw the pieces and put it all together.'

Peter's breathing becomes laboured, so Anna joins her brother, steadying him.

Lorna wraps her arms around herself as the wind picks up.

'So, what? You're like a mutant or something?' Jamie clarifies.

'Jamie,' Brady bites at him.

'I'm kidding.' Jamie holds up his hands. 'I had to make a joke. He was going to go all *Thor* on us again.'

I hit Jamie's chest.

He shakes his head. 'Why are you being so serious?'

'You're not helping.' I narrow my eyes at him.

'Peter, could your parents do the things you can?' Lorna asks.

'No, our mother couldn't. She said our father died before we were even born, but I don't think so.'

'Well, how can you know for sure?' Jamie pipes up again.

'We only have what our mother said.'

Other Nature by Kerry Williams

'The same mother who kept you prisoners?' Jamie's question lingers in the air.

Anna and Peter look at each other, considering the accusation.

'I'm just saying, if I were you, I would start asking some questions. Not about your laser-beam hands, but about your dad. Who was he? Where did he come from? Did he have magical powers? That sort of stuff.'

'Our mother is dead. It's not like we can ask her.'

'Er, you do live with her sister, you know.'

Jamie has a point. Sally probably knows more than she has ever let on about the twins.

'We could go back to the house?' Brady suggests. 'See if we can find anything?'

'I'm not sure that's a good idea.' Peter shakes his head.

'Why not?' Jamie asks.

'Our mother died in that house,' Anna answers for Peter.

The wind whips around, throwing Anna's golden hair into a spiral. She holds onto her brother, worry etched all over her face.

I look back at Jamie. He's good at pushing buttons, but I can't decide if this is good or bad in Peter's case.

Peter keeps his eyes on him.

Jamie considers him in return and changes tack. 'So, make it rain or something.'

'It's not that simple,' Peter says through gritted teeth. 'It's all connected to my emotions. I have no control over it.'

'And how do you know that?'

Peter is starting to get annoyed by Jamie's pushing, a darkness flaring in him. I recognise the look from before he was hit by lightning.

'You want to know what I think, Peter?' Jamie sneers. 'I think you're lazy. I think you were born different, and through fear and arrogance, you never taught yourself to practice.'

'Jamie.' I push him back away from Peter, desperate to avoid another confrontation. 'This isn't helpful. It's not like practising football.'

'Why not? It's all muscle memory. He is so arrogant, Connie. He thinks it should all come so easy to him... like you did. He clicked his fingers, and you were his. Why should this be any different? He thinks it is what it is because he's never had to work for anything in his life.'

Peter advances on Jamie, his eyes dark. 'Do not, for a second, think you understand what my life has been.'

'Prove me wrong.' Jamie stands his ground.

'You want to see what I can do?'

'I don't think you even know how, Peter.'

Peter cracks his neck in frustration and shrugs Anna off. 'Oh, I'm going to show you.'

The air shifts, and some of the electricity I haven't felt in weeks ripples through my body as Peter stomps over to a large tree that has long lost its leaves. With his hand on its trunk, as he takes up Jamie's challenge before our eyes, the branches burst forth with green buds, lighting up like fairy lights. All too soon, their leaves turn green and begin unfurling.

A low whistle comes from Brady beside me as we watch the leaves crisp then brown before falling to the ground.

Jamie's face glows in awe, the same as the rest of us. 'Pretty. What else you got?'

Peter drops to his knees, pushing his hands into the ground. His focus is on Jamie as the ground at Jamie's feet twists, and the vines of the undergrowth begin to climb Jamie's legs, causing him to stagger back a few steps to escape their grasp.

'Peter, that's enough,' Anna calls out.

'I'm just getting warmed up.' Peter dismisses her, pleased he's unnerved the naysayer.

It dawns on me that Peter's *natures* are constantly at war with each other, his control always on a knife edge, and when it's tipped over the edge, it's difficult—impossible even—for him to stop. It only ends when it's too much.

We are all under his power now, unable to look away.

'You really want to see what I can do?' he asks Jamie before turning to me.

As soon as he takes my hand, the electricity surges through me. He holds my hand up and lets his own hover an inch away while he focuses on my hand for a second. The golden volts start to connect us, the glowing currents swirling down my fingers and up my arms. It is different, though. This drug is wholly Peter. His warmth rolling deep inside me, making me feel the way only he can.

Unfurling desire.

Indescribable pleasure.

It's dangerous.

My breaths grow shallow. The feeling starts to build, and as I look at him, trying to keep my focus, satisfaction is all over his face. He knows what he's doing.

His eyes darken, but I can't take mine off him as he licks his lips, so slowly.

'Peter,' I whisper.

'What does this do to you, Connie?' His eyes fixed on mine, hypnotizing, he commands, 'Tell me.'

But I can't talk. A hint of a moan escapes my lips, and Peter bites his lip. I'm about to go over the edge, so I close my eyes.

'That's enough.' Anna breaks the connection between us. 'You've proven your point, Peter.'

Peter looks from his sister to me, then takes a few shaky steps backward before having to take a seat on the ground.

When I look at my friends, they're all staring at me.

'You already knew? About all of this?' Lorna asks me.

'Some,' I say, trying to catch my breath. 'It's been so gradual. But his powers, they *are* getting stronger. I think Jamie's right… we need answers. If Peter is going to be able to control this, he needs to know where it comes from. There has to be other people like him in the world.'

Peter drops his head into his hands.

'What's wrong with him?' Brady asks.

'It drains him.' Anna puts her hands on her brother's back and rubs in comforting circles. 'Using his powers like that saps his energy.'

'Do you have powers?' Brady continues, and Anna shakes her head. 'The other night, what was that light? It seemed to go into him? And made him act crazy.'

'It was different.' Peter looks up at Brady, starting to come to, then back to Lorna. 'I don't know what that was. Like I've said, the things that have been happening to me recently, I don't understand them.'

'Peter, you fixed me. I'm fine. You did a good thing,' Lorna tries to reassure him.

'Lorna, I think I drained you. I think your energy, it passed into me.' Peter hangs his head in shame.

I sit at his feet, pushing the hair off his face.

'Peter, let us help,' I plead with him.

He glances at Anna and then back to me. 'I'm scared of what we'll find.'

I grasp onto his hand. 'I'm not going anywhere. You're not alone anymore.'

Anna's face is still filled with trepidation, but Peter nods slowly. 'Okay, maybe we should go back to the house. But I'll need to prepare myself for that. It can't be today.'

'Are we done?' Anna asks, her tone making it obvious she doesn't think any of this is a good idea.

I attempt to give her a reassuring look.

'Let's go, Peter.' She helps her weary brother to his feet, and he puts his arm around her as she leads the way.

'I'll drive you both home,' Brady offers when he joins them in going back toward the house, Lorna following.

I hang back. Jamie is already walking toward the fence from where he came.

'Hey,' I call after him.

He stops, one leg already over the fence he perches atop.

'I just wanted to say I'm sorry.'

'What? Because I was right and he is a freak after all?' Jamie laughs, but there isn't any malice in his voice.

'Because I didn't talk to you. There was something between us, and I ignored it. I didn't want to confront it because it meant hurting you. But I hurt you anyway. I'm sorry.'

Jamie's eyebrows rise. 'Thanks,' he says. 'I suppose this is what you're thinking with him.' He motions to Peter who's walking up the hill with the rest of our friends. 'If he keeps ignoring this, someone will get hurt.'

'Mainly him. He's so lost, Jamie. I just want to help.'

He considers my words for a second. 'Have you ever thought maybe some secrets are best kept buried?'

'Do you honestly that?'

'Connie, I don't know what to think. I'm still trying to process that your boyfriend has magic powers.'

I laugh at that.

'One thing I do know is he is drunk on power.'

'Jamie—'

'Please, Connie, that little display on you. That was entirely for my benefit. To show me how much you are his and not mine. I mean, I get it. But he's not in control. I hope you're prepared for the can of worms you're about to open. Do you really think anything you find won't send him into a spiral?'

The thought makes me shudder. 'What would you do?'

'My advice, keep him away from that house. Practice. Practice using his powers so you are ready for what you find.'

'You're going to help, right?' I ask as Jamie jumps down the other side of the fence.

'Oh, I wouldn't miss it.'

CHAPTER 21

Anna

Unsure if it's the alcohol or seeing Peter so exposed, I feel sick. My whole life, my mother drilled into me what would happen to Peter in this world. How he'd be treated, how he would never be accepted and taken away from me.

I close my eyes. It was lies, all lies. I clutch at my chest, trying to contain the sob that's forcing itself to break through. It's important to remember everything she told us was lies.

For seventeen years, the words were drilled into me, *'Your brother is special. The world will not understand. You must stay close. He needs you.'*

I press my eyes against my knees in my now cold bath, trying to stem the sound of my flowing tears as I think back to two nights ago. I try to push down the sickness. All my life has revolved around my brother. It's never mattered who I am.

And now he belongs to everyone else.
I have no idea what to do.
Or who I am without him.

Only moments before Lorna's accident, I'd almost kissed my brother's girlfriend. Both of us out of control in our own way.

My brain whirs.

I was drunk.

My emotions and Peter's can get all confused sometimes. That's all. Except, I know it's more. The feelings have been creeping on for weeks.

Another sob escapes my lips again, and I push my eyes harder into my knees.

The bathroom door bursts open, scaring the hell out of me as Peter slams it behind him and stands looming over me, looking almost as terrible as I do.

'You don't want to go back? To the house.' His expression is stern and unreadable as he takes in my streaked face, my damp hair hanging around my shoulders, limp. 'What's wrong with you?'

I don't know how to explain it. When I open my mouth, another sob escapes. 'Just go, Peter,' I manage to get out, dropping my head to my knees again and shaking into my sobs.

I don't hear him leave, but I can sense him doing something to the side of me. It's not until there's a splash that I look up to see him getting into the bath, settling in at the opposite end from me.

I choke down my tears. 'Peter, no. You need to go. You shouldn't...' I can't talk anymore. 'Y-you can't be here—'

'Anna.' He moves closer, trying to hold my face. 'What is it? Talk to me. What have I done?'

I look into his panicked eyes, so like mine—the only person on the planet whom I can't live without. 'Peter, what people say about us. What they think…' I can't carry on, so I squeeze my eyes shut.

'You mean that idiot?'

He takes my lingering silence as confirmation, and he laughs at me.

'He won't be the only one.' I protest. 'They all think we're freaks. And now they've seen you.'

'Who cares?' He laughs. 'Who cares what they think of us? We know who we are, Anna.'

The panic starts to rise in my chest. I shake off his hands, trying to back away. 'That's just it. I don't.' I bring myself to look at him. 'You were the one person I was sure about, how our relationship works, but now even this…' I motion between the two of us, '… is tainted.'

'You can't be serious?' Peter's eyes turn hard. 'Jamie has no idea what life has been like for us. What we've been through.' His chest heaves.

It breaks my heart.

'It's not normal, Peter. We're *not* normal.'

He grabs my wrists. 'Why are you so obsessed with being normal?'

I can't look away from his serious eyes. 'I want it not to be so confusing. You were right, I think about *everything*. I notice everything. Every glance, every person. I can't—' The tears well up, my words catching in my throat. 'I really like Brady. I should be happy. He makes me feel safe, but then, I don't know. Even with Connie, on New Year's Eve…' I pause but then blurt it out, 'I almost kissed her, Peter.'

Peter looks dead at me for a long minute, and I can't tell if he's angry.

I almost kissed his girlfriend.

He should be furious.

Instead, his lips stretch into a smirk. 'Well, I can't say I blame you. She is delicious.'

His humour is even worse.

'Don't laugh at me.' I lean back to cover my face. 'What's wrong with me?'

'Nothing. You were drunk.'

I heave a big sigh. *At least he isn't mad.* 'It's not only that. It's different for you. Not all of us can feel like we can't be anyone but who we are. Peter, I have no idea who I am, or what I want.'

His face becomes graver as he hears what I'm saying, so I continue, 'It's like this… I'm happy with Brady, but then I notice the way his sister sometimes looks at me. Or a girl at school, and my brain…' I grab my hair in frustration, '… and my stupid brain thinks and thinks. Then I look at you with Connie. You're so lucky. You are so focused on her. It's simple.'

Peter smirks again. 'Simple? I doubt Connie would agree. It's a little more than that. I'm obsessed with her.'

This does not comfort me in any conceivable way.

He finally shrugs. 'So you like girls too. Who cares? Girls, boys, whatever, it's all the same.'

I give him an incredulous look.

'Seriously, you should've kissed her. You'd feel better.'

I open my mouth to protest, but he cuts me off, holding up his hand and leaning forward. 'Do you think it matters to me she's a girl? We were raised away from everything and everyone. Why wouldn't we look at everyone else as people?' He takes my hand again, holding it impossibly tight. 'It's me and you, Anna. And then everyone else.'

He gets up, looming over me again as all the water falls off his sodden clothes, and looks at me for a fraction of a second before getting out of the bath.

'It's not that simple, Peter.'

'Why not? Do what you need to make *you* happy, not everyone else. And definitely not me. You don't need to protect me, Anna,' he says but doesn't give me a chance to answer as he leaves the bathroom.

CHAPTER 22

Peter

The return to our mother's house doesn't happen the day after we all met in the field, or the day after that even. A whole week passes, and it isn't mentioned again. Part of me is grateful.

Connie seems to have a better plan, suggesting I should work on controlling my abilities. To test the boundaries of what I can do.

We return to the field pretty much daily, and I not only show everyone what I can do, but we test my limits.

It doesn't feel natural, and this is hardest on Anna.

I've never understood, in full, how protective Anna is of me until this week, where I've been more exposed than ever. Every limit pushed makes my sister more and more uneasy. Anna has always sat by, a casual observer who watched me grow plants and flowers like it's the most normal thing in the world. However, hearing the others suggesting new things for me to try, watching me perform in the open, it's obvious she doesn't think my practising is a good idea.

The benefit of practising is it helps to curb the built-up tension, which, in turn, serves to balance my emotions. The other side—as much as I hate to admit it—is that Jamie was right. Using the power is like a muscle, and while I am gaining more control, the powers are getting stronger. I can extend my reach farther, taking less and less time to recover. By the end of the week, I don't even need to connect my hands into the earth to exert my energy. Like an invisible force, it now pushes out of my fingertips and into the ground, springing the grass seeds into life.

Despite Anna's trepidation, I feel free for the first time in my life. I've always loved my ability to make things grow. It's useful, of course, but also incredibly beautiful to watch the earth spring to life at my touch, the world around me reacting like I'm a human catalyst. I'd never pushed what I could do beyond plants. My newfound friends are fascinated by it. They want to know more, to see more. And while I love seeing my reach extend farther into the earth below, it's the weather around us that impresses them the most. Granted, it's the harder thing to do. To create something out of nothing is more primitive and primal, something harder to disconnect my emotions from. But I'm getting there.

The more I use my abilities, the more the tectonic plates of who I am shift into place. Everything else before has been a phantom. My dreams have always been a dark, shadowy place, but they're becoming bright and alive. Dreams of water come to me, a great river calling me to it, a nameless place always slightly out of reach. The water whooshes around my ears, but it's not drowning me. It's warm and inviting. Beckoning.

I open my eyes to Anna who's sleeping in bed next to me. I'd been sleeping at Connie's all week, but tonight decided to return to my aunt's late. Anna was already fast asleep in my bed when I got here.

Her eyes flicker open and she smiles, putting her arms around my waist. 'Peter, you're home.'

I pull her into a hug.

'I miss you, brother. Everything is so different.'

'You shouldn't worry so much. I don't have to hide anymore,' I reassure my sister. I can't understand why worry is still etched all over her face. 'Anna, no one is going to take me away.'

Her eyes become glassy as she pulls away from me, and her voice is small, timid. 'I feel like you're already slipping away from me.'

'How can you say that? They've been helping me.'

'Helping you? More like worshipping you. Peter. They're egging you on. They don't understand your powers. They don't know what they might do to you.'

'And you do?' I roll over and retreat with my back against the wall putting some distance between us in the bed, the sharpness in my voice coming through. 'You've always been the one to tell me to keep control. Do you know how hard it is to control something you aren't able to use? It's like water against a dam, Anna. It builds inside of me, waiting to explode, seeping out of me. Infecting everything around me. You told me that, Anna. You were the one who told me I infect everything. I need to practice to control it.'

I clamber over her, getting out of bed and move to open the window, allowing the cold air into the room.

'It doesn't look like control. Yesterday, I watched everyone cheer as you changed a gentle breeze to a windstorm, and you loved it. I know you, Peter. I can see it… you loved feeling powerful and performing for them. Admit it. You're enjoying this, showing them what you can do.'

'Why shouldn't I?' I demand. 'I've been kept a prisoner my whole life. Why shouldn't I enjoy what I am, Anna?'

'Are you joking? A prisoner?' Anna spits at me. 'You're the one who wanted to go back. You would have stayed there forever, Peter. You said we were happy.'

'My eyes are wide open now. It was our mother who was wrong. She did neglect us, Anna.' An alien sensation of tears stings my eyes with my rising voice. 'She lied to us. She told us everything was bad in this world, and she caged us. If she hadn't died, we would have died there too. Thinking *that* was living. All we've been doing all this time is surviving.'

The grim reality of my words hang in the air, and the tears that threaten to spill fall over the edge. I let them. I cry, and for the first time, I let all the hurt fall out of me. The denial I have held onto for so long, for months, that we've lived a lifetime of neglect.

'Peter.' Anna rises from the bed and closes the gap, putting her arms around me. 'Our mother was doing what she thought was best.'

'How can *you* think that?' I ask my sister, my anger now subsided. 'You should be the angriest. You didn't even need the life she decided for us. If it wasn't for what I am, you wouldn't have had to be locked away.'

She brushes the tears from my face, her touch a balm. 'When will you understand that I never want to be parted from you? Please stop pushing me away.' Her own tears come now, sliding down her rosy cheeks. 'You're the only thing that makes sense to me.'

I pull her back into my arms and stand there with her for what seems like an eternity. *How does one have a normal life when they are one of a kind?*

'Peter.' Anna releases me and looks into my eyes in earnest. 'Before you go through with this, and we go back to that house, there's one thing we need to do. We need to talk to Aunt Sally about our mother. We lived in this village for seventeen years, right under Sally's nose. We need to ask her how that happened.'

'You know she won't tell us. We've asked before.'

Anna dips into a low nod but keeps her eyes on me, giving me a knowing look.

'I thought you didn't want me to use my powers?' I chide her.

'No, I don't want you to show off. That's dangerous,' she bites back at me, shoving me a few paces. 'If you're going to use them, it might as well be for a good reason.'

I roll my eyes. Anna has an answer for everything. I've only ever used my influence knowingly twice—to kill the gossip at school and on Connie's mum. It's the one power only Anna and I know about. Therefore, the only one I haven't been practising. It's worth a shot, though. *What have we got to lose?*

We wait for James to go out because for this to work, it has to be Sally on her own. I sit cross-legged on my bed, listening to her moving about in the kitchen below. Ready to centre myself, I close my eyes. As I breathe with the world, I am connected to everything. Rather than imagine my will as a seed, I envision it like the vines in the undergrowth, stretching out, invisible, winding their way through the bowels of the house, reaching Sally. They wrap themselves around her, envelop her, bringing her memories of one thing and one thing alone—her sister.

The hairs on the back of my neck stand on end, and my vision blurs as I turn my hands over, looking at my earth-worn palms. I attempt to get a handle on it, grappling with its invisible force.

I'm stronger, a voice rings in the back of my mind. *Do I even want to know what she's going to tell me?*

Too late now.

My bare feet are padding down the stairs, where I poke my head into the living room and motion for Anna to follow me. Sally's in the kitchen, sitting at the table and staring into her coffee. She looks a million miles away from here. Sad.

'Sally?' I hedge, making my voice soothing.

She doesn't look up from her reverie in her coffee cup.

I take the seat opposite her, Anna moving next to me, keeping as quiet as she can. I slide my fingers over my aunt's hand that rests around her cup, warmed by the liquid inside. Only at my touch does she look up, her eyes swimming in sorrow.

'You know, you children look nothing like your mother.'

Neither do you, I think.

I keep my eyes on her while forcing out a fresh wave, an encouragement for her to tell us more. 'Sally, we want to know more about her. What happened to her?'

Sally starts to tremble when she puts her other hand over mine, words bubbling at her lips as her tears start to fall.

I already know these are words she's never spoken to anyone.

'I want you to know that I loved her so much. And I am so sorry about what happened to you two. She said she was leaving the country. She was paranoid, and I hadn't seen her in so long. I'm not sure if she had even been back to England since our own mum and dad died. She certainly didn't come to either of their funerals. She just turned up after ten years with two babies, saying all kinds of crazy things. And then she was gone. She'd been gone for so long already, I didn't even question it.'

'Sally. This is important.' I keep my words even despite my pounding heart. 'What was she saying? No matter how crazy. Tell us what she said.'

'Peter.' Sally tilts her head, looking from me to Anna. 'Your mum, she was unwell. Really unwell. I can't remember her any other way. And mental illness wasn't talked about the same way back then. Our mum and dad, they were very religious, and they didn't handle it well. The village was even smaller then, it was hard for them. Everyone knew about her. I'm embarrassed to say that our mum and dad were ashamed of her. Living here was so hard for your mum.'

'What did they say was wrong with her?' Anna asks.

'You would call it paranoid schizophrenia these days.' There's a momentary pause as we take in our aunt's words. 'She said she could hear voices, and she had delusions of grandeur. Our parents thought they were helping but only made it worse. The drugs made her incoherent, like a zombie. Eventually, they tried shock therapy but, like everything else, it made her delusions worse.'

I see Anna's hand move across her mouth. My mind races. Our mother often rambled, but our old life seems so long ago, the words she spoke so much a part of us, it's hard for our lifetime of truth to be unravelled as delusions.

'What were the delusions?' I force myself to ask, scared of the answers.

'She was seven years my senior. I used to think they were amazing stories when I was young.' Sally gives an uncertain smile. 'Sometimes she could tell me things that were going to happen before they actually did, or she would know when it would rain, she would always be outside whispering to plants and with spiders in her hair, but as we got older, the stories became more elaborate, more biblical. I think it was partly in rebellion to our strict upbringing.'

I lean forward in my chair, the weight of Anna's eyes on me. 'Tell me, Sally. Specifically.'

Sally's tears are starting to dry on her cheeks. She looks at me, weary. 'Just before she ran away, she became paranoid she was being watched.' Her gaze drops down, and she fiddles with the rim of the coffee cup. 'She said she was to be the mother of the Second Coming. That God would walk on this Earth again and she would be his mother.'

Although I register Anna's sharp inhale next to me, I keep my eyes on my aunt. While the information about our mother is disturbing, it's useless, except to confirm she actually was crazy, and probably one hundred percent of what she'd told us was bullshit. Our mother talked in riddles, but it always had to do with nature, the order of the universe. Never about religion.

'What happened when she came back? Did she say where she'd been? What she'd been doing for the past ten years?' I push.

Sally takes a moment to arrange her thoughts. 'I only saw her once, in that house. I couldn't believe it. We'd always said we wanted to live there when we were kids. But it was just more paranoid stories. She said your dad bought it for her before he died to keep you all safe and hidden. That it was vital to keep you two hidden.'

'Did she say why?'

'No, only that you were in danger, that one of you was special and needed protecting. People would come and try to take you. It was crazy. Even after all that time, nothing had changed, except she had you two. Innocent babies. I urged her to get help, said that I would assist in any way I could, but when I came back, the house was bolted up, and I never heard from her again. I had no idea she would lock you all in. I don't understand how she did it.'

'Where had she been? What happened to our father?'

'I'm not sure, Peter. I think she might have been part of some kind of cult, maybe in India or something. It was hard to make sense of what she said. I'm sorry I can't give you answers. In her own way, I think she wanted to protect you the way our parents couldn't protect her.'

I nod my head. My chest is heavy and tight. This was all for nothing. We're no closer to finding anything. I sit back and breathe deep, looking away from my aunt.

'She did give me a photo. I can try to find it for you, if you want?'

'She gave you a photo?' My interest piques again. 'Of what?'

'Of you when you were babies, being held by your father.'

I look at Anna, whose eyes are bulging.

'Yes, do that,' I say, unable to conceal my excitement.

Without hesitation, Sally moves out of her chair and retreats upstairs.

I run my hands through my hair. A photograph would be progress. Our mother never showed us a picture of our father, or even talked about him much, for that matter. It never seemed important to me who our father was, and now he could be the answer to everything. The single clue. At the same time, what use will a photo actually be? Where can it lead? My head is starting to ache.

'Are you okay?' Anna asks, her tender voice breaking me out of my reverie. She looks worried, her eyes like glassy orbs.

I nod.

'You sure?' she presses, motioning toward the window.

I didn't notice when it started raining, the downpour turning the midday black.

I let out a long breath. 'Am I just an open book from now on?'

'Hardly.'

'I'm frustrated. This conversation is getting us nowhere, Anna. She doesn't know anything useful.'

Anna's eyes widen. 'How can you say that? Peter, our mother was like you, and when she told them, they tortured her.'

I shake my head. *No, that's not it.* 'If she was like me, then why didn't she tell me?'

'Because she was protecting you. She knew firsthand what happens when you are different.'

'No.' I shake my head again, adamant that even though her interpretation of our aunt's story makes sense, it doesn't ring true. 'Anna, our mother was not like me. She wasn't scared for me… she was scared *of* me.'

'I don't think that's true, Peter,' she says, holding my gaze.

The heat of fresh tears stings my eyes. *What is with all these tears? I never cry.* All the threads of my life are fraying, hanging loose, like they're just beyond my grasp. I've always been so certain of who I am. What I am. That I *am* good. Simple. I want to live outside and grow my garden, nothing more. But the last six months weigh on me like a ball of string, and the more it unravels, the more it frays, the less everything makes sense. I don't want to say to Anna that maybe our mother was like me, and scared of me, because that means what we are is an illness, and I am crazy, just like she was.

'What if it's all in my head?' I whisper. 'What if the powers, all of it, is in my head?'

Anna moves her chair closer, taking my hand in her warm fingers. 'Peter, I've seen it. And Connie and the others, we know it's real.'

'What if you're all in my head t-too?' I hear my voice crack and shake as I lower my head into trembling hands.

'Peter, you have to pull yourself together. This is real. What's happening to you *is* real.'

I can't help but notice the tinge of alarm in Anna's voice.

'I feel like I'm half in and half out. One foot in reality, the other not.'

Anna moves her forehead to mine, sharing my anguish. 'Peter, we should stop. Let's stop asking questions, stop testing you. Can't we just stop and be happy again?'

My eyes close. Anna's words make my chest ache. Ache for the life she wants but I can't give her. Ache because, like it or not, she's bound to me because I'm too selfish to let her go.

'I can't.'

I'm not sure if she's heard the words. We stay rooted in our place, joined together, but as I open my eyes and she moves back, I see her tear fall onto her lap.

Aunt Sally's footsteps grow louder as she comes back down the stairs, holding a single Polaroid in her hand.

'I knew I had it somewhere,' she says, not noticing the heavy tension in the air. 'It's been so long since I've looked at it.' With a sad smile, she hands me the picture.

My heart is in my throat as I take in the image. Anna leaning over to see as well. It shows a man holding two tiny babies, one in each arm, smiling at the camera. He's a stranger to me. No reassurances of familiarity come from him. I would never have guessed he was our father. Next to him is our mother, looking young and as slender as Anna, her dark brown hair tied in a long braid slung over one shoulder, her blue eyes vivid and serious.

'That's him.' Anna takes the picture from me to get a closer look, studying it.

We've never seen any baby pictures of ourselves. There were no photographs in our house, or none we ever knew about. It's a shame my father is wearing sunglasses in the picture, but he must be where we get our dark eyes from. His skin is darker than ours, his black hair slicked back along with a thick black moustache.

A fresh tear rolls down Anna's cheek.

There we are, a happy family.

It's then I start to notice the background. We're outside, standing on a balcony overlooking a large river. I take the picture from Anna and slide it on the table back to my aunt. 'Where was this taken?'

Sally leans forward and stares hard at the picture, and her brow furrows. 'It looks like it could be India. That could be the Ganges.'

'We were born in India?' Anna asks before I can.

My aunt is rubbing her forehead. Like the information isn't coming easily.

'Was our father born there? What do you know about him? How did he die?' Anna's questions come rapid fire, each one more demanding than the last.

'I don't know, I don't know!' Sally slams her hands onto the kitchen table. 'I can't remember what she said to me. It feels like a lifetime ago. He died, and she was traumatised. It must have sent her into an episode. She thought you were all in danger, and I let her down. I let you two down. I'm so sorry.' Sally's words descend into sobs.

Anna rushes over, throwing her arms around Sally, and they cry together. Holding onto each other. A misunderstood sister, an unknown father, both strangers in a way, now gone. Forever a mystery to us.

I lean back in my chair, resting my hands behind my head. I know our birth certificates are British, stating we were born in Royal Worcester Hospital, but in the photograph, we can only be weeks old. Our mother must have falsified our birth certificates. But why? My thoughts lead me back to the house. We need to go back and search the house.

'It's why I worry so much about you, Peter.'

I catch the end of what my aunt's saying while I've been lost in thought.

'Huh?'

'In so many ways, you remind me of my sister. How you are, you can be quite like her. I don't want to fail you the same way I did her.'

I take a moment to look at my weary aunt as she stands to turn away from the table. 'I'm nothing like her,' I murmur.

'Of course not.' She smiles, patting my hand. It looks like sleep might take her right where she stands. 'Your mother thought she was a witch.'

Chapter 23

Connie

From my bedroom window, I stare at the belting rain battering my beloved apple tree. I glance back at the little clock on my nightstand to see it's only three p.m. and pretty much black outside. Easing open the window, the air smells like Peter. Something's wrong.

After Jamie's words of warning, I couldn't help thinking it was too soon to reintroduce Peter to the house where his mother died. His trauma would be exposed like a raw nerve, which for someone like Peter, is a terrible idea. So, instead, I didn't bring it up again. Rather, focused on him practising his powers, finding balance. Control.

The only problem with Peter is it's hard to tell if he has control or not. It can go from one extreme to the other in a blink, but he's becoming more willing to exercise his abilities in front of us. I have to admit, it's quite something to behold. He'd never been taught to practice before, to push his boundaries, to revel in what he is. It's hard not to be impressed. The elements around him react—flowers bloom under his fingertips, and the breeze dances with the sway of his head. It's strange, the unexplainable abilities right before my eyes, they somehow become acceptable. All of us look on in amazement at what we're seeing.

'Connie.'

His voice makes me jump a mile. I hadn't heard my door open over the sound of the rain.

'Jesus,' I squeal, clutching my fist to my heart. 'What are you doing here?'

Jamie's drenched form hovers in my doorway. 'Your mum was calling for a while. In the end, she just sent me up.'

Leaning against the window frame, I beckon him in and watch him cautiously enter my room.

Jamie hasn't been in my room since we were kids. He looks around, his nerves clear, as I wait for him to speak. Going over to the world map, he studies the pins. Almost absentmindedly, he flicks his dripping hair, which has grown a little long, out of his eyes before moving to my desk, stopping to look at the picture of Peter and me that I've stuck into the corner of my laptop screen. He looks at me hard before going back to the picture.

'He's getting stronger,' he says, matter-of-fact, his eyes still on the image before him.

I don't respond. Unsure what he wants.

He moves on, perusing my bookshelves, hands in his pockets. 'How's things?' he continues, not looking at me, per se. 'We never catch up anymore. Are we okay?' Jamie stops in front of me, a melancholy expression in place.

'Of course.'

'Connie, I wanted to say that I'm sorry too. About how I handled everything. I took you for granted. I thought you would always be there, and then I was mad at you when you weren't. I liked you, I wanted to be with you, and I should've told you that before they came along.'

I hold my breath.

'So that's what I'm here to tell you. I still want that, Connie. I still want to be with you.'

'Jamie, I—' I start, my pulse picking up. There's a tiny part of me stirring at his offer. Spending time with him again in recent days, his helping Peter—something about Jamie is comforting, familiar, and simple. But it can't compete.

'I know.' He cuts me off. 'Not now. But I'll wait, and I want you to know I will be there for you. After.'

'After?'

'Just… after.' He shrugs. 'I know I can make you happy. Not now. But Peter's getting stronger, and he won't stay here. At some point, he'll leave to go and find out more about who he is, what he is, and we'll all be left behind. Life will go back to normal. We can go back to normal.'

Anger flares through me. *There he goes assuming he knows what I want.*

I grit my teeth. 'And what makes you think I want a normal life?'

Jamie takes a few steps back from me, acting like I'm the one being impossible. 'Because that's what people want. Everyone wants a normal life, to have stability and someone to rely on.'

Even though I can see he's being genuine, his assumption that I feel the same is still beyond annoying.

'People think they want the excitement. *You* might think you want that, that all the uncertainty he brings is exciting and an adventure, but eventually, Connie, it will leave you tired. You'll be tired of trying to keep up, tired of being in someone's shadow, tired of it always being about him. What I'm saying is… I will be here. I'll wait for you.' He takes a hesitant step forward. 'You should be with someone who puts you at the centre. I know I haven't done that in the past, but I promise I will do that from now on. I'll be here for you, Connie, always. I'm yours.'

For a moment, I stand here with the wind knocked out of me. I've never given much thought to what the future might hold for Peter and me. Everything about Peter is so much in the moment. However, in *this* moment, time stands still. My eyes can't move from Jamie's. I've never seen them so blue, looking into mine so deep, like this is the first time he's ever truly seen me.

He caresses the side of my face, full of hesitation. 'You're so beautiful, Connie.'

My chest hurts, and in the next moment, I hate myself. Hate myself for what I'm about to say. 'You should go,' I whisper.

He's so close the heat of his breath warms my cheek, and I watch the walls go back up behind those blue eyes. The disdain he wears like a mask is back as he turns from me.

I want to reach out to him, ask him to stay, tell him he's my friend and I love him, even if it's not in the way he wants me to. But that's not fair, not right now.

I follow him down the stairs in silence.

Outside, the rain has become torrential, and it's only as we near the hallway I hear the banging on the front door.

Jamie hears it too, his voice full of confusion as he asks me, 'Do you hear that?'

'Yes. I hear it.' I push past him to open the front door.

Peter is dripping on my porch, the rainstorm raging behind him in a sea of inky blackness. He's only in a black T-shirt, which almost looks washed away by the rain, and his hair hangs down in his face. Both hands lean against the door frame. His breath ragged.

'Peter.' My voice rings with alarm, but my feet stay rooted to where they are.

Jamie doesn't move either, staring at Peter, who looks like a wild thing.

He straightens, somehow making himself look even taller than before. His breathing heavy, he takes one step toward me, then another. Registering his footprints, I notice he is barefoot. He drops to one knee, then the other, in front of me. I push his hair from his face, taking in his big brown eyes, so dark now they're almost black.

'I needed to see you.' His voice is still breathless. He must have run over here in the storm. Peter snakes his arms around my waist, resting his head on my stomach. Taking in a deep breath, he steadies his breathing while I cradle his head to me.

Remembering Jamie's there, I try to give him an apologetic expression. In return, he gives me a look that's impossible to read.

'I'm going to go,' he says with a hint of sarcasm.

Peter releases me and gets to his feet, then looks at Jamie like he's appeared out of thin air. 'What are you doing here?'

'I was just leaving.' Jamie holds his hands up innocently.

'Peter, what happened?' I pull on his hand to bring his attention back toward me.

'The house. It's time to go back,' he says simply.

Of course, now Jamie doesn't appear so eager to leave.

'We talked to Sally. She gave us this.' Peter pulls a crumpled Polaroid from his pocket and hands it to me.

Jamie comes closer to look.

'This is our father. That's the Ganges River in the background, I know it.'

'And you think there might be something that leads you back to him at your house?' Jamie asks.

Peter gives a small nod.

'When do you want to go?' Jamie asks resolutely, and I'm surprised he's behind the idea.

'Tomorrow.' He turns back to me. 'Can I stay here? I need you tonight.'

'Sure,' I say.

Peter is here most nights now, but Jamie doesn't know that. He doesn't say another word to Jamie before heading up the stairs. As he nears the top, I catch him pulling his sodden T-shirt up over his head. The sight of Peter taking his clothes off sends a thrill through me, although this time it's matched with annoyance too. I know the little show is for Jamie's benefit.

'I guess I'll see you tomorrow,' Jamie says stiffly, making his exit.

I follow Peter's footsteps back up the stairs to my bedroom. He's lying on my bed, stretched out and inviting. Now I'm a bit peeved with him for trying to make Jamie jealous *and* for making my bed all soggy.

'I should ask my mum if you can stay,' I say curtly.

'She won't mind.' Peter is running his hands through his hair, staring at the ceiling. The weight of his thoughts hang heavy around him. 'Come here. I need to tell you something.'

I perch on my bed next to him. 'So, tell me.'

'My aunt said my mother was a paranoid schizophrenic. That their parents had her committed.

They even used electroshock therapy on her when she was younger.' His dead eyes stare at my ceiling.

'Jesus. That's awful.'

'She thinks I'm like her, Connie. Our mother, when she was old enough, she ran away. Didn't come back until she had us.'

'That's terrible.' I put my hand on his chest.

'Sally said she claimed to be a witch,' he rushes out, eyes turning to watch my reaction.

'A witch? Could that be possible? Is that what you are?'

He looks at me thoughtfully. 'What? A witch or a schizophrenic? I don't know, maybe both.'

'Peter.' I move in closer, noticing he smells like the rain. 'Why would you say that? We know what you can do.'

'It shouldn't be real, though, should it? Magic or whatever this is that I have… what my mother had.'

I swirl my hands up his chest, and it makes him breathe deep.

'If my very existence is impossible, does that mean I'm not real?'

'Maybe you're a figment of my imagination,' I tease.

He catches my arms and pulls me closer, his deep brown eyes serious. 'Whatever happens next, don't let me get lost, okay?'

How can someone be so powerful and so vulnerable at the same time?

I dance my fingers down his chest. Some remnants of electricity crackles between us. I nod in agreement, but in truth, I have no idea what I'm promising. How will I know how to pull him back from the edge? I know in my core I will always try, and comprehend that Jamie's wrong. Peter won't leave me behind because I'll follow him anywhere.

His breath hitches as my hands make their way downward. He closes his eyes, the pleasure washing over him. The thrill of commanding this way makes its way through my body, starting in my stomach. It's an indescribable sensation that floods over me and rolls in waves. His features are now relaxed as he drags his teeth across his bottom lip.

'I wish I could feel like this always.' His voice is low and gravelly, his dark eyes open now, and hungry. 'Make me forget, Connie. Make me forget about all of this.'

I kiss him, long and slow. And I make him forget.

For one night, it's forgotten.

The next morning is still dull and drizzly when I wake up, my head on Peter's warm chest. I can sense he's already a million miles away.

It's not long until Brady arrives with Anna and Lorna. Anna brings Peter fresh clothes and shoes to wear. Anna looks pale. She doesn't say a word, Brady every now and then giving her an uneasy look. The drizzle today seems to have done the opposite to the deafening noise of the turbulent rain yesterday. The world has turned mute. Lifeless.

'Where's Jamie?' I ask as we sit in quiet contemplation in my front room while Peter ties his shoelaces. I try to make my voice as bright as I can.

'I'm not sure.' Brady looks relieved someone has broken the silence. 'He wasn't there when I went to pick him up this morning. His mum didn't know where he was.'

My stomach sinks. I want to ask more, and wonder if he got home okay last night. He must have, his mum would have called around if she'd been worried. I try not to think about how I've hurt him. Again.

Peter stands, looking glorious in his black jumper, and takes a deep breath. 'We might as well walk. It's not far. I know the way through the woods, and it takes us to the back of the house. It's probably the easiest way in and won't attract any attention.'

'Not many people even drive out that far,' Lorna comments.

'Regardless, it's best to not take any chances of being caught breaking into our old house,' Peter reaffirms. He looks at Anna.

I haven't seen her shake so hard since the first day of school.

Lorna looks from Peter to Anna and back again, and it's not hard for any of us to read the anxiety in both of them.

'Are you sure you want to do this? We don't know if there is anything there. It could just open old wounds,' Lorna presses.

Peter holds his sister's gaze. 'We need to go back. We're different people now from the ones who left that place.'

No one else makes any protests. We're going to the house—to the place of Peter and Anna's trauma. The last time they stepped foot in that building, they'd run from their mother's rotting corpse.

It occurs to me I've never been in a house where I know someone died. Instinct draws my attention to Anna, who's usually so vibrant and chatty. I've not given much thought to how she's handling this. How she feels about going back.

As we walk toward the house, she stays by Peter's side, his arm wrapped around her shoulder while the distance disappears beneath our feet. No one speaks.

Twins, two halves of one whole, Peter had told me once. He can't survive without her close, his words. She's been caught in Peter's orbit her whole life. The way I am now.

Lorna and Brady fall into step on either side of me.

'Did we miss something? Why today?' Brady asks.

'They spoke to their aunt, but she couldn't tell them much.' I try to choose my words carefully. 'Some things we already thought. Others, Sally confirmed. Their mother had mental health problems, and she kind of lost it when their dad died. She thinks the twins were born in India, where their dad was from.'

'They don't look very Indian to me,' Lorna says.

I shrug. 'She doesn't know anything for certain. Their mother wasn't exactly a reliable witness. Their aunt believes she was in a cult. Peter thinks if there are any leads back to India, we'll find them at the house. Sally said their mum claimed she was a witch.'

'A witch?' Brady says incredulously, pushing some sodden branches out of his way. 'But, witches aren't real.'

'As opposed to boys who can channel lightning and heal broken bones,' Lorna retorts.

'So that's it?' Brady looks to me for confirmation. 'He's a witch?'

I sigh. 'Look, I don't know, and he doesn't know. It's the only lead we have. I suppose we have to think everything is a possibility.'

'Do you realise how weird our lives have become?' Brady says, shaking his head.

The walk seems shorter than before, and before I know it, the house is in view. This is where it all started. For Peter, for Anna, even for me. The house looks like a ghostly shell in the mist and rain, decaying and hanging at the seams. We join Peter and Anna, who stand at the edge of where the woods meet the garden, entranced by their dilapidated home. We stand in a row, like warriors preparing for battle.

I push my fingers through Peter's and give a reassuring squeeze.

He takes me in, fixing his determined look. Keeping hold of my hand, he leads me forward, breaking the invisible barrier we've all been observing.

The others dutifully follow.

The back porch creaks under our weight. With all the windows boarded, one would think the house has been empty for a lot longer than under a year, but I suppose that's what their mother wanted—for the world to think it was abandoned.

Peter releases my hand and starts to pull a board from the window at the back door. Without saying a word, Brady joins him. It doesn't take long for the two of them to pry it from the door frame, revealing the old glass. Despite knowing this is Peter's house, what we're doing feels illegal, and I go out of body, like I'm watching from a distance as we watch him find a rock to break the glass with. Peter pauses to glance at us, rock in hand, before he propels it through the window. The shattering of the glass is loud enough to be heard for miles, but of course, it's only an illusion, my mind playing tricks on me. On instinct, I scan around, searching for those who will discover us. No one's here.

Peter puts his hand through the hole in the broken glass and opens the back door, which I can see leads into the kitchen. He peers into the tree line and then looks at Anna.

'Do you want to wait out here?' he asks. The question hangs in the air as she seems to consider the option.

'I'm with you,' she says, walking past him and into the house.

He follows her in, and I do the same, flanked by Brady and Lorna. It's like we've stepped back in time. The kitchen is huge, the pantry door open with thick dust layering the shelves. We separate, searching. Lorna runs her fingers over the pages of an old cookbook lying on the table. The book, like everything else here, is frozen in time. Tin mugs still sit on the table, the ditsy floral tablecloth faded to almost nothing. There are plates in the glass cupboards.

Anna rubs the fabric between her thumb and forefinger, returning her gaze to her brother, who's hovering by the door. 'What now?' she asks him.

Peter steps forward into the room, running his hand along the length of the table and closing his eyes. He doesn't say anything. Instead, he keeps on walking out into the hallway. We all follow. Peter extends his arms on either side, running his fingers against the walls of his own home. He continues down the hall one measured step at a time, leaving his arms stretched slightly behind him, his fingertips trailing the walls while drinking in the ghosts of his past. Each footstep creaks the wooden floor.

The hallway is long. Lorna ducks the spiderwebs, although Peter's form all but clears a path for us. Only when the hallway meets the grand front hall does he stop, open his eyes, and drop his right arm. Letting his left swing on the banister of the stairs, in one poetic movement, he spins to face the ascent.

Anna shoots her hand out, stopping him and making the rest of us jump a mile. She grabs the front of his coat, pulling him toward her. 'You cannot be serious,' she hisses at him.

'I need to see it,' he says, removing her hand and continuing on up the stairs.

'Peter, we're here to look for links to our father, not for you to confront your demons,' Anna declares as she follows him, the sound of his footsteps quickening.

'You don't have to come, Anna.'

Of course, Anna is following, and so am I.

We all join Peter, who's standing in a long landing with at least five doors leading off it. This house must have been grandiose at some time. His back is against the wall as he stares down one of the doors like it's an unsolvable puzzle.

'Well?' Anna says, her hands on her hips. 'Is this what you came here for? To torture yourself?'

Peter closes his eyes and runs his hands through his hair. His hands are visibly shaking.

'We should get this room over with. It'll be the hardest. After that, everything will be easy. Plus, if our mother hid anything, it'll be in here,' he reasons with her.

Anna shifts uncomfortably from one foot to the other, weighing up whether his reasoning offsets her desire not to go in. Her face is always like an open book. In the end, she rolls her eyes and motions for him to go right ahead if that's what he wants to do.

He grabs the handle, twists it, and the door swings open, like our own personal ghost story, to reveal the bedroom. A four-poster covered in a cacophony of spiderwebs looks quite beautiful and ethereal, facing the large double window. Anna enters first and, entranced, goes over to the dressing table in the corner. I follow her in, and she gives me a tentative smile as she picks up a necklace that was left on the top.

'It doesn't feel like I thought it would,' she confides. 'It's quite nice to see her things still here.'

'You should keep it,' I encourage, motioning toward the necklace she's holding.

The others move into the room cautiously, a sense of imposition making us reluctant to move things.

'So what are we looking for?' Lorna asks.

Anna looks around. 'Letters, I guess. Documents, photos, anything with an address or a name.'

Peter moves into the room last, taking three heavy strides and sitting on the bed. A huge plume of dust floats up into the air.

The stench it releases is incredible, sticking in my throat the same way the revolting thought that this is where his mother's body decayed sticks in my mind. The particles float through the air, and I cover my nose and mouth with my arm.

'Do you think if I found her sooner, I could have saved her?' Peter says out loud, looking at his sister, although I'm not sure he wants an answer.

Unbothered by the dust floating like a cloud in the room, Anna steps in front of her brother, setting her hand on her hip. 'So, you *are* here to torture yourself.'

'What did they do with her body?' Peter asks, his voice barely a whisper.

'Jesus, Peter,' is all Anna can reply.

His next breath comes out ragged, and I can almost see him exhale the dust, but then I hear Brady. One hand suddenly at his chest, his breathing shallow, his other hand steadies himself on a nearby bookshelf. In two beats, Lorna does the same, clutching her chest and unable to control her breath.

'Lor, what's happening?' I rush over to her.

'Can't. Breathe,' she manages to get out between ragged gasps of air.

The air around me starts to blow like a window has been opened, but the giant window in the middle of the room is still closed. It looks like Lorna is having a panic attack. I look over to Anna, who's still watching Peter, the wind whipping the hair around her and making her look otherworldly as she stands over him.

'Peter, what are you doing?' she challenges.

Peter's breathing matches Lorna and Brady's, but it's not the dust cloud affecting them.

Understanding comes—they're sharing Peter's panic attack.

I rush to his side. The wind is stronger around him, and I can't figure out where it's coming from. I take his hand, forcing him to look at me. 'Peter. Peter, take a deep breath, okay? Breathe with me.' I start taking deep breaths, nodding for him to follow suit. Deep breath in through my nose, count of three, and then out through my mouth, count of three. 'Stay with me,' I urge. 'Come back to me.'

I keep my attention on him, and soon, his breath starts to steady as the wind dies down, the room becoming peaceful again and the dust settling around us. Until the only sound is Peter's steady breaths, followed by Brady and Lorna's. He's calm again when he places his hand on the side of my face, stunning me with his brilliant smile. Of course, I smile back.

'We should go,' Brady says from behind me.

We haven't found what we are looking for, though. I'm about to say we should keep searching, that everything is okay now, when I hear a new sound—the *click, click, click* of shoes on wood.

Someone's downstairs. Peter is on his feet, moving himself to be a barrier between Anna, me, and the open door.

The footsteps come closer, slow and steady, with no sense of urgency. At first, I think it might be Jamie, but his trainers wouldn't *click* on the parquet floors. The stairs creak under the weight of our unknown guest moving up them and in our direction. Peter's stance in front of us has moved into a protective position. Crouched, like a predator.

My heart hammers in my chest as the gait comes closer to the room and we remain frozen in place. I couldn't move my feet if I wanted to.

Tan leather boots come into view of the doorway, standing out against his dark outfit, jet-black hair slicked back, with eyes as black as coals as he takes in each of us.

The man from the Polaroid.

CHAPTER 24

Peter

As the worn pattern of the snakeskin leather boot comes into view, I already know who it's going to be. *Our father*. The only difference from the photograph is that I can now see his eyes. Even from this distance, I see their darkness. They resemble obsidian. Cold like stone. It takes me a full second to see how wrong this is. In reality, he looks like that picture could have been taken yesterday. No clear evidence of the seventeen years that have passed ageing him at all. I straighten up out of my stance, protecting Anna and the others.

Danger.

Every fibre in my body screams danger about this man. I felt it from the moment his first footstep echoed through the house. *Run, Peter,* my instincts tell me. But I don't. I remain watching, waiting. Everyone's expecting me to do or say something.

He looks from me to Anna, not acknowledging the others. His face stretches into a broad grin, which sends a chill down my spine when he holds his arms out wide, as if expecting us to embrace him.

'Children.' His accent is thick and unfamiliar. 'I'm so glad to have found you. It's been so many years, too many. I am Arjun, your father.'

His words hang in the air, unable to shift themselves from the tension here. His eyes shift from Anna back to me, something penetrating in his gaze. A gut instinct makes me want to be as far away as possible from him. I take a step backward to fall in line with Connie and Anna. His lips twitch and, for some reason, I know I've made a mistake.

'You don't seem surprised to see me,' he says, his broad smile beginning to fade. 'And yet, you do not seem happy about my being here.'

'You're supposed to be dead,' I say, glad my voice sounds more confident than my shaking hands reveal.

'Yes, yes, a horrible mistake. Your mother did truly believe I had perished. And she fled before I had the chance to find her, a mistake that kept my children from me all these years. She did an outstanding job of hiding you all.'

'How did you find us?' Anna asks.

'Surely you know the spell died when she did?'

My heart stops.

Everyone's eyes turn to me.

I wish they didn't.

His lips twitch again.

'Spell?' I ask, desperate not to know.

He smiles wider. 'Yes, that's how she has kept you hidden. She really was the most powerful witch I had ever met. It all came so naturally to her.' He talks as if the statement is the most normal thing in the world, like we should be flattered.

'I think you're mistaken. Our mother wasn't a witch. I think you should leave,' I say. Unfortunately, my self-control isn't good enough to stop the influence from sweeping out of me.

Suddenly, I don't want answers to any of it. I'm not interested in the mystery of the man standing in front of me. I just want him to leave. I want the others to be safe.

All traces of his glee vanish, his footfalls paced and deliberate as he approaches me. The way his black eyes stare into me—through me—chills me to the core. Terror passes through my body, vibrating my bones. *I am terrified of this man.*

His hands clasp me hard on the shoulders. 'It's you, isn't it?' His eyes are flat, no depth, just cold and hard. 'Did she tell you what you are? What you really are?'

'I don't know what you're talking about.' My voice is weak and unconvincing. The pressure from his hands hurts. I turn away from the emptiness of his eyes.

'Stop,' Anna demands, enduring my pain. 'We really don't know anything. Our mother told us nothing.'

Arjun releases me from his grasp and runs his hands through his already slicked-back hair. Taking a minute to think, he says, 'Children, you must have questions. That is why you are here, is it not? And I have answers. Why don't we start there?' His smile is back. 'Let's move from this room. We have a lot to talk about.'

Anna follows him out of the room and down the corridor, Brady trailing, his hand linked to Lorna. Connie falls in beside me.

'Peter, you have to keep control around him. I don't think it's a good idea for him to know what you can do,' she whispers.

'It's too late, Connie. He already knows,' I whisper back, taking her hand and leading her downstairs to join the others.

They're already in the sitting room, a room we barely used even when we did live here. The old moth-eaten sofas are covered with sheets coloured with years' worth of dust and dirt. Brady takes a corner of a sheet and, throwing it off the sofa, sends a plume of dust into the room. Lorna and Anna devolve into a coughing fit, waving the air in front of them. I stand in the doorway with Connie, watching the dust and dirt fill the room.

'I'll open a window,' Brady chokes out.

'Allow me,' Arjun says. Pursing his lips, he gently blows the dust cloud into nothing.

'Are you a witch?' Anna asks, her look of caution turning to one of wonder at Arjun.

'Yes.' He smirks at her.

'How do you still look young?' she asks.

'Being the high priest of a coven has its advantages. There are certain magics that can extend a life. Give the illusion of youth. Did your mother not practice at all around you?'

Anna shakes her head.

Arjun gives a nod of understanding, looking a little troubled.

'What happened?' Against my better judgment, the words are already leaving my mouth. 'Why did she run?'

He takes a long pause, looking around the room at all the eyes on him before speaking, 'The answer to that is complicated. Especially if you know as little as you say you do. But when you were born, it was a true gift to the coven.' He sets his eyes on me. 'A gift of unlimited potential. Before that gift could be realised, there was a fire in our house. Your mother was able to get you two out while I was stuck inside. She always did have the instinct of flight. She would've seen the attack on the house as an attack on the two of you and the power you pose to the coven. I imagine she thought with me dead, the others would come, potentially try to take you both. So she fled.'

'Others?' I can't stop myself. 'Was it another coven? Why would anyone have done that?'

'I doubt she stayed around long enough to find out. Your mother always tended to be paranoid. Which was natural, given what happened to her when she was younger. She was half driven mad when I met her. She wouldn't have trusted anyone, not even her own coven.'

'Why would her own coven turn on her?' I'm squeezing Connie's hand too hard.

'Fear.' Arjun's obsidian eyes gleam. 'You have to understand, the circumstances of your conception, of your birth, it was something that had not been successful in centuries. It took me many years to acquire the ancient ritual, even longer to find a witch powerful enough to be a host. Your mother was a rare powerful creature. I truly did mourn when I felt her passing. When she found out that she was pregnant with twins, we knew the ritual had worked. It's always twins, you see. It has to be twins. You were so young back then, we didn't know which it would be. But I can see it's you, Peter, isn't it? I can feel it, all that power inside you.'

Arjun's excitement is barely containable. His whole body seems to vibrate.

A lump lodges in my throat, my mouth going dry. Connie's hand grips mine tight in spite of me crushing her fingers. My body shakes. I try to keep it all inside, try not to react. Fight not to make the world react to me, to the power now radiating from Arjun, acting like a catalyst to me. Like Lorna's life force before, giving me energy. I don't want him to say the words. I don't want to know what comes next.

The *crack* of the nearest windowpane causes a shriek from Lorna, and everyone turns to look at the source of the noise. Arjun's eyes stay on mine, however, and I know I've already lost. I can't control the energy he's giving off. The plants—which have been climbing up the side of the house—twist and snake through the windows, covering the walls, finding their way to me.

Arjun's smile is wide, but the black fathomless holes of his eyes terrify me. The energy he has obviously been feeding me begins to ebb away, and with it, my own pours out of me. I stumble into Connie. Everything happens so fast. All that practice and I'm undone in an instant.

Connie struggles to steady me. 'Peter! Peter, fight it. You have to control it,' she pleads as green ivy snakes up her leg.

I slow my breathing, the way she'd shown me upstairs, until the room returns to calm. The vines and leaves slow their progress, then stop. Everyone's on their feet, shock and horror twisting their faces.

'It's okay,' I say to myself as much as the group, extending my hand for them to keep their distance. 'I'm okay. I have it under control now.' My ragged breath returns to normal, and I turn to Arjun, who looks elated as the plants rustle again.

'Chlorokinesis.' Arjun's excitement is palpable. 'Wonderful. Just wonderful, Peter.'

'So that's what I am, then? I'm like you? I'm a witch.'

'My boy…' Arjun shakes his head with an amused grin, '… you are a god.'

The silence drags on.

And on.

The smile fixed to Arjun's face as he holds my stare.

I silently curse my mother for leaving me so underprepared. I have no way to fight this man, no mastery over my abilities. He holds all the cards, and I can't shake the notion that none of his motives are good.

He is *not* good.

The others look from me to Arjun, then back to me again. It comes as a mild surprise that the first sound anyone makes is laughter.

Even Arjun turns to Brady, whose quiet sniggers are descending into fits of laughter. He clasps his mouth, trying to hold it in, but that makes it worse.

Lorna, who's sitting next to him, looks at me like I'm the one causing it. This time, it works the other way around. His laughter is infectious, and I start to laugh too.

'What's so damn funny?' Anna demands, yanking on his arm.

Brady tries to steady himself, catching his breath. 'I have never heard anything so ridiculous. This last hour, we've talked about witches, covens, and high priests. And now you're telling me my girlfriend's brother is a god. I can't...' He laughs maniacally. 'I can't cope.' Brady then descends into another hysterical fit of raucous laughter.

I join him, leaning my free hand against the door frame. He's right, it is ridiculous, even if it's true. Despite my mistrust of Arjun, I know he isn't lying. It's the answer to Connie's question, the big question.

What am I?

I am a god.

And that is the craziest, funniest thing I have ever heard.

Besides, the laughter is worth it to wipe the smug look off Arjun's face. My influence may not work on him, but it will work on the others.

'You are a funny man, Arjun,' I say between fits, the others soon joining me and we all turn to Arjun to laugh right in his stupid face. It makes me feel better about being so ill-prepared to deal with him.

'Enough,' Arjun demands with a wave of his hand.

Everyone stops.

Ah, he has influence too. Except, his doesn't work on me, as mine doesn't on him. His face flickers with something resembling frustration.

'So, you do know more than you let on. A whisper from you can change minds, sway emotions, bind someone to you.' His eyes flicker to Connie, who still has a tight grip on my hand.

'Let's just say I'm a fast learner.'

'I bet you are.' His dark eyes sparkle at the thought.

'You said there was a ritual involved,' Anna speaks, her curiosity not satisfied. 'What does that mean? Did it turn one of us from a regular baby into a god?'

Again, Arjun takes his time with his words. 'No, one cannot be turned into a god. Gods are born the same as man, but the magic is complex and ancient, not one that can be easily harnessed in these modern times. Man has new gods… money, technology, fame. I've heard of new gods being born. Rarely, but it has happened. They have been weak and fade all too quick, sadly. Time will tell what fate has in store for you, Peter.'

'What does that mean for Anna? Is she a god too?' Brady asks.

Arjun turns back on me. 'No, although it's Anna who made Peter's existence possible. It is she who bound him to this plane. She's totally human, with a human life. Like me. But Peter… Peter is born of the eternal. The infinite chaos, his connection to the fabric of the cosmos comes from this, as all gods' abilities do.'

'What does that even mean?' Connie asks from beside me, her beautiful emerald eyes locked onto Arjun.

'It means, my dear, that old age will not find him. He is eternal. He could walk this Earth for millennia.'

The pit in my stomach sinks even deeper. The one thing I truly fear is a fate I'm destined to—to be alone. One day, I will lose Connie. One day, I will lose the one thing I cannot live without, my sister. I look at her, aching, like that moment could be now for the pain in my chest.

'That doesn't mean there aren't ways to kill him,' Arjun continues. 'But many of the old ways are lost.'

'Why?' I ask through gritted teeth. 'Why would you want to create a new god? Why would you want to give anyone a fate where they're doomed to be alone?'

'My dear son, for the good of the coven. I can teach you so much, how to use those wonderful powers of yours. I can help you change the world. A god's powers are a gift from nature. I can see that yours help you to give life to the earth. Beautiful, Peter. You're what this metal-loving world needs. I can help you take this world back. Restore it to a paradise.'

'And what exactly does the coven get out of this?' Connie quizzes as my head swims with all the knowledge—too much to take in all at once.

'Witches are children of nature. Why wouldn't we want to help Peter reclaim the Earth?'

'You didn't know that's what he could do until you saw it,' Lorna points out.

Arjun acknowledges her for the first time.

'So you couldn't have known that when you made him. Why make him, then?'

Arjun mulls it over in his head. 'True.' His neck coils like a snake. 'The nature of his gift was unknown to us at the time. All I had to go on were the stories that came before. It was a gamble. A gamble that paid dividends. The gift of Chlorokinesis is powerful and rare.' He smiles.

'You see, a witch studies the ways of nature, the stars, the universe even. Our power comes from the ability to harness such understanding. We can tap into it but not the source. Our spells are limited. As I said, they die with us. Which means that like our human lives, they are temporary. But for a god, cast free of a mortal coil, with the right words to the right people, empires can be built, religions sweep across the lands. A god's reach can be limitless. Your power at this moment, Peter, it's unstable. I can help. I can guide you.'

Arjun's words are fading, getting farther and farther away, harder to take in as I blink a few times, trying to clear the fog in my mind.

The whole of my life spent inside the four walls of this house, I never wanted anything else. I hate crowds. I hate being alone. I like to see the pink of a strawberry ripen before my eyes. I like the warmth of the morning sun on my face.

I take a step back. *I do* not *want this.*

'I'm not human?' I didn't plan on the words coming out. I don't know why it's important to me.

I take another step back, taking Connie with me. I can't let go. Her eyes are soft. My back hits the opposite wall. The rising panic in my face must be showing since I see Anna get to her feet.

'No, Peter. You are not.' Arjun steps forward to place a claiming hand on Anna's shoulder.

Concern radiates off everyone, probably expecting me to lose my grip on my shaky control.

It's a lot to take in.

I am a god.

I'm not human.

I cannot die.

My gaze drops to Connie. Connie, who *will* die. How do I even begin to comprehend that long after she's gone, I will remain? I can't put into words how much this terrifies me, to be so alone. Without thinking, I start walking, leading her out of the house.

Anna calls after me to stop, but Arjun stops her. 'Let him go. He needs some time.'

The winter air cools and restores some of my calm, but I don't stop until we're in the tree line. Once we're in the shelter of the trees, I release Connie's hand and flop down onto the moist ground. I rub my eyes hard, trying to arrange my thoughts.

Connie lingers on her feet, standing above me. 'He could be making it all up.' She stoops to rub the top of my head.

I love how she touches me, so I take a second to focus on nothing else. 'He's not, though, is he? He came here because he wants my power. He's not here to lie about what I am. I'm not human, Connie, and I'm not going to die. That's not natural. My mother taught me death is the most natural thing, that it's a circle. Life isn't our own. It's all borrowed from the universe, and it is beautiful. A beautiful process. She made me believe life is even more beautiful for its fragility. She taught me this, knowing I wouldn't die.' The tears prick my eyes. 'How could she do that to me? Like I'm some sort of experiment. Inhuman. Alone.'

'Peter.' Connie crouches in front of me, placing her hand over my heart. 'How can that be? I can feel your heart beating. I've seen you bleed. I've felt your body next to mine. You're human in all the ways it counts.

Maybe that's why your mother hid you for all this time, to teach you that you can still be human. Maybe she wanted to protect you from becoming this grand creature that man wants you to be. What he's saying… it's just words. You are not alone. I will follow you anywhere, *anywhere*, on this Earth.'

I trace the edge of her delicate face. 'You said you love me.'

'I do.'

'You know, no one ever said those words to me before you. Not my mother, nor my sister.' I take her face in both hands, moving onto my knees, so I'm level with her. 'I love you, Connie. I love you, and that *is* real.'

I rest my hand over hers, close my eyes, and embrace the beat of my heart. I'm flesh and blood like her. Her arms enfold me, her body always welcome against mine. It's solid, real, and reassuring. I let it take me, tilting backward until I see the tortured sky. I hold Connie close and let myself become swathed in the vastness of the clouds above me. Exhaustion takes over and, without warning, I'm drained. Done.

Connie's breathing deepens. She must be asleep.

The paranoia stirs up the bile in my stomach, frothing in the pit, wondering if the influence is not something I can fully control. Haunting me. It scares me that Connie is connected to me, and there's nothing she can do about it. Because she's something I want, and so, she is mine. I try to push the dread deep down, somewhere I can't taste it.

'I can't believe you left us in there.' Anna jabs her finger at the air above where we are lying.

Connie sits bolt upright, rubbing her eyes in confusion. Her silky dark hair is all scrunched on one side from the dampness in the air.

'I needed some air.' I sit up to face Anna, who has Brady and Lorna in tow.

None of them look impressed at being left alone with Arjun.

'What happened?'

'Nothing. He just talked some more.' Lorna shrugs. 'He said he'll stay in the house while you take some time. He can wait for you to go back. Arjun thinks you should travel with him and learn more about your history. That it would help you understand more about your powers and where they come from.'

'I'm not going anywhere with that man,' I say, getting to my feet and helping Connie to do the same.

'Wait, are we really buying what he's selling?' Brady asks, more to Anna than me.

'I think so,' Anna says, keeping her eyes on me. 'Do you believe him, Peter?'

'Yes,' I say in a quiet voice.

Brady looks at me like I've lost my mind. 'You can't be serious? You believe you're a god?'

'Who knows what that actually means, Brady?' Lorna defends me.

I can't help but cringe at how arrogant it sounds.

We all stand in silence, staring at each other.

'I think you should go with him,' Anna finally says to me.

Now it's my turn to look at her in disbelief. Connie tenses up beside me as I reply, 'There's no way I'm leaving you.'

'I'll come too.' Anna shrugs.

I examine her eyes, trying to detect Arjun's influence. It's frustrating that I don't even know what to look for.

She continues, 'Peter, this is what you wanted. We can't keep playing guesswork with your powers. This is how you learn to use them.'

'I know how to use them.'

'Chlorokinesis. Have you heard that word before? Do you know what it means?' I don't answer her, so she goes on, 'Besides, you heard him, your powers are unstable.'

I shake my head. 'Anna, I may believe him, but that doesn't mean I trust him. The powers are all he wants. I can see it written all over his face. It's all he cares about. He's not here to be our father, sister.'

'Maybe. But what other choice do we have?'

Exasperated, I look to Connie for what she thinks.

'I'll come as well,' she says quietly.

I push my hair through my hands. *I don't want the two most important people in my life anywhere near him.*

'No!'

The sound makes me jump.

I've never heard Brady sound angry before.

'No, no, no.' He stalks around the natural circle we've created. 'This is crazy. You can't all be thinking of running off to India, or wherever, with some witch bloke we just met. Connie, do you even own a passport? Can everyone pull themselves together for a second?'

Letting out a low breath, he looks me right in the eyes, pleading. 'Peter, I know this guy has just shown up and dropped a huge bombshell on you, but you have to be smart about this before you put Anna and Connie in the hands of God knows who. For now, we're safe in the village. None of us have ever left.'

'I have,' Lorna pipes up, raising her hand meekly. 'I'm just saying, I'm not from here. I even have family in India.'

'Jesus.' Brady rubs his temples. 'Can we all stop volunteering to run away, please? All I'm asking is that we take some time. If Arjun is genuine and wants to help Peter, then he won't mind sticking around, will he?'

Anna opens her mouth to protest, but I beat her to it. 'I agree with Brady. I think we should stay. And if... *if*... I go, then I go alone.'

'Peter,' Anna and Connie say in unison.

'Anna.' I turn to her, flexing my fingers and resisting the urge to ring her neck. 'I'm all he cares about. I don't trust that he won't put you in danger. I *will* come back to you.'

'It's my choice, Peter, he's my father too,' she calls after me.

But I'm already walking away from the house and back toward the village, pulling Connie along with me. The energy Arjun forced me to use with his little experiment to show my powers continues to take its toll. I'm tired and long to be in the sanctuary of Connie's room.

'I'd come back for you too, Connie,' I say after a while.

Connie is usually quiet, but I hate to think I've hurt her.

'I want to come. I told you I would follow you anywhere.'

I can hear it, the rejection in her voice.

'I know you would.' There's a sense of relief when her house comes into view. 'That's the problem. I don't know how safe I am to be around. Trust me, I don't want to go, especially on my own, but I can't put you or my sister in danger. You're too important. Too fragile,' I add in a confessional whisper.

I've already lost the people I love.

Maybe not today, but one day, it *will* happen. A lump rises in my throat as I attempt to resolve whether to go with Arjun. That I will leave my sister and Connie behind to try to piece together some kind of normal life without me. Arjun said my influence is permanent. I could force them to stay behind, if I must. The question is, will I be able to go through with it? I'm not so sure. Because, unlike my sister and unlike Connie, I'm weak.

I can't bring myself to look at Connie's hurt expression.

It takes me a second to register Jamie sitting on the low stone wall outside Connie's house as we approach. He waves when he sees us, putting his phone back into his pocket and pushing himself off the wall. My jaw clenches at the sight of him.

Connie slows, tugging on my hand as I pull her forward.

'Sorry I'm late. What did I miss? I tried to call you, Con,' he says, making his way around the wall near the back garden.

In the few paces it takes us to reach him, I'm furious. Angered that when I'm gone, it will probably be Jamie who comforts Connie. Considering the life they could have together if I don't come back—knowing he will taste her, of every gasp he may illicit from her, of his hands smoothing over her thighs, how she might say *his* name—is maddening. I long to hurt him, to ensure he never gets the chance to be those things to her.

The old apple tree in the garden has roots that travel deep and reach wide. Without thinking, I flick my hand up.

Jamie takes a step back, confused by the unnatural action. In seconds, the old roots break through the pavement, wrapping around his legs and up his torso, finding their way around his neck. The panic rises in his face when his air supply begins to restrict.

I don't truly want to kill him, just exert enough pressure to let him think I do. And to know that I can.

Connie's screaming at my side, pulling my coat, telling me to stop.

Her screams are lost in the wind.

The alarm in Jamie's eyes is so sweet I can almost taste it. His face is starting to purple. It would be so easy. Alas, with a breath, my anger subsides along with the roots, and they find their way back into the earth, leaving Jamie on his knees, gasping for breath.

I can't quite remember what made me so mad to drive me to such actions.

Connie rushes over to him, her hands moving to the red welts around his neck. She turns on me, her emerald eyes filled with a fire I haven't seen before. 'What the hell is wrong with you?' She uses all the force of her tiny body to shove me backward.

I don't have a word to say to defend myself but am instantly filled with regret.

She shoves me again, screaming, 'Get out of here. Go. If that's what you want, Peter, then go.'

I move back two paces, but when I try to reach out to her, she yells again, 'Do *not* touch me. I *want* you to go. *Now*.' She turns away from me, helping Jamie to his feet.

Together, they head back toward the front of her house.

I stand and watch until I can't see them anymore.

My heart gone, I turn my face to the darkening sky and, thick with my misery, will it to rain.

CHAPTER 25

Connie

'Where were you?' I ask.

The welts on Jamie's neck look sore. He winces as I examine them. Luckily, my mum is out—I have no idea how I would explain this.

'I woke up late.' His words are casual, but he avoids my gaze. 'I take it the trip to the house went as well as expected.'

I turn away from him and get myself a glass of water, wondering how to begin to explain. The pain of Peter leaving almost splits me in two, and standing here in front of me is Jamie, who less than twenty-four hours ago predicted this would happen. I can't bring myself to show it. Instead, I pour another glass of water and leave it next to Jamie, not bringing myself to look at the wounds on his neck. Or him at all.

Jamie shifts uncomfortably on the kitchen countertop. His water untouched.

I haven't spoken for a full minute. Instead, I've been in a staring contest with the wall.

'Con, what happened?' he presses.

'Erm…' I snap out of my trance and turn to Jamie. 'His dad's alive. He's here.' My voice sounds hollow.

'Oh shit. What did he say?'

'A lot of things. I'm not sure I should say.'

'Why? Because he told you not to?' Jamie's voice is laced with spite.

'No, because you'll laugh.' I'm not in the mood for Jamie making fun of me.

This clearly isn't what he's expecting me to say. He slides down from the counter to stand in front of me. I look at the red rings around his neck. I know they don't particularly like each other, but I don't understand why Peter attacked him.

'I won't laugh, Connie. I promise.'

I can't say it, though. The tears prick my eyes. The seriousness in his eyes tells me Jamie won't laugh, but I still can't bring myself to say Peter *is* a god. He's immortal. Which is so ridiculous but also true. And how can I ever compete with that?

'You were right, Jay. He is going to leave.' I try to keep my voice even. 'And he doesn't want me.'

Jamie puts his arms around me, and I let the tears come. 'Connie, you know that's not true,' he whispers into my ear as he keeps his arms around me. 'How could he not want you?' His hot breath in my ear sends a shiver down my spine.

I pull back and consider him. It's not like Jamie to say the right thing. His face so close to mine, his sad blue eyes flick from mine down to my lips.

I freeze. Feelings long forgotten bubble to the surface. I've kissed Jamie a million times. It used to be the most natural thing in the world. It wasn't intense or overwhelming, but it was always fun, simple, and uncomplicated. In the back of my head, I wonder if I'm a bad person for wanting this again, even if only for just for a moment.

My eyes pop open at the sound of knocking at the front door.

Sheesh. Saved by the bell.

I'm out of Jamie's arms in lightning speed, rushing to the door.

Why am I such an idiot?

Kissing Jamie would've been the stupidest thing to do. Peter has already tried to kill him. Twice. I throw back the door.

Of course, Lorna and the others have caught up, all of them particularly soggy. I hadn't noticed the rain.

'Have you been crying?' Lorna asks, clasping me by the arm and moving me out of the doorway. The concern on her face is soon replaced by one of confusion as Jamie walks out of the kitchen.

He appears annoyed.

Maybe he planned the little kiss incident. It occurs to me that I'm caught in some kind of pissing contest between him and Peter, which riles me.

'No, I'm fine.'

'Where's Peter?' Anna asks, throwing a dirty look at Jamie.

'I'm not sure. He left,' I say stupidly.

Way to state the obvious, Connie.

Anna eyes me suspiciously, making me squirm. Also frustrating because I didn't do anything wrong, even if I wanted to for a second.

Jamie's eyes bulge. 'Yes. He left. After he tried to kill me.' Jamie, in dramatic fashion, pulls down his collar to show the red marks on his neck.

'Did he strangle you?' Lorna asks with a tone of humour I appreciate.

'What did you do?' Anna squares on him. She's taller than him, and fierce. Almost as fierce as her brother.

'What did *I* do?' Jamie's look of disbelief is almost comical.

'Yes, what did *you* do, Jamie? The last time Peter was going to kill you, you'd accused us of incest. So, yes, what did *you* do?' With her last words, she gives Jamie a powerful shove, sending him back into the coat rack, much to the surprise of Jamie by the look on his face.

Anna turns on me next.

I try to shrink away from her, but her finger lands heavy on my chest. 'If you seriously choose this guy over my brother, Connie, then you have lost your damn mind.'

In a whirlwind, Anna's gone.

Out of my house.

Leaving us all bewildered and myself feeling somewhat guilty.

Luckily, the awkward exchange in my doorway is enough to make everyone want to leave, so not even Jamie sticks around. For which I'm eternally grateful.

I take a long shower to warm myself up and to try and rid myself of the emotions Anna left me with.

After all of today's revelations, I do nothing but mope for the rest of the day.

I tell my mum I have a headache and don't want dinner when she comes home and checks on me. Perhaps I can get out of school tomorrow. I sit on the edge of my bed and stare into space. There's no energy to do anything else.

Considering a life without Peter in it seems hollow, even though I've only known him for six months. Maybe this is simply how it is with first love, like my mum said. Or maybe this is how it is when you fall for a bloody deity.

Just your luck, Connie.

I lie down, my eyes close, and sweet sleep takes me.

The soft touch of Peter's fingers moving my hair from my face sends electric currents down my spine. I open my eyes to see him crouched next to me.

I smile. I'm whole again.

'What time is it?' I ask, looking at the black sky outside my open window.

'Late.' Peter grins as he strokes my hair.

'I take it you came in through the window?'

His lips curl. His eyes are bright. His very presence… infectious.

Not only infectious—it calls to me. Summons something deep within me. Something I never knew existed until *him*. When he goes, he'll take that part of me with him. A part of me that comes alive with every inch of me when I'm with him.

I shift from my place on my bed and move my lips to his.

He told me once to let him consume me. So I let go. Let go the way I only can with Peter. Melt my lips into his, wanting more.

Peter's hands move to my shoulders, pressing me hard into the bed.

The freezing wind of the night blows my curtains, giving them a ghostly appearance. I tuck myself in as close as I can to steal his body heat as he enjoys the lazy melody of the quiet song playing from my speakers. His fingers move in time to the music across my chest. Peter's eyes examine my body like it's the most wondrous thing on the planet.

I bite my lip, dreading what I'm about to ask, 'You're leaving, aren't you?'

He stops his patterns and lays his head on his arm to meet my eyes. 'You saw me today. I can't stay. I don't trust Arjun enough to risk your life, Connie. I am sorry, though… sorry that I hurt Jamie.'

'Why did you?'

'Jealously. He'll be here with you, and I won't.'

I can't help but laugh. 'Peter Burke, you are a god and jealous of Jamie Singer. Over me.' My fingertips dance up his arm. 'That's the craziest thing I've heard all day, and it's been a strange day.'

Peter's dark eyes gleam in the dim light of my room. 'It's entirely selfish, Connie. That he'll be the one here to comfort you. How, when I go, you'll move on. When what I want is, for *my name* to be the only one you whisper into the darkness.'

My heart hammers in my chest. 'So stay. Stay with me for just a little while longer.'

Peter drops his head onto my chest, and I wrap my arms around him, hoping if I don't let go, he will stay forever.

'Okay, Connie. I'll stay, for a while. For you.'

CHAPTER 26

Peter

Ever aware of *his* presence, I don't return to the house.

Arjun.

My so-called father.

Not just a shadow that lingers in the back of my mind, but physically, his energy emanates across the village, finding its way to me like a serpent, his power reacting to mine.

I'm exposed, responding like a raw nerve.

My powers are bubbling under the surface. All the control I've learnt comes to nothing. In fact, worse. Things have started to react to me without any push on my part. Dying flowers spring back to life as I walk past, grass shoots up past the edge of my boots where I tread. I'm lucky no one has noticed. Yet.

I'm positive Arjun is doing it on purpose, emitting a beacon of power to drive me over the edge and force me to come to him. Then again, maybe it's because he's a powerful witch, and his presence is all I need to throw my powers out of balance. What vexes me most is not knowing.

In truth, what annoys me even more is Anna. She's gone back to the house more than once to speak to him, to gain understanding. What she learns, she passes on to me, trying to convince me he's not bad, just strange, different, like me. Like us. I hate it. I hate her being there with him. I try to warn her he has influence too, that she needs to be careful, but I can see in her eyes what this is about.

Father.

She has a father.

She wants a family.

For us to be a family.

As the week goes on, Anna starts to pull away from me, irritated with my stubbornness of not going to see *him*. In truth, it's my own fault. I put up the brick wall first. I suppose I've been shutting her out bit by bit, retreating into Connie. I'd promised Anna I would be fairer with my time, but that hasn't happened.

I take a minute to stare up into the black night, my leg cocked over the edge of Connie's bedroom window, my body already halfway out. Connie is fast asleep, and I can make out the soft shape of her naked back. Some feral instinct in me wants to turn around, get back into bed with her, and wake her up. But I should go. I wasn't supposed to be here tonight, not that I think her mum would care at this point, but old habits die hard.

I think again of Anna and know I should return home. I promised Connie I would stay for her, but it's a temporary arrangement, and I don't want to leave with Anna mad at me. I push further out of the window, not paying enough attention, and miss my footing on the ivy-covered trellis. With my body already too far out of the window, I fall.

Too quick to make a sound, the world rushes past me. I brace myself for impact, one that doesn't come. The balls of my feet hit the ground with the same force as if I'd jumped from the backdoor step. Adrenaline floods through my body. Connie's dormer window must be a clear twenty feet off the ground, and I landed it like a cat. I look around again, thinking it's almost a shame no one was around to see it.

Walking through the village at the darkest point of the night, I could be the only person on the planet. Everything is peaceful, still, save for the odd fox that crosses my path.

The assent to my room is the same as always, an easy climb up the nearby drainpipe. I drop in without noise, pry off my trainers, and pull my hoodie up over my head. It takes me a moment before I notice Anna isn't here. Panic rises in my chest. *Anna's always here*. I push it down because it doesn't take a strong emotion for the world around me to have a reaction these days.

I tiptoe across the landing and ease open her bedroom door. My heart rate returns to normal at the sight of her curled up in a ball. I climb in next to her. From the big sigh she lets out, I've woken her up and she's aware of my presence. I wrap my arms around her body, holding her back to my chest.

'You weren't there,' I whisper to the back of her head.

'What do you expect, Peter? You're never here. I can't spend my life waiting for you.'

I close my eyes against the blackness of the night. 'Anna,' I reply weakly, with no idea what to say next. I've never been a fan of talking. Words don't come easy. *How do I put into words how much she means to me?*

'I love you,' I say, something I've never told her before.

She immediately wiggles around to look at me, her eyes bright. 'Stop pushing me away, then. What have I done wrong? Is it what I said before, after new year?'

'No, of course not. You could never do anything wrong, not to me.'

Her eyes are like deep dark pools, nothing like the hollowness of Arjun's. Instead, they're full of warmth and humanity.

'I don't trust Arjun.'

'Then trust me. Besides, he knows so much we don't. You should hear his stories about our mother for yourself. It's like seeing her through his eyes, learning how powerful she was, a natural witch. He is our family.'

I don't say anything, just grunt into the dark.

'Peter. I'm my own person, and if I say I'm coming with you, I mean it. You can't stop me.'

'Actually, Anna, I can.'

Anna sucks in a sharp breath as the weight of my words hang in the air, lingering like poison. I regret saying it as soon as the words leave my mouth. I know I would never knowingly use my influence on her.

'I didn't mean that.' I breathe in, closing my eyes, trying to calm my raging thoughts. 'What I mean is, I don't trust him *not* to put you in danger. I don't trust myself *not* to put you in danger. Brady's right. We know nothing of this world. I don't know how to protect you.'

'And who protects you, Peter?'

'Immortal, remember?' I grimace even if she can't see me.

'Arjun says there are still ways you can die,' Anna whispers in response.

'Which, conveniently, he hasn't told us.'

'So, what if it is a trap?'

'All the more reason for you to stay here,' I reply in an instant.

Anna ponders my response for a moment before sliding her hand into mine. 'You're everything to me, Peter. I don't know if I could live without you.'

All the instincts that have been drilled into me for the last seventeen years rear their ugly head, and all I want is to relent, tell her she should come with me. That I want her at my side—I'll always want her at my side. Instead, I say, 'You have the chance at a normal life, Anna, with Brady. With our aunt and uncle. Just be normal and see what that's like for a while. I will come back, I promise.'

We don't say much more. What else is there? But I know the time is nearing.

My aunt has been rather quiet since she told us about our mother. Guilt plagues me because she'll be devastated when I leave. Gone. The same as her sister all those years ago.

My sleep is restless. The shadows have returned, creeping in at the edges, winding like vines, trying to find me. I barely manage to stay free of their grasp, but they're always right behind me. The water is back, the huge expanse of the Ganges wide and unforgiving. I want to step into it. But when I do, I'm instantly submerged, the water overwhelming me. I sink deeper and deeper, my breath becoming thin. Maybe drowning is a way I can die. The water is heavy, and the shadows have followed me, their reach like decaying fingers extending toward me. I am powerless.

My bed is soaked in sweat as the vibrating of my phone under the bed jolts me awake. I don't even remember coming back to my own room. The brightness of the morning confuses my senses, as well as the incessant vibrations. Nobody ever calls me. I grapple under my bed for the phone, trying to shake my nightmare away.

'Hello?' My voice is thick with sleep.

'Peter?' Connie's voice has an edge to it I don't like.

'What's wrong?'

'Erm... what happened last night?'

My mind races. *What happened last night?* Nothing out of the ordinary. No one even knew I was there unless someone saw me. But then, Connie would have said that.

'Are you there?' she asks when I don't respond.

'Yes. I'm here. I'm trying to think. Nothing happened. What's going on, Connie?'

'I was worried. When I saw the apple tree, I thought something must have happened. My mum is all in a tizz about it. Well, she thinks it's lovely, but she's confused, obviously.'

'What are you talking about?'

'The apple tree... it's in bloom. It's pretty. There are even tiny frostbitten apples on it. It's like something out of a fairy tale.'

The tree. I fell.

The adrenaline—it must have been the adrenaline. I hadn't noticed in the dark. It was only a matter of time before something like this happened.

'I'll be right over,' I tell her and hang up.

I get dressed and leave the house, managing not to see anyone, heading to Connie's as fast as my feet will take me. When I arrive, Connie is already in the garden, standing under her apple tree, which is exactly as she said—in full beautiful bloom. The blush pink of the blossoms even more delicate for the twinkling frost adorning it. Connie looks ethereal standing underneath it, and her face sparkles as I approach. Seeing her so not worried about it eases the burden in my chest.

'Are you mad?' I ask, pulling her into a hug.

'How can I be mad? It's beautiful. It's magic, Peter. You are magic.'

I smile down at her, but it's a smile that doesn't reach my eyes. 'I can fix it.' I hold out my hand to the trunk of the tree, but Connie pushes it away.

'No, don't. I love it. Plus, my mum will be even more confused if it suddenly goes away.'

'What will you tell her?'

Connie gives an incredulous laugh, looking up at me through her thick lashes. 'Peter, why would my mum expect me to have the answers?'

Of course, why would her daughter's strange boyfriend have anything to do with this?

'Okay. Then it stays.' I kiss her forehead. 'Something to remember me by.'

Connie's reaction is immediate, pulling herself away from me in three quick steps. Her jewel-like eyes wide. 'This is it? You came to say goodbye? I thought we had more time.'

'Connie, your mum may not be asking you questions now. But how many things have to happen before someone does? I can't stay a-anymore.' My voice cracks, I want to tell her to come. My selfish heart needs her, but I push those words down. 'I love you, Connie. I want you to be happy.'

'You're coming back, though, right?'

'Yes, I'll come back. I don't know how long it will take, and if you have moved on, then I won't want to mess that up.' The words hurt me to say. I don't want her to move on. I want her to wait, but it's not fair of me to ask.

Connie's expression turns to confusion. 'Is this about Jamie? Because I've known him all my life, and he's my friend, but I've never felt for him what I feel for you. I love you, Peter. I don't want anyone else.'

'What if I'm gone for years? I can't expect you to put your life on hold.'

'Why not? It's my life.'

'You'll never have a normal life with me, Connie.'

'Who wants normal?' She closes the distance between us. 'It's my choice, and I choose you.'

Connie stands on her tiptoes to kiss me. I let the warmth fill me, giving me relief and solace in her love but not knowing if I have truly earned it. The voice in the back of my head that has lived there since I learned about my influence whispers its bile, saying that none of this is real. *How can it be her choice if I chose her first?*

I push it down, way down.

I leave before I change my mind and once again make the walk through the woods to my home. The frosted ground of the woodlands crunches under my feet and echoes through my mind. I try not to let my thoughts drift to Anna.

I didn't say goodbye.

It's better this way. Less painful. She wouldn't have to let me go if she knew I was leaving.

The house still looks as dead as the last time I saw it, but I know he's in there.

I'm not ready.

The pain of walking away from the only home I've ever known burns inside me. It could consume me. I hold tight to the back door frame, the ability to walk forward becoming more and more difficult. The wheezy laugh that escapes is not my own. Here I am, a god with all this power, and I would give all of it up for a home, to be loved. I clutch my chest, hoping somehow to be able to put out the fire that's started to burn there.

'Peter.'

I look up to see Arjun standing in the hallway beyond the kitchen. He's smiling, knowing it was only a matter of time. All he had to do was wait me out.

'How can you tell?' I ask. Now that I'm here, I'm desperate for the answers. 'How can I tell if she loves me or if she thinks she does because I want it?'

Arjun takes a deep breath, his stance softening as he approaches me. He wraps a fatherly arm around my shoulders and leads me inside. 'My boy, you can't. While the gifts you possess are a blessing, they can be a curse for those close to you. The human race will always act on your will, mostly.' He gives a cold, dead smile. 'I can teach you to direct your will with more purpose, should we say. But your will is your will, and there's no stopping that. However, there are certain spells that can protect individuals from the influence of your will. It will give them clarity, you might say.'

'You can teach me this spell?'

Arjun lets out a low chuckle. 'I have to say I'm a little disappointed in you, Peter. A god, with the world at his feet and a high priest at his disposal, and your concern is if this girl's feelings are true or not? Stop thinking so small, my boy. The universe is vast, and so will your years be.'

I edge away from Arjun, taking in the miniature shanty he has constructed in what was our living room. White paint peels from the walls and the clock on the mantel is falling apart, one of its hands missing. *My home.*

'My world has been this house for so long, I only know small.'

Arjun's hard eyes soften a little. 'Of course. That could all change. I could show you. Take you back to the country where you were born, open you up to wonders you cannot possibly imagine. Show you this world. My son, it's a world full of unimaginable beauty. There's so much to see, to learn. Lifetimes worth of history, all ripe for the picking. And true magic, Peter, it is woven into the very fibre of your being. This house, you have outgrown it. Come with me.'

My heart pounds as my head nods at Arjun's words. I dare not open my mouth, the fear rippling through me makes me shiver.

Push it down, Peter. Push it down.

Connie's words come back to me, helping me to breathe through and focus. Fighting me, Arjun's elation at my agreement is hard to contend with. I see the vines and roots remaining around the room, start to shiver and coil. I flex my back in an attempt to bring it back under control, but it's already in motion as the roots begin their crawl across the floor toward me.

Arjun notices, peering from the winding root and up to me.

'Can you do anything to suppress this?' I manage, but his expression is unreadable at the longing in my voice, the need to make it stop. To make it easier.

Arjun makes his way over as my body continues to shake. His bare hand is ice cold when he places it on the side of my neck. The black holes of his eyes reach for the panic in mine. 'My boy,' he utters. The effect of his touch, at first cold, starts to spread a calm that travels through me.

I take a deep breath.

My first in days.

'How did you do that?' I ask. My next few breaths huff out in a cloud.

'Years of study,' Arjun says, turning away from me. 'We should leave immediately. My car is a few miles from here. It'll take us a little bit of time to walk to it.'

I nod, tucking my hands into my pockets as I suppress a laugh. I don't know what I expected, like Arjun had flown here on a broomstick. It's obvious we would be driving.

'Shall we drive back to collect your sister, or will she be joining us here?' He is busy bundling his things into a large leather bag.

Surprised, I turn back to him. 'Anna's staying here.'

Arjun freezes in his crouched position. 'What?' he whispers without looking at me.

'I told her to stay,' I reaffirm, then I take a step back, instinct telling me this is something that's made him angry.

'Your sister should join us, Peter.'

A sinking feeling in the pit of my stomach sends me another pace away from him. 'No. It's safer for her here. Anna doesn't want to come.'

'Foolish child,' he mutters under his breath as he turns on me. Pushing back his slick hair, he asks, 'Do you really think you can lie to me? Anna *will* be coming with us.'

Now he looks furious, and I scramble for my words.

'She should stay here and try to be happy. This has nothing to do with her.'

Arjun throws back his head and laughs. 'You have the arrogance of a god. It has everything to do with her.' His face becomes a sneer. 'Do you know what it's like for her? You have no idea, do you? The thought has never crossed your mind. She's unable to break free of you. She *has* to come with us.'

'No,' I say as firm as I can muster. 'I will let her go.'

'You fool,' Arjun spits, venom in his eyes. 'It's not even possible. She is tethered to you, doomed to follow you until the day she dies.'

'What?' I whisper.

'Your sister is the very thing that made your birth possible. She brought you into this world, Peter. The mortal side of you. She is your humanity, your human half. She's part of you. It's not possible for you to leave her behind. She's the key to your control. Anna is doomed to live in your shadow, and you will never have full mastery of your power while she lives.'

I shudder as he continues, dread and longing dancing along my skin, 'You two have existed side by side for too long, Peter. It is time for you to become one.'

My thoughts are foggy, the effect of Arjun's touch suppressing my powers and my ability to think. 'Become one? How?'

'Anna needs to die, Peter.'

I freeze. 'This was your plan all along, wasn't it? You came here to kill her?' My voice comes out more as a whisper while my feet take me backward.

Arjun remains in his place. I can't look away from him.

'I came here for you.' Arjun's face twists into a sly grimace as he advances toward me slowly. 'You will be the one to kill her.'

A laugh leaves my lips, a sick, disbelieving laugh. 'If you think I can kill my sister, you know nothing about me.'

'It *will* be so.'

The world spins as I move backward, my legs like jelly.

'It's her energy. Her life force will stabilise you. It is the only way, Peter.'

I shake my head. *It can't be true.* Arjun's words bring forth a memory of Lorna after I'd mended her broken leg. In the process, something switched, and I absorbed the white light from her. The rushing of it was intoxicating—it was her life force becoming mine.

My stomach churns.

This is what I'm supposed to do, absorb the life out of Anna and into me. This is how we become one, the way I'd almost done to Lorna.

Arjun stops a few feet from me, his keen eyes taking me in, his mouth spreading unnaturally wide into the most sinister of grins. My back hits the wall, my knees go weak, and I cower before him.

'You've done it before, haven't you, boy?'

CHAPTER 27

Peter

Never have I felt so disconnected. From my body, who I am, and the world around me.

Sheer will to be out from under Arjun's glare is the only way I'm able to crawl on my hands and knees away from him.

I find myself putting my bare hands onto the cold ground outside. Whatever Arjun has done to suppress my powers is holding, but barely. The dormant grass beneath my palms springs to life.

I gingerly stagger to my feet. One step. Two steps. I make for the tree line.

I try to ignore the lush grassy footprints appearing wherever I step, leaving a trail. I make it to a tree, and wrapping my arms around it, it shivers, springing to life before losing its leaves again.

Over and over again.

Pull it together, Peter.

The tree shudders under duress at being forced into its life cycle over and over again. I drag my hand down my face. I need to think. My head is spinning.

Breathe. Just breathe, Peter.

My stomach lurches, driving the bile that has been sitting inside it out, covering the ground at my feet.

Arjun came here for me. For my powers. His plan for me to kill my sister—that will not *happen.* I look back at the desolate house. There's no sign of him. *Why isn't he following me?* Being sick has cleared my mind a fraction.

There's only one thing left to do. *Run.*

So I do exactly that. Slowly at first, as my body regains its strength from the shock, but eventually faster, stronger, and with more purpose.

I need to get Anna, and we need to flee.

We won't be able to run for long but at least long enough to think of a plan.

It's good to be moving, giving me an illusion of control. *I can beat this. I can beat him.* A wave of relief begins to wash over me.

Change of plans—I'm not leaving with him. I'm leaving with her.

The pain of leaving Anna behind is one I don't have to worry about. Just keeping her alive I can do. He's crazy to think I could ever kill her.

I round up to the house full of fresh purpose. We're leaving together. *Now.* I burst through the front door, hanging onto the door handle, trying to catch my breath, my clothes wet with sweat.

Sally appears in the hall, placing her hand on my back. 'Peter, what on earth is wrong?' Her voice is full of concern.

Anna emerges from upstairs, still in her pyjamas. She stops dead at the sight of me.

'We're leaving. *Now*. Go and get changed,' I direct Anna between ragged breaths.

But Anna only stares daggers at me. 'You went to him? You were going to leave without saying goodbye.' She practically stomps her foot.

Anger flashes through me. *How can she be petulant at a time like this?* I close the distance, taking the two bottom stairs to meet her, and roughly grab both of her arms.

'It doesn't matter now. We have to go. Just the two of us. The way it should be, Anna. You and me, but we need to go *now*. Please, Anna. Please. Please. We need to go,' I beg.

If I have to, I'll use every ounce of my stupid influence. I don't care.

'What did he say to you?' Her deep, brown eyes implore mine.

Now is not the time for explanations.

'We're in danger. We can't stay… we need to go.'

She nods.

I rest against the wall, catching my breath.

'Would someone mind telling me what's happening? You two are not going anywhere.' Sally puts her hands on her hips, pointing her finger between Anna and me.

'You are in danger too, if we stay.'

Sally shakes her head, struggling to understand.

I wonder at all the things my mother said to her that she didn't understand. Going to her, I take her hands in mine. 'It was all true, Sally. Everything Mother said was true. We have to go. You have to let us.'

Sally's eyes fill with tears. 'Peter, you need help. None of this is real.'

I stagger back to the wall for support as my breathing begins to return to normal, searching for the words to say to my aunt. I want to explain how everything she thought was a lie is true—that her sister wasn't sick—but I don't have the words. My energy is already fading.

'I can't let you go,' Sally says after a few moments of silence.

'You don't have a choice.' Gazing into her eyes, I pull together enough energy to know my influence will work and she will let us go. I wrap the idea around her. 'And we'll need all of the money you have in your purse,' I add.

Her head moves up and down, and she leaves me alone with Anna.

I crumble to the floor.

Anna comes to support me. 'Was that necessary? You're robbing her now?'

'If we're running, we won't get far without money.'

'Peter—'

'Don't, Anna. We need to start moving and then I'll explain. I promise.'

Anna considers me for a moment. I've sunk to a ball on the floor. Luckily, my lack of energy has nullified my powers for the time being and I don't have to worry about tree branches crashing in and taking over the house.

'If you truly want to run, then we should call Brady.'

'Absolutely not.'

'How far will we get without a car?'

I rest my face in my hands. 'I don't want to put him in danger,' I say through gritted teeth.

'Don't you think that's Brady's choice?'

'Fine, call him. But it's now or never. We're not waiting.'

Frantic, Anna nods and turns to run upstairs to call him. Against what I know is the right thing to do, I'm on my feet and heading to my room to also make a call. My thumb hovers over her name for a second before I call her.

'Hi.'

Her voice is happy, light, and I try not to will her to say yes.

'I didn't think I'd hear from you so soon.'

'There's been a change of plans.'

'You're staying?' The hopeful tone in her voice almost breaks my heart.

'No. I'm still going. It's hard to explain right now. But…' I take a deep breath, '… Anna's coming with me. And you can too, if you want. We're going now. I know it's an impossible thing to ask, but it's your choice, not mine.'

Silence.

I bite my lip. It's for the best. She should stay away from me. Have a normal life with Jamie. I could have killed her best friend without meaning to. That's how easy it is for me to take a life. I close my eyes. *It's time to let her go.*

'Connie, it's okay. Staying is the right thing to do.'

Anna comes into my room, a silent nod telling me Brady is coming to get us.

'I have to go now, but—'

'Peter, stop. I want to come with you,' Connie says in a rush, and despite my panic, I'm elated to hear it.

'Okay, Brady's coming for you. Be ready.'

I hang up the phone and look at Anna. She's now dressed, wearing a thick winter coat and holding a packed bag.

'He said yes,' I state.

'So did she,' Anna returns with a wry smile.

'What did you tell him?'

'That we're in trouble and need his help.'

I rub my eyes at the truth in her simple statement. We have no idea where we're running to or even how to do it. I pack a few things into a bag. There's no time to shower, but I do change out of my sweat-drenched clothes. I look in the mirror. My reflection is similar to how I looked when we'd first been taken from our mother's house. My hair, shorter now, is tangled and my face is dirty. The dark circles under my eyes are new additions. I head downstairs to wait for Brady and Connie. While I feel a tad guilty about taking money from Sally, it's not like I asked her to empty her bank account.

Forty minutes pass, and I'm starting to get restless.

I pace the hallway while Anna sits on the stairs, more patient than me. I try not to let my mind wander to the edge of panic fizzing inside of me. I curse my mother again for leaving us so unprepared. Of course, she thought Arjun was dead, but our lack of knowledge about the world has made us vulnerable. She may have thought she was protecting us by keeping us hidden but, in reality, she made us weaker.

Brady pulls up in front of the house.

Anna pauses at the door, as if to turn back and say something to our aunt who's in the living room, but I usher her out. Some things are better left unsaid. I'm relieved to leave the silence of the house and to be moving, putting distance between ourselves and Arjun.

Connie throws open her passenger door and is in my arms in a quick few steps. I pull her in close. Of all possible outcomes, this should be my ideal, both Anna and Connie at my side. But the instinct to run is never a good one. Connie's embrace only lasts a minute before I'm guiding her into the back seat with me, letting Anna take the front with Brady.

'Drive,' I insist.

He does as requested, backing the car out of the driveway and putting the house in the rear-view mirror.

My heart rate starts to return to normal with the sway of the car. I melt into the seat, not releasing Connie's hand. I notice Brady's eyes flicking to me every few seconds in the mirror as Anna looks straight ahead, not saying a word.

I could sleep for a week. Two weeks even. But there's a long road ahead of us.

'Thank you,' I say eventually. 'Thank you, both of you, for coming and for helping us. The truth is, we don't have much idea of how to do this.'

Brady looks at me in his mirror. 'Truth be told, Peter, I don't think me or Connie have any idea what we're doing either. But we're here, for whatever you guys need.'

'Thanks,' I say again, some composure coming back to me. It'd be nice to close my eyes for a few minutes.

'So, any idea where we're going? And how long for?' Brady asks with slight trepidation.

Guilt hits me for the position he's putting himself in with his family by running away.

I shake my head. 'I don't know, as long as it takes. As for where first, I'm open to suggestions. We just need to put as much distance as possible between us and Arjun.'

Brady's eyes stay on me in the rear-view. 'How do we run from a man like that? He found you once before. Surely, he can do it again.'

'We won't be able to stay in one place long. He's still just a man. We need to get ahead of him and then we can figure it out as we go. Once I clear my head, then I can think about what to do next.'

'Maybe we can head to the coast?' Connie suggests. 'In the direction of Wales? It's a few hours' drive, but we can spend the night there and then regroup with our next move.'

Brady agrees with a nod, his eyes still flicking back to me every now and then. I must look pretty dishevelled. I'm glad I changed out of my sweat-and sick-stained clothes. Having a sickly-looking god in the back seat of your car must be unnerving. I don't blame Brady for doubting our chances against Arjun.

'What did he say to you?' Anna's voice is quiet but firm, a question I hadn't answered earlier, and now, there's no escaping.

Everyone's attention lands on me as we leave the outskirts of the village and merge onto a long highway. *This is the farthest I've ever been from home.*

'Answer me,' Anna demands, shifting in her seat to look at me.

I close my eyes. I can't even look at her when I say it. 'It's you who's in danger, Anna.'

'What. Did. He. Say. Peter?' Anna's voice is at a boiling point. 'Look at me.'

I take a deep breath and open my eyes while the whole car holds its breath.

'He wants me to kill you, Anna.'

The familiar sound of Brady laughing rings through the car once again. Anna's eyes stay on me.

'That's so ridiculous.' Brady laughs.

I can't pretend. The sick feeling bubbles in my stomach again. *I have to tell her.*

'Anna, he said that you're the human half of me. We are bound to each other. You cannot live without me. And I'll never be in full control of my powers while you're alive.'

I hear Connie's sharp intake of breath beside me.

Anna's expression is blank, now staring through me rather than at me.

Brady's laughter—no longer raucous—instead changes to nervousness, and his glances come more frequently. 'But that's just bullshit, right?' he directs at me through the mirror. 'He's crazy. That isn't true, right, Peter?'

'Right,' I say, fighting down the urge to vomit again. The image of Lorna's life force snaking up my arm tries to come back, and I push it down. I don't want to relive it. 'Arjun believes it, though. We have to assume he'll come for Anna, so we run and keep her safe.'

Anna turns away from me to look at the long winding road in front of us Brady has turned onto, tree-lined and with fields as far as the eye can see. It would be beautiful if I didn't feel so wretched.

The hint of a plan starts to form in my mind. My powers might be out of balance while Anna's alive, but there are ways of suppressing them. Arjun had done it with a touch, and the more I think about it, the more I think it's likely my mother must have done it my whole life. Using her own powers to suppress mine.

What we need is another witch.

But first, I need sleep, a little bit of sleep.

'Brady, look out!' Anna's voice screeches.

My eyes snap open wide enough in time to see Arjun's dark form in the middle of the road. It all happens too fast. My stomach lurches as Arjun's arm stretches out in front of the car, exerting an invisible force. The hood buckles and twists, sending the car into the air. The screams of Connie and Anna fill my ears. The wreck we're all expecting doesn't come, though. Instead, the car rolls into a nearby field.

No one is hurt.

Because this is what Arjun wants.

Brady's car is destroyed though. The bonnet bent out of recognition, smoke rising in front of the windscreen as Brady works to calm a shaking Anna.

Adrenaline floods me, forcing the remnants of Arjun's spell out of my body. Like a muscle, I flex a surge of power that runs through me like a wave. The electric current is powerful, mine to command.

We can't run, so I'll fight. I will become the creature my mother attempted to cage.

Fear ripples through me. I need to use it—every ounce of it—to keep my sister alive. The only thing left is to kill him before he kills her. I unbuckle my seatbelt, checking Connie to make sure she's okay, and tell everyone to stay in the car.

Connie isn't looking at me. Her gaze wanders past me, fear in her eyes as she watches Arjun advance toward us. There may be a thousand things I want to say to her in this moment, but the words do not come. Instead, I open the car door and move into the path of my father.

He laughs a humourless laugh. 'Now, I know you didn't think you could outrun me, Peter.'

'Can you blame me for trying?' I try to hide my body's shaking, but all the power comes, no control now. All that's left for it to do is to wash over me with no restraint.

All the fear is fuel.

The wind picks up and the storm clouds roll in as the earth starts to rumble beneath us. Grass comes to life in the stretch of earth between Arjun and me.

'That's a nice trick. Why don't the others join us?' With a flick of his wrist, the car doors open.

'No.' I turn to look, but they are already exiting the car, Anna's face now pale. 'Stay in the car,' I try to command.

'I can't help it, Peter,' Anna says on a sob.

Arjun's influence outmatches my own.

'What do you want? You're more powerful than me, so what do you want with me?' I turn to Arjun, desperately doing anything I can to slow him down, drawing roots from deep underground, wrapping them around his legs and chest, winding them up to his neck the way I once did with Jamie. But he dispenses with them as if they're nothing, giving me a satisfied look instead.

'For too long, I have watched this Earth turn to ash at the hands of humanity. You and I are going to put it back to its rightful state. Don't you want that, Peter? A more beautiful Earth. An Eden, where you can be at peace.'

His crooked finger beckons Anna to him, silent tears now staining her face as she's powerless to stop her forward motion.

'But you have to complete the cycle. She gave you life, and you are her death. You need to understand how this works. It's all a cycle, you see? It will be done. One way or another.'

His finger moves to wipe away one of her falling tears. The sight of him touching her makes my stomach lurch once again, only this time, as I call for him to stop, the rumble of thunder explodes in the darkening clouds above us.

Arjun turns his face toward the heavens, as if noticing them for the first time, while I move closer, eager to get between him and Anna. Distracted by the unforgiving sky, he glances from me to the angry clouds above, which are fit to burst. The spell holding Anna appears to be broken, and she rushes to my side.

Arjun sinks his hands on his knees. Anna and I look at each other, confused by the realisation that the guttural sound coming from him is laughter. Real laughter this time. It's the first time I notice he has a knife in his hand, compact and silver. A thrill goes through me, making the clouds swirl. He truly is insane.

Anna takes a step behind me.

Arjun throws his hands in the air, taking a breath from his laughing before pointing the knife to the sky. To me, he asks, 'Is this you?'

I don't say anything.

He laughs some more.

'It is you. My boy. My dear boy. To be gifted with Chlorokinesis is something, but this.' He wipes his eyes with the back of his knife-wielding hand. 'You are more powerful than you can ever possibly imagine.' He looks up to the skies, the way I worship the rain. 'The elements, my boy, you have influence of the elements. Can you imagine? The power of the wind and the rain. My son, you are the maker and the destroyer of worlds.'

I shake my head, stepping back and taking Anna with me.

Arjun is deliberate with his steps now, moving in front of me. I don't think I've seen him look happy in the short time we've known him. 'Peter, do not be cruel. Release your twin from her prison. She cannot contain this. She shouldn't have to. You, my son, are a ticking time bomb for everyone you're around. Oh, your mother, she did a good job. She bound all that energy down deep inside of you, didn't she? Clever woman. But there's no stopping you now, Peter. Without Anna's life force, you will destroy everything.'

Anna's hand clamps hard on my shoulder, and the clouds above us burst, showering us. 'Don't listen to him, Peter. That's not who you are.'

Arjun's laugh comes again, louder than the rain. 'It is *what* you are, Peter. A force of nature, connected to the very energy that fuels our sun. Your power will burn them all, boy.'

'Don't give him what he wants, Peter,' Anna whispers.

It's too late, though. Everything's already moving. The earth, the skies, and the roots and vines from the nearby trees wrapping around the car, myself, Anna, and Arjun.

'Control it,' she pleads.

'I can't,' I whisper. I try not to think about Lorna's leg. While the sight of blood-induced sickness, the sensation after, the white light, the ecstasy, it'd been crave-worthy. Madness inducing.

Don't think about it, Peter.

The vines aren't enough to hold Arjun. He rips them off like tissue paper as he makes his way to Anna, pulling her away from me and throwing her against the vine-covered car.

Brady and Connie's screams come from where they're pinned against the vehicle.

No sooner does her back hit the car than my hand is at his throat. I know the knife is still in his hand, the vines twirling and wilting around our limbs like a diseased fairy tale. I can't make anything stick to him, but he does stop to regard me.

'It's inevitable. She's mortal. One day she'll die, and her life force will bind to yours. This is how it's supposed to be.'

Arjun forces my hand from his throat, slipping the knife into it instead. The metal of the knife cool under my hot skin. My fingers flex around it like it was made for them. It's heavier than I would've expected. Its weight reassuring in my palm. I swallow hard. *Don't think about the life force. Of claiming it, of it flowing into your body. It's not natural to take a life.* Yet, I can almost taste it. I know that, underneath it all, it would be so sweet.

Arjun holds Anna fast to the car, his eyes with their look of triumph on me. Anna's fear-stricken face is on mine, urging the coils inside of me. *I must be quick.*

Holding tight to the blade, I slash through the air.

Arjun releases Anna in time to block my attack.

And, in a move too quick for me to grasp what has happened, he plunges the knife deep into my stomach.

CHAPTER 28

Peter

So much for being immortal.

I feel like I'm dying.

With the blade still deep in my stomach, Arjun's icy fingers slip around my neck to whisper in my ear, 'One of the ways to kill a god, my son, is a sacred blade.'

Arjun retreats a few steps as I drop to my knees.

The once-cool blade now sears my insides. Rich grass in front of me turns crimson as my blood spills through its blades, enriching the soil. The pain is consuming, thunder cracks overhead, and I know this won't take long.

Yet, relief floods my body.

Anna's on her knees next to me and I can sort of hear Connie shouting. But all I can focus on is the blood. There's so much of it, and I've never liked the sight of it. I rest on my heels to look at Anna, her sobs uncontrollable.

'I love you, Anna,' I tell her, my hand leaving red fingerprints on her tear-stained cheek.

Her desperate eyes meet mine. 'This can't be happening.'

'It's better this way.' I wince at the knife still lodged in my gut, wrapping my fingers around it.

'No,' Anna whispers, throwing her arms around me. 'You healed Lorna before… you can do it to yourself.'

I sink further into my heels, shaking my head the slightest amount. 'I have nothing left to give.'

A fresh sob leaves her body, her hands sinking into the ground soaked with my essence. The knife burns as I pull it out, a fresh river of blood mixing with the rain to soak into the earth. I let the knife fall to the ground. I will die and go back to the earth. The way it should be.

Anna draws herself back onto her knees, my blood soaking her delicate fingers, taking the knife with her. 'Use me. Use me, Peter, to heal yourself.'

Even through the pain, I can't believe what she's suggesting. I glance at Arjun, who's surveying us from above, his serpent eyes watching our every move.

'This is what he wants, Anna.'

Anna slices down the palm of her hand. 'I don't believe you can kill me, Peter. Just take what you need.' Anna defiantly sticks her chin out at Arjun, and I glance back.

The corners of his mouth twitch a fraction. This is what he wants. This is what he *planned.*

'No, Anna. He knows I don't have enough control to stop.' I look away from her.

Anna's already forcing her cut hand into mine. 'I trust you.'

I withdraw from her. *I want this—this death is mine.*

'Peter. I'll die without you, remember? You die, I die, and do you honestly think he'll let Connie and Brady go if we both perish here?'

'She's telling the truth, Peter,' Arjun sneers from his place above me. 'Either she dies today or you all do.'

The rain is coming down so hard now I can't tell the raindrops from Anna's tears. Her voice is thick as she says, 'It's okay, Peter, it's okay.'

My life is ebbing away as I fall into the pool of my own blood at Arjun's feet. Anna slowly slips her hand into mine, this time with no resistance from me.

She manages to keep her composure. I grip her hand tight, bringing it up to my heart. I cover my eyes with my free hand because I want to recoil at myself from the horror of my true nature. It's already happening, like instinct. The cells of the cut vibrate against my palm. Tuning into them, it doesn't take long to fix. Fixing it is only a ploy to access what I truly want. Her life. Altogether different from Lorna's, Anna's feels like home. From the connection of our hands, all the life that has been ebbing out of me returns. Not just returns but makes me stronger.

Anna's life tastes like fresh berries in spring, the cold water of the lake in summer. It's everything right with the world. Better than the sun, better than food, better than sex. Enriching me, becoming part of me. My eyes are open now, looking down at her, our positions reversed. I kneel at her side while Anna lies on the sodden ground. She looks happy. Like she wants to give me this.

Her life is mine to take.

'I love you too, Peter,' she says through her smile. The light that flows from her to me makes her glow. She looks like an angel.

This way we will always be together. I will never be alone.

I move so fast it catches even Arjun off guard, severing the connection and slamming my back hard into the car. My breath ragged, I shake my head, trying to steady myself, to comprehend the crazy.

The ecstasy.

I can't tell if it's worked or not as I lift my face to the heavens, letting the rain wash the blood away. Wash everything away. The fear is gone now. I could be light itself.

I open my eyes enough to see Arjun is furious.

The world moves in slow motion.

Arjun is moving like a snake toward Anna.

She's still looking at me from her place on the ground. Beaming, like she never doubted me for a second.

While I'm glad I managed to stop in time, she hasn't noticed he's right behind her, the sacred knife back in his hand.

For once, I'm two steps ahead of him with a clarity I've never known before. The world around me is mine for the controlling, no emotion needed. I turn back to my dark sky and call forth the lightning, letting the full force of the strike travel deep down into my chest. It crackles and ripples across my body as I set my gaze once again on Arjun.

The sight of me harnessing the lightning stops his advance.

I don't think twice, throwing my arms out toward him. The power of the lightning strike hits him, sending him hurtling through the air and landing in a heap. The steam of the burn rises from his singed flesh.

It's not enough to kill him. Unfortunately, I can still see his chest rising.

Before I can do anything else, Anna's body slams into my chest, which is only a little sore from the lightning strike. Her arms squeeze me as tight as they can muster.

'Peter, you did it. I knew you could.'

I return her embrace. 'Are you okay?'

More arms fly around me before Anna answers. Connie and Brady.

'It's not over yet,' I say against the weight of them.

'What are you going to do with him?' Connie asks, turning to look at Arjun's smoking form.

'I'm going to finish it,' I say, breaking free of their embrace.

I stalk over to where Arjun lies. He's clinging to consciousness, weak but still aware enough to see me standing over him. To know what's about to happen as I bend down to pry the knife out of his hand.

Arjun stutters to speak.

'What was that?' I ask in a mocking tone, putting my knife-wielding hand to my ear for effect.

'Destroyer of worlds,' he chokes out with some effort.

My calm is restored, maybe not forever but satiated for now.

'Too bad you won't be around to see it.' I impart my final words to him before plunging the blade into his chest. His body convulses at the intrusion. He doesn't have long. His coal black eyes stay on mine, too empty to convey any emotion. I only hope he's scared.

I yank the knife out and place my hand over the wound, then drink in his life force. So different to Anna's, his is cold and acidic, but powerful nonetheless. Just as addicting.

Slowly, I rise, trying to contain the rush of absorbing all his power. Arjun's witch magic is quite different—it courses through my body. Strong. Controlled. As I let out a low breath, the storm dies down and the rain ceases.

I look down at Arjun's lifeless body. He looks even more like a thing now.

I turn to the others, Anna, with her face buried in Brady's chest, his own gaze averted from what's just happened in front of him. It's only Connie whose attention remains fixed on me.

Unflinching.

CHAPTER 29

Connie

Lorna's eyes bulge as I finish telling her what happened. When I'd finally arrived home yesterday, I only had enough energy left to text her and let her know I wouldn't be at school. Obviously, when Brady, Jamie, Anna, Peter, and I didn't show, she knew there was more to the story.

Her lips struggle to form words. I place my hand over hers from my place in my bed, where I've spent the whole day. As far as our parents are concerned, we were in a car crash, but Lorna knows the whole truth.

Relaying the story made it even more real, yet somehow, the words still sound unbelievable in my mouth. We were running away. Anna's life had been in danger. How Arjun had the power to flip the car. How he'd stabbed Peter. How Peter used Anna. Peter channelled lightning once more, this time using it to take down Arjun. How we all watched as Peter drove the same knife that almost killed him into Arjun's chest.

'How is this our life now?' Lorna takes a deep breath.

'I don't think I've processed it all yet. We've seen Peter do some amazing things, but this was on a whole new level.'

'Have you spoken to him since it all happened?'

'No. We were all on autopilot, I think.'

I recall the last thing Peter said to me, how he had some explaining to do with their aunt. Anna was understandably the most exhausted of us all. She was all but asleep in Brady's arms by the end of the night.

'And I can't believe Jamie did that. Who would've thought?'

I can't do much else but nod in agreement. Jamie had come through for us. When Peter killed Arjun, the grim reality was that we were still not in the clear. We had a body on our hands, Peter and Anna were covered in blood, and Brady's car was completely wrecked.

It was my idea to call Jamie. Peter only hesitated for a second before agreeing. To my surprise, Jamie agreed to the massive favour I requested with very few questions. He didn't bat an eye. We were in trouble and needed his help. I asked him to take his mum's car and bring us any spare clothes his mum wouldn't miss, along with bed sheets. I'd inwardly cringed as the words left my mouth, waiting for him to say something sarcastic. After a few minutes of dead line, he simply asked where we were and promised he would be there.

It was a nervous wait for him to arrive. Brady took Anna to the car for her to sit down and rest while I joined Peter, who was standing a little way from Arjun's body. Peter had been guarding it, as if half-expecting Arjun would rise from the dead.

'We thought he was dead before,' he had said to me, confirming my thoughts. *'But I think he really is this time.'*

I'd never seen a body before but recalled what Peter once said about seeing his mother after she died, how she was more like a shell.

Who she was before was no longer there.

Now I understood what he meant.

Arjun looked like more like an object. All the presence and threat he once carried reduced to nothing. His eyes like glass, unseeing. I moved to his side and closed his eyes.

I recall the events as they played out…

Peter watches me closely.

'I killed a man today, Connie.'

I nod. Yes, he did.

'You saw me do it.'

I nod again. Yes, I had.

'He tried to kill you,' I say quietly, joining him at his side. 'He definitely would've killed Anna.'

'You think he deserved it?' Peter's eyes are hard on me.

'I don't think you had much of a choice,' I reply, choosing my words with care, not sure what he's getting at.

Peter doesn't elaborate.

When Jamie finally arrives, I run over to him to try and prepare him somehow. At first, his focus is completely on Brady's wrecked car.

'Jesus, Connie, what happened?' He looked horrified by the sight of the car.

'Listen, Jamie. What you're about to see, this is a secret you take to the grave, okay?'

'What am I here for?' he asks.

My heart hammers in my chest. It's such a big risk. Jamie could very well tell me to go to hell and call the police right here and now.

As I lead him over to where Peter stands, I keep glancing at him, trying to read his reaction as he takes in Peter's form. From his chest down, Peter is covered in blood, his shirt torn from where he'd been stabbed.

'Shit,' Jamie mutters under his breath.

Peter closes the last few steps between us, saying to Jamie, 'I hate to get you involved in this.'

Jamie's gaze lingers on the body on the floor and then shifts back to Peter. 'I'm here to help you dispose of th-that, right?'

It almost pains me to remember the crack in Jamie's voice at the question.

But it's exactly what Jamie did—he helped.

Despite his dislike of Peter, either out of fear or out of his feelings for me, he helped us cover up what had happened. He gave Peter and Anna the spare clothes and took the bloody ones away to burn. Peter insisted on going with him for the task of disposing of the body.

Then, the final part of the plan was to move the car to the side of the road to make it look like a crash.

At first, it appeared this would have been the hardest part of the plan. We'd all moved into position to push the side of the car. Anna stopped first, realising her efforts weren't needed. Then me, then Brady, until Jamie noticed we'd all stopped, and he stood back to watch Peter single-handedly push the car onto the side of the road. Whether it was what he took from Anna, or Arjun—or both—Peter's different. Even stronger than before.

'So, what happens now?' Lorna asks, bringing me out of my fascination.

'I have no idea,' I say truthfully.

Mum knocks and pokes her head around my bedroom door. 'How are you, sweetie?' Her voice soft, she asks, 'You up for another visitor?'

I incline my head with a half smile.

She insisted I visit the hospital yesterday to get checked over. Of course, I was completely fine. I hear her tell someone they're okay to come up. Their footsteps take two stairs at a time until we see Jamie peek around the door before he opens it to stand in the doorway.

'Hey. How are you?' I ask him.

'I'm processing,' he says before looking at Lorna. 'She told you what happened?'

'Yes,' Lorna responds. 'And I think it's amazing what you did, Jamie.'

'You do?' Jamie responds with some surprise. He moves to sit next to Lorna on my bed.

'Sure,' she continues. 'You actually did something for others without thinking of yourself. I call that progress.'

Jamie's thoughtful at Lorna's admission, turning his pale blue eyes to me.

'I did it for you, Connie. I told you I'd be here for you. I meant it.'

'Thanks, Jay,' I say, taking his hand.

Jamie stares down at our hands. I can tell he's gearing up to verbalise what he came here to say as his thumb grazes tentatively over my knuckles.

'Spit it out,' I encourage, half-knowing what's coming.

'Con, you need to step away from this now.' His eyes don't leave our joined hands. 'I know he means a lot to you, and I'll admit you mean a lot to him. But that kind of danger will follow him wherever he goes. I don't want you to get hurt or end up dead from being caught in the crossfire.'

'Jamie, she's been through a lot. Maybe give it a rest?' Lorna protests on my behalf.

'Lorna, he killed someone. No, he killed his own father. Look, I appreciate you're all grateful for what I did. But what I did was help cover up a murder. Peter's a murderer now, and we're all accomplices. You're seriously telling me you don't have a problem with your best friend being around this person?'

'You know what happened, Jamie. It was self-defence.'

'He didn't care.'

'No, Jamie.' My voice comes out stronger than I've felt all day. 'You don't understand. *I* don't care.' I stare hard into his eyes, the familiarity between us all but gone. I know normal is not what I want to go back to. Ever.

Jamie's hand slips from mine.

As he gets to his feet, the weight of everything else he wants to say weighs heavy in the air. But he doesn't say it. He simply leaves.

Lorna watches me for a moment, but whatever she's thinking, she doesn't say. Instead, she lets out a heavy breath, her exhale deflating me while I let my head drop back onto my pillow. After a moment, she flops down next to me, and we both stare at the ceiling for a moment before she says, 'Seriously, dude, how did it come to this?'

Despite spending the whole day in bed, sleep comes easy.

Deep, peaceful sleep.

It takes me a while before I register the *click, click, click* sound at my window. When I do open my eyes, the call of the sound brings a sly smile across my face in the darkness.

Some habits die hard.

I make my way to the window, the dreamlike quality of the nights months prior hanging in the air, my nostalgia for them floating around me. Opening the window wide, I see Peter standing in my garden, hands in pockets, gazing up at me.

He doesn't say a word, but he glows in the moonlight. I take a few steps back from the window—an invisible invitation—and in a few moments, he's in the room. His tall form stands over me, his dark eyes bright. I stay rooted in my place, waiting for him to talk first. I can't fight my heartbeat. My chest hammers like it has a life of its own. In an instant, his lips are on mine and his hands on my hips, pushing me backward, and it's intoxicating. I wrap my arms around him while deepening our kiss. His hands support me to lift me up like I'm nothing, and my legs squeeze around him as he drops me back onto my bed.

And once more, I lose myself to him.

'I can't stay tonight,' Peter says after an eternity. 'I promised I'd come back. Anna doesn't want to be alone. But I had to see you.'

'How's she doing?'

Peter's eyebrows pull together in a frown. 'Not so good. She's frightened, trying to get her head around what happened.'

'What did your aunt say?'

'Pretty similar story. She's trying to process it, but it's hard for her to accept.' Peter runs his finger over my hip bone, sending an all-too-familiar shiver down my spine. 'She feels like it means she did abandon her sister. A hard pill to swallow.'

I study him in the dim light of my room. He seems so different to the Peter who was here a few nights ago. 'Did you tell her about Arjun?'

'No. But I told her the truth about everything else. About me, our mother.' A wicked smile passes over his lips. 'I even gave her a little demonstration.'

My eyes widen. 'How did that go down?'

Peter chuckles. 'Still lots of disbelief. There's going to be an adjustment period.'

I nod, tracing my fingers across his chest, over the bruising from where the lightning hit, splintering down and across his arms like a full-body tattoo of purple and yellow. Only this time, Peter's unbothered by its presence.

'And you?' I ask, looking up at him through my lashes.

'Would you believe me if I told you I am fine? Great even? Whatever magic I absorbed from Arjun has levelled out my powers, giving me back some control. For now.'

My heartbeat starts to pick up again. 'Do you think it'll last?'

Peter's fingers dig into my hip. 'No, I don't. Connie, one thing hasn't changed. I still need to leave.'

I swallow hard.

'It's not going to be right away,' Peter continues. 'I need to give Anna some time to recover, and we need to do things right. I'm going to ask my aunt about selling our mother's house, wait until we turn eighteen, get passports. So much to think about, but if I do it the right way, then Anna can live a long and full life. I just need to find a way to control that side of me.'

'Where will you go?' I manage to ask, hoping my voice doesn't sound too strangled.

'India. I keep having this dream about this great expanse of water. I think it's calling to me. Plus, Arjun said that's where we were born, so it's as good as any place to start. I think I need to find another witch.'

I keep my hand on his chest, focusing on his heat. 'What will you do? Will you absorb their magic too?'

Peter catches my wrist, jerking me forward so my face is inches from his. 'Of course not. To find a spell to subdue my powers. Connie, do you think I want to kill anyone else?'

I stare into his big brown eyes as he searches mine. What do I see there? Hurt? Confusion? I don't know what he's looking for in mine.

'Will you come with me?' he asks.

CHAPTER 30

Anna

Peter pads into my room, quiet as a mouse. Although I pretend to be asleep, I'm glad he has come back. I know he has no way to curb his addiction to Connie.

'I know you're still awake,' he says to the back of my head.

I open my eyes and stare at the wall. This is easier to say while I'm not looking at him. 'It turns out I am a part after all.'

'Anna, don't—'

'No, Peter, you listen to me for a change. I *am* a part. That is all I am.' I promise myself I won't cry. 'This past year, all I've done is struggle. To find out who I am, questioning everything while knowing I have no idea how to be without you. Of *who* I am without you. Now, it all makes sense. Why I've been so scared to let you go.'

'Anna. That's not how it is,' he says softly.

'You killed him.' My lip betrays me and trembles. 'You killed our father. You did that for me.'

'And I would do it again,' he declares.

I squeeze my eyes shut as the tears come. He doesn't say anything. He simply puts his arms around me and lets me cry.

'You're the human half of me, Anna. The human. I'm the *thing*, not you. You're not a part… you're everything that's real. So, you don't have my one-track, black-and-white mind, you're confused, and you struggle, and you're real. I need you.' His words sound tight. 'I need you to remind me how to be human.'

'I can't unsee it, what you did.' I cry.

'He's not worth your tears. Anna, this is why I need you. I need you as you, a whole person who's always at my side, not because you have to be but because *I* need you there. I need *you*. Not the other way around.'

I sniff and turn to face him, his eyes look black in the darkness, full of concern.

'You're worth ten of me, Anna,' he says.

'How can you say that? You're a god.' I half laugh. 'Who the hell am I? I'm nothing without you.'

Peter closes his eyes. 'Please don't say that. I love you more than anything. I'd rather die than let anything happen to you.'

My lip trembles as I bury my face in his chest. 'I don't want to die, Peter.'

I cry and cry into him until I finally fall asleep.

Peter

Five months later...

The lush green landscape soon changes to an endless rolling tarmac, the world passing by me unbelievably quickly. My stomach dances with excitement at the thought of freedom, true freedom. From our mother and our aunt. The responsibilities of our lives firmly on our own shoulders for the first time.

This is not the start of the voyage, though. That's not for a few weeks. We've been busy planning, and in three short weeks, we'll be travelling to the country where Anna and I were born. Myself, along with Sally and James, have worked hard over the last few months to make my mother's house more saleable. Once it looked habitable, it hadn't taken long for it to sell.

That chapter is closed.

The sale of the house brought with it a huge sense of relief. There's no going back. The only thing to do is move forward. Onward with the journey. What's in the past can stay there.

The thrill of the unknown washes over me.

The money from the sale of the house is more than enough to give some to Sally and James for their troubles, and enough for the four of us to live modestly while abroad in India for a year. Connie and Lorna have deferred university, having convinced their parents—with only some gentle nudging from me—that a year off to travel is a great idea before beginning three years of university.

Brady isn't ready to leave, so he's staying behind.

I promised Anna to give me a year to find answers in India, to find a witch powerful enough to suppress my powers, and then we'll return to Wixford. Where she can have a life.

Anna has taken a long time to recover from the aftermath of Arjun. His death weighs heavily on her soul even though she accepts that I didn't have a choice. She took to her bed for over a month, the way our mother used to. The reality of her mortality is another issue that weighs heavily on her.

I try not to wonder if I've shortened her life with what I've taken from her, or the struggles she wrestles with. Another reason to find a witch is to see if there's any way I can give back the life I've borrowed. It perturbs me, but I can't access the magic absorbed from Arjun. His knowledge died with him. The positive is the magic does help to maintain my balance, giving me focus and keeping my powers in check.

I find it helps to keep busy, and so this is what I do. I get busy making myself useful, planning the trip, and organising our passports for when we turn eighteen. We don't talk about the obvious fact that Anna has to come with me. I only hope my promise that we'll return has softened this for her.

For now, it's nice to see Anna smiling again as she sits in front of me, the window rolled all the way down. She lets her hand glide through the whooshing air, laughing in the front seat next to Brady.

The trip was Connie's suggestion, and it's a good idea. Both Anna and I are unbelievably excited by the prospect of seeing the sea for the first time. Plus, this is something good for Anna and Brady. A proper goodbye, something to replace the horror of our experience with Arjun.

In a few short hours, we reach our destination on the Welsh coast. By now, the nerves have set in at being so far from home. As Brady parks his car a short distance from the seafront, Anna gives a delighted squeal.

Brady turns to beam at her before addressing Connie and me in the back. 'Are you ready for this, kids?' he jokes, his grin stretching from ear to ear.

'Oh yes,' I return, meaning it as we exit the car.

The air tastes different, fresher, salty, and even though there isn't a cloud in sight to keep us from the sun's glare, it doesn't feel suffocating. It feels glorious.

Connie wraps her arm around my waist as Brady leads us toward the front.

'Is it weird I can't tell if I'm excited or nervous about seeing the sea for the first time?' I ask her.

Her eyes sparkle even more than usual in the sunlight. 'Not at all. I don't know who's more excited. You and Anna at seeing the sea for the first time, or Brady and me for being able to watch you both experience it.'

She beams up at me, and I place a chaste kiss on her lips as we walk. I push down the bitter aftertaste of a lingering paranoia I'm trying my hardest not to think about. An ulterior motive I haven't told anyone as yet.

Connie.

The other need for me to find a witch? To discover the spell to remove Connie from any effects of my influence. As long as I want her, can she ever not want me in return? I can't sentence Connie to a lifetime of being bound to me, forever wondering if I'm truly what she wants. I have to know for sure.

'This is it,' Brady says ahead of us on the path as we turn the corner, bringing the beach into our open view.

Something in me shifts, like the wind is knocked out of me. Anna's hand slips into mine. Any tension between us evaporates as we take in the glorious expanse of sea that extends as far as the eye can see. So blue. Massive. Calm. Seemingly endless.

Out of the corner of my eye, the jubilant faces of Connie and Brady light up, clearly loving how we're at a loss for words.

Still speechless, our world just got so much bigger and will continue to do so—this is beautiful.

Anna turns to me, the lightness reflecting out of her. My heart swells seeing her this way once again. She watches, waiting for me. Slowly, I stretch my mouth into a broad smile, biding my time. Waiting until the moment is just right. Until she can't bear me not saying a word for a second longer, and only then do I run, as fast as my legs will take me, straight toward the water. I hear her laugh, her quick footsteps sounding behind me.

Without any hesitation, my feet hit the shoreline. The sea water on my ankles is cold in the best possible way in the heat of the day. Two steps, three steps. I throw my hands out in front of my head and dive straight into the sparkling water.

Heaven.

I stay submerged for as long as I can, weightless in the cool water around me.

When I resurface, Anna's head is bobbing in front of me. She's giggling, and I can't help it. I'm laughing too. Some of the families we must have startled are playing at the water's edge, now chuckling as well. I let myself lie back and float on the shimmering surface, gazing up at the sky, which is gloriously clear and flawless. We needed this, one perfect day before we face whatever is coming next.

I gradually make my way back to the shore where Connie and Brady are standing. They've taken their shoes off and are paddling in the shallows. As I pass Anna, she calls out, 'Hey, Brady, come swim with me.'

With a shrug, Brady swims past me and goes to her.

My Converse squelch into the wet sand as I approach Connie.

She shakes her head at me. 'You're crazy.'

I throw my arms out wide, mockingly rolling my eyes. 'It took you this long to figure that out?'

She laughs as I gather her up in my arms, then squeals as I launch us both back into the water, prompting fresh laughter from the onlookers. Connie gasps for air, pushing me away only for a moment before pulling me back to her, her lips finding mine.

In times like these, it's easy not to worry if what Connie feels is anything but genuine. And I let myself believe it, even if it's only for a minute.

'Thank you,' I tell her. 'I needed this.'

'How is everything?' she asks sincerely, bringing her fingers to my temple. 'In here.'

'Better. I'm starting to understand why my mother did what she did. She thought she was doing the right thing. Keeping me in check, keeping Anna alive. I suppose she kept the truth from us for so long she didn't know what else to do.'

Connie considers me, tilting her head to get a better view in the sunlight. 'That's progress. Peter. Whatever we find in India, there's the possibility Arjun wasn't telling the whole truth. It may not be true about Anna.'

'I'm certain you're right. I'm sure there are a great many things Arjun was not truthful about, but I'm afraid Anna is not one of them. When her life was in my hands, it scared me more than anything.' I kiss the top of her head and push back into the water.

Today is a good day. I don't want to ruin it, nor dwell on any urge I had to kill my sister, no matter how fleeting. 'So that's why we'll find another way. We will find our witch in India… a good witch, who'll help us, and Anna will live a long, long life and have about ten children with Brady, and all will be right with the world.'

Connie beams, pushing out into the water after me. 'And what about you, Peter Burke? What becomes of you?'

'I will be a very strange uncle, who never ages, tending to my garden, simple and happy with my power subdued for as long as it takes. And maybe, if you'll have me, you will put up with me too.'

I let Connie close the distance between us, her lips almost on me.

'It sounds almost too good to be true,' she whispers.

Her emerald eyes are my undoing.

I am hers wholly.

Mind, body, and soul—if I have one—all belong to her.

'Connie, I don't think I'll ever not want you.'

She doesn't say another word as her lips melt to mine.

The rest of our day is idyllic, spent lazing on the beach, drinking ciders, sunbathing, and after changing into our swimming gear, taking more dips in the sea. We stay until it turns cold, finding our little beachfront hotel to get changed and grab dinner before returning to the beach to watch the stars.

The next morning, the atmosphere in the car couldn't be more different from when we travelled down. Our hearts are light as air. A fleeting moment of absolute happiness. My sister sits in the front seat, singing along with the radio at the top of her voice with Brady. Connie laughs with them before starting to sing along as well.

My smile hurts my face. I want to sing, but I don't know the words. Instead, I turn to Connie, knowing Anna and Brady can't hear me over their singing.

'I love you,' I say to her.

'I love you too.' She beams back.

She doesn't have a chance to react to the change in my facial expression. It only takes seconds. Too late by the time I register what I'm seeing as Brady prepares to merge onto the motorway.

The car from the middle lane is sliding. Not sliding—it's spinning, moving toward us.

A second.

Less than a second.

It hits our car.

Impacting the right, beside Brady and Connie.

Ridiculously, my first thought is for Brady's shiny new car.

The force flips the car onto its side.

I've been here before. But this time, it's different. There's nothing gentle about it.

The car fills with our screams.

Another flip.

My head smashes against the window and hot liquid gushes down my face.

The world doesn't make sense. My neck twists. I think my arm is broken. Out of my window, I can see the wreck behind me. Cars turned onto their roofs. The glass glittering across the tarmac looks unreal, like diamonds, and for some reason oddly beautiful. The blood flowing from my head drips into a little puddle on the ceiling.

My world is bloody again.

Worse than the screams, now there's no sound from the inside of the car. The silence is haunting as I strain to look around. Anna's long blonde hair pools against the ceiling in front of me, her hand hanging lifeless next to it, the blood slowly making its way down to her fingertips.

Panic starts rising in my throat as I try to steady my breathing.

I don't want to look to my right. I don't have to look—my instincts are honing in on Connie. Connie's heartbeat. Her *fading* heartbeat. Forcing myself, I turn to see her bloodied face, where she hangs limply in her seatbelt.

The noise that leaves me isn't words. It's sounds coming from somewhere deep inside of me.

My world is fading heartbeats. All of them. No one will get here in time.

'No,' I finally say out loud.

No, I refuse.

I refuse for this to be how they end.

If I can take a life, then I can also give it.

I refuse to live while they die.

I reach out to Connie, who's closest, and grab her hand. With contact, I can feel it all, how broken she is. Her broken ribs and shattered collarbone, the internal bleeding. I start to pull, drawing it all back together, slowly making her whole again while her skin burns hot under my fingers.

I can't reach Anna.

I hold my arm as close as I can get. It'll have to be enough. It has to be enough. The cut on my face is already healed, but I fight against my broken shoulder. Instead, I focus on Anna, her cells, her injuries, the white healing light leaving my fingertips and enveloping her skin. Maybe if I give her my life, it will mean she can live.

I turn to Brady. Brady's injuries are bad. His rib cage is crushed against the airbag. The impact was too great. It's so much. So much is broken, but I have to try to put him back together.

I attempt to focus my energy, pushing everything out. All the life I can give, all of the magic, I let them have it. A deep guttural noise comes from somewhere deep in my chest.

I refuse to let them die.

I give it all.

The light burns hot.

So hot.

It soon takes on a life of its own, and I'm no longer in control. The white light fills the car, blinding me until I can't see my world anymore.

When it comes, it is weightless.

There's nothing else to do but let go.

Nothing.

Just…

… darkness.

Acknowledgements

Thank you so much for reading.

If you loved this book, please do take a moment to drop me a review on Amazon and Goodreads - I can't tell you how much this means to authors.

I hope you love part 2, Gemini, just as much. Be warned, the themes begin to mature as the characters get older and (not so) wiser. As the legendary Holly Black once said on second books, 'Why I love second books. First books do all the work of the set up so that we can go straight into pure misery. Delicious misery.' I've never resonated with something more when writing this trilogy.

It would be criminal if I didn't give a shout out to Shandi Boyes formerly of Skye High Publishing, without her I wouldn't be where I am now.

Thank you to my lovely friend, Maria Dean who has kept me sane on this publishing journey. To my partner Ben for being my biggest cheerleader through the ups and downs. Of course, always to my wonderful family, in particular my sister, my mom and Diane for always being my test readers.

About the Author

Kerry Williams is a UK author based in the heart of England and writer of romantic fantasy novels.

Copywriter by day, she gets lost in a world of magic at night, either in her writing or in what she reads. Her creative roots were cultivated by the writing of the unforgettable Anne Rice, she also adores the work of Erin Morgenstern, Holly Black and J. K. Rowling. These days you will often find her with her nose buried in a romantic fantasy book.

She graduated from Brunel University with a 2:1(hons) in Creative Writing. She is an avid cat lady, die hard tea drinker and eternal star gazer. Always known to her family as a daydreamer, she and her young daughter, Ivy, can often be found looking at the moon.

www.kerrywilliamsauthor.co.uk

Printed in Great Britain
by Amazon